PENGUIN BOOKS

You're The One That I Want

Actress and freelance journalist, Giovanna is married to Tom Fletcher from McFly. She grew up in Essex with her Italian dad Mario, mum Kim, big sister Giorgina and little brother Mario, and spent most of her childhood talking to herself or reading books. Her debut novel, *Billy and Me*, is also published by Penguin.

To see what makes Giovanna smile, take a look at her blog at www.giovannasworld.com or her Twitter page @MrsGiFletcher.

You're The One That I Want

GIOVANNA FLETCHER

PENGUIN BOOKS

PENGUIN BOOKS

Published by the Penguin Group
Penguin Books Ltd, 80 Strand, London WC2R ORL, England
Penguin Group (USA) Inc., 375 Hudson Street, New York, New York 10014, USA
Penguin Group (Canada), 90 Eglinton Avenue East, Suite 700, Toronto, Ontario, Canada M4P 2Y3
(a division of Pearson Penguin Canada Inc.)
Penguin Ireland, 25 St Stephen's Green, Dublin 2, Ireland (a division of Penguin Books Ltd)
Penguin Group (Australia), 707 Collins Street, Melbourne, Victoria 3008, Australia
(a division of Pearson Australia Group Pty Ltd)
Penguin Books India Pvt Ltd, 11 Community Centre, Panchsheel Park, New Delhi – 110 017, India
Penguin Group (NZ), 67 Apollo Drive, Rosedale, Auckland 0632, New Zealand
(a division of Pearson New Zealand Ltd)
Penguin Books (South Africa) (Pty) Ltd, Block D, Rosebank Office Park, 181 Jan Smuts Avenue,
Parktown North, Gauteng 2193, South Africa

Penguin Books Ltd, Registered Offices: 80 Strand, London WC2R ORL, England

www.penguin.com

First published 2014
001

Copyright © Giovanna Fletcher, 2014
All rights reserved

Lyrics from 'Love Is Easy' written by Thomas Fletcher, Daniel Jones,
Dougie Poynter and Anthony Brant © Published by Kobalt Music Publishing Ltd

The moral right of the author has been asserted

Typeset by Palimpsest Book Production Ltd, Falkirk, Stirlingshire
Printed and bound in Great Britain by Clays Ltd, St Ives plc

ISBN: 978–1–405–90997–6

www.greenpenguin.co.uk

To Giorgina and Mario, for making my childhood so much fun. Whether we were making up radio shows on our brown Fisher-Price recorder, counting out a bag of marshmallows to share (Giorgie, I know you always cheated and had more), or jumping on the sofa as we sang along to *Grease* – life was always great with you two by my side. Love you.

If this is love then love is easy,
It's the easiest thing to do.
If this is love then love completes me,
Because it feels like I've been missing you.
A simple equation,
With no complications to leave you confused.
If this is love, love, love,
Oh, it's the easiest thing to do.

McFLY

Firstly, on behalf of my wife and I, I'd like to thank you all for being here. It means so much to be surrounded by our family and friends on what can only be described as the most important day of our lives.

Maddy

Twenty-six years old . . .

Only fifty-two feet stood between me and my husband-to-be. All that was left for me to complete the transformation from Miss Maddy Hurst to Mrs Maddy Miles was to walk that fifty-two feet and say my vows. Then I'd be able to leave the past behind and look to the future with security, dignity and the love of a good man, knowing that I deserved to be receiving it.

But even though I knew it was what I wanted, it was still the most difficult fifty-two feet I'd ever had to walk. I knew I was walking away from someone who had the potential to take me to new dizzying heights with his love – a love that was mine for the taking, but never truly within my reach. Perhaps if the circumstances were different we'd have had something magical. It pained me to be walking away from those feelings, from him, but I'd said all I needed to say. He knew I loved him and that my love for him was unconditional, as it had always been.

'Give me Joy in my Heart' started playing inside the church, tearing me away from my wandering thoughts, and letting me know it was time for my entrance. One by one the bridesmaids calmly walked through the giant wooden archway. Pearl, the last of the bunch, turned to give me a big wink before following suit, the little train of her mint chiffon dress floating behind her.

'You ready?' asked my dad, who looked incredibly cute in his light grey suit, and emerald-green tie – which I noticed was slightly wonky. His salt-and-pepper-coloured hair was mostly covered up by a big top hat, which bizarrely made him appear shorter than usual, even though it gave him extra height. He looked as nervous as I did – something I wasn't prepared for!

I straightened his tie and gave him a little nod.

He checked over my veil in the way Mum had clearly instructed him to – so that it creased at the sides and not in front of my face. Then he stood beside me and lifted my arm before hooking it through his.

'You look beautiful, Maddy,' he whispered.

'Thanks, Dad,' I managed to say, the nerves seeming to have taken hold of me.

'Feeling nervous?'

Another nod.

'You'll feel better when you see him. Come on, grip hold of your old man. It's time for your groom to see his bride,' he said, firmly squeezing my arm into his side.

At our cue, we started to walk at the steady pace we had agreed on – not so fast that we were almost running to the altar, but not so slow that people started yawning with boredom either. We'd practised it that morning to ensure it wasn't a complete disaster.

I found myself clutching tightly on to Dad's arm as we turned into the church and walked through its doors. A sea of faces welcomed us – all of the congregation were on their feet, looking at me with the broadest smiles I'd ever seen. And there were so many of them! It was a wonder to think we even knew that many people.

During my wedding dress fittings I was told numerous times to enjoy that particular moment, to look at those faces, the ones of the people we both loved and admired, and bask in their warmth. Their love that day was for us. I'd been told to embrace it. But as I took in their faces, their happy smiles, filled with joy, they made the feeling that had been mounting in my chest for weeks tighten further.

That was it.

There was no going back.

A surge of happiness bolted through me as I spotted him, staring back at me from the altar, looking simply divine. My wonderful man, Robert Miles – strong, reliable and loving. My best friend. I pursed my lips as my cheeks rose and tears sprang to my eyes at the very sight of him, looking more handsome than ever in his grey suit. His tall muscular frame visibly relaxed as his dazzling green eyes found mine, his luscious lips breaking into a smile that I couldn't help but respond to.

And then I stole a glance to the right of Robert, to see my other love, Ben Gilbert – kind, generous and able to make my heart melt with just one look. But he wasn't looking back at me. Instead, he had his head bowed and was concentrating on the floor in front of him; all I could see was the back of his waxed brown hair – the smooth olive skin of his face and his chocolate-dipped eyes were turned away.

His hesitance to look up struck a chord within me, momentarily making me wobble on my decision.

Suddenly, something within me urged him to look at me. Part of me wanted him to stop the wedding, to show me exactly how much he cared. Wanted him to stop me from making a terrible mistake . . . but is that what I thought I was actually making? A terrible mistake?

I loved Robert, but I loved Ben too. Both men had known me for seventeen years – each of them had seen me at my worst, picked me up when I'd been caught in despair, been my shoulders to cry on when I'd needed to sob. They were my rocks. Plural. Not singular.

Yes, I'd made my decision. I'd accepted Robert's proposal, I'd worn the big white dress and walked up the aisle – however, if Ben had spoken up, if he'd even coughed suggestively, then there's a possibility I'd have stopped the wedding.

Even at that point.

But, as the service got underway, as the congregation was asked for any reasons why we should not have been joined in matrimony without a peep from Ben, it started to sink in that he was not about to start fighting.

He was letting me go . . .

Maddy caught my attention on the very first day I clapped eyes on her. She looked adorable with her scruffily wild bob and red cheeks. She also looked as though she was going to burst into tears at any minute. I'm not sure what she made of me and my wingman, with our chubby faces and overly keen ways — well, actually, I think she was pretty terrified. But we won her over eventually. We're still not sure how we managed to pull that one off . . .

Ben

Nine years old . . .

It was during the arduous task of deciding whether a red or green felt tip pen was best for the snake hair of my Medusa drawing (a very important decision and not one to have been made lightly) that I noticed her – looking around the class with her big blue eyes. Her cheeks and nose were rosy from her walk to school in the frosty February air and the ends of her not-so-perfect auburn bob flicked in and out uncontrollably in a careless fashion. Her school uniform, the same as every other girl in the class (which was the same as us boys, but we wore trousers) – grey pleated skirt, white t-shirt and green jumper with our school logo of the local church – was far too big for her. The skirt hung way past her knees and the sleeves of the jumper were gathered at her elbows to stop them from covering her hands, both of which were clutching hold of her green book bag so tightly that her knuckles appeared to whiten with the strain. Her lips were clasped together as though she was trying to stop herself from crying. She was visibly squirming in her new surroundings – which wasn't too surprising seeing as the majority of us had stopped what we were doing and were gawping at her.

Our form teacher, Mr Watson, who always looked like he was in a foul mood as he glared at us through his wire-rimmed spectacles, took her to her new desk. It was the spot none of us had wanted – facing the wall and the class toilet – a double whammy of depressiveness. Not only did you have to sit looking at the sick-coloured wall that was thirty centimetres away from your face, but every now and then, if someone decided to go for a number two in the loo, you'd get a whiff of it – occasionally the smell lingered for a couple of hours too. It was pretty gross.

I'd wanted to go to her then. I wanted to make her feel welcome so that she didn't feel so alone. But nine-year-old boys didn't do things like that. So I resisted the urge. I just continued to sit and stare like everyone else who'd spotted her.

'Have you got the green pen?' asked Robert, my best friend who sat to my right every day. We were inseparable. Had been since our mums met in the local park when we were still in our prams and sucking on dummies – prompting them to meet up daily for tea, biscuits and some light relief from baby chatter. They'd revelled in having another adult to talk to after months of just Robert or me for company while our dads were out at work. According to my mum, Robert handed me a single raisin from his Sun-Maid box on that first day, and that was it – firm buddies for life. Well, they say it's the simple things . . .

Sat at our desk, I flustered at his question – I hadn't decided which colour to use for the snakes yet, but ended up handing him the green pen anyway. It no longer mattered – I was more focused on the new arrival. Medusa could wait.

'What you staring at?' Robert asked, brushing his blond hair out of his eyes.

I said nothing but his beady green eyes followed the direction of my gaze.

'Oooooh . . . nice,' he giggled.

Robert lowered the newly acquired felt tip pen back onto our desk and joined me in staring at the newbie. We didn't say a word. We just sat and watched. She really did look quite nice, I decided, agreeing with Robert.

'Okay, everyone,' boomed Mr Watson, scratching the side of his rounded tummy that threatened to spill out from beneath his white shirt, as he demanded our attention. 'I'd like you to say a warm good morning to your new classmate, Maddy. She has just moved to the area from London.'

'Good morning, Maddy. Good morning, everyone,' we all chorused together in unison – a trick we'd been trained to do since our first day there at Peaswood Primary School. I wonder when, as a society, we grow out of things like that – you don't get grown-ups barking at you in the same manner when you start new jobs. If I walked into a new place of work and had everyone turn to me and shout, 'Good morning, Ben Gilbert,' with sickly sweet smiles, I think I'd run a mile. It's quite cult-like. But, I have to say, I thoroughly enjoyed saying good morning to Maddy Hurst on her first day.

I watched as she looked up while we chorused in her direction, and was left stunned when her eyes found mine for a tiny second. My cheeks suddenly sprang to life and I felt them lift into a huge goofy grin. She smiled briefly before her gaze fell next to me for a second and then back down to the ground – her cheeks pinking further. I turned to Robert to see that he was wearing the same silly grin as I was. He looked up at me and let out a second giggle.

Robert never giggled. He laughed, but never giggled. The new girlish squeal he'd been unable to hold in was quite amusing.

At lunchtime Robert and I wasted no time in going over to Maddy and saying hello. We took her to the dinner hall (where we tucked into potato croquettes, dinosaur-shaped breaded turkey and baked beans – food back then was awesome) and gathered as much information as we could about the girl we'd decided would be our new friend.

Our hearts almost exploded when she revealed she lived around the corner from our homes – we both looked at her with open-mouthed grins, not believing our luck, as we wondered how soon we'd be able to knock for her to play out with us.

It would be fair to say we became instantly aware that Maddy possessed something different to any other girl we'd ever met – something that had us spellbound from our first glimpse of her nervous frame as the class's new girl. She just had this air about her, this inexplicable quality that drew us in like two obedient puppy dogs.

Not a single part of me wanted to fight against that attraction.

I was happily won over.

Immediately smitten.

Maddy

Nine years old . . .

I wasn't very happy when Mum and Dad announced we were moving 'to the sticks' – even if they said it was for a 'better way of life'. In my head I imagined we were going to be living in a wooden shack with no one else around us for miles and miles, surrounded by fields of hay and smelly chickens – like something from *Little House on the Prairie*. But actually, it wasn't so bad in Peaswood – our house was made of brick for a start, we had neighbours, and there wasn't a chicken in sight. There was a bustling High Street, which was within walking distance no matter where you lived in the village, filled with shops and pubs (there were four pubs – a tad excessive for such a small place), and a big community centre at one end. The local C of E church stood in the middle of the busy street, flanked by the florist and the baker's – the smell of freshly baked bread and cakes making tummies rumble as people knelt and prayed.

I had been nervous about starting a new school and making new friends. It wasn't like I was the popular kid in my previous class, but I had a nice bunch of mates who I was sad to say goodbye to when we moved. Like any girl at that age, all I'd wanted was for my new classmates to like me.

On my first day I was feeling extremely nervous and flustered as Mr Watson brought me to everyone's attention in his brisk manner. It's mind-boggling that teachers don't realize how stressful and awkward that moment is for a kid – knowing that everyone's sizing you up and deciding whether they're interested in making you their new BFF or whether you'll be doomed to be the class loser for ever more. It's excruciating. I felt my face redden and my bladder weaken in seconds – it took every ounce of self-control to stop myself peeing on the spot. That would have been a great start.

Spotting Robert and Ben, once I'd finally plucked up enough courage to look up from the thinning brown carpet at my feet, both sending the cheesiest smiles in my direction, had made me feel much more relaxed. My inner turmoil momentarily gave way, enabling me to flash them a smile before, once again, looking down at the brown below.

Even though we'd exchanged smiles, I was still surprised they were the first to come over to talk to me. I thought the girls of the class would be. I assumed one of them would be happy to have someone new to hang out with, but it appeared not. None of them bothered with me at all on my first day. Instead, it was the two boys who took an interest.

I can remember thinking they were a funny pair, Robert and Ben. Robert, who I noticed was clearly the more confident of the two, wore his straw-like blond hair in straight silky curtains that ran either side of his face, down to his cheekbones. His sparkly green eyes, splattered with flecks of gold, never seemed too alert – it was like he was half asleep with two little slits on his lightly freckled face. Ben was painfully shy, but reminded me of Bambi – his chestnut hair was gelled into perfect spikes and he had these humungous brown eyes, which appeared all the richer due to his olive skin.

Thanks to their ridiculously big smiles and kind manners when taking me to lunch, I quickly felt my worry at being in a new school melt away. I was also thankful not to have been completely rejected by my new classmates.

Although, saying that, I was more than surprised when the pair turned up at my door that night, asking if I could go out to play as they both sat on their matching blue BMX bikes, using the tips of their trainers to rock forwards and backwards on their wheels. I couldn't help but smile back excitedly at them. It was the first time anybody had ever stood at my door asking after me.

Unfortunately, Mum decided it was too soon for me to be wandering the streets of Peaswood with two boys she didn't know. So as a compromise she invited them inside to play instead – once they'd called their mums and told them of their whereabouts, of course. The boys gleefully accepted the offer and discarded their bikes in our front garden without a moment's hesitation. I can remember looking down at their bikes and smiling to myself at the thought of how safe our new neighbourhood must be, before shutting the door and joining my new friends inside. I'd felt wanted and included.

My relationship with the boys kickstarted with great gusto and enthusiasm, whereas trying to strike up a friendship with the girls in my class was much more problematic. They were a tight bunch, made all the cosier by the fact that they (Laura the ringleader, Michelle, Becky and Nicola) had a special name for themselves – the Pink Dreamers. A name that was also used for the girl band they were in. I can't express how much I wanted to be included when I heard that, but it seemed the friendships I'd already sparked up with the boys were going to put my chances of primary-school popstardom and any friendship with the girls in jeopardy. Yes, even at nine years old, social politics were rife.

They hated the fact that I hung around with the boys and would tell me so while asking if I fancied one of them or had kissed them. It was horrible to feel so interrogated and like such an outsider. Unfortunately, when my brain was taken over by some crazy acceptance-needing twerp, I decided the best thing for me to do would be to cut all ties with Robert and Ben. I'm ashamed to say I ignored them, sat away from them at lunchtimes, ran away from them at breaktimes – I figured it was the only way to make the Pink Dreamers (I can't believe I cared so much for a bunch of girls who called themselves that) want me to be a part of their group.

And I thought I'd succeeded at one point.

One day at lunch I was called over by Laura to join the girls. At last, I thought, I'm in.

Oh what a foolish girl I was.

The whole thing was a set-up.

I sat on the spare plastic orange chair, ready to enjoy my first lunch with my new BFFs, only to feel the chair give way beneath me. I flew backwards through the air with an almighty screech and landed on my back with my legs in the air – white cotton knickers on display, my dignity splattered alongside me on the floor. I'd never felt so humiliated.

Off I ran to the toilets, riddled with humiliation, only to be followed by Robert and Ben. Bless them, they even came *into* the girls' loos to see if I was okay. Not many little boys would venture into such formidable territory, without caring whether they were caught by our peers or not.

In that little loo our friendship was restored. We pinkie promised that I'd never be such a loser again and that the three of us would stick together as a threesome until the end of time. It was a deliciously cute moment and one that firmly cemented us as a united force.

I had my boys, I needed nothing more.

Ben

Nine years old . . .

It wasn't long after that uplifting moment of friendship that my dad walked out on me and my mum. He just upped and left with no explanation, no apology and no emotional farewell. It seemed easy for him to sever his family ties and start a new life elsewhere. Not caring that he may never see the innocent little boy who worshipped the ground he walked on, ever again.

He'd found another woman. Someone he worked with in the police force – another officer. I don't think she was younger than my mum, as is the usual stereotype. I don't even think she was prettier, nicer or more intelligent – but then, I wouldn't, would I? I've always thought of my mum as beautiful with her short raven bob and dark brown eyes, her tiny frame making her seem delicate and break-able – but, in actual fact, her bones were made of steel, something I learned over the years. She was tough enough to take a few knocks from life. Perhaps the new woman in Dad's life understood the pressures of the job better than my mum had, but then I don't want to justify what he did by admitting that.

The thing that hurt me most was that she had a kid of her own, this new woman. A son named George who was a couple of years younger than me. Dad took him on as his own – as though he was a replacement for the son he'd left behind. It was that easy, it seemed.

Obviously, we didn't know any of that information when it first happened, we just heard bits of gossip from my nan and aunts as time went by. They weren't meant to tell us, of course, but it slipped out occasionally. Little nuggets of information that I managed to piece together.

You know, he didn't even leave a note to inform us that he'd left. We only knew because most of his stuff had disappeared. He'd done it when I was at school and Mum was at work. What a coward of a man.

When Mum collected me from school that afternoon I asked if Robert could come over for dinner (Maddy was busy doing something, I can't remember what), and not knowing the void that was waiting for us at home, she happily said yes, as usual. Robert was always welcome.

We knew that something was wrong as soon as we walked through the front door. It felt colder, or as though something was missing. The same feeling that might be aroused if you were to come home and find you'd been burgled. It was unsettling and different.

Mum sighed. That was her reaction to the whole thing, to sigh as if she knew it was coming. Knew that the waste of space she called a husband would desert us in such a loveless manner after thirteen years of marriage.

'Boys, do you want to play out in the garden while I put dinner on?' she asked, managing to keep her voice strong and steady.

'Should I get changed out of my school stuff?' I asked. I was never allowed to play in my uniform, usually my t-shirt was in the wash as soon as I'd taken it off – Mum ran a tight ship.

'No, you're all right, love.'

She wanted to stop me from going upstairs in case Dad's getaway was apparent – wardrobes left open with no clothes in, empty hangers splayed across the room carelessly as he made his quick escape. She'd wanted to save me from that hurt, that embarrassment.

I knew, of course. They always say kids have a sixth sense about those sorts of things, and I certainly did.

I nodded and shuffled outside with Robert. Silently, we went down to the bottom of the garden, away from the house, and climbed up into my treehouse. Dad had assembled it as a present on my previous birthday, the last one he was ever around for. It was a four-foot-by-four-foot square of timber, completed with a flat roof and small window looking back at our home – Mum had offered to put curtains in it at one point, but I thought that would take away the boy-ness of it all. Hanging from the roof, through a hole in its base and to the ground below, was a thick, knotted blue rope – perfect for me to scramble in and out of my new den. Dad had told me I was big enough at nine years old to have my own bit of space – although Mum was always fretting about my safety, unable to cope with her little boy being capable of climbing up and down freely with confidence.

While we sat up there on that bleak afternoon, I turned and looked at Robert. I noticed that he was anxiously pulling his bottom lip through his teeth and it dawned on me that he knew too.

'I think my dad's gone,' I said quietly. It felt odd to say

it out loud. Hearing the words come from my mouth forced me to see the truth of the matter, allowing the sadness to creep in and grip firmly around my heart. I felt so . . . disappointed.

'Yeah . . .' Robert said, looking at me with concern.

We sat in silence for a while, side by side, looking up at my family home. Until that moment it had always been a place of safety, but it quickly and violently became a place of uncertainty. Of course, we'd all heard about parents getting divorced; I wasn't the first one in my year it had happened to. One girl in our class hadn't even met her dad, he'd buggered off before she was born, so, yes, we knew about it, and we feared it. Every time there was a squabble at the kitchen table or a disagreement in the car about bad directions, we'd feel the worry tiptoe in. For me, in that moment, the nightmare had turned into a reality. Millions of questions floated around my brain as I wondered why he'd left, if I'd done something wrong to upset him, if we'd have to move house and leave Peaswood, if I'd ever see him again and whether he still loved me.

I thought about that morning with my dad, the last time I ever saw him, and searched it for clues – a task I repeated over the years whenever he made an unwelcome appearance in my thoughts. I wondered whether he had done anything to suggest he was anxious about the big decision he was about to make, whether he showed me any more affection than normal or if he seemed sorry to leave me. As far as I could tell there was nothing. No looks or strange utterings to decipher. Just the normal morning routine – breakfast while he read the newspaper, then off he went to work.

'You'll be okay,' Robert eventually said with a nod.

'Yeah . . .'

'You'll always have me.'

'Thank you,' I managed before bursting into tears, no longer able to keep the sadness in.

Robert put his arm around me and firmly held me, silently becoming my anchor of support as I crumbled.

We sat like that for the next thirty minutes.

Nothing more was said.

We never talked of my tears once I'd finished, but that afternoon had altered things between us. We'd been exposed to something our fragile young minds weren't ready for, a grief that, in an ideal world, we should have been protected from. My dad had left me, discarded me like a worn and used jumper. He'd done nothing to try and save me from the pain of his leaving – in fact, Robert, at just nine years old, did more to comfort me than my own dad had. How pitiful. It was the vulnerability that the situation provoked in us both which caused a firmer alliance to be built between us. From that moment Robert had turned from my best friend to my rock, and I worshipped him for it.

Maddy

Eleven years old . . .

Two years after stepping through the doors of Peaswood Primary School I was happily settled thanks to my two bestest buds, Robert and Ben. We went everywhere and did everything together. It was rare to see one of us without the other two in tow. This was helped by the fact that our parents had become close too, meaning that while they had their grown-up dinner parties and weekly Friday nights at the community club, we were allowed to wander off and play. On top of that, hardly a day went by without us doing something together after school. Our mums would come and collect us at the school gates, take us to our individual homes, and within minutes one of us would be knocking on the others' front doors, asking if they wanted to play out.

Thankfully, things had changed in class – mostly because I no longer had any desire to become a Pink Dreamer, although it wasn't an easy conclusion for me to come to. After various spats, I suddenly saw sense – much to the boys' relief. In turn, because I stopped caring so much, Laura and co stopped picking on me. Thankfully we'd come to some sort of truce.

On 15 May, in our final year at primary school, our whole class was stood at the bottom of the school playing field in the spring sunshine, next to the great big fir trees, waiting to watch Becky Davies (one of the nicer girls in the Pink Dreamers) and Greg Reed (the most popular boy in class) do a very grown-up thing . . . get married. It was all taken very seriously with Laura as the priest and the rest of her gang playing the bridesmaids (hardly a surprise).

'I don't understand why we have to watch this,' huffed Robert from my right.

'Because! It's romantic!' I said back.

'It's stupid.'

I didn't respond any further to his moaning because I was pretty sure that Robert had a bit of a soft spot for Becky. That was the real reason for him thinking the whole thing was ridiculous. He was jealous.

'I like it . . .' said Ben from my left with a beaming smile.

'Really?' questioned Robert in disgust, flicking the ends of his hair out of his eyes with irritation.

'Yes,' Ben nodded, eagerly.

Laura was standing beside Greg in what was our childish makeshift version of a romantic spot to get married in – a collection of sticks, daisies, bluebells and dandelions had been arranged into a circle, like a little love nest.

We edged a little nearer to them when the ceremony was about to start, much to Robert's annoyance.

'Please welcome the bride and her bridesmaids,' Laura shouted, as she theatrically swept her hand in the air towards the incoming group of girls, who'd been hiding behind a few of the trees.

Nicola and Michelle, the other two Pink Dreamers, walked up to the circle carrying small bunches of daisies, as they hummed 'Here Comes the Bride' with great enthusiasm. Behind them walked Becky wearing a big white shiny dress over her school uniform.

Laughter came from my right.

I turned to see Robert with his hand covering his reddening face as he failed to suppress more mocking laughter.

I elbowed him in the ribs.

'Ouch.'

'Ladies and gentlemen, boys and girls,' Laura boomed louder, her voice sounding more serious and grown up than normal. 'Thank you all for joining us here today. Becky and Greg are delighted to be sharing this wonderful moment with their friends.'

Robert sighed next to me, unable to hide his irritation.

'Marriage is about two people saying they like each other very much and showing it to the world,' she said to the crowd. 'It's them saying they love each other more than anyone else they know. That they are happy to be there for each other from now until the day they die.'

I couldn't help smiling as I glanced at Robert, who was flicking bits of grass around with his foot in boredom, and then at Ben, who was paying close attention – his expression full of awe as he soaked up the meaning of the words.

Once Laura had come to the end of her speech and the bride and groom had finished repeating Laura's words, she came to the finale of the service. 'Becky and Greg, by the power in me, I now call you man and wife . . . Greg, you may now kiss the bride.'

We all watched in stunned silence as Greg placed his

hands on Becky's cheeks, pulled her into him and kissed her straight on the lips. It was, and still is, the friskiest first kiss I've ever experienced at a wedding. It lasted a couple of seconds and was followed by a big grin from the newly married couple as the gathered crowd erupted in whoops and cheers.

'That was a bit much,' huffed Robert, rolling his eyes.

While the crowd continued to go crazy, a warm and clammy hand found its way into mine. It was Ben's. He gave my hand three little squeezes before pulling his hand away.

I looked up at his face as he flashed me a bashful smile.

Ben

Eleven years old . . .

I.

LOVE.

YOU.

That was what I'd wanted to say in those three little squeezes.

I knew I meant it.

I really did . . .

Being in that setting, with the emphasis of the occasion one of love and happiness, it was hard to escape the intense desire that took hold of me – making it impossible to ignore. I had an overwhelming urge to open my mouth and say the words out loud, but I couldn't. Instead I found another way to express what I was undoubtedly sure I felt. The words pulsed through my body and out of my hands into hers, the one I loved inexplicably.

Of course, it would be easy to brush the whole thing off and insist it was a crush, a silly little case of puppy love, but it wasn't. It was far more than that.

From the moment I saw Maddy she'd captured me. She had me completely gripped. I was fascinated with everything about her – the way she looked with her fire-like hair and flushed cheeks, the way her heart-shaped lips spoke with a softness and warmth, and the way she appeared so vulnerable as she exposed her caring heart. I adored her – it was that simple.

With Maddy in my life I felt whole. She added a magical sparkle that I'd never want to live without. And so I told her, with those three little squeezes. I had no agenda, no hidden plan or desire for anything to change between us – my only thought was to relieve myself of those feelings by communicating them in the only way I felt I could.

Three squeezes of love.

From me.

To her.

Being friends with two boys wasn't always the easiest thing for Maddy to have to put up with. There were times when just being friends with us cost her more than a few tears and heartache. Especially since, as everyone knows, girls and boys can't be just friends. But we liked to think of ourselves as an exception to that rule. And when the shit hit the fan, which inevitably it did, we decided — over a pinkie promise, if I remember rightly — to stick together like glue. It was a symbol that we would always be there for each other and that we'd never waver on that promise, no matter what life threw our way. Of course, as soon as puberty struck, our teen years were filled with wild mis-demeanour. Well, hanging from trees counts, right? But, for Maddy and me, a school trip to Paris was where our story really started. Whether there had been something between us all along, or whether the city of love cast a spell and claimed our hearts, it's hard to say. All I knew was that things would never be the same again . . .

Ben

Fifteen years old . . .

'What do you think of Maddy?' I asked Robert as we kicked a football around his garden. It was a Saturday afternoon in mid-June, but a cool, cloudy day. Maddy wasn't about, she'd gone to visit her nan who still lived in Harrow, so it was just us two for a change. Football wasn't really her thing, so we made the most of having a kick-around when we could do – without being grumbled at. I took the opportunity to talk to Robert about something that had been playing on my mind. Maddy.

'What do you mean?' he asked, confused by my vague question. He rolled the ball back on to his toe and flicked it upwards so that it landed on his knee, enabling him to bounce it from one to the other, on to his chest and then back over to me with considerable control. Robert was ridiculously talented with a ball – in fact, he was great at any sport, ball or no ball. He always won, no matter what the game – something that was helped by his competitive streak. He liked being the best, whereas I was too laid-back to care. Perhaps that's why we worked so well together.

'I dunno . . .' I shrugged, putting my foot on top of the ball to stop it before slowly passing it back in his direction as I struggled to formulate my words. 'She's not like the other girls in our class . . .'

We'd been attending Peaswood High for the past four years. It was a lot bigger than our primary school, with loads more children, but all three of us had managed to get into the same form class – thanks to us begging our parents to ask the headmaster. So nothing much had changed when it came to our friendship. We still lived in each others' pockets and were as tight as ever. Occasionally one of us would get close to another kid and they'd join us for a bit – but they'd wander off eventually, put off by how close we all were, I reckon. So the three of us had stuck together, as we'd promised we would. We'd even come up with our own group name – 'The Tripod'. Yeah, it was only mildly better than Laura and her Pink Dreamers, but it meant something. The name came from our first science lesson with Mrs Fellows – an extremely strict teacher with an irritatingly high-pitched nasal voice. One of the kids in class had been playing with his tripod, instead of listening to her riveting lesson on the periodic table, and bent one of its metal legs. The teacher made him stand on his chair as punishment and, as if that wasn't embarrassing enough, proceeded to give him a massive lecture on respecting school equipment before detailing the important qualities of the tripod. She said, 'Tripods have three legs. They rely on each other for support. If they stand together they are strong and united. BUT if one breaks, they are all rendered useless . . .' We turned to each other with little smirks, all thinking the same thing – yeah, we're a fricking tripod!

'What's made you ask, anyway?' Robert probed as he flicked the ball in the air and head-butted it repeatedly, continuously keeping an eye on it as he jerked his body around to wherever the ball was headed – always a step ahead and ready to tap it skywards.

'Nothing . . . It's just I heard Antony and John talking about her,' I shrugged.

'Yeah? What did they say?' he asked with a frown, catching the ball in his hands and looking at me – my revelation grabbing his full attention.

'That they thought she was fit.'

'Really?' He raised both his eyebrows and puffed out his cheeks as he mulled over the comment.

Going to 'big school' and mixing with people from outside of Peaswood (they all arrived on coaches every morning – streamed in by their hundreds), we suddenly discovered how sheltered our lives were. Our idea of a fun night was riding around on our bikes down our road and grabbing some penny sweets or collectable stickers from the newsagents, but in those first few years at secondary school we were shocked as we heard many tales of raunchy things happening at under-eighteen discos. Even the school discos or birthday parties we went to were eye-opening – kids would go around snogging as many people as they could, tallying them up in some sort of tongue-wagging competition. The three of us would be awkwardly stood on the dance floor, getting our groove on to 'Cotton Eye Joe', as we tried to stop ourselves from gawping at the sight of it all. Before going to Peaswood High, that kiss between Greg and Becky was the rudest thing we'd ever seen and that was nothing to our new classmates. Even four years in we struggled to keep up – we were too busy being the children we were supposed to be. Some of the other kids were simply much more advanced than us – kids like Anthony and John, who we knew had both been 'all the way' with various girls in our year. Knowing that they were now talking about Maddy in that way, that she was on their radar, made me feel really protective of her. And irritated.

'Well, she's not ugly . . .'

'Definitely not.'

'In fact, yeah, she is cute, I guess,' shrugged Robert, his face returning to its earlier frown as he contemplated our best friend in a way he clearly hadn't before.

Robert had been flirting with a girl in our class called Daniella that week. They both knew they fancied each other and that they'd be snogging each other's faces off at the next party, it was only a matter of time. I think his own concerns for our female friend were fuelled with the knowledge of the racy thoughts that had been going through his teenage mind about his looming first sexual encounter with Daniella.

'It's strange to hear that said about her, though, you know?' he added.

'Yeah, that's what I thought.'

'Makes me feel weird.'

'Same . . .' I nodded.

'Do you think Maddy likes one of them?'

The question threw me. It was toe-curling enough thinking of them fancying her, but I hadn't even thought about Maddy fancying one of them. We didn't really talk about that sort of stuff with her – she could ask us any questions she liked, for instance she'd been quizzing Rob no end about him fancying Daniella, but we'd never probed her on the topic of the opposite sex. Well, I didn't anyway.

'I dunno . . .' I muttered.

'Maybe you should ask her.'

'Do you reckon?'

'Why not? I bet she'd like hearing that they called her fit,' he grinned.

Standing there, just the two of us, in the safety of his back garden, I thought about telling him how I felt – confessing that I thought Maddy was more than fit, that I thought she was the most amazing girl ever to have graced the planet, but I didn't. I'd been feeling that way for so long and our friendship, the one the three of us shared, stopped me from saying anything, like it had done in the past whenever the words were on the tip of my tongue. We were a tripod. We stuck together to help each other through whatever dramas life chucked our way, we weren't meant to be creating them or making things complicated between each other. I'd always thought that if I were to tell Maddy how I really felt it would have caused things to change between the three of us. It could have ruined everything and driven a humungous wedge between us that we'd never be able to get rid of. I never wanted that to happen to us. I carried those fears with me and they kept my heart in check – stopping me from blurting out declarations of love that, for all I knew, I could have ended up regretting.

Anthony and John paying her attention had got my back up, perhaps because they had the freedom to say what they felt and more of a chance with her than I did – and I knew they'd use that chance to get as far with her as they could. They'd have no respect for the kind and wonderful girl I knew her to be. They were teenage boys with one thing in mind. Sex. I couldn't stand it.

* * *

Our morning routine had been set on our first day at Peaswood High – Maddy walked round to mine, then we'd both continue round to pick up Robert before heading into school. It had originally started with our mums taking us in convoy, but within a month we'd managed to persuade them that we were fine to do the five-minute walk alone. So, on the Monday morning after speaking to Robert, as soon as I'd closed my front door and taken one of the pink peardrop sweets she was offering me, I decided to bring up the conversation.

'Erm . . . I heard Anthony and John talking about you the other day,' I said, popping the sweet into my mouth, my eyes instantly watering at the sweetness of it.

'Those two idiots,' she sighed, rolling her eyes. 'What were they saying?'

'They called you fit.'

'Haaa!' she shrieked, as she grabbed hold of my arm and stopped on the pavement. Shaking with laughter, she tilted her head back, covering her face with her hands to quieten the sound.

'What's so funny?'

'Anthony Burke and John Martin?' she giggled.

I shrugged – not understanding her apparent aversion to them.

'Pass me a bucket!'

She laughed the whole way into school.

I couldn't help but smile. She wasn't about to start dating one of them if that was what she thought of them . . .

Or so I'd thought.

It's possible that my little chat with Maddy had resulted in her mind being awoken to the possibility of fancying

John – the dim-witted yet more pleasant of the two rogues. Such is the fickle nature of a teenager's heart, what wasn't there one minute had grown into a colossal flirtation the next. At least, that's what it felt like for me – and the change came suddenly. That very same day, when we were in afternoon registration, John walked over and whispered something to Maddy. I have no idea what was said, but was surprised to witness her cheeks pinking as she pouted out her lips into a smile before tapping him gently on the arm. She was visibly flirting. And I knew that was the case because she couldn't look at me for several minutes afterwards – no doubt she could sense my unbelieving eyes staring at her incredulously, questioning her behaviour.

It simmered along in that playful manner for a few weeks, suggestive gazes and whisperings going back and forth, until Julia Hicks's birthday party. On that night of childish antics, not only did Rob go off to snog Daniella, but Maddy ended up tucked away in a dark corner of the room playing tonsil tennis with John.

The never-ending stream of cocktail sausages at the buffet table were my only comfort that night.

I wouldn't say I was happy a week later when John decided Maddy wasn't his type after all. Watching her become deflated and embarrassed at being carelessly dumped was certainly uncomfortable, but I definitely felt relieved that their coquettish behaviour had come to an end. I selfishly found it reassuring and comforting to have things go back to normal. Well, almost back to normal – John may not have taken his relationship with Maddy much further, but Robert and Daniella had become an official item. This was a pairing I didn't mind so much. It didn't leave me seething and depressed; in fact, it was almost the opposite. I enjoyed having Maddy to myself a little more when Rob's attention had been diverted away from us. I liked us becoming a twosome.

Maddy

Fifteen years old . . .

The summer before going into year eleven was a glorious one. Every day seemed to be spent running around in the sweltering sunshine with careless abandon. The long days stretched the daylight hours, increasing the time we had to explore and play. More than any other summer holiday I can remember, that one was gay and merry – our last chance to be proper kids before heading back to school, turning sixteen and starting the gruelling lead-up to our GCSE exams. For the last time in our lives we were free from worries, responsibilities and expectations. It was a summer filled with smiles of contentment . . . for the most part, anyway.

We were that little bit older by then and our mums felt at ease about us going out independently, allowing us to go into the village on our own – as long as we promised to stay together and headed home before it got dark. They implied they were doing us a favour but, let's face it, we were a handful and it was a relief for them to get rid of us for a few hours when they could. There was only so much they could take of us being under their feet after they had been used to sending us off to school each day. With us out of their hair they were left to enjoy the peace that had only existed before we came into the world kicking and screaming.

Robert and Daniella (the school's current golden couple) had frequently been found snogging each other's faces off whenever they had the chance during term time. Despite their keenness, though, they hadn't actually managed to see each other so far during that summer break. Instead they had been texting almost every day and spent an hour every night on MSN. Much to Ben's and my disdain.

Our local park, to which we'd become regular visitors, had a variety of trees lining the pathways and clustered around its edges, most of which we'd succeeded in climbing. The boys had developed a little routine when it came to tackling their vertical beams, one that was aggravating to say the least. Essentially, they would clamber up as quickly as they could, perch from up high and grin down at me, heckling for me to start climbing. I had no doubt that Robert and Ben never saw my being a girl as something that made me a lesser human being, but when it came to climbing trees I was slower and more fearful – something that amused them. Now, I wasn't a girlie girl, I wasn't scared of getting grubby. I just wasn't overly keen on heights! Usually I overcame my fear and cautiously ascended, taking care not to look down until I was on a sturdy branch but, occasionally, if the tree just seemed too big and freaked me out, I'd decline the challenge and remain grounded, much to the boys' annoyance. I'd lie beneath the tree, basking in the gorgeous sunshine, ignoring the leaves and twigs that they playfully threw down at me until they got bored and descended, joining me at ground level.

Three weeks into our six weeks of freedom we were

once again in the park, towards its back end, with the boys deciding what tree to take on.

'This one!' shouted Ben as he approached a sparse-looking beech tree, and started to fly up it with ease.

Robert followed suit. Only once they were both dangling from its branches, swinging with youthful serenity, did they look down at me, Ben grinning manically, while Robert simply raised his eyebrows, daring me to join them.

'Come on,' called Ben. 'Hurry up!'

'Don't rush me,' I warned in a huff as I placed my baby blue rucksack next to the base of the tree, took out a bottle of Coke and downed a big gulp of it, the fizz burning my insides in my haste.

'I don't understand what takes you so long.'

'I'm just getting ready.'

'You've climbed bigger!' encouraged Ben.

'I know, I know . . .' I faltered, peering up at the pair of them, each in their grubby army-like camouflage shorts and khaki-green t-shirts. Their look was certainly Action Man inspired, my own was a touch more Sporty Spice, with dark blue Adidas trackie bottoms that had three florescent orange stripes running down each leg. Stupidly I'd put on a white t-shirt that day, and there was no way it would still be gleaming white by the time I got home, so I knew I'd get a telling off from Mum for getting it dirty.

'It's an easy one!' Ben encouraged.

'Get up here!' yelled Robert, taking a more forceful approach. After a heavy pause he slowly, and teasingly, added, 'Don't be such a girl, Maddy.'

Well, that was enough to get me out of my strop and up the tree instantly. Talk about succumbing to peer pressure. Ben was right, it wasn't as hard as some of the others they'd forced me up and, as long as I looked up it and not down at my feet, the height didn't seem so bad. I just took my time.

'I knew that would get you up here,' Robert laughed with a cheeky wink, once I'd joined them on the steady branch they were both perched on.

'Very clever,' I smiled, looking out at the rest of the park.

Putting my fears aside, there was nothing like being up high in a tree with Robert and Ben. Even though we were realistically only seven or eight feet in the air, to us that seemed ginormous – we might as well have been at the top of the Empire State Building, it would have evoked the same feeling of wonder. The air seemed different up there, cooler and fresher, and the view more beautiful than when we were grounded. We could see the whole park. There was also something about becoming invisible to others as we hid behind the tree's leaves and branches that felt magical. I completely understood why the boys loved being up there so much. An overwhelming sense of peace would take over us for a moment or two when we first sat there, as though we'd entered a new world.

Inevitably, at some point, the peace and tranquillity we'd marvelled over would descend into chaos with the boys shaking the branches and trying to do forward rolls on them. I'd clamp my arms and legs onto the branch and scream my head off at them to stop, scared that we were on the verge of falling and breaking all of our bones. They never listened to me, they just cackled, finding my fears hilarious.

Getting down was always fun too . . . NOT. The boys would courageously swing and leap to the ground, landing with ease, whereas I'd painstakingly hold on for as long as I could while the boys shouted at me to jump – occasionally pulling at one of my legs if they got really bored of waiting for me.

That's how it had been on that day in the middle of our summer holidays – the boys had teased me just as much to get down the tree as they had to get up it. That's why, as we were walking back through the park heading home, I decided it was time to get my own back on the overly confident duo. I hated being the weaker one. It was time for them to squirm instead. And so, as we walked towards a tree we'd nicknamed 'The Big Green', a monster of an oak tree that had been too difficult for any of us to master with its wide girth and sporadic branches, an idea popped into my head.

'Go on, then,' I said to them both, pointing towards the giant feat, feeling pleased with myself for thinking up such a great plan. 'I dare you.'

'What?' shrieked Ben, laughing at the ridiculousness of what I'd suggested, shaking his head so vigorously that his cheeks wobbled. 'No chance.'

'Why not?' I demanded.

'Because!'

'That's not a proper answer,' I said.

'It's dinner time. We have to get back,' he replied, his voice becoming shrill with panic.

'Don't be such a wimp.'

'I'm not being a wimp.'

'You are,' I goaded.

'I'm not!'

'Are.'

'Not.'

'Are!'

'Not!'

'I'll do it,' Robert said calmly, breaking in on our bickering, causing Ben and I to whip our heads round to face him.

'Really?' Ben asked, clearly as shocked as I was by his bravery. Or stupidity.

'Of course,' he shrugged, as though it was nothing.

I was impressed, although sure he'd change his mind as we made our way closer to the Big Green; after all, the nearer we got, the more of a monster it became. Just standing beneath it and looking up at its expansiveness was enough to make me nervous and dizzy, even though I wasn't the one about to climb it. There's no questioning the fact that Robert was the most confident of the three of us – that was something we'd always been aware of – but surely even he had his limits! I'd expected the pair of them to quake at the very thought of it – not for one of them to give it a go!

'You sure?' I gulped.

'Yep,' he barked, without the slightest quiver in his voice.

And off he went, up the tree, hugging it as he pulled himself higher and higher. His legs and arms were strong as he scrambled up to near where its branches began to poke out.

Ben and I stood below, gawping at him as he kept going higher and higher, inch by inch.

'Whoa!' I muttered.

'I know,' he whispered.

Within seconds that wonder turned into panic. Maybe it was because he was getting cocky from our admiration and trying to show off, making him less careful, or perhaps the challenge was simply too great for him after all.

Somehow Robert's left foot slipped, the rubber of his Hi-tech trainers grinding along the bark to make a terrifying scraping sound as it did so. He tried, with a giant reach, to grasp hold of the tree, of its branches, of anything he could, but failed. Instead, his hands grabbed at the air as he fell backwards, legs and arms flailing around helplessly, before landing on the ground next to us with a thud and an almighty crack. He writhed in pain, clutching hold of his thigh, his face distorted with agony.

'Argh!' he screamed.

Ben rushed to his side first and knelt down beside him, placing a hand on his shoulder to comfort him. Once the shock allowed me to move again I joined him, taking hold of one of Robert's hands. It was the only thing I could think of that might soothe him in some way. He gripped it tightly. So tightly it caused me to clench my jaw to steady myself.

'Rob, you okay?' Ben asked. 'Where does it hurt?'

'My leg!' he yelped, the torturous pain causing him to roll from side to side on his back.

Looking at his leg we could clearly see he'd broken it. A bone was sticking out in a grotesque manner. I couldn't help but wince at the sight of it.

I looked up at Ben as panic started to rise within me. Surprisingly, for the boy who was eager to be led rather than followed, he looked calm and composed as he took control and decided what we had to do.

'You stay here. I'll go to get help,' he said, looking from me to our injured friend, firmly gripping him on the shoulder. 'I won't be long, Robbie.'

'Quick!' he screamed, before inhaling sharply between his teeth.

'You gonna be okay?' Ben asked me, getting to his feet and grabbing for my hand, which he squeezed three times as though he was pumping courage and strength through his touch.

I nodded and watched as he turned away from me and sprinted across the park. My heart ached as I looked down at Robert and saw his face scrunched up as he battled with the pain, groaning as he held on to my hand a little tighter, his breathing becoming erratic and forced.

'Shh . . .' I breathed, trying to keep myself from bursting into tears as I attempted to comfort him. Not only was I horrified at seeing my best friend in such pain, and lost over how to help him, but I also felt enormously guilty. I was the one who'd sent him up that ridiculous tree, after all. I'd only wanted to show them that we all had limitations and that I shouldn't have been given such a hard time for my own. I hadn't expected Robert to climb it and I certainly didn't think he'd break something as a result.

'I'm so sorry,' I sobbed eventually, after watching his suffering for a few minutes, unable to keep in my shame any longer. Robert was the strong one of the three of us, and I'd reduced him to a vulnerable mess with my stupidity.

'What are you crying for, you loser?' he croaked.

'Because it's my fault.'

'What?'

'I told you to go up there. This wouldn't have happened if I hadn't done that . . .'

'Don't be such a girl, Maddy,' he groaned, flinching in pain as laughter trickled out of him.

I stopped crying and just stared at him open mouthed, wondering how he could possibly use that line on me when he was in such a state himself.

'*Me* being a girl? What about *you*?' I teased, giving his shoulder a gentle shove.

'Huh?'

'If Daniella saw you now she'd think you were the biggest girl she's ever seen,' I continued. 'I mean, she'd probably dump you on the spot,' I shrugged.

'Maddy . . .'

'What? At least I *am* a girl! What's your excuse?'

'Really? You're choosing this moment to verbally abuse me?'

'You started it.'

'I fell out of a tree and broke my leg,' he said incredulously, his face still twisted in agony at the pain. 'Please, just . . . be nice!' he exhaled.

He laughed then. Laughed so hysterically that I couldn't tell if he was laughing or crying for a moment or two. Perhaps it was a mixture of both as they battled against each other, but the laughter eventually won. His chuckle filled the air around us as he leaned back and closed his eyes, bringing his free hand up to cover his crinkled face.

Looking at him, at the ridiculousness of the situation, at our bickering, I couldn't help but dissolve into a fit of giggles myself. My body doubled over, causing my forehead to gently rest on Rob's chest before I rolled off on to my back. With our heads and shoulders touching, and hands still gripping hold of each other, we laughed uncontrollably side by side as our cackles drifted skywards and entwined into the leaves of the Big Green.

It was a perfect moment, born from something horrific and shocking, that briefly brought us closer than we'd ever ventured before.

By the time Ben came back with Robert's dad, we had tears streaming down our faces and couldn't stop smiling. Ben looked at us not only as though we'd gone mad, but also with a bemused sadness, as though he was troubled to be left out of whatever was going on. He quizzed us both eagerly, asked what we were laughing about, but his confused face, and the fact that we were effectively being giddy over nothing, made me laugh harder – so hard that my body convulsed once more with laughter, moving me on to my side so that my mouth was nuzzled into Rob's neck, as I tried to calm myself down.

It was when Robert's dad started to inspect his injury that he yelped out in pain again, stopping the moment in its tracks and sobering us instantly.

A quick dash to the hospital told us that, as predicted, Robert's leg was broken. Thanks to me, he spent the first few weeks of life in year eleven on crutches with a massive bright orange cast on his wounded leg – which we all signed and put rude messages on. He might have been temporarily disabled, but he rarely complained. That's mainly because it guaranteed him ample attention from everyone – the football team who missed him, the girls who cooed after him like he was a poorly puppy and the teachers who gave him preferential treatment. He got out of lessons early to avoid getting crushed by the crowds in the crammed corridors and was granted access to the front of the dinner queue . . . Well, as far as silver linings go, his wasn't bad.

The only thing it didn't help was his relationship with Daniella. She'd started going ice-skating every Saturday with her mates. Rob couldn't exactly go along and, as a result, she met Russell. He was one of those more capable skaters who rushed around the ring as though he was about to knock everyone over with his menacing speed, putting the fear of God into all the nervous skaters on the ice. Evidently Daniella liked that sort of thing.

She dumped Robert by text.

Nice.

That had been my first experience of Robert having a girlfriend, and I hadn't liked it one bit – especially after the incident under the tree. I teased him about his relationship and jibed him for being 'under the thumb' whenever her name popped up in conversation. That probably makes me sound like a spoilt brat, longing for his attention, but I just had this urge to get under his skin on the topic and to make sure I wasn't being forgotten about.

With much guilt (although I don't think it's a surprising confession), I'll admit that I was relieved Robert was no longer spending hours at his computer sending Daniella soppy messages. Being dumped hadn't fazed him at all — he was as funny, witty and charming as ever.

I was thrilled to have him back!

Ben

Sixteen years old . . .

Robert's new-found single status meant that he was back with me and Maddy once more. I was chuffed to have him with us again, obviously, but it meant I wasn't getting as much alone time with Maddy as I had since the start of the autumn term – and I can't hide the fact that I'd been enjoying it. I'll even admit that I felt deflated somehow at having to 'share' her again. It was the first time I'd become what can only be described as possessive over her.

Being a three again led me to feel a bit paranoid, and that irritating feeling had started to creep in even before Rob got dumped. The day he fell and broke his leg, I'd left a shaken Maddy and pain-stricken Robert beneath that tree to go and get help. I thought I was being heroic . . . taking control and being the leader for once. But when I got back, I was taken aback to find them wrapped up in each other looking like they hadn't a care in the world – laughing and taking pleasure in each other's silliness. I felt like I was intruding on something, and that was an unfamiliar and uncomfortable sensation.

If it weren't for the bone visibly protruding from his leg, I'd have thought I'd dreamed Robert falling and needing my help.

It irked me, even though I told myself it was nothing,

reasoned with myself that Robert was with Daniella and didn't see Maddy in the same way that I did.

I was being hypersensitive . . . a douchebag! Still, it took a while for those feelings to simmer down and disappear and for me to feel like everything was normal between the three of us – between the two of them.

That summer changed my outlook on my own feelings, and not just because of the way I'd found them underneath the Big Green. I'd been to see *Pearl Harbour* at the cinema (I'd taken my mum out for her birthday), and was left feeling as though my heart had been ripped out. It might sound pathetic, but the message was clear – seize the day, love like there's no tomorrow and declare your feelings before it's too late. That's how I'd come to realize that I could no longer bottle things inside. What, I wondered, was I trying to prove by living in the torturous barricade of my own heart? I'd let myself be tormented by what I hadn't said, rather than what I had . . . paranoid about what others might be feeling, rather than just asking outright. Yes, I'd decided to take control, to put my feelings out there to be reciprocated or rebuffed. Either way, *something* was better than nothing.

With a trip planned in year eleven to the most romantic city in the world, I decided to bite my tongue a little longer. It was only a few months, I told myself, and I wanted the moment I finally decided to lift my silence and speak up to be memorable. And so, for months I thought of nothing but Paris. Vivid images filled my mind – of us together at the top of the Eiffel Tower, surrounded by the romantic view, and the look of adoration on Maddy's face as I opened my mouth to utter my love confession. It fuelled my sleepless nights that summer and gave me a giddy feeling of excitement in my gut.

It felt as though Paris had become, in many ways, the pinnacle of my very existence. Nights were spent ploughing through information on the web to formulate my plan, hours were spent with a pen and paper writing out what I was going to say when the moment of truth finally came. It was as though years of wonder and desire had led me to that point and to that precise spot I needed to reach at the top of the Eiffel Tower. I wanted, more than anything, for it to go right. It had to be perfect.

Maddy

Sixteen years old . . .

The best thing about taking Art as a GCSE was that you got to go on an art trip to Paris in year eleven. A week away from parents, exam stress and school work, traipsing around the millions of museums and eating trillions of crêpes and macaroons, understandably sounded very tempting. And that was why the three of us all decided to take up art when it came to filling out our options for the years ahead – yes, we all sat down and had a big chat about certain subjects we should all go for so that we'd get time together. Along with our compulsory subjects, we all opted for French over Spanish, Art over Drama, and History over Religious Education. I however went for Food, while Robert went for Physical Education and Ben went for Graphic Design – something he was insanely good at. Our plans did backfire a little bit when it turned out that each year group was separated into new class sets for the mandatory core subjects as well as those we'd optioned, but we found ourselves together in Art, and at least we all got most of the same homework to plough through together.

In the weeks leading up to that art trip I felt an endless wave of apprehension. No, I wasn't worried about being stranded in the capital (that would have simply been an adventure) and I wasn't worried I'd get homesick (I couldn't wait to get out of the house) ... Nope, I was nervous because of a feeling that had been brewing inside during the previous months. Those feelings had nothing to do with Paris, but everything to do with Robert. A fact I was struggling to comprehend.

As a result of that afternoon underneath the Big Green, I was drawn to him like a piece of flimsy metal to a powerful magnet – there was no way of avoiding its strength. No way to resist. That unspeakable energy tingled away beneath the surface, giving me a surge of something unidentifiable every time I thought of him. It felt like we were on the cusp of a momentous change, but I wasn't sure how I felt about it.

Robert treated me as he always had – like one of the boys he could have a laugh with, or, at times, a little sister he was fiercely over-protective of. He was always draping an arm over my shoulder, or gently mocking me for something I'd said or done. It was how we'd always been. So, was I the only one looking further into every touch shared? Every gaze he placed in my direction? Embarrassingly, it seemed so.

Robert's enchanting ways (which had naturally transpired from his confident role as our group's leader) continued to capture more girls' hearts than ever. He'd always been a charmer (his flirty and confident ways had been buried deep within his gorgeous exterior), but seeing him tease or fool around with any other girl after that moment under the tree was excruciating. Each suggestive glance, wink and mutter that he flung in another girl's direction stung my teenage heart – a fact that confused me beyond belief. Then there was the gossip that lingered around him – girls speculating over who he'd end up snogging while we were away. For obvious reasons I was never even suggested, but for once, that omission left me feeling jealous. Envious not to be seen as having a chance . . .

Of course I knew what those alien emotions meant, but I also knew that I wasn't going to be the one to act on them. I wasn't going to show Robert that I'd succumbed to his charms and found myself plonked in the middle of his fan club with tens of other girls. Oh yes, he really did have a fan club. The girls in our year, in fact our whole school, swooned over him relentlessly – more so when he'd broken his leg! Huddles of girls would frantically walk around the school to find him on his lunch break, they'd giggle as he passed them on the stairway, dribble at the smallest glimpse of him in the corridor, and if there was ever any accidental body contact, like arms brushing as he walked past, there'd be a near-fainting situation . . . It was mind-boggling and quite sickening to watch, but Robert loved the attention from his adoring fans and often played up to them, much to their delight. Due to their lovesick nature, his admirers continuously treated me with caution – I was, after all, a girl with unlimited access to Robert. It was something they could only dream of. I wasn't too bothered by their occasional evil glances. In fact, I found the whole thing funny. Yes, I knew Robert up close and personal – but that didn't just mean I got to see his handsome (there's no disputing his good looks) face on a regular basis behind closed doors, but I also got to see him scratching his arse, popping his hand down between his boxers and trousers for a quick squeeze (as though to check his bits were still intact) and a million other little idiosyncrasies that would leave other's minds boggled. The Robert they saw, the charming, suave and well-groomed prince, was a tad different to my grubby friend Rob – and I loved it that way.

I had a secret piece of him.

Did I really want to give up that piece and turn into every other girl looking at him through rose-tinted glasses? Sadly, it seemed it was way out of my control. That's what led me to be full of nervousness about going to Paris. If something *was* going to happen between us, then it was sure to occur there when we were cocooned in a bubble of holiday abandon. Right?

And if it didn't?

If he ended up kissing someone else right in front of me?

Well, I just wanted to get on that trip so I could witness which of the two scenarios would win out. At least then the anxiety of not knowing could be put to rest.

On the morning we left for the trip, I experienced a rush of excitement as I wheeled my suitcase through the school gates and saw the green coach waiting to take us all across the English Channel. Instead of walking into school with Robert or Ben, my mum had decided to go with me. Partly because of the early start – it was six o'clock in the morning and still dark thanks to it being November – but mostly because it was my first ever trip abroad without her and my dad and she wanted to see me off safely. I could already see the tears of concern threatening to spill in her eyes and had to stop myself from rolling my eyes at her – horrified that she was on the verge of embarrassing me with an emotional goodbye.

'You just make sure you stick with the group, okay?'

'Yes, Mum,' I said, trying to stop her from worrying – although it was no use, she'd had her knickers in a twist ever since she and Dad got the first letter about the trip at the start of the school year. Honestly, you would have thought she'd be happy to have me, her premenstrual-screaming-raging-teenage-daughter-who-is-lovely-to-everyone-else-but-the-actual-devil-at-home, out of the house for a little bit. But it appeared *not* having me at home caused her just as much stress as having me there did.

'And listen to everything that your teacher says . . .'

'Mum, it's going to be fine!' I said for the umpteenth time. 'I'm not a kid!'

'Don't you take that tone with me, madam!'

Luckily, Robert started walking towards us. Not only did a pang of nerves shoot through me, but it also stopped Mum in her scolding as she planted a welcoming smile on her face.

'Hello, Robbie!' Mum beamed, opening her arms and giving him a big hug. She was always delighted to see him.

When we were nine years old Robert and Ben melted Mum's heart as they sat on their bikes at our front door asking for me to play outside – seven years later and they still had the same effect on her, although their relationships varied. Robert had my mum wrapped around his little finger. He was incredibly cheeky with her, always winding her up or telling naughty jokes – she couldn't help but laugh at his funny ways. As for Ben, she was always going on about how respectful and polite he was whenever he came over. The first thing he used to do in our house was ask Mum if she wanted him to make her a cup of tea or if he could help with whatever she was doing, like dinner if she was cooking, or the gardening if she was weeding on the patio. Their glowing personalities made them look like angels and me look like a hormonal brat, although I think that was just the joy of having a teenage daughter – gone was the little princess she'd dressed up in frilly outfits, replaced by an adolescent who huffed and puffed her way through home life. With that in mind, it's unsurprising that Mum treated the boys as though they were her own delightful kids – the sons she never had. It was clearly a case of wishful thinking.

At sixteen years old, Robert had changed a considerable amount since I'd first met him. I'm pretty sure that, back when we were nine, we were roughly the same height. Not any more. During the summer the year before he'd shot up and become over six feet tall – the difference was astounding. The only trouble was that his body had put so much effort into growing upwards that it had forgotten to grow a little bit outwards too. He was incredibly lanky and clumsy with these long limbs that he'd miraculously accumulated overnight, but there was clearly something endearing about him as females swooned in his presence.

'You excited?' Mum asked Robert.

'Yeah! Can't wait. Have you got your camera?' he asked me.

'Of course!'

'I've only let her take three disposable ones,' Mum informed him. 'That way she won't have to worry if she loses them. You know what she's like . . . careless.'

'Thanks for clarifying that, Mum,' I grumbled.

'Have you forgotten what you did with your dad's binoculars when you went to Dorset?'

I rolled my eyes. Here we go again, I thought to myself. She'd revel in any excuse to bring up how useless I was.

'Yes, you brought them back covered in cow pat, and then you didn't even bother to wash them – you just placed them back in the cupboard, where they waited for me and your dad to find them a month later. The smell, Robbie, was atrocious.'

Robert grinned at me as he shook his head.

Other people might have worried about their parents speaking to them, and treating them, like a child in public, but Robert and Ben had seen my mum talk to me in that way countless times, in fact she'd even spoken to them in that tone on numerous occasions (like the time we'd played tag in the garden and ruined some of her newly bloomed flowers – big mistake), so they found it amusing rather than embarrassing. A good thing when my mum was around.

'So you've only let her have *three* cameras?' Robert asked my mum with a smirk.

'Is it a bit much?' she frowned. 'You know she likes to take an account of every little detail.'

'You're telling me. I'm surprised her face hasn't morphed into a camera after covering her face with one for so long.'

'Oh, Robbie,' my mum giggled in response.

After badgering my parents endlessly, I'd been given a top-of-the-range camera for Christmas the previous year. They probably thought I'd get bored of it and discard it like every other present I'd begged for in the past, but instead I took it everywhere I went. It was irritating that I wasn't allowed to take it to Paris with me, the disposable cameras would be crap in comparison, but I also didn't want anything to happen to my most prized possession, so I didn't put up too much of a fight when they insisted I left it behind. Not that I'd have let them know that – such is the prerogative of a teenage daughter. I thought I was meant to argue against every boundary they set.

'I was just wondering how on earth she'll be able to annoy us when those three films have run out,' continued Robert with a playful shrug.

'Oi,' I shrieked, acting insulted.

'Come on,' Robert laughed, grabbing for my suitcase. 'I'll take it round.'

'You're such a gent,' Mum beamed.

'I try,' Rob smiled back before gesturing to the other side of the bus. 'My mum's over there talking to Ben and June.'

'Oh, I didn't realize your mums were coming too,' said Mum, clearly happy not to be the only one that'd shown up.

'What? When there's a chance to embarrass us? Of course they're here.'

'You cheeky little monkey,' Mum laughed. 'I'll tell your mum you said that.'

'What have you got in this?' Robert asked me as he tried to do the macho lift with my suitcase, rather than drag it along on its wheels like a girl.

'Stuff,' I shrugged. I'd definitely over-packed. I hadn't had a clue what to take with me so had ended up bunging in loads of extra clothes that morning, even though I knew I wouldn't end up wearing half of it.

'We're only going for a week . . .'

'Yeah, yeah . . . it has wheels, you know. Just use them if your muscles haven't fully developed yet,' I teased.

With this he lifted the whole suitcase up onto his shoulder and walked off to put it on the bus.

'Show off!' I called after him.

He turned and gave me a wink. I knew the hearts of other girls would have melted at the gesture, but I grimaced back to make him think mine hadn't. Although, as soon as his back was turned, I couldn't help a small smile forming on my lips – the nervous excitement bubbling away once again, no matter how much I tried to squash it.

As we walked around the bus we spotted Robert's mum, Carol, Ben and his mum, June, huddled together in a small group and headed towards them.

Like Robert, Ben had also changed a lot over the years – he'd grown a good couple of feet as well, but he wasn't quite as tall. Instead, his body had stayed in proportion as it *did* manage to grow outwards at the same time, giving him a much sturdier appearance. Much to Ben's annoyance, though, he'd also kept hold of some of his puppy fat – that's not to say he was fat, there was just a little more of him. Yes, I would have described Robert as a long stick and Ben as a round ball that you just want to squidge. He was soft and cuddly. And his dark facial features had maintained the cuteness that they'd always had. He might not have got the same sort of attention from the ladies as Robert did, but he was well loved by them all nonetheless . . . they were more likely to go to him for advice (or a squeeze – he was the best hugger, he really held you tight) than to flirt. I don't think that bothered Ben as he never really seemed into any of the girls that he talked to. My dad had actually asked me at dinner one night if he 'batted for the other team'. I almost choked on my cottage pie. I told Ben what Dad had said on our way to school the next morning and he'd almost choked on the sweet he'd been sucking . . . Choking was obviously the standard reaction when questioning Ben's sexuality. It put an end to that little query, anyway. He was straight, he liked girls, but seemed too laid-back to want to do anything about it.

As we were nearing our group, Ben let out a huge yawn – one that he didn't bother to cover up with his hands. It seemed to go on forever, highlighting just how tired he was.

'Bit early for you, love?' Mum laughed.

'Just a tad.'

'Well, you should've seen him jump out of bed this morning,' said June, pointing her thumb sideways in Ben's direction. 'I've not seen him like that in a while. Anyone would think he couldn't wait to get away.'

Ben shrugged in innocence with a sheepish grin, wrapped his arm around her and rested his head on hers – he was at least a foot taller than her. I always loved seeing little moments like that pass between Ben and June. Unlike Robert and me, who both went through stages of being embarrassed by our mums (or declaring we hated them), Ben hadn't. He worshipped her and gladly showed that in public.

'You would not believe how hard it was to get her up today,' tutted Mum, giving me a gentle poke in the ribs and making me yelp in shock.

'Ooh, quick photo of our leaving party before we go?' I pleaded, pulling one of the cardboard-covered cameras from my coat pocket and winding the film along.

'Do we have to?' moaned Mum.

'Yes.'

'But I haven't even got my face on yet . . . here, give me the ruddy thing. I'll get one of you and Ben instead,' she demanded, grabbing the camera off me before I managed to get a quick picture of her make-up free.

I wrapped my arms around Ben's neck and smiled, but just before Mum captured our pose Robert jumped on us from behind – turning it into a laughing picture of the three of us.

'I see she's started already then?' Rob jokingly asked Ben while frowning at my camera.

'Only just,' Ben laughed. 'Hope you've been practising your fake smiles.'

'Yes, my speciality. Well, now that's done . . . Miss James is about to let everyone on the bus. Quick!' Robert whispered. 'Bye, Mum,' he added with a cheeky grin and a wave before turning on his heels and running back around to the door of the bus.

Ben and I instantly sprang to life, the race for the back seat was on. Yes, the downside to being a threesome was that, on coaches, one of us had to sit on our own unless we managed to bagsy the back seat. It wasn't an easy task when there were so many other groups of friends wanting to get it too – it took some cleverly planned timing and for one of your team to be as quick as a bullet! With Robert first in line, he made the prospect of us getting our desired seats highly likely.

Robert's mum was close on his heels.

'If he thinks he's going to get away with saying a crappy goodbye like that without giving me a proper kiss, when he's leaving me for a bloody week, he's got another think coming,' tutted Carol, as she shook her head and wandered off after him, causing us all to laugh.

'Bye, Mum,' Ben said, leaning down and hugging June tightly before giving her a peck on the cheek.

'Oh, come here,' said Mum as she took me in her arms for my own cuddle goodbye, which I happily entered into. Despite my huffy appearance, I was nervous about the week away and I knew I'd miss my mum and her crazy ways.

Ben

Sixteen years old . . .

The excitement on the bus, even at that time in the morning, was sky high. We were getting away from school life, from exam stress and from our parents for a whole week. We were off to chill with our friends in Paris, to marvel at some wonderful art while sketching it (badly) into our workbooks, eat loads of crêpes and to test out our French on actual French people – it was time to see whether we'd actually learned anything in our lessons. I wasn't holding my breath on that score and had packed my mini French phrase book, just in case – so had Robert and Maddy. For some reason I was doubtful that the one French phrase that stuck in my head, 'Où est la piscine?' (where is the swimming pool?) was going to get me very far.

Once Miss James had called the register and found everybody had made it on board, even though it was frightfully early, we were free. Maddy, Robert and I squished up against the window at the back of the bus, and waved goodbye to our mums – all of whom were teary-eyed and rubbing each other's backs in support. We couldn't help but laugh at them, making them giggle back at the stupidity of their emotional outbursts. We were only going away for a week – you'd have thought we were moving to the other side of the world indefinitely the way they were carrying on.

As the coach started moving, carrying us away from our mums, away from the school and away from Peaswood, I experienced an unexpected lull – as though reality had hit, causing me to abandon my joyfulness momentarily. I worried about my mum. I shouldn't have, I knew she was far tougher than I was and could cope with far more than me, but it was the thought of her in that empty house on her own, without me there for company. The other mums had their husbands to rely on, but she obviously didn't. Dad leaving had made us closer than ever – we looked after each other, made sure we didn't dwell too heavily and moved each other into the light any time his absence hit us hard. It worried me that she'd have no one to do that for her without me there.

I looked up at the others to find Robert looking back at me. He winked and gave me an encouraging nod. He knew what was on my mind even though I hadn't said it, and I knew what he was saying even if the words hadn't worked their way out of his mouth. Mum would be fine. Everything would be okay.

But as soon as my thoughts of Mum had subsided a different feeling arose from the pit of my stomach. This is it, I thought to myself, this is the trip I've been waiting for, the trip that will change my future and hopefully give me the girl of my dreams. I took a deep breath to steady the nerves building up inside.

'You okay?' Maddy asked to the right of me, her hand resting on my arm.

'Yeah! Knackered . . .'

'Me too,' she smiled, before taking my hand in hers, resting her head on my shoulder and nuzzling her body into mine.

It felt lovely.

I couldn't help but smile as I intuitively squeezed her hand. Three times. 'I love you,' I declared in what I hoped was the last time I'd have to do so in my coded way. Paris was going to give me the freedom to verbalize it, at last.

'I love the way you always do that,' she smiled, rubbing my arm in response to my gesture, clueless as to what it actually meant. 'Three squeezes. It's your thing.'

'Is it?'

'Yeah,' she laughed. 'You must be aware that you're doing it?'

I stared at her with this gormless expression on my face, but before I could respond she started talking again.

'Did you see Lauren and Daniel getting on the bus?'

'I think they're here somewhere,' I said with relief, stretching my back and craning my neck to see over the tops of the seats in front of us.

'No,' she giggled, pulling me back into my seat. 'I mean, did you see the way he asked her if she wanted to sit next to him?'

'Oh. No. Why?'

'It was a bit . . . odd.'

'Was it?'

'I don't even think I've ever seen them talk before.' She was trying to talk as quietly as she could, but her eyes were practically popping out of her head as she willed me to grasp whatever it was she was saying.

I looked at her blankly. It was too early for guessing games.

'I think he likes her,' she eventually spelled out.

'Really?'

'What's this you're whispering about?' asked Robert, leaning across both our laps so that his face was right in front of ours. He was so close I found it hard to focus on him.

'Lauren and Daniel,' Maddy mouthed, smiling.

'Yup. Spotted it,' he nodded knowingly, pursing his lips.

'Really?' asked Maddy, excited at having a little gossip, especially as it was on the topic of love. She wasn't a girlie girl, but she was certainly a romantic. 'Do you think they'll get it on?'

'Don't see why not,' shrugged Robert.

'Anyone else you think might?' Maddy asked, her eyes widening in delight.

'Let's see,' Robert said, taking a quick peek around at the rest of our classmates on the bus, as though to remind himself of who else had joined us on the trip.

'I think Aaron has a thing for Jessica.'

'Yeah, but she wouldn't go near him,' Maddy protested, shaking her head. 'Rebecca would, though.'

'Obviously. She'd have anyone who gave her a chance. So what about you?' Rob asked her. 'Anyone you've got your eye on?'

'Nooo . . .' she blushed, visibly embarrassed by the question.

'Well, I wonder if anyone has theirs on you . . .'

'Doubt it,' she muttered, nibbling on her lip.

'Jackson? Williams? Tipper? Mr Brown?' he offered,

listing the surnames of some of the guys on the bus, his eyebrows rising more with each suggestion given.

Maddy screwed up her face in reply.

'Might be your lucky trip, Maddy Hurst. I bet someone's got their eye on you,' he grinned.

'Doubt it. We can't all be as popular as you,' she teased.

'It's quality that matters, not quantity, Maddy.'

'Is that right?'

'Yep.'

'If your fan club could hear you now.'

'I'm not being ungrateful!' he protested with his eyes wide. 'They're all lovely, but . . .'

'What?'

'Well, I'm just waiting to be swept off my feet by the right girl.'

'And you think you'll find her in Paris?'

'It's a nice place to start looking.'

I stayed quiet. In fact, I think I may have even stopped listening (and breathing). I couldn't look at them. We were all seated so close together, Robert was still lying across us. I felt wedged in with no escape. I panicked that the conversation was going to be turned around to me and who *I* fancied. I had no idea what I'd have said. All I could think about was my plan being messed up if I so much as uttered the wrong thing. I zoned in and out of their conversation, a bead of sweat appearing on my upper lip as I continued to freak out.

But the conversation just ended.

Just like that.

Robert sat upright and dived into his rucksack, chucking out a chocolate Curly Wurly bar for us each and that was it.

The only thing remaining of the exchange was Maddy's pink-stained cheeks.

The moment had clearly been forgotten by Robert who, instead, decided to unload the rest of his bag and impress us by revealing its contents – a mountain of treats: biscuits, crisps, chocolate and sweets. A staple diet for any growing teenager.

'No way I'm eating frog's legs or snails!' he declared, with a cheeky grin.

'Yuck!' chorused Maddy and I, pulling disgusted faces.

Yes, shamefully we all believed the stereotype that, at some point on that trip, we'd be forced to eat such dishes – something we were all terrified of. But for a few minutes, as we sat back in our seats and started to munch on the chewy caramel chocolate, our fears melted away.

Even though I was relieved that the conversation had quickly moved on, I didn't fail to notice Maddy's eyes twinkling as they roamed along our classmates and visibly continued to dream up different possibilities and matches in her head.

I wondered if she was thinking about her own chance of romance . . . and if she was thinking of me.

'You're so lucky that you get to share a rooooom!' whined Maddy as she stomped her way through our hotel room door and plonked herself on my bed.

The room was pretty basic but better than we imagined. Our twin room had two single beds (made up with cream-coloured sheets and blankets rather than a comfy duvet – our first Parisian grumble) along opposite walls with a wooden bedside table placed between them. The walls were off-white and blue curtains hung at the windows, which looked out at a brick wall of the building next door rather than a breath-taking view of the city. The most wonderful thing about our room was the en-suite, which was exciting enough, but it also had a shower in it. We only had a bath at home back then. What a luxury!

'I have to share with Kelly Sinclair – I don't even know her! Why can't I be in here with you?' Maddy continued, her face all screwed up as she moaned.

'You know why,' shrugged Robert, a cheeky smile appearing – the one he always used before saying something naughty. 'The teachers know you wouldn't be able to keep your hands off me if you slept in here.'

I was used to Rob winding Maddy up in this way, but never had he said something quite so sexually suggestive. It shocked me. To my horror, I started to wonder if I wasn't the only one to harbour feelings for our best friend – although, if that was that case, I wondered if Rob would really choose to be so blatant about it. Surely he was just winding her up, I hoped. Nevertheless, my paranoia started to return.

A second or two seemed to pass with me gawping at the two of them while Maddy widened her eyes at a smirking Robert in disbelief.

'Argh, you're so gross!' she eventually whined, much to my relief, as she pulled one of my pillows from the bed and flung it at him. 'What's this?' she asked, holding up a scruffy stuffed toy rabbit by its ears. I'd brought it with me and quickly hidden it under there when Robert had gone to the loo earlier. I didn't expect Maddy to come in and find it mere moments later.

'Erm . . .' I hesitated.

'Wait, I recognize it,' she said, as she brought it round to face her, ruffling its shabby lilac hair. 'I got you it for your birthday. Years ago.'

'Yeah . . .' I raised my eyebrows and sighed, shaking my head and acting as though I was as confused by its appearance in our Parisian hotel room as she was.

Maddy had given it to me on my tenth birthday and at that time it was the most precious thing I owned. It's not like I went to bed with it every night or anything, I'd only done that for the first year, but when I was packing to go away I saw it sitting glumly on my bedside table and thought it might be a nice thing to have with me – my lucky mascot, if you will. I wrongly thought it would go unnoticed.

'I've no idea what it's doing here. Mum must've put it in my bag. You know what she's like,' I said with a quick shake of the head and a roll of my eyes.

'Yes, I do.'

'Nutter . . .' I added without much gusto. I wasn't used to talking badly of Mum.

'And who put it under your pillow?' she asked after a pause.

'What?'

'Your pillow?'

'Huh?' I heard her the first time and knew exactly what she was getting at.

'It was under your pillow, so somehow it hopped out of your suitcase and dived into your bed before either of you noticed . . .'

I looked at her with my mouth wide open, willing my

73

brain to form some sort of an explanation. Nothing came. Suddenly *I* was the rabbit, caught in the big flaming headlights of embarrassment.

'Leave him alone!' yelled Robert, coming to my aid and throwing the pillow back in Maddy's direction. 'Are you trying to tell us that you've not brought one yourself?'

Maddy covered her face with her hands, unable to stop a girlish giggle from escaping.

Later on that night, once Maddy had left to go to her own room and we were lying in our beds, one topic whirled around inside my head: Maddy and Robert.

'Do you fancy Maddy?' I asked, much to my own surprise. I couldn't stop my mouth from opening and the question firing out as the overriding urge to quiz Robert fought against my brain's resistance.

'Huh?' he questioned, sounding half asleep, even though we'd only just turned the lights off.

'Maddy?' I couldn't face asking the whole question again, so I hoped he'd heard the majority of it, and opted to just repeat her name instead. I was so thankful that I'd waited until the lights were out – I could feel my face burning up, making me feel flustered.

'Oh . . . not that I'm aware of,' he laughed, sounding more awake. 'Why?'

'You were being quite flirty with her earlier.'

'Was I?' he asked.

'More than normal,' I said, in what I hoped was a laid-back tone of voice.

'You know what she's like,' he sighed. 'She gets so uptight and bashful, I was just winding her up.'

'That's what I thought . . .' I nodded to myself.

'Did I take it too far?'

'Maybe . . .'

'I hope I didn't offend her.' He sounded genuinely worried at the idea.

'I'm sure you didn't,' I reasoned, mentally bashing myself around the head for having said anything in the first place – one thing I'd started to understand about love was that it made me feel more suspicious than anything else ever had. It was torturous.

'Still, I'll apologize tomorrow. I was only messing around . . . it's nice that you're protective over her,' he added after a brief pause.

'You are too.'

'I guess we can't help it.'

The conversation ended there. I wasn't sure if Robert had simply fallen back to sleep or whether he, like me, was lying there thinking of Maddy.

I hoped it was the former.

The next morning we were forced out of bed ridiculously early (which probably wasn't that early, but seeing as none of us had bothered to move our watches forward an hour it seemed like it was still the middle of the night). We might have thought we were on holiday, but our teachers were hell-bent on getting us out of bed and on to the streets of Paris as soon as they could. We'd mumbled good mornings to each other at the breakfast table as we slumped into our seats.

'Okay, sleepy heads,' welcomed Miss James with a smile before handing around printed worksheets. 'Here's a rough itinerary for the next few days and the work I expect you to do in each museum or place we visit.'

'Work?' queried Robert. 'But I thought the idea was just to look at the art, Miss. Surely that's what the artists would want.'

'Nice try, Mr Miles.'

I swear I saw her blush.

I quickly skimmed my way through the itinerary and longed for the words to pop from the page, but I didn't see them.

'Miss? Where's the Eiffel Tower?' I asked, unable to hide the panic in my voice. 'Surely we're going to go there . . .?'

To my relief a few of the others grumbled their own protests at the omission.

'I was planning on talking to you all about that. I thought it might be a nice thing to do the morning we leave to go home – a splendid way to round off what I'm sure will be a great trip. Although that does mean getting up very early, and getting on the bus to go straight back home from there, rather than going from here. Does that sound okay with you lot?'

There was a split reaction from the group – the girls all nodded in approval, beaming great big smiles at the thought of gracing the super romantic spot, and the boys grunted – either because they weren't as bothered or because it was still too early. Needless to say I was with the girls on this one. Going there on the last day would be all right, I decided. I'd have preferred to go there straight away and get the whole thing over with as soon as I could, rather than having to wait for the entire trip and agonizing over what was to come, but the important thing was we *were* going there. All I had to do was hold it together until then.

Gazing over the plans for our busy week, we tried to eat the crusty rolls and slices of ham and cheese given to us (none of us were too impressed with that continental malarkey), and then our crazy week of cramming in every tourist attraction Paris had to offer commenced. We gazed up at Notre Dame cathedral while singing the songs from the Disney classic which included a lonely hunchback (then had to stop ourselves from continuing to sing when we were inside the holy building – although I'm pretty sure I heard Robert humming along to himself). We explored the Rodin Museum and copied the moody pose of *The Thinker*, walked around the Picasso Museum and debated whether he was a genius or just off his rocker. Got dragged through Père-Lachaise cemetery as Miss James listed details of a load of dead people we didn't know – actually we had heard of Jim Morrison and Oscar Wilde, but even then it was hardly riveting stuff – they're dead! Plus, it was freezing cold and standing around bored was irritating. We marvelled over work in the Musée Marmottan Monet, complained how small the *Mona Lisa* was in the Louvre (after queuing for ages to see her – plus the glass case in front of her was dirty) and questioned the respectability of almost every piece in the Pompidou Centre ('How can *that* be art?') – all the while making notes and scribbling sketches in our notebooks so that our teachers would think we were actually doing some work, but more so that we had something to show our parents when we got home, giving them the satisfaction that their money had been well spent. Hardly any crêpes were eaten – one of my biggest disappointments of the trip when it came to experiencing the joys of Paris. Well, that and the fact that our trip to the Eiffel Tower never felt like it was getting any closer.

The days crawled by at a snail's pace, as if they were purposefully trying to torment my lovesick heart. However, every now and then, in the distance over a bridge or from a viewing platform at one of the museums, I'd catch a glimpse of that metallic beacon of beauty and romance and feel a surge of happiness ping through my heart. Every day, every minute and every second inched me closer and closer to its magic, reminding me that my plan was still intact, that the trip's grand finale was just around the corner. I had no doubt that the Parisian air had the power to propel us into something new. Something different that would change our lives forever.

In many ways, I was right.

Maddy

Sixteen years old . . .

It was our last night in Paris and, as a treat, Miss James and the other chaperones decided to take us out to a little French restaurant for dinner. While we were getting ready and putting on our make-up, my roommate, Kelly Sinclair (one of the cooler kids from our year who always looked perfect with her dark smouldering eye make-up and long tousled brown hair) turned to me – her head leaning to one side as she squinted her eyes at me suspiciously.

'You and Robert were looking close on the way back today.'

Her comment was nothing new, I was used to being quizzed in such a manner when it came to me and the boys. Sometimes it was Ben and I cuddling that got people talking, other times it was the playful banter between Rob and I that caught their attention. I could usually brush it off, insisting that I didn't believe in the assumption that girls and boys could never be *just* friends, but on that trip I'd become even more aware of things shifting. Everything between us felt more charged, like we were both just waiting for something to happen. Like the chat on the bus about him waiting for the right girl – was that a hint? And was he questioning me about other guys in our class to suss out my reaction?

I was more than embarrassed when he lay there and mocked my supposed inability to keep my hands off him – I wondered if he could sense what was going on in my head. And if he could, well, that was just humiliating. He apologized for that, actually. The morning after the hands-off incident he'd gone out of his way to pull me to one side and say sorry, but not in a macho can't-believe-I'm-doing-this way. It contained real concern as he placed his hands on the tops of my arms and held my gaze while he made sure he hadn't upset me. It did nothing to ease the growing feeling inside – instead it put it on high alert. If I were to be quizzed on Robert's whereabouts at any point on the whole of that trip, I'd have been able to answer straight away. I was in a permanent state of awareness. Although, funnily enough, there was one moment at the Rodin Museum when I was lost in thought sketching the great bronze statue of *The Thinker*. I must have been sitting on the bench, hidden in the museum's gardens, concentrating for quite some time (it was the only piece of work I'd almost managed to complete). Being the main attraction of the museum, many people came, saw, replicated for a photo and left – there was a constant buzz around the piece. Once I was nearly finished I looked to the person on my right (they'd been sat there for a while) and found Robert staring at me.

'Did you know you bite your lip when you're concentrating?' he asked with a frown.

'Do I?'

'You've been doing it for the last half an hour.'

'You've been sat there that long?'

He nodded keenly.

'Just staring at me like a nutter?'

'Oh no, I drew you too.'

'What?'

Before I had a chance to be amazed by his revelation, he turned his sketchbook round to face me. He'd opted for the 'stick man' approach. The only part of me that he'd gone into any detail with was my hair – for which he'd used the colour red to draw an aggressive-looking bird's nest on top of my head. The windy air was clearly doing me no favours.

'Nice,' I muttered, raising my hand to smooth down my wild hair.

'Don't,' he insisted as he took my hand and placed it back on my lap. 'It's cute.'

I raised an eyebrow at him, questioning his comment.

'I think I've captured you perfectly,' he smiled proudly down at his work. 'I've called it My Red-headed Thinker.'

The use of the word *my* did not go unnoticed by my hammering heart.

The day Kelly chose to question me there had definitely been another moment between us as we made our way back from the Louvre.

This time I'd started it.

As we walked side by side to the hotel a silence had fallen between us. It wasn't an uncomfortable one, but nonetheless, I felt the need to fill it with something to stop my wandering thoughts. So I playfully pinched his thick blue scarf and wrapped it around my own neck. I hadn't expected it to escalate into him grappling me to the ground in the middle of the sanded pathway in the Jardin des Tuileries and me being tickled into hysteria until I handed it back.

It was more than just the two of us mucking around as normal – this time it was physical. It was feisty and intense. However, Kelly pointing it out made me feel protective over the whole thing. I didn't want to be asked about it. I wanted her to butt out.

I shook my head and rolled my eyes as I pinched in my cheeks and swept on some pink Rimmel blusher.

'Oh really,' I sighed nonchalantly, hoping Kelly would get the hint that it was a topic I was bored of explaining.

'You were flirting,' she continued.

'No, we weren't,' I protested, my voice hitting slightly higher notes than I wanted it to.

'You were jumping all over each other.'

'No. It was flipping freezing so I nicked his scarf. He was trying to grab it back off me. That's all.'

'It was classic flirting.'

'Kelly . . .' I flustered, shaking my head.

'I think he likes you.'

'Don't be silly. He's my friend and that's all there is to it,' I said matter-of-factly, trying to end the conversation there.

'Yes, I know. But you're not kids any more, Maddy. You must be able to see the way he looks at you and the fact that there's shitloads of chemistry between you.'

'There really isn't,' I said firmly, almost losing my patience in a way I never had on the topic.

'Right . . .' she sighed, gazing back at her reflection in the mirror. I thought she'd finally relented, but then she added, 'He is so fricking hot.'

'I don't see it . . .' I lied with a shrug, watching her as

82

she expertly applied purple eyeshadow to her already dark eyes, wishing I knew how to do the same to mine. No matter how hard I tried I knew I never matched up to the other girls in the way they took care to groom themselves to perfection – perhaps it was the only downside to being friends with boys over girls. We spent our time in trackies outside, taking on new adventures, while girls experimented with make-up and learned to make the best of what was given to them. I was years behind and it showed. I'd never known what to do with my fair skin – fake tan made me look like an oompa loompa, and I'd acquired far too many freckles to cover up with foundation. My red hair was the only thing I liked – it was thick and manageable, although it was usually thrown up in a ponytail to keep it off my face (even then, wispy bits always broke free and created a frizzy ring around my face – as Rob had nicely pointed out in his drawing). Why would Robert be attracted to someone boyish like me, I wondered, when he could have someone beautiful like Kelly? As soon as I heard the question bounce around the walls of my inner mind, I knew I was in more trouble than I cared to admit. Self-doubt just wasn't in my nature. Well, not over a boy anyway.

'You don't see that Robert is the fittest guy in our year? Really?' Kelly asked further, looking at me in disbelief.

'Yes, really!' I shrugged.

'Perhaps you should start looking then . . .'

I smiled at her as I picked up my mascara and unscrewed the wand.

'Because I've got to say, if you don't look, I might be

forced to make him look in my direction instead,' she said with a saucy wink.

All at once I started to feel nauseous.

I felt extremely awkward when I joined Robert and Ben in the lobby half an hour later. All I could think about was what Kelly had said, and the realization that I'd definitely developed ulterior feelings for my best friend. I felt irritated by how self-conscious it made me feel – for instance, I was aware of every part of myself, which made me feel like an inexperienced Bambi walking on ice as I approached them. The way Robert looked me up and down with a delirious expression on his face didn't help (it made my insides flip inside themselves), and neither did the pair of them wolf-whistling at me as I approached.

'Cut it out,' I hissed, giving them both a firm shove on the shoulder.

Yes, being with Kelly had prompted me to make a bit more effort than usual – I was wearing more blusher and eyeshadow than my mum would have liked, along with an emerald mini-dress, tights and heels – Kelly's heels, not mine. I'd felt good as I left my room, sexy and mature, but now their gaze was on me I felt silly and exposed.

'What? You look hot,' laughed Ben, smiling at me as he took my hand and gave me his usual comforting three squeezes.

'Ouch,' said Robert as he cheekily rubbed the opposite shoulder to the one I'd pushed, giving me a smirk. He was always trying to treat me like a feeble girl, simply because he knew it wound me up. Or was he flirting, I wondered. And, if so, had he always been?

'I'll do it harder if you like,' I warned, perhaps with a bit more gusto than I'd meant.

'Promise?'

I couldn't fail to spot the glisten in his eye as he raised an eyebrow at me, tilted his head ever so slightly and licked his lips as they formed a smile. The action had me transfixed and I literally had to pinch myself to pull myself away from the magnetic force of his whole being. It was more than him being his usual cocky and suggestive self, and that knowledge caused a rush of excitement to whizz through my body. I could feel my cheeks beginning to blush at the unexpected sensation.

As I turned away from them both and busied myself with putting my gloves on, I cursed Kelly for putting the thoughts I'd been grappling with into the forefront of my mind. Pull yourself together, I told myself, you do not fancy Robert and he certainly does not fancy you . . . you silly, silly girl.

Well, there's nothing like trying to fool yourself into believing something that's a blatant lie.

We were taken to La Ferme des Beauvais – a little Parisian restaurant on the corner of one of the side streets north of the Louvre. Windows covered the breadth of the external walls, displaying its name in silver-framed red lettering that curved like a rainbow on each pane of glass. Inside, the wooden tables were lined in rows to make the most of the limited space and covered with red cloth, tealights and a single red rose on each one. On the walls were photographs of Paris taken throughout the years, all in black and white. There was no doubt it was a cheap place to eat, we were on a school trip after all, but it was these little touches that helped make the place more atmospheric and inviting.

The majority of the group opted to eat pasta on our final night, as we had most nights. It was always the safest option – although it was washed down with pieces of French bread, so it did at least have something traditionally French about it.

As our feast was being gobbled up, Kelly turned to Miss James, who was in deep conversation with Miss Stokes, another teacher. We'd never been taught by her before and she'd been very quiet the whole trip – we'd almost forgotten she was there.

'Miss James,' Kelly called from beside me.

'Yes?' she shouted back.

'Seeing as we're in France and we've been good all week, can we have a glass of wine each?' she tried with a cheeky shrug.

Miss James cackled at the request.

'Come on,' pushed Robert, hoping his charm would help win her over. 'We're eating anyway, it's not like we're going to get drunk. It'll just wash it down nicely.'

'Nice try,' she smiled. 'As lovely and good as you all are there's no way I'm letting any of you drink alcohol.'

'You're having some,' stated Kelly.

'I'm an adult.'

'Oh, go on,' she pleaded.

'I'm afraid there'll be no underage drinking on my watch,' she finished, turning back to the conversation that had been interrupted.

'That's what she thinks,' Kelly whispered, winking at

Robert before slinking off to the toilet. When she came back she discreetly pulled a bottle of vodka out from underneath her jumper.

'Where'd you get that?' I squeaked in shock.

Ben's eyes, like my own, widened with surprise. Robert looked impressed – something that didn't go unnoticed by me.

'Never you mind,' she laughed, before winking over at one of the waiters at the bar. 'Pass us your glasses.' As we did so, she quickly added the alcohol into our Cokes before carefully passing the bottle along to the next table. 'There's more where that came from too . . .' she teased with a wicked smirk.

I was never one to break the rules, not really, but on that occasion, as I watched Kelly, Ben and Robert grin at each other as they picked up their glasses and gulped away, I certainly didn't want to be the only person not involved. After just a few mouthfuls the worry I'd been feeling earlier that evening started to slide away, leaving me to feel giddily free and naughty – a feeling that was increased when I lowered my glass to find Robert winking at me. God, I fancy you, I thought, with such clarity that I stunned myself.

Once dinner was finished the tables were cleared away, and cheesy pop songs started blaring from the restaurant speakers, replacing the sounds of Edith Piaf that we'd endured throughout dinner. Miss James had organized a surprise mini disco for us to round off what had already been an amazing trip. None of us needed any encouragement to dance (probably thanks to a certain tipple lubricating our inhibitions), we were up on our feet as soon as the first intro started. Thankfully we were the only diners in the dimly lit restaurant, so we didn't have to worry about us teenagers upsetting anyone with our dizzy behaviour. We could just be carelessly joyful and silly as we danced along to the nineties classics being played. Hits by artists like Sugar Ray, Madonna and No Doubt boomed through the room, putting us on even more of a high. Robert, Ben and I were pulling the craziest moves we could muster, singing raucously and making each other laugh hysterically. It felt incredibly liberating.

At some point towards the end of the night, Hanson's 'Mmmbop' started blaring out of the speakers, putting us all into more of a childish frenzy. We jumped around, making even sillier shapes with our bodies, waving our hands in the air and shaking our heads to the music. We might not have looked cool, but it was so much fun we didn't care.

'I'm just off to the loo!' Ben shouted at us as he hopped his way through the excited group, continuing with his wacky moves as he went.

As we carried on singing along to the music, Robert grabbed my hand and thrust it up in the air, gesturing for me to spin under it. I did so. He then threw me around, spinning and twirling, several times with dizzying speed, causing me to get light-headed. I ended up laughing manically as I fell into his chest to steady myself.

As the song came to an end and the next song started playing, the mood suddenly changed.

The familiar piano intro to K-Ci and JoJo's 'All My Life' filled the air, replacing the childlike mood with an intense one, laden with sentiment and emotion . . . and a whole heap of sexual tension.

As my head was already on his chest and my body close to his, Robert gently placed a hand on my lower back, holding me securely into him, before picking up my hand and cradling it in his. With his head bowed, he rested his cheek on the side of my head.

I closed my eyes and savoured every detail of the delicious moment.

I could feel his heart pumping through his chest.

I could feel his hot breath in my ear.

I was aware of every single movement and spasm that our bodies were involuntarily making as we swayed to the music – his hand as it slowly moved across my back, his thumb as it rubbed up and down mine, and the fact that I'd almost stopped breathing.

Understandably, we were nervous. We'd never been this close before. This intimate. I willed it to continue – I didn't want Robert to change his mind and stop. My whole body was in a state of suspense, waiting for him to make the next move – it had to come from him, there was no way I could have instigated anything. I had to know I hadn't been stupidly making up the whole thing in my head.

He lowered his head further. With my eyes closed, I could feel the corner of his mouth rest at the side of my face. He stayed there for a few seconds before slowly sliding further down my cheek, his lips causing my body to tingle as they tantalizingly brushed my skin. I knew what was coming and I held my breath, waiting for it to happen. Willing it to.

He kissed me.

Actually kissed me.

Robert's big juicy lips were on mine, as his hands roamed up and down my back, and in that moment I completely melted. I devoured the new sensations of heat and electricity running between us both, knowing there was nowhere else I'd rather be.

Okay, I told myself, you're right – you do fancy Robert. But, not only that – it would seem that he flipping well fancies you too.

Ben

Sixteen years old . . .

I stood frozen in the middle of the crowd as I watched the tender moment between my two best friends. My heart ached as it understood its significance and a feeling of sadness swelled through me. I felt lost – unsure of what to do with myself. Should I have gone over and made a joke of their locking lips, ruining whatever magic was passing between them? Should I have retreated back to the loos and come back out a bit later, pretending I hadn't seen anything? Well, that's what I wanted to do, but before I had a chance to do anything the song was over, they'd pulled apart and noticed me – both of them looking at me with great big grins on their faces, insanely happy with themselves.

I had no choice but to grab the nearest girl to me, who just happened to be Maddy's roommate on that trip, Kelly, and give her a quick snog. It was horrible and sloppy, we even banged teeth in my haste, but at least I didn't have to look at their elated faces, I thought. At least I didn't have to talk to them.

It had been the last song of the night and as soon as it was over Miss James was ushering people to get their coats on and head outside. I managed to keep my distance from Maddy and Robert by diving in, getting my stuff and walking outside before they'd even moved from their romantic spot in the middle of the makeshift dance floor.

I trailed behind at the back of the group as we walked to the hotel, aware of the irritatingly joyous chatter going on in front of me. Everyone was talking animatedly about how much fun the night had been and how wonderful they'd found the whole trip — I didn't give a flying crap. I would have given anything to be able to teleport home and get far away from Paris and every single one of them.

Even though there were at least sixteen people between us, I could see that my two best friends were still holding hands. I was so inexplicably angry; angry at them for kissing, angry at them for thinking it was all jolly and fun and that there wouldn't be any consequences, angry at Robert for kissing Maddy when he could have picked any other girl at school — but most of all I felt sorry for myself, because I'd missed out. My hopes and desires for that trip came tumbling down around me. I'd been a mere twelve hours or less from standing at the top of the Eiffel Tower and telling Maddy how I felt, but I'd been beaten to it. Accusing questions formed in my head as I started to beat myself up over my mammoth disappointment. Why did I think I needed some romantic gesture or setting to go along with my declaration of love? Why didn't I just tell her months earlier when I first thought of doing so? Why did I allow time to get in the way and steal her from me?

It quickly dawned on me that I'd lost her. Either way, whether things continued between Maddy and Robert or not, there'd be no chance for us. Maddy, the girl who glittered beautifully, who carried an indescribable magic in her very being, would never be in my grasp. I was heart-broken.

When we got to the hotel I scampered off to our room with great speed, but not before I painfully caught a glimpse of Robert and Maddy kissing once more as they said goodnight.

I got to our room, stripped off and got straight into bed, trying to hide myself in the hope that Robert wouldn't want to talk when he came in. I was wrong, of course. Even though I was feigning sleep he sauntered in and started talking loudly as soon as he walked through the door.

'There you are,' he said, standing in the middle of the room with the biggest grin on his face. 'What a night that was.'

'Yeah,' I muttered, pretending to be half asleep.

'I tell you what, I wasn't expecting that to happen when we went out tonight. I mean, it's Maddy! Maddy!' he practically squealed, puffing air from his cheeks as he mulled it over. 'Maddy and me! Who'd have thought.'

Not me, that's for sure. Well, I had, but I'd been talked out of thinking such paranoid thoughts. How ironic.

'Why did you say you didn't like her in that way?'

I was annoyed with myself as soon as I'd said it. Not only had I dropped the whole tired guise, I'd also asked him a question, prompting him to talk about the whole thing further. I'd given him the encouragement he'd needed to cheerily talk his head off about it.

'Mate, I wasn't sure how I felt. Until I could understand it myself, I thought I'd best stay quiet about the whole thing,' he exclaimed, coming over and sitting on the edge of my bed, happiness irritatingly radiating all around him. 'I don't even know what happened tonight – we were just dancing stupidly, you were there, you saw that. And then, that song came on and it got really . . . I dunno, heated. Seriously, it was weird. I had this urge. Well, actually, I've had that urge for a while, but tonight – I couldn't stop myself,' he shrugged in amazement as bewilderment flickered across his face.

I wondered whether he was already replaying the little moments between them – the gazes, the feel of her lips on his, her taste. The very thought crushed me.

'I know she's our best friend and all that, but, my God, Ben! I mean, it was electric. *She* is electric. How on earth have we not noticed that before?'

His face had become dopey, full of surprise and wonder at the night's events. I'd never seen him like that. The more I looked at him, the sadder I felt. It seemed I wasn't the only one who'd fallen for Maddy's charms.

I'd had years to make some sort of sense of my overwhelming feelings so that I could tell her exactly how I felt, but I hadn't. I'd hesitated and allowed life to get in the way – because of that I knew I had no right to be angry with either of them. They didn't know that she was my world. That I'd loved her since the day she walked into class with her manic bob and cute red nose. I was a coward for keeping those feelings to myself and foolish for not realizing that I had to act on them sooner. I was gutted for myself that Robert's confidence had led him where I desperately wanted to be – with Maddy.

I didn't sleep that night. Instead, I repeated their embrace in my mind again and again, as though it was some kind of mystery that needed to be solved. When I left them they were busting their stupidest dance moves to a bloody Hanson track and then, one pee stop later and that had changed into a lovers' clinch. It didn't make sense to me.

Confusion whizzed around in my brain as I tried to process how it had all happened and what would happen next. I dreaded them becoming an official item, I wasn't sure how I'd cope seeing what I saw that night all day, every day. It was like I was trapped in some sort of nightmare. I wanted it to stop. I longed to wake up.

My only flutter of relief came when it dawned on me that if Robert was what Maddy was after, then I'd have had no chance anyway. In fact, the timing had done me a favour and saved me from a bitterly embarrassing situation. Like I said, it was only a 'flutter' of relief. It didn't make it hurt any less.

Maddy

Sixteen years old . . .

I was deliriously giddy and couldn't remove the smirk from my face as I kissed Robert goodnight. I hadn't wanted to leave him, I could have easily stood in the hotel lobby and kissed him all night long, but Miss James wouldn't have allowed it. Instead she sent us off in separate directions to our rooms, much to our dismay.

'So you don't fancy Robert, then?' laughed Kelly, as we walked away from him and headed up to our room.

'No, definitely not,' I giggled, suddenly feeling like the biggest girl in the world as a strange feeling danced around in my tummy. Yes, you guessed it, butterflies. Robert Miles – my best friend of seven years, had given me butterflies. I loved the sensation.

'Can you believe you kissed him?'

'I really can't,' I said, shaking my head at the madness of it all.

'Did it feel weird? Was it anything like kissing a brother?' she asked with a perplexed look. 'That's the one thing I was worried about with you guys.'

'Definitely not brotherly, no.'

'Good! That could've been really awkward.'

'You know what, it just felt right. We fit together.'

'You lucky bitch,' she howled.

I didn't even bother trying to sleep that night – I couldn't, someone had to stay awake and keep an eye on the grin that had exploded onto my face and refused to leave. Instead I spent the night looking at the ceiling, thinking of Robert. I wondered what thoughts were in his head at that moment, whether, like me, he was feeling light-headed from it all, or whether he'd regretted it as soon as he'd left me. I was sure it wouldn't have been the latter, not so soon afterwards anyway. The whole thing had been too delicious to think negatively on.

Ben

Sixteen years old . . .

Dread filled me as I woke up on the last morning in Paris and realized we were still going to be taking a group trip to the Eiffel Tower. It was the last place I wanted to go – I didn't want to be anywhere near it. It was hard enough knowing that my plan had failed, I couldn't have faced Robert and Maddy canoodling up there in front of me and soaking up all the romance I thought would be there for me.

It seemed, for once, my prayers were answered.

As soon as our suitcases were packed and closed there was a knock on the door from Miss James, coming to tell us that due to torrential rain, she thought it best if we cancelled our Eiffel Tower trip, although she did promise to get the bus to drive right by it so that we could take some snaps.

I didn't grumble or moan.

I was relieved.

Due to Maddy and Robert being busy sucking each other's faces off as they said good morning, I was put in charge of getting us the back row of the coach on the way home. I purposefully failed to get it, which thankfully meant we had to sit apart. I managed to smile at them both as I suggested they sat together, telling them I was knackered and would probably sleep the whole way anyway. They agreed and found a spot towards the back of the bus, obviously away from Miss James in case they wanted to continue to lock lips. Deciding to go towards the front of the bus, I sat facing the window, glumly watching the world pass me by.

I didn't look when Miss James announced we were approaching the Eiffel Tower, with the warning to get our cameras out ... I closed my eyes and tried my best to ignore the gasps of admiration coming from everyone else around me.

It was remarkable how differently I felt about the place within the space of just a few hours. Before that trip it had been the iconic objectification of love, as it was and is to millions of people around the world, but on that cold, wet and miserable morning, it became the symbol of devastation and despair – a representation of a lost love, of a squandered hope.

I couldn't bear to be so close as it highlighted my failure and mocked me callously.

I was ready to pretend the whole thing hadn't happened. I was hoping (rather foolishly) that Maddy and Robert would denounce it as some crazy holiday fling spurned on by the romantic setting, which they'd come to regret once we were home. But it didn't happen.

The following Monday, when Maddy knocked for me on the way to school, I noticed there was something different about her. I couldn't quite pinpoint it at first, I just noticed she looked glossier and more glammed up. Turns out she was wearing more make-up than usual. Not loads, the school would never have allowed that, but her cheeks were rosier from blusher, her lips were smoother from balm and, to complete her look, her hair was perfectly placed, gliding over her shoulders in silky auburn waves.

'You look nice,' I offered.

She looked at the ground coyly, unable to stop a smile from forming.

It was for Robert, I realized with sickening clarity.

As we walked together in silence I could tell she was nervous about seeing him. Unless they'd met up without telling me, that morning was their first encounter following their Parisian love affair. I loathed having to be there for it, and wished I could have had the foresight to pull a sicky that day instead.

Once we knocked for him, they held hands straight away, confirming their couple status as Maddy bashfully smiled in my direction. I had no choice but to smile brightly back at her, like some crazily over-enthusiastic kid's entertainer, before we silently continued our journey.

Once at school it was impossible to avoid the situation; even if they weren't with me, it was all anybody wanted to talk about. Those who were in Paris wanted to share what they'd seen like it was some modern-day mythical tale, and those who weren't wanted to know all about it – drinking up the details with surprise and awe as though it was the most romantic thing they'd ever heard.

Unsurprisingly, when I was with them it was worse. Walking around the school you could hear the whisperings of gossip as we passed – that and the sound of teenage hearts being crushed as they realized their heart-throb, Robert Miles, was off the market.

* * *

As soon as I walked through my front door that night, my mum was there, quizzing me about what had happened in Paris. She didn't even give me time to take my school shoes off before words excitedly flew from her mouth.

'Oi, you! Why didn't you tell me about Robert and Maddy?' she demanded. 'Her mum called today and was saying how Maddy's been non-stop talking about him since she got back – Carol said that Robert's been the same!'

'Oh, I just . . .' I started with a shrug, leaning down under the pretence of undoing my shoelaces, but actually trying to hide my face, unable to keep up the cheery façade any longer. I had to let the smile that had been frozen to my cheeks all day drop. I was exhausted.

'Who'd have thought it. I mean, I didn't see it coming. I expect they look cute together, though . . .'

I burst out crying then, failed to hold it back any longer. Sobbed into my worn-out leather shoes as my mum awkwardly hugged me from above, letting every ounce of emotion I'd held inside me since their first kiss, the regret and sorrow, spill its way out of me. I couldn't remember ever crying in that way before; even when my dad upped and left, it wasn't as bad as that. It was like I'd lost all control.

Mum said nothing for a good five minutes. It must have shocked her to see her teenage son in such a fragile state, so different from the jovial, carefree child she thought of me as. She just held me tightly into her skinny body, rocking me from side to side, shushing me whenever a fresh sob bubbled out of me. How ridiculous.

'Sorry, Mum . . .' I mumbled, slowly uncurling myself, leaning against the hallway wall for support.

'Don't be daft. Want to talk about it?' she asked, gently rubbing my arm.

'It's nothing. It's just . . .' I sighed as fresh tears sprang to my eyes, the loss of restraint irritating me. 'I'm such a dick.'

'Oi!' she reprimanded, gently slapping me on the arm.

'Sorry,' I mumbled.

'I get it, Benny,' she said, placing her hand under my chin and raising my face so that I was looking at her. 'You guys have been friends since you were little – three peas in a pod. You're worried that if them two get together you'll be left out. Or, if things go pear-shaped, like they did with me and your dad, that you might lose one of them.'

I hadn't even thought of it like that, but I didn't want to tell Mum the truth. I didn't want to tell her that the possible love of my life had kissed our mutual best friend, and that because they had kissed it meant I was unlikely to have my own chance with her.

'It'll be okay, darling. You'll see.'

'Will it, though?'

'Ben, sometimes life chucks these things in your way and you just have to go for it. No questions asked.'

'Isn't that what Dad did? Act on his feelings and not give a toss about us?'

'Robert and Maddy aren't your dad,' she said calmly, not showing any sign that my words had hurt her, but that was Mum all over. She was, hands down, the strongest woman I'd ever known. She didn't crumble when the love of her life walked out on her, she just got on with it. It's only growing up that I realized she wasn't really left with any other choice, she couldn't give up – she had me to look after. 'They're two young people, without any baggage, who've discovered they like each other,' she continued. 'Do you realize how brave it is of those two to do this?'

I looked down at the red rug on the floor, concentrating on the loose bits of fabric the cat had scratched up, willing the conversation to end so that I could go up to my room and sulk.

'What they really need from you right now is your support, Ben,' she sighed. 'They don't need you going all weird and making things harder.'

'I wouldn't do that . . .'

'I know, I know,' she said, grabbing my hand. 'Just never doubt their love for you, because that'll never change.'

I nodded my head and gave Mum a little smile. What else could I have done?

'You're coming with us tonight, right?' asked Robert later on that week at lunch.

We were stood in the school corridor in a raucous queue outside the canteen, waiting for Maddy to join us after her food tech class.

A group trip to the cinema had been planned for weeks. *Bridget Jones: the Edge of Reason* had just been released and Maddy was adamant that we all go and embrace our feminine sides with a girlie film, insisting it was payback for us always making her watch countless action and sci-fi films. Before Paris I was quite looking forward to it, but now, the idea of watching a rom-com with the new lovebirds made me feel queasy.

'Er . . .'

'You could bring Kelly?' he smirked, giving me a wink.

'Naaaah . . .'

'She really likes you.'

'She's not my type,' I replied dismissively, looking ahead at the queue, willing it to go faster.

'Didn't look that way in Paris . . . it could be a double date.'

'Look, if you guys want to go on your own I'll totally understand,' I offered, the words, 'double date' ringing in my ears as visions of them smooching the whole way through the film filled my brain. If that evening's trip turned into being Robert and Maddy's first ever date then that was the last place I wanted to be, especially as we'd be watching a rom-com – proper date material.

'Don't be daft.'

'Well, it's going to happen at some point – I can't be with you every single time you're alone together. I'll be a proper gooseberry.'

'What are you two talking about?' asked Maddy, as she arrived and squeezed in between us.

'Tonight and the cinema,' informed Robert, raising his eyebrows before pulling her into him and planting a kiss on her forehead.

'Ooh, have you asked him about Kelly?' she said with a grin on her face as she looked from Robert to me.

'Nothing's happening with Kelly,' I said, irritated that the pair of them had clearly talked and decided to couple me off with someone.

'Why not? She's nice.'

'She's not his type apparently – and, he was just about to bail on us.'

'What? No way! You're coming!' she demanded.

'But –'

'I've been waiting for months to see this and haven't once moaned when you two have dragged me along to your boy films.'

'It's a chick flick . . .' I protested.

'And?'

'And you guys are on a date.'

'Do you want to sit in the middle?' she offered.

'Erm . . .' started Robert, a frown forming on his face at the very thought of it.

'No!'

'Because you can . . . if you want to.'

'I don't want to.'

'That's a relief,' laughed Robert.

Maddy rolled her eyes at him, before smiling at me.

'Ben, tonight is not a date.'

'It is,' tried Robert.

'It's not,' she repeated, shooting a warning look in his direction. 'It's us three going to the cinema together as usual. Okay?'

'Fine,' I said, caving in. There was no way I could get out of the night without upsetting her and, despite my urge to get out of it, I didn't want to do that.

'But, it still could be a date,' smirked Robert. 'If you brought Kelly . . . please bring Kelly!'

'Leave him alone,' laughed Maddy, looping her arm through mine as we made our way into the canteen.

Maddy

Sixteen years old . . .

Robert wasn't my first ever boyfriend (how I wish I could forget my brief, yet embarrassing, relationship with John Martin), but I instantly knew that he was going to be my first *proper* boyfriend. That we would be together for a long time, that he'd be the first boy I'd ever say 'I love you' to and that our being a couple would have a huge effect on both our lives. I think knowing that was what had made me so aroused by the whole thing.

The night we got back from Paris, I was up in my room reliving the previous night, dreamily hugging my pillow, unable to wipe the smile from my face yet again. I'd only been home about ten minutes or so when Dad shouted up the stairs that Robert was on the phone.

I sprinted down the stairs.

'Hey . . .' he purred when I picked up.

'Hey, you,' I said back as I curled myself into the corner of the hallway floor and coyly fiddled with the telephone cord, grinning to myself with giddiness.

'I can't stop thinking about you.'

'You only saw me ten minutes ago,' I laughed, relieved that I wasn't alone in my thoughts.

We hadn't really talked on the coach coming home, we were both shattered from our busy week and all the excitement on our last night. Instead I'd tucked myself into Robert's toned chest (yes, what a delicious treat), and we'd both slept most of the way. Okay, there was some more kissing too . . . but my point is there was not a lot of talking.

'I miss you.'

'Already?'

'Yep.'

'I'm sorry, who is this? What have you done to Robert?'

A gentle laugh came from the other end of the line, making a smile spring to my cheeks.

It's surprising how content you can feel, even in a silence, and there was a lot of silence on that first phone call as a new sense of shyness fell over us both.

Eventually Robert attempted to get to the root of why he'd phoned, 'I was calling because . . . I don't want you to feel like you're just . . . I dunno . . . just another girl . . . because, you know . . . you're not like anyone else,' he sighed. 'You know I think the world of you. I really like you . . .'

'Robert?'

'Yes?'

'What are you trying to say?'

'Do you want to be my girlfriend?' he blurted.

I cackled into the phone.

'You're not meant to laugh!'

'But it's you – you asking me that! Robert who's known me forever, one of my best mates!'

'And?'

'It's weird.'

'Bad weird?'

'No!'

'What then?'

'What if it all goes wrong?'

'It won't.'

'How do you know that?'

'Because I won't let it,' he said quietly.

I smiled into the phone.

From the tone of his voice I could tell he was smiling too when he asked again, 'So, will you be my girlfriend?'

How could I possibly refuse?

After years of poking fun at the hoards of girls who swooned at Robert's charms, I'd found myself giving up the fight and joining in. I was swooning, swooning bad! It was quite unsettling.

And so, as a result of that conversation and us becoming an official item, I knew the cinema trip had turned into our first date for Robert. At first I wanted it to be too, if I'm honest, but I was aware Ben was meant to be coming with us and that we couldn't just ditch him or make him feel unwanted because we'd hooked up. I also knew about his little breakdown – mums talk, after all. June phoned my mum the next day, unsure of what to do – it can't have been easy seeing her happy-go-lucky son crumble like that. I felt bad knowing about it, especially as I knew Ben would hate that I knew, but at least it meant I could try my best to make sure Ben wasn't feeling left out or made to feel uncomfortable. I didn't want him to feel like everything was changing. Our friendship group was always going to be the most important thing for me, and I didn't want him questioning that.

I knew Robert would understand why we had to tread

carefully, but I decided not to tell him about Ben's breakdown. Perhaps I should have done, then they could have had some awkward lad conversation and talked it all through, but I thought it would be cruel to talk about him behind his back. I just hoped I could balance everything enough to keep them both happy.

Obviously, that night in the cinema was a bit tricky to start with, but I wasn't sure if that was because I kept looking for signs that Ben was uncomfortable. I thought he was at first – as he stood alongside us, waiting to buy tickets, he fixed his gaze on the surrounding posters of future films with an overly keen interest. I was sure he was doing it to avoid having to interact with us, but I couldn't be sure.

I might have been trying to play it cool, but Robert clearly wanted us to act like a couple; he was extremely touchy-feely. He barely let go of me, continuously placing a hand around my waist or taking my hand in his. It was difficult, I didn't want to just brush him off and leave him feeling rejected, that would have been a crap start to our relationship, but I didn't want the whole thing to be thrust in Ben's face either. I wanted it to feel normal.

'I'll get yours,' Robert said as we got to the counter.

'Oh . . .'

'Thanks,' joked Ben, managing a smile.

'Nice try.'

'You don't have to get mine,' I argued, putting my hand over the ten-pound note he was holding out to the cashier.

'Er, yeah I do,' he said, gently pushing my hand away. 'That's what boyfriends do. Get used to it.'

I looked up at Ben and gave him a meek smile, which

he winked back at before pulling out a fiver to pay for his own ticket.

The wink took me by surprise, it was confident and reassuring. After that he seemed to relax a little, although I wasn't entirely sure why. Despite his initial outburst to his mum, it seemed as though Ben was feeling calmer about the whole situation. He even managed to joke around with us when we were eventually sat in our seats, saying things like, 'I can hear you,' when we were kissing, and, 'You promised it wasn't a date,' which obviously killed the moment as it made us laugh, but I was thankful for the humour.

It was gorgeous being there with Robert, holding hands and kissing (when we could). I felt ridiculously comfortable and happy sat next to him, loving the new feelings passing between us and the warmth radiating from his body.

There was one awkward moment, though, which happened during the film – annoyingly, it could have easily been avoided if it wasn't for our teenage lust. Needless to say, things heated up between us in that darkened cinema room, which resulted in Robert and me getting a little carried away. We'd completely given up watching the film – exploring each other's mouths was far more interesting, as was Robert stroking my skin and his hand working its way up my top.

I'd wrongly assumed that Ben was preoccupied with the action onscreen.

He wasn't.

Our groping did not go unnoticed. Instead, rather embarrassingly, Ben leaned over and asked for the popcorn just as Robert's hand had finally cupped hold of my boob. Rob flapped around for a few seconds trying to free his hand (which had become trapped under my bra), before handing over the snack with a shameful look on his face.

I almost died on the spot. It was like being caught by my mum.

We were all sitting in my lounge the following day, watching *Friends* on repeat. The weather had turned bitterly cold, and none of us could be bothered to walk to the High Street. Instead, we set up camp in our comfies and splayed our homework around us, languidly making our way through it. Both boys were on the sofa, while I was on the floor cutting out pictures of different types of bread for my food tech coursework, with little effort or thought put into it.

'I think I'm going to ask Kelly if she wants to go out with us all,' said Ben coyly, as he wrote in his notepad.

'Really?' I squealed.

'Yeah.'

'You mean on like a double date?' smirked Robert.

'Why not,' Ben shrugged, still not looking at either of us.

'I knew you liked her,' I said, pointing the tips of my scissors in his direction. 'I can sense these things.'

'You're just like Cilla Black,' mocked Robert, grinning at me.

'Maybe we could go ice-skating or something?' I said, ignoring him. 'We could go tomorrow?'

'Let's not rush things!' he said worriedly, looking up at me. 'I'll have a chat with her on Monday and see if she wants to plan something for next weekend, yeah?'

'Spoilsport,' I jokily pouted.

'She might not even want to!'

Bless him, I thought, he'd clearly not pursued things with her because he was worried about being rejected. I'd assumed that was what had stopped him from asking her to the cinema with us, and possibly part of his meltdown – Ben wasn't the most confident person when it came to the opposite sex.

'Oh . . . she'll want to,' I said, grinning at him.

Kelly might have boldly told me on our last night away that she thought Robert was fit, but, as a result of Ben pouncing on her, she'd quickly switched the target of her affections. As soon as we got back to school on the Monday she was asking questions about him; what he was like, whether he'd mentioned their kiss, or whether I thought he liked her, etc. I knew he'd have no trouble getting her to go out with him, although the thought of them together petrified me – Ben was sure to be eaten alive by the foxy minx.

The upshot? Me and Robert would be free to go on an actual date without feeling awkward.

Ben

Sixteen years old . . .

I had seen Robert's hand up Maddy's top in the cinema. In fact, I was ridiculously aware of every single movement the pair made; when they started to hold hands, when their legs entwined, when they first kissed – the film hadn't even started by that point; his tongue was down her throat before the lights had gone down. I couldn't help but stare at them in my peripheral vision. A couple of times I purposefully asked for the popcorn bucket, or interjected with some little remark, but that was only to gently remind them that I was there – and that they had promised it wasn't a date. The breast-touching-hand beside me, though, suggested differently. God knows what happened to Bridget and that Mr Darcy bloke, I wasn't paying the slightest bit of attention to what was going down on the massive screen in front of me. I was far too distracted.

Earlier on in the night I could tell she was panicking, she kept staring at me with this worried expression, paying close attention to my every move – I guessed my mum had spoken to hers about my tearful outburst. I knew that I had to man up. I had to put her mind at rest, otherwise I'd crack up under such scrutiny. Even though it killed me inside, I had to put on a brave face and act like I wasn't bothered by the changes going on.

The whole thing was a bit of a nightmare for me, and that was why I agreed to ask Kelly out. At least it would keep my mind occupied when we were all out together and stop me from feeling like the world's biggest pervert because, disturbingly, when I saw his hand up there, the first thought that went through my head was, 'I wonder what that feels like'. My hand tingled as I contemplated it and a hotness rushed through me, causing a stirring down below. Yes, the first time I'd got an erection from thinking of Maddy in a sexual way was when she was being fondled by my best friend. Up until then my feelings had been mostly innocent. I couldn't be thinking thoughts like that!

Inviting Kelly along seemed the most sensible thing to do, but as Monday loomed and I realized I was going to have to approach her, I couldn't help but feel queasy. I was such a wimp. It was ridiculous. It didn't help that Robert and Maddy kept pulling faces at me the whole way through our art class, gesturing for me to go over to her. I never performed well under pressure. Still don't.

I seized the opportunity to have a quiet word with her when she was over by the sink washing her brushes. I picked up one of mine and casually strolled over.

'Hi, Kelly . . .' I smiled, as I stood alongside her, running my brush underneath the warm flowing tap.

As she looked up and saw it was me, I noticed her deep red lips push out into a pout. Kelly was one of the hot chicks in our year, and she knew it. There was something about her that was dangerously sexy – she was wild and carefree, something her untamed long hair and dark eyes helped to amplify.

It was at that point, while I was lingering next to her at

the tap, that I remembered our teeth bashing when I'd pulled her in for a snog in Paris. I couldn't help but shrink into myself as I internally cringed with embarrassment.

'Maddy and Robert, huh? What a shocker . . .' she laughed, blowing a loose strand of black hair out of her face.

'Tell me about it.'

Kelly picked up a cloth and started to dry her clean brushes. I kept mine underneath the tap, thinking of different ways to approach the subject.

'You know, if you want,' she started, releasing her words slowly as she gazed at me with her smouldering eyes. 'I could always hang with you guys. I'd hate to see you feel left out when they're smooching each other's faces off.'

I laughed in relief at not having to ask, she'd simply offered it.

'We can't let them have all the fun . . . can we?' she whispered wickedly as she leaned forward and took the brush from my hands in what can only be described as a suggestive manner – circling her fingers loosely around the end closest to me and slowly skimming her hold along the shaft before gripping completely at the end and pulling it off me. It was practically pornographic to my teenage mind.

And that was the start of my fling with Kelly.

I'm not going to say that I ever loved her in the same way I loved Maddy, I really didn't, but she moved me in a very different way. She excited me and kept me guessing. She awoke something new in me – the desire for physical connection. I hadn't really realized its significance until she came along.

Put frankly, she made me fucking horny.

I tried to bury my head in the sand, or, more accurately, in Kelly's massive tits, when it came to Maddy and Robert. It had been difficult to watch them get together in the first instance, but it was far worse watching them fall in love. That hurt more than anything. Every day they stayed together affirmed the notion that I'd never have a chance with Maddy. She would never be mine, never know how much I loved her. I wished I'd been brave enough to tell her my feelings before we'd gone to Paris. I wished I'd told her after telling her Anthony and John thought she was fit, or when her dad queried whether I was gay or not . . . or at that childish wedding back at primary school when I'd only had the guts to tell her with those three desperate squeezes that I constantly used throughout our childhood, hoping one day she'd suddenly hear me and understand their meaning. I was a coward and I hated myself for being that way.

Maddy

Sixteen years old . . .

From the moment Robert and I kissed in Paris I knew I'd lose my virginity to him. I wasn't sure when it would occur – in a week's time, a month's time, six months, a year – I just knew it was going to happen. It was a thrillingly scary thought.

We'd talk about it, a lot. Of course we did. What teenage couple didn't talk about the possibility of having sex? But one thing Robert was brilliant at was reassuring me. He was in no rush to lose his V-card (it's what the cool kids were calling it), and neither was I. That was until he told me he loved me . . . from that point on I just wanted to do it more than anything. There was a desire that surged through me, threatening to cause an almighty explosion if something wasn't done sharpish.

It ended up happening over the Christmas holidays, just a month after we got back from Paris – yes, I'm aware that it would have been nice to wait a little longer, but there was no stopping our lascivious behaviour once the cogs were in motion. Plus, we'd known each other since we were nine years old – we trusted each other unconditionally. So many qualities you'd hope to build in a new relationship already existed between us. I didn't feel the need to wait any longer.

It happened on a Tuesday.

Our parents were at work.

Ben had taken himself off somewhere for the day – I've no idea if this had been planned between the two boys, or if he'd arranged it himself not knowing what we were about to get up to.

I spent the morning making myself look and feel wonderful. I shaved my legs, armpits and everywhere else I thought shouldn't have been displaying hair, put on some simple, but matching black underwear (it's not as though I had anything lacy or provocative at that age – my mum would have killed me), some make-up, a pair of black trousers, vest top and a red cropped jumper and tidied my hair back in a pretty, loose fishtail plait. I hoped I looked effortlessly cosy and gorgeous – like the girl next door that all boys seem to want to sleep with.

On the short walk to his house I started to worry. What if I wasn't very good at it, I wondered. What if I was so bad Robert decided he never wanted to do it with me again?

My heart was beating so fast by the time Rob opened his front door – but one tiny smile from him brought back all the desire I'd experienced in the lead up; it was all the reassurance I needed. I was nervous, more nervous than I'd ever been about anything, but I knew it was what I wanted.

Robert took me by the hand and guided me over the threshold. As soon as the door was shut he cupped my face in his hands and kissed me, slowly and with such a pensive look on his face – I realized it wasn't just me who was nervous.

'Should we go upstairs?' I heard myself squeak.

He just nodded, took my hand and led me to his room in silence.

Once we were in his blue box of a room with the door shut, he exhaled sharply and drew me into him for a hug – a tight, loving embrace. I felt it was to comfort not just me, but himself. All the cheekiness and cocky behaviour Robert possessed was just a façade to win others over, I knew that, but it was still a surprise to see that front completely dropped – to have the vulnerable part of Robert stood in front of me feeling, perhaps, that he didn't want to be the leader for once. He needed to make sure it was what I wanted. That it was right.

Still held in his clasp, I took his fingers in mine and brought them to my lips, kissing each of them individually in what I hoped was a tantalizing manner, as I looked into Robert's eyes intently. They questioned me, asked if I was sure. In response I backed on to the bed away from him, before reaching my hand out and beckoning him over.

He didn't come. Instead he put his hands on his hips and stared at me in his new-found shy manner.

'Should I put some music on?' he mumbled, before turning to his stereo and playing with some buttons until he finally settled on a radio station playing cheesy love songs.

'Sounds good,' I encouraged, willing him to stop acting so weird.

'Let me just shut the curtains . . .' he faffed, going over to the window. 'There . . .' he declared once they were closed and the room was a little dimmer.

As soon as he was next to me on the bed, our lips about to kiss, something else popped into his brain and he was back on his feet once more.

'Candles. Shit, I forgot I bought candles,' he said urgently, before practically falling from the bed in a clumsy manner as he reached for his rucksack. He pulled out a fifty pack of vanilla-scented tealights from Ikea.

'You're not planning on lighting all of those, are you?' I asked, wondering how long it would take.

'Sorry . . . I was going to have it all done before you arrived but . . .' he said with a panic-stricken face, as he rested the bag on the bed.

'It doesn't matter,' I insisted.

'It doesn't?'

'No.'

'I just wanted it to be perfect, though.'

'It's already perfect because I'm here with you, you big softie,' I laughed, grabbing his hips and pulling him back on the bed with me.

He pouted at me, his perfect face still full of concern, before breaking into a little smile. 'I'm being a girl . . .'

'You are,' I smiled, loving that our old joke could still lighten the mood. I ran my fingers through his hair and pulled his head towards mine so that our lips found each other.

'I love you,' he mumbled.

'Then that's all I need.'

The first time we had sex I kept my eyes closed the whole way through, well, for at least the majority of it. I'd read somewhere that you should always kiss with your eyes closed, so it made sense to me to stick to that rule when doing that greater deed too. I'll admit that I did decide to sneak them open at one point but the look of intensity and determination on Rob's face surprised me, so I decided to shut them again for fear of getting nervous giggles.

Once it was over I felt relieved. So did Rob. Half an hour later we did it again. It lasted far longer and was much more pleasurable knowing what the unknown actually was. Gone were any remaining nerves, what was left was just . . . lovely.

Afterwards, Robert brought up our lunch on a tray — chicken dippers, potato Alphabites and spaghetti hoops. A feast to celebrate the day we both lost our virginity and moved onto the next, more serious stage of being a couple.

As we sat curled up in his bed, utterly naked, tucking into the sophisticated meal, I felt completely relaxed and content. Growing up I'd heard of girls regretting their first times (they were drunk, it was too soon in a relationship, it was with someone they didn't really care for), but I felt an overwhelming sense of pride that it wasn't the case for me.

Robert was a natural leader, something that was apparent in our friendship group, but as a lover I'd discovered him to be even more caring and giving than I thought possible. My cheeky friend had the sweetest heart with the most gorgeous love to give — I felt blessed to be the one receiving it.

Dating someone who'd seen me at my worst, and who I'd seen at her worst, was a whole new experience for us both. We couldn't lie and pretend to be perfect like some couples do in those early days. We knew each other inside out. It changed things between us drastically, as you'd expect. There was no way I could pretend Maddy was one of the boys any more. Well, I certainly wasn't treating her like one of the boys any more, that's for sure. Something I'd like to apologize to our fellow tripod member, Ben, for. There were certainly a few moments in our younger years where Ben copped a load of something he shouldn't have.

Maddy

Eighteen years old . . .

Ben and Kelly's relationship didn't last long. Well, they fooled around together for nine months before she left to go to college – but as we all stayed at Peaswood High in the sixth form to do our A-levels, their relationship came to an amicable resolve. But just because Ben and Kelly didn't last, it didn't mean that Ben was back to being on his own with us and looking like a tag-along. Kelly had given him a new-found confidence with the ladies, and so had losing his puppy fat. He'd become effortlessly slender and the way he Brylcreemed his hair back made him look like a Mediterranean Superman with his olive skin and dark eyes. He was popular, but he wasn't a womanizer – he didn't treated anyone badly or just use them for sex, it's simply that he was never short of female company. Years of being the perfect listener to many of the girls in our year, added to the fact that he'd grown some self-belief and learned how to flirt, had given him a tantalizing charm – made all the greater by the fact that he didn't realize what a catch he was.

I asked Robert if he was envious of him once.

'Why would I be?' he'd asked innocently.

'Because he gets to be with all these girls while you're stuck with me, that's why.'

'It's never even crossed my mind,' he muttered, pulling me into his chest and kissing the top of my head.

I had no doubt that Robert was happy with me, but the fact that their roles had almost been reversed must have had some sort of impact on him, even if he didn't want to admit it. After all, Ben, with his many admirers and string of dates, was leading the life all three of us would have predicted Robert, with his cheeky ways and army of fans, would have had, if it weren't for our relationship.

'You know what's funny?' he said into my hair.

'What?'

'I don't miss it at all.'

'Being popular?'

'Ha!' he spat, pulling me closer and tickling me until I begged him to stop. 'It never meant anything to me, but you? Now, you mean the world to me.'

And just like that, my strong, loving, thoughtful boyfriend eradicated my fears . . . well, at least for the time being.

We'd come to the end of school life and our university days were looming around the corner, ready to take us on the next big journey of our lives. There was a huge chance that the three of us would end up at different places around the country, a fact we'd decided not to worry too much about until our results were collected and offers accepted – but the wait was agonizing, even if we didn't admit it.

We all had different universities down as our top choices, having decided to focus on different subjects. It meant that, if we all got the grades we'd been predicted, our friendship group would be separated for the first time in nine years. Robert, who had taken PE, Biology and English Language A levels, was hoping to go to Nottingham Trent to study Sport and Exercise Science. Ben, who'd taken Graphic Design, Art and English Language, was hoping to go up north to Northumbria to study Graphic Design. And I, having studied Art, English Literature and Psychology, wanted to go to Bristol and study Photography. If everything went to plan we'd be miles apart. It was a sobering thought.

A fry-up was the only way to start results day. Our grades, and our future fate, wouldn't be accessible until ten o'clock and, seeing as we knew we'd all be up anxiously pacing around our homes, we figured getting together would keep our brains occupied. A sombre mood filled the kitchen in my house as we cooked in silence. Each of us lost in our own thoughts.

'How are we all feeling?' I asked, once we were seated and had started tucking in to our bacon, sausages, eggs, beans and toast.

Two shrugs were given as answers. It was a gesture I was used to receiving, but on that particular day I'd expected more from them.

'I'm the only one crapping myself, then?' I huffed.

'Mad, there's no point worrying until we know what we're worrying about,' said Ben with an appeasing smile.

'Well said,' nodded Robert, although I could see the worry in his face, highlighted by the frown on his brow. Robert needed to get the highest marks of our group to get onto his chosen course – two As and one B. I knew he was feeling the pressure, even if he wanted to pretend that he was laid-back about the whole thing.

'Where are we going tonight, then?' asked Ben, changing the subject to something more jovial.

'Tonight? I think we should start straight away,' Robert laughed, pulling three miniature bottles of Jack Daniels from his pocket and handing one to each of us. 'To the tripod,' he toasted, unscrewing the lid of his bottle and thrusting it in the air.

'To the tripod,' Ben and I repeated, giggling as we knocked them back.

The school was in chaos when we arrived, with people running around screaming in delight or crying in despair – their future fate decided. It caused a lump of nerves to form in my throat as we strolled to reception and picked up the awaiting white envelopes.

'Should we go somewhere quiet?' asked Robert. 'Away from everyone?'

'Over here,' I gestured, leading us away from the crowds and into an empty classroom.

'Here goes,' sighed Robert.

'Moment of truth,' I laughed weakly.

'On the count of three . . .?' suggested Ben, to which we nodded. 'One, two, three . . .'

We all hastily opened our envelopes, and took out the result papers, taking time to understand the meaning of them before any reactions were given.

'Three fucking As!' screamed Robert, fist pumping the air.

'One A and two Bs!' I squealed – it was more than I needed to get into Bristol. I threw myself on Robert in excitement, thrilled that everything was on track for us both.

But one of us wasn't celebrating. I turned to face Ben to see that he was still staring at his paper, looking disappointed.

'You all right, mate?' asked Robert, clamping a hand on his shoulder. 'How did you do?'

He looked up and shook his head.

Ben had needed to get an A and two Bs to get into Northumbria, but instead he'd got three Bs.

'Fuck!' offered Robert.

'What are you going to do?'

'I'll phone up and see about clearing, I guess, but . . .'

'There's a "but", that's good!' encouraged Robert.

'Well, it's good enough for my second choice . . .' he said looking at me with an apprehensive smile. 'Bristol.'

'Ahhhh!' I screamed, running in for a hug. 'Please come with me! Please!'

'I might not have a choice,' he laughed, trying to struggle away from me.

'Oh great, so now I'm the only one who's going to be on my own. I'll be a loner!' moaned Robert.

'Oh, people will love you,' I giggled. 'You'll be the popular kid as usual!'

'You won't have us two geeks dragging you down,' offered Ben.

'Well, when you put it like that,' he chuckled, putting an arm around each of us. 'I'll try not to have too much fun without you guys.'

Leaving Peaswood High behind us, we wandered down to the local park – the same park that lent me, Robert and Ben its trees to climb and play on when we were younger. We spent the majority of the afternoon in the sunshine, along with most of the upper sixth. We sat in several circles (with the majority of people sticking with their friends – even at the end people refrained from socializing too much with other peer groups), and drank our way through copious amounts of wine and beer while listening to indie music. Bands like the Kooks, the Zutons and Kaiser Chiefs pumped from a portable stereo like we were at a mini music festival. Whether people had received good news or bad regarding their future, we were united in saying goodbye to the school that had been our home for the last seven years. Freedom and new beginnings were ahead of us – the world was our oyster. I can remember looking around at one point, seeing the sunshine beam down on everyone laughing and singing, and feeling like I'd entered a euphoric state. It felt warm, weightless and hippy-like.

Those feelings stayed with us over the summer months before we headed off to university, endless summer evenings drifting by with ease. The daytimes were a different matter. With three months to kill there was no way our mums would have let us bum around aimlessly; we were forced to go into Tamsgate, our nearest town, and get jobs. I wound up in a department store called Magpies in the home department (relentlessly refolding towels all day long and sighing with frustration every time a customer carelessly came and messed them up), while Robert and Ben were both at Spin – a cool music shop– having a whale of a time. It was possibly one of the only times in our whole friendship that I felt left out and jealous, but seeing as Robert was going to have to put up with me and Ben being together for the next three years, I kept my petty grumbling thoughts to myself.

The plus side to them working in Spin was that they got me a massive discount on any CDs or DVDs that I wanted. We'd all started driving that year and nothing beat the feeling of cruising along (let's face it, we'd drive even when there was nowhere to go) with our windows down as great music pumped from the stereo. Thanks to the boys all of our cars were filled with current albums.

In return I got us all a load of sheets and towels, which might sound pretty lame, but it came in really handy when we were getting ready for our new lives in student halls . . .

Ben

Eighteen years old . . .

On my eighteenth birthday Robert found me perched in my treehouse at the bottom of my garden. I'd been sat in that spot for at least an hour and was in a grumpy, contemplative mood as I stared at an old photo of my dad and me together on my ninth birthday, taken after he'd led me outside into the garden to see his gift for me – that treehouse, built from scratch with his own bare hands. In that vintage and rare photo, my arms are wrapped around his neck with glee, excited that I had a cool den to play in. He's laughing at my reaction with his eyes closed, a lovely image of a dad getting a hug from his grateful child. There wasn't even a hint of the trauma that was to come just five months later. Perhaps leaving us wasn't even on his mind at that point.

'Happy birthday, mate,' Rob grinned at me as he popped his head up through the floor of my wooden house and pulled himself inside.

I said nothing but tried my best to return the cheeky expression he was wearing. I clearly wasn't very good at it, though – he frowned at me straight away, sensing something wasn't quite right.

'What's up?' he asked, crouching his body in two as he made his way through the small structure to my side – it was a tight squeeze now we were on the verge of adult-hood. 'Oh,' he pouted as he caught a glimpse of the picture I was holding.

'Yeah . . .' I nodded dejectedly.

Robert sighed and sat down next to me.

'Why doesn't he want anything to do with me?'

'Maybe he does . . .' Rob shrugged feebly.

'Dude, he knows where I live – it's the same place he tucked me into bed for almost ten years before he fucked off with some other family. He's got a replacement son and can't be arsed keeping in touch with his own blood. It doesn't bother him that I'm the product of his one singu-lar winning sperm.'

'Eurgh!' chuckled Robert, giving me a gentle nudge.

'I can't get my head around the fact that he's never been in touch,' I exhaled. 'Even today? All those birthdays he's missed out on over the years, but today stings the most. It's a special one.'

'I get that.'

'In theory, from this point forward, I'm an adult. He missed most of me being a kid, and now it looks like he's going to miss the rest of my life along with it.'

My words lingered in the silence that fell upon us.

'So what?' he asked, matter-of-factly.

'Huh?'

'You have a great life. You're surrounded by people who love you, you've got a wicked relationship with your mum and you're fucking talented. So why care about someone who hasn't taken the time to realize how awe-some you are?'

I looked at the picture in my hands and said nothing,

instead concentrating on nibbling at a tiny bit of loose skin on my bottom lip. It wasn't quite the reaction I'd been expecting from Robert – it was far more diplomatic than the bashing of my dad's crummy morals that I was after.

'Is someone who could walk out on you when you were just a kid really worth pining over? Is he really worth the energy or effort?'

'I wish it was that simple.'

'Maybe it can be,' he shrugged, turning to me with wide green eyes.

'But not having him makes me feel trapped and desperate,' I confessed, feeling defeated at having to share my niggling thoughts. 'Some days I come up here and I feel like that little nine-year-old all over again, wanting him to come back and apologize, to tell me and Mum he still loves us . . . I know it sounds ridiculous.'

'No,' Rob breathed, shaking his head.

'This place pulls me in, acts like a safe haven, and then reminds me of his betrayal,' I added, as I took in the ageing and weathered wood around us.

'Then why come up here?'

'It calls out to me. It's just too tempting not to. I spot it from the kitchen or from my bedroom window. I've always thought of it as a place to be closer to him – but I've been feeding myself a sack of shit. All it does is remind me of what I no longer have.'

Rob puffed out his cheeks as he exhaled and ran his fingers through his hair, pulling the blond strands away from his eyes.

'I'll be back in a bit,' he said quickly, as he shuffled along the floor, grabbed hold of the blue rope and jumped down and out of the hole to the grass below. I watched him as he walked around the house and out of the side gate. When he returned ten minutes later he was carrying a bright yellow plastic toolbox.

'What's that for?' I yelled down, sitting up and trying to get a better view of what he was up to.

'Call it a special birthday present,' he grinned, opening up the box and taking out a hammer and saw.

'What?'

'A few pieces of wood shouldn't make you query how loved you are – or taunt you about what might have been if your dad wasn't such a dick. Now, come down here, grab some tools and let's demolish the crap out of it.'

'Seriously?'

'I want to free you of your chains,' he smirked.

'I feel like Rapunzel,' I joked as I hung out of the window of my childhood treehouse.

'That makes me your prince charming, then,' Rob winked. 'Are you coming down? Or do you want me to carry you?'

Eagerly, I made my way down from the treehouse for the last time. Adrenaline pumped through me as I took the saw from Robert and reached up to start hacking away at one of my hidden demons. We ripped, smashed, crushed and split every piece of that wooden structure until there was nothing but a simple apple tree left behind. It must have taken less than half an hour, but I enjoyed every second – at one point I even threw the tools aside and just started pulling at it with my hands, yanking rusty nails away from their embedded homes. Never had I felt so pumped and full of energy.

'Now what?' I asked in my out-of-breath state as I stared at the treehouse's carcass in a heap on the ground.

'We burn it,' he grinned, pulling out lighter blocks from the plastic box, along with a box of matches.

I'll admit that the whole thing had an air of teenage girl drama about it. You know, girl gets ditched by arsehole boyfriend and burns every picture of them together in some ritualistic voodoo cursing manner ... but as I watched those pieces of wood go up in flames, and flicked that picture from the day it was created on top of the burning pile, I felt a sense of release.

I put my arm around Rob's shoulders and thanked him for giving me the best birthday present I could have asked for.

'Anything for you,' he winked, ruffling my hair. 'Now, let's go find that girlfriend of mine ... I believe she's been making you a cake.'

Maddy

Eighteen years old . . .

And so, the time came to head for university. We were all leaving Peaswood on the same Saturday morning in early October. Gloriously warm sunshine beamed down on us as the sun dug its heels in and refused to give in to the winter weather that was heading our way.

Robert was to travel in his own car to Nottingham while his parents followed behind in theirs. You'd have thought that as he was the youngest of three boys, both of whom had previously been sent off to university, they'd be blasé about him going away, but he was still their baby, therefore they insisted on going with him and getting him settled. Much to his annoyance.

Me and Ben were going in separate cars, while our mums and my dad followed behind.

All three of us were going to have our cars with us, which we were hoping would make the miles between Bristol, Nottingham and home appear more bearable. Plus driving still felt cool and gave us great freedom – we weren't too keen on giving that up so soon and relying on public transport.

As agreed, at eleven o'clock Ben, Robert and the parents drove over to ours to say a final farewell. I'd said a proper goodbye to Robert the night before. He'd come over to help me pack, but he proved to be quite a distraction and kept picking me up and dragging me away from my suitcase. He'd always been athletic and strong, but in our last year at Peaswood High his pole-like frame had suddenly bulked up and become more manly, once again capturing the attention of not only the girls at school, but any female we passed on the street – occasionally males too. As ever, he liked to show off his strength, which was why he kept picking me up and plonking me back on my bed, no matter how much I protested.

As we lay on my bed, once I'd given up fighting back, he turned to me with a sad sigh.

'I can't believe you're going to Bristol and that Ben's going with you!'

'At least you'll have someone to keep an eye on me now.'

'As if I needed that anyway,' he said, pulling me closer.

'You never know, I might be swept off my feet by some arty type,' I laughed.

'Don't even joke,' he said with a pout.

'Oh, and there's not going to be a swarm of girls falling over themselves to get to you, Mr Muscles?'

'I'm blind to everyone else . . . you know that.'

'Yeah, just wait until you get to Freshers' Week and you see just how short the skirts are and just how high the boobs have been pushed up.'

He raised his eyebrows at me and laughed, 'How high are we talking?'

Prompting me to whack him on the head with a pillow, leading to a play fight.

Eventually, as we calmly snugged in together once more, he whispered in my ear, 'We'll be okay.'

'We will, won't we?'

'Absolutely . . . there's only one girl for me and I love her with every beat of my heart.'

'So cheesy.'

'So true,' he whispered, pulling me on top of him and kissing me in a way we both knew would lead to some very naughty behaviour – even with my parents downstairs.

We fell asleep at some point, causing my mum to come in a couple of hours later and shout her head off like a crazed madwoman as she spotted my unpacked suitcase. Robert later snuck off home, after more snuggling at the doorway, deciding it was about time he started his own packing – although I was sure his mum would have done the whole lot for him already.

There was nothing final about our goodbye that Saturday – even though we were entering into new worlds and new lives, it was joyous rather than sad. Well, for us it was, but you wouldn't have thought so if you looked at our mums, who were all sniffing into their tissues before we'd even got into our cars.

The three of us stood in a huddle and hugged goodbye, Robert holding me around the waist while Ben took my hand and squeezed it three times in his ever-comforting way – I was thrilled that he'd be going to Bristol with me, that I'd still have him for constant support.

'So, we'll see you next weekend or the one after, then?' I asked Robert, as we broke away, bouncing my car keys in my hand in excitement and doing a little jig with my knees.

'Yes! We'll play it by ear. See what's planned for us all in our Freshers' Weeks.'

'Watch out for those girls, Mr Miles,' I warned.

'How high did you say they were again?' he grinned, placing one hand on his chest to mockingly measure the assumed freshers'-week-boob-height, before putting his hands around my waist and pulling me close.

'Oooh, you little monkey,' I laughed.

He gave me a tender kiss before turning to give Ben an embrace, slapping him on the back in that brotherly way guys do to each other.

'Look after her,' I heard Robert say quietly.

'Of course,' promised Ben with a nod.

It was a sweet moment between the two of them, even if they were acting as though I wasn't there and that I was some feeble girl who needed looking after. I had no doubt I would be fine – it was the boys I was worried about, after all, their mums did practically everything for them. I had no idea how they were going to cook and clean unaided. Not that I said as much.

After the three of us joined together for one final huddle, I got into my little red Ford Ka and manically waved goodbye. We beeped our horns the whole way to the motorway, excitedly starting the journeys to our futures.

I'd picked Bristol as my top choice for university mainly because of its beautiful location and scenic views – I'd been there years before with my family and had thought of it as a magical place ever since. Although, obviously, the photography course I'd be studying sounded great too. Ever since Mum and Dad had bought me that first camera, I'd never been able to shake off my love for the art. I knew Dad would have loved me to study something more solid, like business or English – something that offered more prospects once the degree was complete and would secure me a future, but he never tried to sway me from doing the course. At eighteen, I had no idea what I planned to do with a photography degree, but I figured something would pop up somewhere along the line. Taking pictures was what I loved doing. Plus, not to blow my own trumpet, I was good at it. Now I'm not saying that I thought I was about to become the new Mario Testino, or anything like that, but I was better at doing and creating rather than forcing my mind to think about mundane tasks and sums. A doer, not a thinker, perhaps.

Bristol was just as beautiful as I'd remembered it from my childhood. The area that had stuck in my mind most vividly was Totterdown, with its multi-coloured houses sitting all pretty in the hills. In my head I'd assumed I'd be living in one of them when I went to university there, so I was mildly disappointed to learn it wasn't a possibility. It was student halls for me. Although that didn't stop me over the years wandering down to Totterdown and pretending it was my neighbourhood – I liked living in that little fantasy whenever I could.

The rest of Bristol itself was far from ugly with its historic-looking buildings at the heart of it; with the rivers winding their way through everything – the campus, shops and houses – it felt like you were never far from the water. Plus, there were loads of beaches a cycle ride or a drive away (depending on how adventurous you felt), where we could sunbathe over ice cream, dinky doughnuts or a bag a chips. Perfect. I knew I'd be spending most of my time inland in the busy part of the city, but it was lovely knowing that those views were only minutes away and easily accessible.

On the day I arrived there, once the cars were unpacked, my room was set up, and we'd met a few other students who were staying in the same halls, I finally managed to persuade Mum and Dad that it was okay for them to leave me in this strange place called Bristol.

As soon as I waved them off and returned to my room (after a million goodbye hugs and kisses), I found myself disturbed by the silence. It was eerie. I lay on my single bed and looked around my new home. The bland white walls were hardly warm and inviting, but I knew I could spruce it up with some photos from home Blu-tacked to them. Along one side there was a white wardrobe and a chest of drawers, which were already brimming with clothes – I'd had no idea what to pack, so decided to bring the majority of my wardrobe. Next to those was a wooden desk, on which I'd already lined up my course books as well as my new computer and camera. I was also given the gift of an en-suite – something I was truly grateful for as it would spare me the awkwardness of half-naked encounters with strangers in the hallway after showers and, perhaps more importantly, the embarrassment of having to hide the smell of my number twos when going to the loo. Yes, I knew an en-suite would make my life there much more comfortable.

I took in the new space around me and let out a sigh, suddenly feeling a bit empty – or perhaps it was boredom seeping in after such a hectic and thrilling day. It was, after all, fairly anti-climactic. I'd been so excited to get to Bristol and for university life to start, but we still had a whole thirty-eight hours to go until we walked through those university doors and officially became its students.

I picked up my phone and called Ben. His accommodation wasn't in the same block as mine, but was luckily only a couple of minutes' walk away.

'Hey,' he said, picking up instantly.

'Are you unpacked?'

'Yeah, all done. Mum left ages ago. I've been helping some of the others bring their suitcases up the stairs and stuff.'

'Very nice and sociable of you.'

'I'm going to be living with them for a year – always good to make a good impression.'

'Fair point,' I answered, suddenly wondering what my new companions thought of me. I'd briefly met three students from my halls, Pearl, Jennifer and Flo. They seemed nice enough, although we hadn't all got together and had a proper chat yet, we'd been too busy organizing our new rooms while our parents faffed around us. I thought about going in and getting to know one of them a bit better, kicking off one of those firm friendships that people always talked about creating at uni, but the comfort of having Ben there, who I knew so well already, drew me in. 'What are you doing now?'

'Nothing. Just chilling in my room.'

'Same here. Fancy going to the pub for one?'

'Yeah, why not.'

One drink turned into two, turned into three, turned into four, turned into Ben having to carry me back to my place, only I couldn't for the life of me remember what floor I was on or what room I was in. It was funny for all of two minutes and then, as we were shattered and too drunk to care, we gave up trying to find my new bed and took a little walk to Ben's room instead. We curled up on the single bed and passed out instantly.

And so started our student life.

It didn't take me long to form firm friendships with the girls in my halls, which wasn't like me, but Pearl, Flo and Jennifer were awesome. Pearl, from East London, was a proper cockney – tough and feisty. She might have been just a little over five feet, but she had some gob on her and was as blunt as anything – a quality that was alarming at first but equally refreshing. Flo was from the Wirral, and was our group's English rose. Her honey-like hair fell down in waves to just below her shoulders and her milky skin was flawless, not freckled like mine. She too had a boyfriend that she was separated from – he was a brick-layer and was staying up north – so I instantly felt drawn to her through our similar situations. Jennifer, an exotic-looking beauty with Indian roots on her mother's side, was, rather ironically, from Nottingham, making her an endless source of information when Robert started heading out to all these places that I'd never heard of.

The morning after the night I'd slept in Ben's bed instead of my own, I wandered in to find them all standing in the hallway, each leaning against their bedroom doors – Pearl's room was next to mine on the left, Jennifer's was adjacent to hers and Flo's was directly opposite mine. They were all still in their pyjamas, looking like they'd not long since woken up, gulping on mugs of tea. They were mid-conversation but stopped when they saw me walk in wearing my previous night's clothes, confirming that I hadn't just got home late and then ventured out first thing before they'd woken up – I'd slept out.

'There you are!' sighed Flo, sounding relieved, before eying up my clothes with a troubled look. 'We've been worried!'

'Really?'

'Of course we have, Maddy,' Jennifer added with a sympathetic smile. 'We thought you might've got cold feet and decided to leave us already.'

'So . . . where have you been?' asked Flo.

'God, I got so drunk . . .'

'Did you shag someone?' asked Pearl.

See? Where others might have been more restrained on a topic, she was always ready to wade in and get to the root of a matter without hesitation.

'What? No!'

'Oh! I was sure this was going to be our first walk of shame,' she laughed with mock disappointment. 'What a pity!'

'She's not stopped going on about it,' added Jennifer, rolling her eyes.

'I have a boyfriend.' I protested.

'Well, that doesn't stop some people!' smirked Pearl.

'I told her you weren't doing that,' chimed in Flo almost to herself as she gazed into her mug, looking uncomfortable with the conversation – I had a feeling that she, like me, wasn't keen on any sort of confrontation.

'So where were you, then?' prodded Jennifer.

'With Ben,' I shrugged.

'Your extremely fit BFF?' asked Jennifer, her dark brown eyes widening in surprise.

I nodded, prompting the girls to look at each other and giggle.

'What?'

'Oh, nothing . . . I just hope I find a hunky friend to share a bed with, at some point,' laughed Pearl, twirling her brown hair through her fingertips.

'But it's not like that,' I argued, getting ready to defend our boy/girl friendship once more, something I was very used to doing. Hoping that it wasn't going to be made into a massive issue. I liked these girls and didn't want there to be a question mark hanging over me and my loyalty every time I hung out with Ben. That's what had led me to feel judged and isolated in the past – and I didn't want history to start repeating itself yet again.

'Shush, you,' broke in Jennifer, interrupting my frantic thoughts. 'She's pulling your leg.'

'Yep. I've seen a photo of your boyfriend . . . Phwoar!' Pearl growled.

'Thanks,' I sighed.

'Any brothers I should know about?'

'Two!'

'Like heaven to my ears!' Pearl cackled.

'Want a cuppa?' asked Flo, moving towards our communal kitchen. 'Kettle's just boiled.'

'Sounds fab. I'll just go shower first, though.' I felt stale and horrid from the previous night's over-indulgence – I knew I still smelt of alcohol too, it hovered around me, prompting unexpected waves of nausea every time I caught a whiff of it.

I showered quickly and threw on a new pair of stripy purple and white pyjamas (I'd bought them especially for uni), guessing the day was going to be written off in terms of exploring the city, and left my hair wet – I couldn't bear the thought of drying it in my hungover state, and didn't even care that it would dry frizzy and wild.

'Here you go, tea, two sugars,' Flo beamed, handing me a mug as soon as I walked out of my room, back into the hallway.

'Feeling better?' asked Pearl, still standing in the same spot I'd left her.

'Much.'

'Fancy a chocolate Hobnob?' she asked, pulling a massive packet from the pocket of her dark-blue dressing gown.

'That is just what I need!' I sighed, happily taking one.

'I've got two mega packs,' she grinned, swinging out her hip and showing me another packet hiding in her other pocket.

'We've decided a girlie flick is in order,' smiled Flo.

'Yes, come join us in my little boudoir. We're watching that new one with Billy Buskin in – *Halo*,' Jennifer said, opening her bedroom door to reveal the den she'd created. Radiant red and aubergine-coloured fabric was hanging from the walls, hiding the dull white-painted surfaces behind, and incense was burning, making it look like an Arabian haven. It was beautiful.

'How have you managed to make it look so cool?' I asked, mentally comparing it to my own bleak hideout. I thought I'd done a pretty good job personalizing it and making it my own, but Jennifer had shown me otherwise.

'Mum made me pack a whole bunch of saris, just in case the perfect Indian boy turned up on campus . . .' she chuckled. 'I figured I might as well put them to good use instead, plus I was running out of space in my wardrobe.'

'They look incredible!'

'I'll be frantically taking them down whenever she decides to come visit . . . and wearing them!' she laughed. 'Right, grab a space, girls,' she said, gesturing towards the bed as she switched on her television and located the chosen DVD.

We scrambled onto her neatly made bed, which was lavishly covered in red silk sheets and embroidered cream pillows, and nestled ourselves into comfortable positions with our cups of tea cradled in our hands and Pearl's chocolate Hobnobs temptingly placed out in front of us to nibble on.

That, at eighteen years old, was my first ever girlie afternoon. It's bizarre to think that I'd gone that long without one. As we sighed at the romantic storyline between Sid Quest and Scarlett James (cooing over Billy Buskin's charming ways), giggled awkwardly at the sex scenes (can anyone watch them in the company of others and not feel über weird?) and cried our eyes out uncontrollably at the ending (seriously, it's so sad – how could they leave it there?), I realized how fun it was going to be living with the girls and being part of a girlie friendship group for once. Now, being with the boys had always been effortlessly comfortable, and I knew nothing would ever replace or better that, but the new bond that I felt growing was a whole new experience for me, and I liked it.

Robert came to visit us for two nights the following weekend – we didn't quite manage to last the two weeks apart we'd loosely planned – something I was rather pleased about. It was nice to know that he hadn't forgotten about me as soon as he got to Nottingham and was out of reach. We'd all survived Freshers' Week and avoided any disasters, other than gaining splitting headaches from our raging hangovers – students could drink!

'Just what I thought,' Robert said, wandering into my room, nodding as he inspected the place. 'It's basically the same as mine, but with your added girlie touch.'

'It's not girlie!'

'No, you're right,' he said, picking up one of my floral pillowcases from my bed as he sat on it – just to prove his point.

I wouldn't have normally gone in for the floral thing, I was the least girlie person in the world, but I'd become obsessed with all the colourful sheets and towels when working in Magpies that summer. I don't know what had come over me.

'Compared to your boyish lair, which no doubt has nothing out other than your weights, I think you mean it's more welcoming and homely,' I said, jumping on top of him and wrapping my arms around his neck – I was so excited to have him there.

'Ah, yeah . . . that's totally what I meant,' he said with a wink before kissing me. 'Your housemates seem fun.'

'They're great. Love you already, I can tell.'

'They seem like a nice bunch.'

'They are.'

'Make sure that Pearl doesn't lead you astray.'

'What? How do you mean?' I asked, instantly feeling defensive over my new friend.

'She's a wild one,' he shrugged. 'I bet she'll be getting you lot into all sorts of trouble.'

I thought back to the previous night – us girls and Ben had all gone to Castle Park to sit and relax on the green while taking in the gorgeous views of the castle and the river. We hadn't been there long before Pearl whipped out five plastic cups, a family-sized carton of Tropicana orange juice (with the bits) and a litre bottle of vodka. Remembering the sore head I'd woken up with that morning, I realized Robert might have had a point – not that I was going to tell him that.

'What makes you think I'm so easily led?' I bluffed. 'You never know, I could be the ringleader.'

Robert raised both eyebrows at me.

'Yeah, fair point,' I giggled.

'I'm sure if you got your camera out right now there'd be all sorts of incriminating evidence.'

I smiled and gave him an innocent shrug, remembering that, as was usually the case, the evening had been well documented – I was always snap happy, but more so when I'd had a bit to drink. I made a mental note to leave my camera at home on nights that might take a turn to the drunk-photos-are-never-a-good-idea zone.

'So, you've managed to find your way back here okay since your first-night adventures?'

'Yes!' I groaned. 'Ben now has my room number memorized, so he's able to point me in the right direction and get me back safely.'

'Ha! Just as well he's here with you. Can you imagine what would've happened if you were alone?'

'I'd have been fine . . . Well, I would have found my way eventually, I'm sure.'

'Hmmm . . .'

'Although Ben's bed is actually far more comfortable than mine.'

'Should I be worried?'

I rolled my eyes. 'Yes, Robert. You should totally be worried that, due to the fact that he has a comfier bed, I'm going to run off with our mutual best friend.'

'Why, you little . . .' he laughed at my cheekiness, squinting his eyes at me before placing his fingers on my ribs and tickling me, making me jerk around with laughter. He lifted me from his lap and swung me around so that we were lying next to each other, leaning in for a kiss with that look in his eyes that left no doubt as to where the moment was leading. His hand expertly found its way under my t-shirt to my skin, where it roamed around in a playfully teasing manner. God I missed having him with me every day, I thought.

'MATE!' Ben screamed, opening my unlocked door without knocking, and jumping on top of us with a diving hug, squandering our hopes of a quick fumble. 'We've missed you, buddy!'

'So I see,' Robert laughed, returning the hug.

'We're just so boring without you – it's like we've lost the ability to have fun,' I joked.

'I bet.'

'We're like Samson when he chopped off all his hair!'

'Well, unless Pearl's around,' argued Ben. 'Did you tell him about last night?'

I groaned.

Robert turned to me with a smile – what was it he'd been saying about Pearl? 'No, she hasn't . . . spill!'

'She got us roaringly drunk. I only signed up for a chilled night with a couple of cans – but somehow we ended up skipping through the city centre at four a.m. pretending we were animals from *Snow White* – no idea why.'

'Sounds like quite a night.'

'It was – she's crazy.'

'What's the plan?' I asked Ben, changing the subject as I ignored the look Robert was throwing in my direction, clearly finding it funny that I'd been caught out. Yes, Pearl was a little on the wild side, but she was fun. It wasn't like I was going to go off and do something stupid just because someone jeered me on – I wasn't nine years old any more. Plus, I knew he'd have been getting up to the same drunken behaviour in Nottingham, the only difference being that I didn't have a trusted friend there who'd spill the beans on him. Although, I'd no doubt that, with his new gang, he certainly would be the leader, just like he had always been with Ben and me. With us, it really had been a case of he jumped and we followed. Usually without hesitation.

'You tell me,' shrugged Ben, in his usual carefree manner. 'I'm up for anything.'

'I thought we could go on a bike ride, give Rob a tour,' I suggested. 'We have ours here and Flo said there's a place you can rent one up the road. Fancy it?'

'Sounds good,' Robert nodded, still smirking at me.

'I'm in!' agreed Ben, jumping up off the bed and heading out into the hallway, keen to get going straight away.

Getting up from the bed I gave Robert a playful shove, making him fall backwards into my flowery pillows.

'What was that for?' he laughed.

'For being so smug!'

'Come here,' he smiled, sitting on the edge of the bed and grabbing hold of my waist, looking up at me as he pulled me close. 'I'm glad you've got a nice bunch of people around you.'

'Good.'

'I just worry.'

'About what?'

'That you'll forget about me.'

'Like that's gonna happen.'

'Or that you'll end up like one of *those* girls.'

'What girls?'

'You know, the ones with boobs up to here,' he smiled, bringing his hand up to below his neck.

'Have you met many?'

'Several. It's been awful.'

'You poor thing.'

'I know,' he pouted. 'I'm mentally scarred.'

'I'll tell you what,' I purred, running my fingers through his hair. 'I'll keep mine under lock and key tonight, to save you from further trauma.'

'What?' he practically squeaked.

'I think it's for the best.'

'Huh?'

'It's a shame really, I had a whole night of fun planned –

special outfits and everything,' I teased with a smile. 'But, well, I don't want you to think I'm one of *those* girls . . .'

I winked and cackled wickedly, as I freed myself from his embrace and walked out the door.

The majority of trips to see each other during our uni years were Robert driving to us, rather than us going to him. We did go to Nottingham a few times, but seeing as there were two of us in Bristol, it seemed to make sense to do it that way round. As a result I never really got to know the people he lived with, the life he led there or Nottingham itself. I did like it there, though, it felt steeped in history and the main part of the city was absolutely gorgeous with all its old buildings and the big water feature in the square.

I quite liked the fact that he was always coming to me. It felt like he really wanted to see me. Whenever I went there I felt a bit of a nuisance; it was very much a boys' place – as I'd predicted, the only things out on show in his room were his weights. Oh, and a framed picture of us from our sixth form ball which had been neatly placed on his nightstand. I couldn't help but smile when I first saw it.

We spoke to each other all the time – a few times every day in fact. He was the first person I spoke to in the mornings, and the last person I spoke to at night. There was not one part of me that queried his loyalty to me. Not one part that worried about him being out and getting drunk with other girls around. Not one part of me that feared he'd go off and cheat. Would it have changed anything if I had? Probably not.

I took for granted the fact that he was my one and that, one day, we'd get married, have babies and grow old together. I didn't think anything would come along and jeopardize that. I'd never seriously worried about him being around *those* girls. Perhaps I should have.

Instead I was content with life. I loved my photography degree and happily snapped away whenever I could (not just when I was given coursework), had my wonderful boyfriend who visited me whenever he could (and was only a phone call away at other times), and a best friend who made me feel like I was back at home whenever he was around (which was most of the time). I knew my uni experience would have been very different if I hadn't had Ben there to share it with.

I loved how my life was shaping up. Everything seemed to be falling into place.

I should have realized it was all too good to be true.

Ben

Eighteen years old . . .

I loved uni life – everything about it. The fact that we were suddenly in charge of our own lives; of feeding ourselves, washing our clothes, keeping ourselves occupied with no guidance from our parents, well, from my mum. It felt like anything was possible – if we wanted to go out until eight the following morning, we could. If we wanted to eat McDonald's for breakfast and Pot Noodles for dinner, we could. If we wanted to wear the same t-shirt three days in a row, we could (although Maddy would have told me off for that one). We were in control and, as long as we turned up for lectures ready to learn and got all our coursework in on time, we were left to our own devices. We'd been taken from our feeble existence in Peaswood and planted in the midst of university mayhem. What wasn't to love?

Bristol was incredible. At night we were your typical mischievous students, jumping from pubs to clubs, to house parties, and wandering back to our rooms when the sun had already started to rise. But daytimes were a stark contrast – the city offered hundreds of different things to keep us occupied when we weren't busy in lectures or studying. There was something therapeutic about the place. Bristol was inviting and vibrant and its leafy appearance made it seem more like a big town than an overbearing city. It also had more of a laid-back air to it rather than the fast pace found in most others – instantly making it friendlier.

I'm ashamed to admit that I loved it being just Maddy and me, too – a thought I kept berating myself for having as soon as it popped into my head. I just liked hanging out with her. For us it was just like before, except now we were in this little bubble – a bubble for two. It felt like we were sewn together, living in each other's pockets. Despite living in different halls, taking different courses and having different lectures, we saw each other daily. We'd grab dinner together, go to the library and study together, go out and get drunk together. And, rather frequently, we'd just chill out together. We'd curl up under my duvet and whack on boxsets of some of our favourite shows – *Friends* (mutual choice), *24* (my choice), *Prison Break* (mine again), *Gossip Girl* (hers, totally hers) and *Dawson's Creek* (hers, but I have to say, it turned into my guilty pleasure). Hours of our time were spent like that and I loved it – it was even better than when Robert dated Daniella when we were fourteen, leaving us as a two. It just felt lovely . . .

That first instance of her sleeping in my room hadn't been a one-off, in fact it kicked off a regular occurrence – something that was never planned, but always a likelihood if she was too drunk, or if we stayed up late watching something on the television and she hadn't the energy to venture back to her own bed. It was easy and there was absolutely nothing sordid in it, certainly not from her part. As she lay beside me, gently snoring (she'd hate me saying that), it was almost weird to think that I wasn't her boyfriend. That she belonged to someone else . . . our other best friend.

It pained me to realize that the reason she was doing that with me was because she felt so comfortable, because she had no idea of the feelings lurking inside of me. The ones I'd been suppressing since the moment I met her. I'd often lie there wondering how she would react if I just blurted it out and told her. Would she freak out? Be angry that I'd kept it from her? Pity me? Love me back?

Even as I thought about it, I knew I'd never just come out and say it – because of Robert. Not just because she was with him, but because I knew he trusted me more than anything. There was no other guy in the world he'd trust to be in his girlfriend's life to the extent that I was. I've often wondered if he found it weird, us being together so much. He never voiced any aversion to it, so I assumed not.

For a large chunk of our lives, when they went off to uni together, Maddy saw Ben more than she saw me – something that worried me and pleased me in equal measure. I've known Ben my whole life, so I know what a great guy our best friend is. My worry was that she'd suddenly have an epiphany and realize she was with the wrong friend.

Ben

Twenty-one years old . . .

Our third year came along and chomped us on the arse with terrifying speed, leaving us with only a few months to figure out where we wanted to live once we'd finished and what we were actually going to do with our lives once we were handed our scrolled-up certificates and sent on our merry way into the big bad world of reality. On top of that we were craning our necks trying to complete dissertations and final assignments, as well as attending our normal lectures.

On April 16th, a Friday afternoon (I remember the date clearly for reasons you'll come to understand), I found myself free from lectures. Rather than sitting indoors and fretting over my remaining work, I'd decided to make the most of the freak springtime heatwave and go on a mammoth bike ride along the coast. I'd asked Maddy if she wanted to come but she'd declined, insisting she was too busy finishing off coursework – I pictured her sat on her bed, frantically editing her latest photographs, a worry line forming on her brow. She was such a perfectionist, but it paid off. Her work was always awesome. She had a natural eye for capturing little moments, even if photography was something she insisted was something she 'fell into' through being clueless about her future plans.

So, there I was, enjoying the glorious weather and the salty wind blowing through my hair, when Robert called. Needless to say we still spoke on the phone daily, some days two or three times. Maddy always joked that I spoke to him more than she did; I think, back in those days, she could have been right. I pulled over and got off my bike before picking up, perching on a stony wall that was separating me from the sandy beach below.

'Mate!' I breathed into the phone, my lungs only just starting to recover. 'You coming down tomorrow night?'

'Something's happened,' he blurted, steamrolling my chatter with haste.

Everything inside me froze as I heard the fear in his voice. It was far from the calm and cheeky tone I was used to hearing – I knew it was something serious.

'What's happened? Are you okay?'

'No . . .'

'Rob, what is it?' I instantly thought the worst. I thought he was about to tell me something had happened to my mum.

'I've done something really stupid.'

'What?'

'I've slept with someone . . .'

'You've what?'

To say I was shocked would be an understatement. I was hit by a wave of nausea as my surroundings slipped away from me, all my senses focusing on Robert's voice.

'You heard,' he muttered, not wishing to repeat it.

'When?'

'Last night.'

'Fuck!'

'Yeah . . . what a cock,' he berated himself.

'But what about Maddy?'

'I know.'

'What are you going to do?'

'I don't know.'

'Have you told her?'

'No! I wanted to tell you first.'

'Why? I'm not telling her for you,' I stammered, not wanting to be the one to break her heart – he could do that himself.

'Of course not, I wasn't going to ask you to. I just wanted you to know so that you can be there, you know, when I do.'

'Right, yeah. When you going to do that?'

'Now. When I get off the phone to you.'

I thought of Maddy going about her day as usual, blissfully unaware that her boyfriend was about to drop the biggest bombshell on her. I couldn't believe Robert, the guy who we thought we knew so well, who was loyal and trustworthy, could do such a thing.

'Why'd you do it, Rob? Who is she?'

'I can't answer why, it just happened. She's just a girl. A random, stupid, girl.'

'Fuck!'

Neither of us spoke for a few minutes – a million different thoughts raced through my head as I tried to make sense of it all.

'Look, I've got to phone Maddy. I've got to tell her.'

'What are you going to say?'

'I don't know. I'm so confused by the whole thing.'

'Right . . .'

'Look, just be there, okay?'

'Of course . . . aren't you going to come see her?'

'I think I should do it on the phone. Just get it over with. Get it out there.'

'But –'

'I can't, Ben. I just can't,' he said forcefully.

Anxiety took a hold of me as we said goodbye. I stayed there for a few minutes, perched on the wall looking out to sea, trying to calm myself down and compose myself as I watched the waves relentlessly crash and foam.

I was angry at Robert, angry that he'd messed up in such a huge way. Maddy wasn't just some girl he'd been dating for a few years, although that would have been bad enough, she was his best friend. Our best friend. One of us. How could he be such an idiot? Why would he risk losing her for some random girl?

I felt helplessly sad for Maddy. She'd never been the jealous type, never uttered a word of worry to me about what Robert was up to in Nottingham without us to hang out with. I knew the news would crush her.

Cursing Robert for not having the guts to come and face up to his actions, I shakily jumped on my bike and started to make my way to hers, ready to pick up the pieces of her broken heart that my trusted friend had so thoughtlessly trampled on.

We'd moved out of our halls and into actual houses in our second year. Despite the fact that we spent almost all our free time together, we'd decided to stay living apart – mainly because we didn't want to start irritating each other with our bad habits (I was messy, she was a clean freak) but also because her flatmates, Flo, Pearl and Jennifer, wanted to have some sort of all-female, spotlessly clean sorority house. The deal was sealed for Maddy when she discovered that the bedrooms had en-suites – a luxury she was reluctant to let go of. We were still only a few minutes away from one another, both only a couple of miles from the centre of town.

Maddy was in her room when I got to her house an hour later, after a hectic cycle back into town. I found her curled up on her bed in the foetal position, hugging her pillow, with a handful of snotty tissues in her palm. Her mascara had been smeared all over her cheeks thanks to her tears, and her face was blotchy and swollen. Her lips looked redder and fuller than ever as they pouted outwards with misery.

I'd not seen her in such a state since primary school.

'Hey,' I said softly, walking towards her. Suddenly feeling awkward in the space I knew so well and in front of the other person in my life I thought I knew inside out.

She sat up slightly, her big blue eyes looking at me in such a forlorn manner my heart dropped to the floor.

'Do you know?' she asked feebly.

'Yeah, he called a little while ago.' I hated admitting that. Knowing before her made me feel like I was Robert's accomplice somehow, even if I had only known a few minutes before. It made me feel guilty by association, or like I'd been there and not stopped it from happening.

'Oh . . .' she said, nodding her head as she sighed. 'What a twat.'

She moved over onto one side of the single bed, and stretched out an arm to me, beckoning me to her. I took

Maddy into my arms and gave her a squeeze, trying my best to comfort her.

'Why'd he do it?' she whimpered after a moment or two, shifting her body so that her head rested on my chest.

'I don't know.'

'He's such a fucking dickhead.'

'I think he's saying the same thing.'

'He's not.'

'What do you mean?'

'I think he wants a break . . .'

'He didn't tell me that.'

'He said he needs time to think things through,' she whispered with a quivering voice.

'Oh . . .'

I had thought it would be a broken Maddy splitting up with Robert when she heard what he'd done. I hadn't expected it to be him throwing in the towel instead. I'd assumed it was just a one-night thing, a drunken mistake, I wondered if there was more to it than I'd been told. Otherwise, Robert would surely be there fighting to stay with her – mopping up her tears as he begged for her forgiveness. It upset me that he wasn't. I couldn't help but feel disappointed with him as Maddy lay there heartbroken in my arms.

I tried not to think about how Robert's actions would affect the three of us, but I couldn't help worrying. After all, it wasn't just their lives that would be altered – it would be mine too. I knew a fracture within the group would change everything. I wasn't sure how we'd cope. Or, more to the point, how I'd cope if the two of them could no longer bear to be in each other's presence. They were my

166

rocks, the other two legs of my tripod. The disorder felt, in many ways, worse than when my dad had left – at least back then I had my mum for support. I knew she wasn't going anywhere. But with Maddy and Robert, there was a possibility that there'd never be a sense of calm again. They were selfish thoughts, though, and, at least for that night, I knew I had to be there for Maddy, when Robert had decided he didn't want to be.

'Do you think he still loves me?' Maddy asked softly, after a heavy silence.

'Of course he does,' I lied. I didn't know what was going on in his head and that was the alarming thing. I'd never felt so out of touch with the guy I'd thought of more as a brother than as a friend. His actions were so out of character. 'But do you still love him? Could you forgive him?'

She let out a sigh before sobbing, 'Oh Ben. Why on earth has this happened?'

We stayed curled up together on her bed for hours. I let her cry, moan and shout angry words at our best friend – she really did call him every name under the sun. I'd never heard her swear so much, but heartbreak had unleashed a new side to her.

'Right, I'm done.' she said dramatically, hours later, picking herself up off the bed and stretching her face as she swept her hands over her cheeks, shaking her body as though she was shaking the stress away. 'No more tears, that's it. We're going out.'

'Really?'

'Yes. He's not here, Ben. He hasn't realized his monu-mental mistake and arrived demanding to sort things out.

Hell, he hasn't even called or texted since he told me,' she said, picking up her phone and showing me the empty home screen.

'Well, I –'

'He doesn't give a crap,' she said forcefully. 'I'm not prepared to go all weak and helpless just because I've been dumped by the flipping love of my life.'

As she said it I saw her lip wobble and her eyes glass over with fresh tears, belying the strength she was trying to convey.

'Mad, it's okay . . .'

'I'm fine,' she said sternly, mostly to herself as she commanded the tears to back off. 'Now, I'm going to chuck some fresh make-up on and then I'm going out to get wasted. Coming or not?'

I let out a nervous laugh, 'Are you sure that's what you want to do?'

'Abso-fucking-lutely,' she boomed.

Maddy

Twenty-one years old . . .

I took us to the nearest pub I could find. It wasn't one
we'd ever been to before; we usually headed out to places
that were nearer to campus where there would be loads of
people we knew and a good vibe, but that night I didn't
care for friends or atmosphere. I just wanted to get shit-
faced. That's how we ended up in the Red Fox, a dingy
little pub, only minutes away from mine. We must have
walked passed it hundreds of times in our three years in
Bristol, but never had any desire to venture through its
doors. Outside, the pub's crest-shaped sign swung wildly
in the breeze from one hook, rather than two, it's paint-
work was flaky and peeling off, and burly men with
'England 'til I die' tattoos puffed on cigarettes while arguing about the football. Inside wasn't much better with its
den-like appearance. A lack of windows made it dark and
the little peach-coloured lamps were near useless in their
bid to brighten the place up. A pokey-sized place filled
with wooden benches, covered in worn-down cushions,
and sticky tables. It was uninviting, but I didn't care. It
served alcohol and that was all I wanted.

It didn't take me long to accomplish my goal for the
night, especially since I was ordering double Sambuca shots
with every drink we ordered. Curled away in a dark corner

of the pub, hidden from the locals, we drank, whined about everything that was wrong with life and laughed at the stupidity of it all. The world was starting to turn into a blurry mess, and that was exactly what I wanted. I wanted to numb myself to the heartache Robert had caused, to distance myself from his infidelity. To forget. It didn't work; eventually I'd slip back into thinking about him, cursing myself as I did so. I couldn't help it. It was a pretty big deal to be dropped so carelessly by someone you'd loved for so long. And worse, for them to do so over the phone, telling you that not only did they mislay your trust but, perhaps, it would be best if they were to become a 'free spirit' for now, while they were still young and devoid of responsibility. Yes. That was the terminology Robert used. Free spirit . . . he'd picked a fine time to turn into a hippy.

I hadn't seen it coming. Even though we lived miles apart, there was never a single time in those three years when I fretted about other girls, not seriously, nothing that was more than playful banter between the two of us. I'd trusted him, I thought I had no reason not to.

Hours into our heartbreak-drinking session, silence engulfed me as I stared into the bottom of my glass, hoping it would give me answers to the never-ending stream of questions that bubbled away inside me, that threatened to make me blub once more.

'Penny for your thoughts,' Ben smiled, pulling out a one-pence piece from his jeans pocket and placing it on the table in front of me. He couldn't help but laugh at his own joke.

'You know, I was just wondering why he'd do that to me.'

'Oh Mad . . .' he said sadly, his face falling with concern.

'Am I not clever enough?'

'Don't be silly.'

'Maybe she was one of his sporting pals, all trim and toned – am I not fit enough?'

'You're being ridiculous, there's nothing wrong with you.'

'Maybe I should've joined you on more bike rides,' I moaned sarcastically.

'Nah . . .'

'Am I not pretty enough?' I slurred.

'Of course you are,' he said with exasperation.

'Am I not sexy enough?'

'Well, I –'

'I mean, I've changed a lot over the years – there he is looking like the bloody Hulk and here's me, always eating one or two chocolate Hobnobs more than I should.'

'Why are you talking about chocolate Hobnobs?'

'Because they're always on my mind,' I moaned. 'See? Mr Fitness Freak with little Miss Piggy was never going to work.'

'You're not little Miss Piggy.'

'Am I not good enough to be with him?' I continued. 'He was the popular kid, what did I think I was doing. He's so out of my league.'

'He really isn't.'

'What did I do wrong, Ben?' I begged, persisting to badger him with my self-doubt, longing for my friend to tell me what I'd done to get myself into such a sorry mess.

'Nothing. You did nothing wrong,' he said, reaching

across the table to take my hand, which he firmly squeezed three times – for once it failed to comfort me.

'I must have,' I shrugged. 'He shacked up with someone else. Some floozy.'

'You didn't do anything. You're absolutely perfect, Maddy.'

'Hardly.'

'No, you are. It's so annoying that you can't see that.'

'Oh Ben, lovely Ben,' I cooed, leaning into him and resting my head on his shoulder. 'I can always rely on you to make me smile.'

'You really can, Maddy . . . I'll always be here.'

'If you were my boyfriend, I know you'd make me smile every day. You'd never give me any of this crap.'

'I'd try my best to make you happy, that's for sure . . .'

'And you would!' I chirped over the top of him. 'You'd never have done this to me – you're too kind and loving.'

'You're not so bad yourself. As people go.'

'Tell me, Ben. Tell me what else you would've done if you were Mr Maddy Hurst,' I said, sitting up and facing him, enjoying the silliness of the conversation.

'I'd have made sure you knew exactly how special you are and how much you meant to me,' he said, smiling at me.

'And how would you have done that?'

He took a few seconds to think about his answer before saying, 'I'd have started by telling you how much I've loved you since the very first day I saw you.'

'Nice touch, bringing up our history – that's priceless. Not a soul can compete with a lifetime of memories.'

He laughed before picking up his half-full pint of beer and downing its contents.

'You'd have been a lovely boyfriend,' I said, placing a hand on his arm. 'I totally picked the wrong best friend to snog in Paris.'

'Cheers,' he said quietly, playing with his empty glass before holding it up to show me it needed refilling. 'Fancy another?'

'Do you even have to ask?' I cheekily grinned, as I held up my own depleted drink.

I watched him plod off to the bar and wait for the barmaid to come – it was quiet, even though it was a Friday night, but that didn't make her serve him any quicker, as she languidly continued to clean glasses while talking to one of her locals, oblivious to Ben standing there. Not that he was trying to get her attention, though. He wasn't even looking at her. Instead, he had his elbows up on the bar and was resting his head in his hands, rubbing his forehead. Something was clearly on his mind – he appeared agitated.

In my drunken state, it dawned on me that he'd spoken to Robert before I had, that he'd already confessed everything to Ben before calling me with the delightful news. I wondered if Robert had gone into more detail with him. Told him something that Ben felt uncomfortable knowing – perhaps also promising not to tell me. In the few minutes it had taken Ben to acquire the barmaid's attention and come back with our drinks, I had convinced myself that it was the case. He knew things I didn't, and I wanted to find out what they were.

'Out with it,' I practically barked at him as soon as his bum was back on the cushioned bench.

'What?'

'There's something you're not telling me.'

'No, there's not,' he protested, but the reddening of his cheeks told me otherwise. They goaded me on, told me he was lying, that there was more he was keeping from me.

'I know you know something about Robert,' I insisted.

'I don't.'

'He told you something, didn't he?'

'No, he really didn't.'

'Did he tell you not to tell me?'

'What is this? There's nothing to tell you, Mad,' he said, his voice rising in panic at being put on the spot. His eyes were wider than ever as they proclaimed his innocence, but the clenching of his jaw and the guilty swallowing of bile fought against his claim.

'You can't keep a secret from me, Ben.'

'There's no secret.'

'There is. Don't lie.'

'I'm not lying.'

'Then why have you gone red?'

'Because you're being an idiot.'

'I can't believe you're covering for him.'

'Mad, I'm not,' he sighed, looking more and more distressed.

'You're my best friend too, Ben. I know you two have this brotherly love thing going on, but you're meant to be looking out for me as well.'

'I'm always looking out for you,' he frowned, hurt by my accusation.

'Clearly not if you're willing to side with him and keep secrets from me. What has he told you? Was it more than one time? Different girls? Is it more than sex? Has he finished with me for her? Because you might as well tell me, I'll find out sooner or later. I'll be seeing them together. It's better if it comes from you,' I ranted, the alcohol and hurt causing me to push him further than I would normally.

'It's not about Robert,' he blurted, looking shocked that the words had leapt from his mouth.

'So there is something?'

'Maddy. Please, just leave it,' he groaned, looking around the pub as though he was looking for a way out of the very tight spot I had him trapped in.

'Ben, what is it?'

I was relieved it was nothing to do with Robert, but the way Ben was acting troubled me. He was acting all sketchy and weird – there was definitely something troubling him and I wanted to find out what.

'Ben, you can tell me. Whatever it is, I'm here for you.'

'I can't.'

'You can tell me anything . . .'

'You don't get it, do you?' he asked, his large Bambi-like eyes searching my face to see if I had even the smallest inkling of what he was hiding. I didn't. I hadn't the foggiest. He looked back down at the floor in despair.

'Get what?' I pleaded, taking his hand, my voice calmer than before. I hated seeing the torment on his face.

He took a deep breath to steady himself before he looked up and faced me, his eyes looking straight into mine.

'I love you.'

'Of course you do. I love you too,' I smiled, stupidly

tapping him on the nose in a childish manner, a cringe-worthy reaction to his words.

'No, not like that,' he said, getting frustrated with himself, or perhaps at me. 'Maddy, I mean it, I really love you.'

I suddenly felt very sober as I watched my best friend literally spill his heart out. It was the last thing I expected to hear that day, but then again, I didn't expect to get a call from my boyfriend telling me he'd cheated as he promptly ended our relationship either. It was a day of surprises.

'But –'

'Yes, I know, I know. Things are how they are . . . but if I had to wait a lifetime to be with you I would, because you're the one I've always wanted to be with.'

'You don't mean that, Ben.'

'I do.'

'You can't . . . you're just drunk.' I tried to laugh but the seriousness of the situation caused it to bubble in my throat and wither away.

'I always have, though. You've always been the girl for me.'

With that, he leaned forward and gently placed his hand on my cheek, his thumb brushing lightly against my skin. He paused and looked at me, really looked at me, inspecting my face with what could only be described as love and wonder. It was a look filled with meaning, the first time he was allowed to look at me with his heart open and the pretence dropped. The change and intensity enticed me. I could feel myself mirroring him, fascinated by the shift of emotion that felt strange yet familiar all at once – I knew that face, I knew him, but there was a new depth that I felt compelled to explore. It excited me. Thrilled me. Drew me in.

He edged his face closer to mine, focusing his eyes on my lips, that were just centimetres from his, and paused once more – something that wasn't done on purpose to add suspense, but because he was nervous. As was I.

'You okay?' he asked, looking back up at my eyes.

I nodded, knowing what was about to happen, not wanting to stop it.

'Good,' he whispered, as he slowly leaned closer and kissed me. The touch sent an unexpected surge through my body. I pulled away and looked back into his eyes – noticing the love had been replaced by hunger. In that moment I felt like I wanted and needed him more than I'd ever wanted anything else.

The second time we kissed, it was me who leaned forward and cushioned my lips against his. As I pulled away I couldn't help but grin at him, making me shake my head and sigh into my hands.

'What is it?' he smiled.

'I can't believe we're doing this.'

'Neither can I,' he said softly, removing my hands from my face and kissing me back.

We sat at that corner table in the pub, gazing at each other with our new-found admiration and kissing like giddy love-struck teenagers, until closing time. When we were eventually kicked out (the barmaid made no effort to disguise her haste to get home as she swooped up our half-finished drinks), we aimlessly wandered around Bristol holding hands as though it was the most natural thing for us to be doing.

Ben stopped when we got to the river and pulled me

round so that my back was against the railings with him stood in front of me.

'You're so beautiful,' he beamed.

I smiled, it was strange hearing him say that.

'I mean it. I've always thought so,' he said, lowering his head for another kiss. 'It feels so good to do that . . .' he grinned. 'I can't tell you how long I've wanted to.'

'Ben, why haven't you said anything before? I mean, if you've seriously felt this way since we were kids, why did you keep it a secret?'

'I was scared it would ruin our friendship if you rejected me.'

I couldn't help but laugh.

'. . . and then you got with Robert.'

'Oh . . .' Just the mention of his name caused a tug inside me. There's only so long you can live in a fantasy world before the reality comes along to sharply put you back in your place. I pushed those thoughts away. Reminding myself that he didn't want me, he'd slept with someone else. I didn't owe him anything, I thought, as I concentrated on Ben – lovely Ben, who did want me and who I knew would never hurt me in the same way.

'You should've said something.'

'Well, I've always told you I loved you, even if you didn't realize I was saying it,' Ben smiled, managing to ignore the fact that Robert had been mentioned.

I looked up at him in confusion. 'Telepathically?' I asked sardonically. 'Because it really didn't work.'

'Three squeezes,' he laughed, taking my hand and squeezing it three times in the way I was so used to him doing.

I shrugged, not understanding the meaning.

'I,' he said as he squeezed my hand, 'love,' with another squeeze, 'you,' he finished with the third squeeze.

I couldn't help but laugh as I recalled the number of times I'd been aware of him making that gesture, the first one being at the childish wedding in primary school – the last time being when we were sat in the bar, just moments before he said the words out loud for the first time. Ben had told me he loved me so many times, I just wasn't listening properly.

'You've been telling me you love me all that time?'

He shrugged and bit his lip as his cheeks blushed. With his eyes down he concentrated on my hands, really inspecting them, as his thumb made circular motions on my palm. 'I know, it's stupid,' he muttered.

'No, it's sweet . . . I can't believe I didn't twig.'

His eyes flicked up at me before quickly looking back at our fondling hands. His expression changed to one filled with uncertainty.

'What are we doing?' he asked abruptly, a pensive look descending on his face as he slowly stepped backwards, away from me. 'We shouldn't be doing this.'

'I know . . .'

'It's wrong. I shouldn't have said anything.'

I watched as he walked a few feet away and stared out at the river, leaving his back to me.

I should have felt guilty by that point, or been hit by remorse – Ben backing away should have shocked some sense into me and made me question what I was doing. I'd been so angry at Robert for cheating, I'd spent the whole night slamming him for what he'd done, but my actions had made me just as bad, if not worse. We were his two best friends. Even as I realized that, I knew I wasn't prepared to let the feelings I'd discovered go. Not yet. I was enjoying it too much – all I felt was the desire to have Ben near.

'Ben, I know it shouldn't, but it just feels so right to me . . .' I said meekly, walking towards him and placing a hand on his shoulder blade, slowly running it up and down his back, trying to bring him back to me.

'Same here,' he whispered.

'I don't want to stop.'

'Neither do I,' he said, slowly turning round to face me.

'Then let's not,' I implored, pulling his face down to mine, allowing my body to melt into his as we kissed.

'Maddy . . .' he croaked, starting to shake his head.

'It's okay. I want this.'

We stayed at his that night, but not before we walked for long enough to hear the birds singing and see the morning sky start to waken with orange light. It must have been about five o'clock by the time we got to his bedroom.

I'd become used to borrowing a t-shirt and sleeping in Ben's bed after a night out or if I couldn't be bothered to make the short walk back to mine – but this was different, suddenly everything was so electrified. As soon as the door was closed we just stood there and nervously stared at each other, each knowing what was about to happen, but wanting the other one to make the first move.

I started it.

I cautiously undid the buttons on my shirt-dress, aware that Ben's face looked full of nerves as I removed it from my shoulders and let it drop to the floor, leaving me in just my bra and knickers. The movement left me feeling exposed, but ridiculously sexy, something I was aware I hadn't felt in a long time – the thrill of being with someone new after years of being with the same guy, added to the way Ben hungrily looked at my body, as though he wanted to devour every inch of it.

Stepping towards him, I reached the bottom of his t-shirt and brought it over his head, instantly hugging his body into mine, enjoying its warmth, wanting every part of our naked bodies to connect. Expertly he unhooked my bra and ran his fingers over my breasts as he knelt in front of me, licking my nipples playfully before taking them into his mouth, causing me to let out a gasp of excitement as he nibbled gently.

Still on his knees, Ben inched down my knickers, removing them slowly as his eyes locked onto mine. I could hardly breathe at the suspense. Discarding my underwear, his hands reached behind me, sliding over my bum cheeks as he pulled me forward, his tongue tracing my hip bone, his lips brushing over my stomach, building my desire as his hands continued to feel their way around the contours of my body – everywhere but the place I longed for him the most. Back on his feet, his mouth made its way back up my body, past my breasts, along my neck and sucked on my earlobe, his gentle moaning vibrating through my body, massively turning me on. I nibbled on his lobe with desire as I grabbed at his belt, undoing it with speed, unbuttoned his flies and let his jeans drop to the ground.

To my surprise, Ben was commando.

He grabbed for my hands and held them out to our sides, stopping me from touching further, leaving us with just our mouths to roam and explore each other's bare skin, the bodies that we'd seen regularly but were only just discovering.

Putting force onto my palms, Ben guided me to shuffle backwards onto his bed, which we clumsily climbed. Ben lay on top of me and slowed the pace as he stroked my hair away from my face.

'Are you sure?' he asked, searching my eyes with concern.

'Yes,' I smiled. 'You?'

He nodded, as he took a deep breath and looked away from me, brushing my arms with his fingertips, 'I can't tell you how much I want this, Maddy . . .'

I took his head in my hands and pulled us together as I kissed him, excitement rising as I felt more of his body connect with mine.

'I love you so much,' he whispered. 'I completely love you, Maddy Hurst.'

'And I completely and utterly love you, Ben Gilbert,' I promised.

At those words he closed his eyes as though he was in physical pain, taking a gulp of air and drawing away so that his body moved away from mine. Draping the bedsheets over himself, he covered his face with his hands.

'I'm sorry . . .' he began.

'Ben? It's okay,' I pleaded, moving towards him.

'It's not, Maddy. It's really not.'

The firmness in his voice stopped me.

'What do you mean?'

'We can't do this!'

'What? Why?'

'It's . . .' he started, but couldn't finish. Instead he shook his head.

'Because you feel a sense of loyalty to Robert? Because he doesn't know the meaning of the word? I wouldn't worry about him.' I ranted.

'No, well, partly, yes. He's like my brother . . .' he whimpered.

I stared at him, watching as he battled with his emotions once more.

'But mostly because I also don't want us to start out like this,' he mumbled, unable to look at me. 'If we're to be anything – which we don't know because we're still drunk and you're in the midst of heartbreak, but if we were . . . I don't know. This moment is something I've dreamed about for years. Seriously, it is. I don't want it to be some quick drunken shag.'

'It won't be.'

'Look at us,' he said, looking up at my face. 'That's exactly what it would be. I don't want to be the guy you slept with to get over Robert, or worse, something you end up regretting. I want to be something more.'

'But you said you love me.'

I sounded like a child, but sitting there naked, opposite Ben, I felt stupid and exposed. My best friend told me he loved me, kissed me, got me naked and then rejected me. How pitiful.

'I don't just love you, Maddy . . . I'm in love with you,' he sighed. 'There's a huge difference between those two things.'

'I know.'

'Do you?' he implored. 'Loving someone is something you can do from afar, admiring someone and appreciating their existence in your life – but being in love's different. It's all-consuming to the point where being away from that person seems unbearable. There's no stopping that feeling . . . It's been so long and I've tried everything to stop feeling the way I do, but I can't. Do you see?'

'I think so.'

In that moment, I knew I was experiencing a dangerous amount of lust, but I was also aware of the way my tummy whirled around chaotically, churning up new feelings of admiration. I reasoned with myself that if Ben had been feeling even a sliver of those emotions for all those years, then I owed it to him to make sure whatever we did, we did it right, on his terms. Feeling the way I did, I had no doubt that what we had together had the potential to grow into something more, that I could love Ben in a way I'd never experienced before – if that was what I wanted.

'Maddy, I just don't want to fuck things up. That's the reason why I've never said anything in the past. I'd rather have you in my life and not be with you than you not in my life at all. We have to take things slowly to make sure it's what you actually want . . .'

His words lingered between us.

'Wait until it's right?'

'Yes. Until we both know that there's nothing else clouding our judgement. No rushing in like drunken buffoons.'

Stopping there was a wise move. We weren't bad people,

we had morals despite our earlier flutter suggesting otherwise. Sleeping with each other in such a careless manner would have been a mistake. If a relationship were to blossom from that night, it would do better not to stem from the darkness.

'So what do we do now?'

'I don't know . . .' he said, reaching across for my hand, which he lovingly cradled in his own.

We each stared at our cupped hands in silence, deep in thought.

After a few minutes I watched Ben as he walked to his cupboard and pulled out a t-shirt, before picking up my discarded knickers and his boxers and bringing them back to the bed.

'Stand up,' he said quietly.

I did as he said.

Ben bent down in front of me, picking up one leg at a time as he carefully placed my feet through the leg-holes of my knickers, before sliding the black-laced fabric up my legs, back to where they had sat half an hour before. Next he put on his own underwear before picking up the grey t-shirt, pulling it over my head and guiding my arms through the sleeves, slowly pulling it down to cover my boobs and stomach.

With our modesty protected he stopped and looked down at me, pulled me towards him and hugged me close.

'If we do this, we do it properly,' he sighed. 'Believe me, this is taking a huge amount of restraint.'

I couldn't help but laugh, 'What a difference a day makes.'

'Well, I certainly didn't think I'd have a naked Maddy

Hurst in my room wanting to sleep with me when the day started.'

'Kiss me . . .' I asked quietly, looking up at him, not sure if the request was out of bounds now that we had stopped proceedings.

He tilted his head down towards me.

'Gladly,' he whispered, before he gently placed his lips on mine, his fingers running through my hair, down to the base of my neck.

At some point we decided to get back into bed under the covers, although this time the speedy need for sex was replaced by a little bubble of wonder – of nerves and excitement. Snuggling into each other's warm bodies, our arms and legs entwined, we took pleasure in the new feelings being shared between us – an intimacy that felt alarmingly natural.

'Tell me how you're feeling, in one word,' he whispered, kissing my nose.

'Just one?' I smiled.

'Yes, that's the rule.'

I said the first thing that came into my head, 'Happy.'

'That's a nice word.'

'You?'

'Loved.'

I closed my eyes and enjoyed the word, one I could have easily used too.

For those few hours I had no fear. I wasn't worried that things would become awkward, or that, at some point, we'd be forced back into reality and made to suffer the consequences of our actions. What we thought would become of us outside our cocoon, I really didn't know. It wasn't something I thought about in that room on that night. We didn't talk about life outside of that bed, by which I mean Robert wasn't mentioned again. Somehow I'd managed to cut myself off and detach myself from real life. It was unsettlingly easy to do, but Ben made me feel safe, secure and loved, like I needed nothing else in that particular moment.

We didn't sleep a wink, preferring to talk about everything and nothing instead, smiling at each other like super-happy-psychotic Cheshire cats. Ben smiled at me in a way he'd never done before – wider, bigger, more doe-eyed and lovelier than I'd ever seen. It was like he'd saved that smile just to give to me on that special night. A secret smile, just for me. It filled my heart with an unbelievable joy to watch it spread so infectiously across his face. It was beautiful. As was he.

It pained me to leave him the following morning, but when I did it literally felt like I was walking on air. I know that's what people in movies say, 'walking on air', and I agree that it's a saying that would ordinarily make me want to puke my guts up, but there's no other description for the light and giddy feeling that overtook me as I drifted (there was no way I walked, my feet didn't touch the ground once) from his to mine, recalling flashes of images from the previous night as I went – some innocent, some not.

Being with Ben was completely different to what I'd experienced before. It was tender and romantic – I felt special, sexy and wonderful. Possibly the biggest surprise was that it was Ben who'd made me feel that way. Ben who I'd spent almost every day with for the previous twelve years of my life. How he'd managed to keep his feelings hidden I'd never know – they were threatening to spill out of me that morning at every opportunity. I passed strangers on the street and couldn't help but smile at them, or say good morning, as though I was bursting with kindness and a love for life.

What I wasn't expecting was to walk into my house and find Robert on my bed, looking like he'd been staring at the door for hours, waiting for me to return; his worried face puffy and wide-eyed from a lack of sleep, his hair manically pointing in all directions. I had visions of him running his fingers through his hair in panic at my absence, an action I knew he did whenever he was anxious.

We stood frozen. Staring at each other as though we didn't know who the other person was, we'd become strangers, but maybe that was just how I felt about him moments after being with Ben. After all, to him I was still his Maddy, the same girl I was before I kissed our best friend. He didn't know any different.

The floaty feeling I'd been experiencing just moments prior vanished. It deserted me and left me to drop to the ground with a terrifying speed. I felt heavy and trapped as I lingered in the doorway, not wanting to go inside.

'Hey . . .' he started, his face full of shame and regret. I'd almost forgotten he was carrying his own burden.

'Hi,' I mumbled.

'Where have you been?'

'Out.'

'I know that. With who?'

'Why does it matter?'

'Mad . . .' he sighed.

'Ben,' I said sternly. 'I was with Ben.'

'That's a relief,' he almost laughed, putting his hands through his ruffled hair. 'I've been having all sorts go through my head. I thought you might have been, you know – with some random guy or something. Getting back at me. Not that I'd have blamed you, of course, I'd have deserved that.'

'Right . . .' I said dryly, slowly walking in and shutting the door.

A faint smell of Ben's aftershave wafted off me as I moved, catching me off guard. It didn't soothe me. Instead, as I looked up at Robert and the guilt began to creep in, I was left irritated. I didn't want to feel ashamed, I didn't want to be regretful of my actions, I didn't want to feel like what I'd done was wrong, even though I knew it was. We might have stopped, but we didn't want to – we wanted to take it further, and that was the problem; as a result it wasn't just a physical connection we'd made, it was an emotional one too. We hadn't just had sex and woken up in the morning feeling embarrassed about what we'd done, looking for absolution as we awkwardly parted ways – we'd stayed up and developed something else. Standing there, in front of Robert, with a feeling of defiance over the previous night, I knew that what we'd done was worse.

'Why are you here?' I asked, unable to hide my annoyance, my voice surprisingly cold.

'To make things right.'

'Why didn't you come yesterday?'

'I was confused. I wasn't thinking straight,' he conceded.

'And now you are?'

He looked up at me with a sorrowful expression. 'I sat at home for a few hours thinking about it all – not only what I did, but about what I said to you afterwards. I drove over as soon as I'd talked some sense into myself. I've been here all night.'

'So I see.'

'I know I fucked up,' he said exasperatedly, starting to get up off the bed. 'I know I've been a complete dick, but we can get through this, Maddy. I know we –'

'What if I don't want to?' I interrupted.

The colour drained from his face as it dawned on him that the situation wasn't as simple as he'd thought – he couldn't just waltz in and expect all to be forgiven.

'What do you mean? Mad, he said –'

'I'm going to have a shower,' I said quickly, ducking away from him as he came closer, swiftly closing the bathroom door behind me before he had a chance to reach for me.

'I was wrong. I'm so sorry,' he said through the door. 'Please forgive me.'

I stood and listened to him as he started to quietly sob. I hadn't heard Robert cry in years – not since he fell and he broke his leg, but even then he managed to maintain a certain amount of composure. A gentle bang as his head rested on the door and the sound of his hands brushing against the frame broke my heart further as I pictured him standing just inches away from me, caressing the wood as he tried to get to me, to bring me back to him. Ignorant to the fact that not only had he chucked my heart away, but that someone else had been there, ready to catch it when he had.

The awful thing was that although he was feeling sorry for his crime, I wasn't for mine – and that devastated me. Yes, he'd done wrong, but at least he was facing up to it. Thanks to Ben, I totally understood how quickly and easily something like cheating could happen. Yes, what I had done was far worse because I had an absolute lack of remorse. At least Robert had the human decency to show guilt.

'Please, Maddy. You have to forgive me . . .'

I was forced into feeling ashamed as I stood in my bathroom and listened to my woeful boyfriend. When I couldn't bear to hear any more I stripped off and got in the shower. Battling with my thoughts as I placed my head under its piping-hot water, sinking down to sit in the shower tray as the liquid continued to run over my body. Doubt seeped in as I became more and more unsure of what it was that I wanted – or, more importantly, who.

I wondered whether I should have come clean with Robert, and begged for forgiveness, just like he was doing, in the hope that we'd be able to start again and move forward. He did tell me that he thought we should go on a break; that he didn't know if he wanted to be with me any more. Would it really be that awful to say that I'd messed up too? Realistically I knew it was more than that. I also knew that if I did come clean, I wouldn't be able to tell him it was with Ben – that fact would destroy Robert, Ben and me as a unit, ruining years of friendship and any chance of us getting back together. But then, I didn't even know if getting back with Robert was what I wanted. After being so brutally dropped I wasn't sure if I could just forgive and forget. Perhaps, as we'd grown up, we'd drifted apart. We'd been in different cities for the past three years, living completely separate lives . . . perhaps it would have come to a natural end at some point anyway. Although, something I couldn't quickly forget was that Robert, first and foremost, was one of my best friends. I'd no doubt that cutting him out of my life would be more painful that I cared to imagine.

My night with Ben continued to linger in my mind, making it impossible to just forget it had happened. If I stayed with Robert, would I able to blot out what I'd felt with him? I wasn't sure I could do that to Ben and his kind and loving heart. He'd put his feelings out there and opened up after years of keeping them a secret – I couldn't face the thought of rejecting him, after all, that fear was what had caused him to hide his love away.

I wondered whether Ben was worth the sacrifice – it would change everything, not just who I dated. It would affect our friendship group, our families – I was aware it would have a massive impact on them too.

My head had become cloudy and confused. Plagued by a million scenarios, concerns and questions, it struggled to make sense of anything.

I was in the bathroom for far longer than necessary, trying to avoid facing Robert and having to make any sort of decision. When I finally opened the door, none the wiser over what to do, Robert shot up from the spot he'd been sitting in on the floor and frantically grabbed for me.

'Don't touch me, Robert. Please. Don't,' I begged, pulling my arms around myself. I didn't want him near me, couldn't stand the thought of being held by those hands that had roamed over someone else's body.

'Maddy, please . . . I love you. It was a mistake; you've got to believe me. I don't even know the girl, and yes, I know that makes it worse in a way, that I'd do that and risk losing everything we have, I just . . . it was a split-second decision, Mad. I was a fucking prick,' he ranted in desperation. 'I don't expect you to understand why I did it, or what could possibly make me act out in that way . . . but if I could take it back, I would.'

'It's not that simple, though, is it?' I snapped, his words touching a nerve.

Robert mutely shook his head, looking sheepish and scared.

'You talked about going on a break . . .'

'But, I don't want that, I don't need one,' he said with urgency.

'What about wanting to be a "free spirit"?'

'That was just nonsense. It wasn't even about you, it was more that I couldn't believe I could do that to you. That I had it in me to do that to the person I love, to you.'

'And then you just snapped out of those thoughts?'

'I love you. I love you, Maddy. I want to be with you. We've almost finished uni – I want us to move in together. I want to give you everything you ever wanted, for us to grow old together and have loads of kids. I was wrong, I made a stupid mistake, but I know what I want now. It's what I've always wanted.'

As the words tumbled from his mouth I stared at him in sadness and disbelief. If I'd have heard him say those words two days before I'd have been elated, but at that point I just felt pity, not just for him, for myself too. I was sad at the crappy situation we'd suddenly found ourselves in.

'I don't want you to want those things just because you're feeling guilty, Rob,' I said calmly.

'I'm not!' He dropped to his knees and pulled me in to him so that his face was buried into my stomach, his hands grabbing me with desperation. This time I didn't back away from him. 'Please, please, give me another chance. You know me! You know me better than anyone in the world. You get me. You know me.'

'Which is why this is so hard!' I moaned.

'You have to forgive me, Maddy. Please.'

'I don't know if I can . . .'

'But say you'll try . . .' he looked up at me and I saw a glimpse of the nine-year-old boy I first met, all bravado and cockiness evaporated. His little slit eyes were the widest I'd ever seen them as they desperately begged, literally begged. I was shocked to see him looking so broken. How on earth had we come to that? Our relationship had been so placid, so strong, so secure – referred to as perfect by others – and then, in the space of twenty-four tiny hours, all those years of togetherness had been blown apart. It didn't seem to have any logic to it.

I was so confused. All I knew in that moment was that I didn't want to hurt Robert. After years of being with him, I didn't want to crush him the way he'd crushed me. I loved him. I couldn't refuse him and break his heart. I couldn't be that cold.

I cupped his head and pulled it in to me, cradling it against my stomach. I couldn't find any words, but the gesture was enough for him.

'Thank you, Maddy. Thank you,' he wept, squeezing his arms even tighter around my body. 'I promise I'll never be such an idiot ever again. I never want to lose you.'

I felt three tears roll down my cheeks as I thought of Ben.

That afternoon we sat next to each other on my floral bed and pretended to be fixated by the television screen. Four hours worth of *Come Dine With Me* was watched as though it was the most interesting thing to ever grace the airwaves. In reality, neither of us cared whether Moira from Hull's triple-baked cheese soufflés rose to the occasion or not, but focusing on it stopped us from having to focus on each other and the mess we were in. Although, it didn't stop Robert from trying his best to lift us out of the sombre mood– trying to make light conversation (about Moira and her soufflés, 'Oh no, they're going to collapse, poor woman'), or by offering to make us cups of tea every five minutes. I wasn't ready to pretend everything was normal and happy, but I didn't want to spend all afternoon talking about it either. I was tired, irritated and, I'd almost forgotten, hungover. I just wanted to sit in silence and avoid life for as long as I could.

Bodily contact between us was kept at a minimum, something which was unusual for us, as we were always snuggling up or at least holding hands. We were always connected in some way, but that afternoon we sat apart – Robert with his body facing mine (looking eager to lessen the distance between us in his remorseful way), me sat rigid, with my legs curled up, facing the telly straight on. It pains me to say it, but I basically ignored him as much as I could.

I told myself that once Robert had left for Nottingham I'd have time to think things through properly, maybe even talk to Pearl. I knew she was hard to shock, able to keep a secret and good with her advice. If I wanted to talk to any of the girls about it, she'd be the best to go to, definitely – especially as she wouldn't judge me or get all self-righteous. She was far from a saint herself – something Robert was right about.

I also wanted to talk to Ben, see what he was thinking or feeling. Up until that point, in the twelve years Robert and Ben had been in my life, not a single major decision had been made before talking to one or both of them. Now that it was all on my own head, I felt bewildered and panicked.

'These are awesome,' Robert encouraged as he attempted to start up yet another meaningless conversation after coming back from the kitchen with yet another tea round. He was looking up at my latest photographs that I'd hung on the walls.

They were portraits of a whole mixture of people (students, teachers, shopkeepers, children, etc.), anyone I could rope into having their faces painted with an array of wild animals and walk through town – there was even a priest with a tiger guise, a shot I was particularly proud of. All of them were rather striking and meant to encapsulate the wild side in all humans that we keep hidden, the idea being that the animalistic side of us is still there somewhere deep inside – we've just learned to conform to what is socially acceptable.

Ben was one of my volunteers and I'd asked him to be a deer – it had been my one and only time to turn him into the Bambi I'd always thought of him as with his big brown eyes. As Robert pointed out the portraits and scanned the different faces, Ben's face seemed to be bigger than anyone else's. It grabbed my attention and made me feel paranoid as it looked back at me, teasing me as if the picture was about to tell Robert the truth. I knew it was my mind playing tricks on me, that all the portraits were identical in size, but that didn't stop it from freaking me out with its torment. It made me feel itchy.

'They're really great,' he nodded with forced enthusiasm.

'Cheers . . .' I mumbled.

I watched him in my peripheral vision, biting his lip and running his fingers through his hair and knew he was desperately searching for something else to say. Some new reason to talk and engage me in any way that wasn't instantly crushed by the sense of foreboding that we were clearly drowning in. It wasn't that he was deluded to hope for things to go back to normal instantly, more that the reality of the whole thing was too depressing for him to dwell on. He was a doer – put a problem in front of Rob and he tried his best to fix it. It was no doubt infuriating for him to be in a situation (one formed from his own doing) that couldn't be sorted so easily. Even by Rob.

'Do you want to go somewhere? Do something?' he endeavoured, turning to me, clearly finding the day as agonizingly painful as I was. 'We could call Ben. See if he wants to do something.'

He looked back up to the picture on the wall. He had seen it. To some extent I was right, that glossy little print had screwed me over, but in reality I knew he was suggesting it in the hope of digging us out of the awkward hole we'd painfully dug ourselves into. He was suggesting anything he could think of in the hope that something would work to erase the unpleasant feeling in the room. Little did he know he was making it worse.

'I'm sure he mentioned some work he has due in for Monday . . .' I lied.

'We could still ask. Knowing him, he's already done it anyway.'

'You know what, I'm happy here,' I shrugged, snuggling back into my pillows.

'It's a sunny day, Maddy, a bit of air would probably do us good,' he said, reaching for his phone.

'We don't have to ask Ben along, though.'

It was an odd thing for me to say to Robert, and I knew it. I'd never had a problem with asking Ben to join us before. In fact, it was usually me encouraging Robert to invite him. The comment didn't go unnoticed; Robert became shame-faced once more. His upbeat pretence dropped.

'Is everything okay? Is he mad at me?'

'No. I don't think so,' I said, trying to hide the panic from my voice. I did not want to be talking about Ben to Robert. I also did not want to be in a situation where the three of us had to hang out together.

'Are you sure? I feel bad the way I put him in the middle like that. I shouldn't have. I didn't even think before phoning him. He no doubt thinks I'm a complete dick now. I would.'

'Robert, I'm sure he's fine. He's just busy, that's all.'

He looked from me down to his phone with hesitation.

'You know what, I'll call him anyway. It would be good to just speak to him. He'll be worried.'

My heart sank as Robert dialled, put the phone to his ear and wandered out of my room. From the hallway I could hear him talking but he was back in the room within seconds.

'Answer machine,' he muttered.

I felt relieved.

When the following evening finally came and it was time for Robert to head back to Nottingham, he didn't want to go. He put it off as late as possible, hating having to leave when everything felt so unresolved. He had tried his best to hold everything together, to bandage us back into one piece with his earnest attitude, but even he wasn't sure if he'd done enough. He couldn't take our mistakes away, no matter how hard he wished he could.

When it was time to say goodbye he hugged me tighter than ever, still trying his best to knock down the barrier that had been built between us. It was futile to try so early. I needed time, space.

What am I saying?

I wasn't sure what I needed.

I just wanted him gone.

I hadn't been alone for more than fifteen minutes when a letter was slid through the crack at the bottom of my door. It was from Robert.

Maddy,

When we first kissed in Paris our love required a leap of faith.
We didn't know what was going to become of those strange teenage

emotions that had taken over. It was scary voyaging into the unknown but we had each other for support as we put aside our fears and trusted that our feelings would lead us to the place we were meant to be.

I've never regretted that moment, or doubted the love in our relationship, nor have I ever questioned our future together. I need you to know that what happened was not because I do not want to be with you, more that I'm a fool who made the most momentous mistake of his life.

I'm prepared to spend the rest of forever fighting to put things right – to make you see that I'm your Robert. The one you deservedly put so much trust in, and who promised to love you forever.

All I ask is that you take another leap of faith with me, like you did five years ago, although this time, I promise to never let you go.

Yours forever,

Robert xxx

In fact, I was pretty sure she did end up preferring his company to mine on occasions, but he brought her back to me in one piece once our university days were through, so I'd like to take this opportunity to say thank you to Ben, for that. Without him there, who knows what might have happened. She could have been whisked off her feet by an utter charmer and this day would never have happened.

Ben

Twenty-one years old . . .

'Hey, mate. Look, so sorry about all this. I shouldn't have phoned you first and put you in the middle like that. I'm over at Maddy's now. Wanted you to know everything's okay, we're just talking things through. Really want to see you before I go back. Give me a call. Oh, and thanks for looking after her last night. You're a true gent.'

I was still in bed when he called. I'd been replaying little scenes from the previous night in my head, over and over again – I was still in disbelief that it had actually happened, that I hadn't just dreamed the whole thing. For years I'd held in my feelings and not told a soul about how I'd truly felt, too worried that I'd ruin the great thing we had going – worried that I'd be rejected if I confessed anything, not that I'd ever admitted that to myself. I'd told myself I would never get to tell her how I felt, too much time had gone by and then she was with Robert for years, so I was getting used to the fact that she'd never know the truth, that she'd never be attainable to me. I thought that ship had well and truly sailed, but then when she kept pushing me to tell her what was on my mind, pushing and pushing, I suddenly went for it. Put my cards on the table like a freshly opened deck, too tempting to ignore.

I told her everything, about how I loved her, about the

three squeezes, it all came tumbling out ... once I'd started I couldn't stop. I needed her to see its importance, understand that I wasn't just drunk. There she was, the love of my life, listening to my every word. Moved by what I was telling her. It was better than I'd ever imagined.

And when I kissed her? Wow. The way I felt, the emotion inside me, made everything so intense, so much better. Everything about her was as wonderful as I'd imagined; the softness of her milky-white skin, the sweetness of its taste as I ran my mouth over her body. Her voluptuous bum, her smooth breasts, her small blush nipples – I couldn't get it out of my mind. It had taken every ounce of self-control I had to stop myself from having sex with her. Something I was pleased with myself for. I didn't want her to wake up the next day regretting it. But also, I wasn't a total rogue, there was something nagging away inside of me. Typically known to all as my conscience. I couldn't stop Robert from popping up in my brain, reminding me what a tosser I was being to him, my best mate, the guy who'd do anything for me. That was his girlfriend that I was with, and whether they were technically still together or not was beside the point. I was being an arsehole. They had not been apart more than a few hours before I'd swooped in. But then, as I sat there thinking about her plump pink lips, I wondered if he would care. After all, he'd discarded her, got with someone else and talked about breaking up.

I was being ridiculous.

Of course he would care.

My blood ran cold as soon as I saw Robert's name pop

up on my phone. I completely froze. I wasn't sure what to do. It was such a normal thing, him calling me, but suddenly it felt like the most alien and bizarre thing in the world to happen. My mind entered into a mad spin as I tried to work out why he could possibly be calling me.

I thought he might have found out and that was why he was phoning. I imagined maybe Maddy had called and told him everything as a way of getting back at him, or something. That made me feel really sick, which was pathetic – if anything were to happen with me and Maddy, which I was sure I wanted, then of course Robert was going to find out. We'd have to tell him. It was something I hadn't thought about until his name popped up. I would have to tell him and that could potentially ruin over twenty years of friendship. I could lose him. Is that what I wanted? I wondered if I loved Maddy that much. I'd always thought I would sacrifice everything for love, but the reality wasn't as clear-cut. I wasn't sure if I was ready to give up on Robert, but then, I couldn't be sure if it was loyalty or guilt making me feel that way.

If I'm honest, I wasn't sure where I saw me and Maddy going, and that hurt. It pained me that, after years of wanting her so badly, I wasn't sure what the future had in store for us. I'd spent years with her not knowing the truth, of plodding along with her and Robert as my best friends. Having her know the truth after so long was more complicated than I'd feared, leaving me to feel more confused than I thought I ever could over the possibility of being with Maddy.

With all those thoughts and worries whirling through my mind, I didn't pick up the phone to Robert. I knew I needed to speak to Maddy first – to find out exactly where we stood and what was going to happen next.

A loud bleep let me know he'd left a voicemail. I took a deep breath, reached for my phone and nervously held it to my ear as Robert's jolly voice boomed through the speaker.

I sat up in bed as I listened to the twenty-nine second message over and over again.

Everything was okay, he'd said.

He was with her.

They'd talked things through.

They were back on track.

Where the hell did that leave me, I wondered.

Somehow, in the mere hours since Maddy had left my room, she'd gone back to Robert. She'd forgiven him for his misdemeanour. I was just a pit stop along the way to her reaching that conclusion. The night rendered forgettable and meaningless – it hadn't been as special for her as it had for me. But then, what did I expect? They'd been a couple for years, shared a bond that could stand a few knocks. My pathetic few hours with her would never have been able to compete with that. I was foolish for thinking otherwise. Stupid for believing she could love me back in the same way.

The rejection hurt just as much as I feared it would.

I almost had her, and then Robert came back to reclaim her, pushing all thoughts of me and the night we'd shared out of her mind. Yes, Robert had caused me to have my own doubts, but all I'd needed to do was talk to Maddy, to try to decipher the complicated situation we were in. I hadn't expected her to move away from me so swiftly, to turn her back on our night together so coldly.

I sat in silence on my bed, looking around my room. Hours before, it had been a place of love and warmth, now it was bleak and barren. Deserted. I needed to get out, to be surrounded by noise.

I didn't even wash, I just chucked on a pair of jeans and a crumpled shirt and walked back to the Red Fox. I didn't care that it was dirty, I just liked the fact that I knew I'd be left to mope into my pint of Carling . . . of which I had several.

I was already fairly smashed when I got a call from Roger, a guy on my course, reminding me about a house party he was having that night and wondering where I was. In my inebriated state, going along sounded like a top idea.

When I turned up at his place, which was only meant to be a fifteen-minute walk away but took me half an hour to get to because I couldn't quite walk in a straight line – plus I got lost twice – it was rammed full of people, most of whom I didn't recognize. They cluttered up the narrow hallway, the stairs and the kitchen, making it difficult to find Roger. I gave up looking for him fairly quickly, actually, and instead looked around the room and wondered where to place myself.

I decided to join a group of about ten people who were passionately playing drinking games around a dining-room table, boisterously cheering as their friends were made to neck various combinations of alcohol. I watched them finish their game of 'Arrogance', essentially a dangerous game of heads or tails, before joining them to play 'Finger in the middle' – a game where players pour a hefty amount of their own drink into the central cup, then have to guess how many people are going to leave their fingers on the rim of the cup after the count of three. It sounds boring but it becomes fascinatingly funny when you're drunk – which we all were.

Luckily for me, I won the first round – no idea how – and so just had to watch the others battle it out.

It was the loser of the game that caught my eye – a cute little thing with an enormous smile. I'd seen her around campus before and at a few parties. She was hard to miss with her elfin features and petite little body. I had no idea who she was, we'd never spoken, but in that moment she had my attention hooked on her.

I'd watched her as she giggled her way through the game, laughing playfully and covering her face with her hands every time she guessed wrong. Her joy quickly turned to dismay, though, as she lost and realized she'd have to down the entire contents of the half-full pint glass. She grimaced at its grey-coloured liquid, which had curdled thanks to somebody adding Bailey's into the mix of beer, wine and spirits. Every time she went to drink it she burst out laughing as the gathered crowd cheered in encouragement, 'Down it, down it, down it.'

'Do I have to?' she laughed.

'Yes,' shouted back the excitable crowd, not giving her any allowances for being a girl – if you were in to play, you were in for the forfeit. That was the rule.

She looked over at me and I winked at her, the alcohol giving me more confidence than normal.

In return she flashed me a massively beautiful smile.

She pushed her long blonde hair back behind her ears and lifted the cup to her mouth, her hazel eyes flicking back in my direction before she downed the lot – causing the gathered crowd to cheer in approval before dispersing in search of more alcohol for their next game.

'Argh, that was awful,' she said to me seconds afterwards as she stumbled towards me, wiping her mouth in disgust. 'I promised myself I wouldn't do that tonight.'

'Oh really?'

'I'm a sucker for peer pressure,' she giggled, grabbing my bottle of beer from me and taking a mouthful. 'Sorry – trying to get rid of the taste.'

'More alcohol is definitely what you need after that,' I grinned.

'Tell me about it,' she grimaced, handing me back my drink.

'So, what brings you here?' I asked.

'It's my house,' she smiled.

'Ah . . .'

'You?'

'Doing Graphic Arts with Roger.'

'Oh, I see. You're . . .?'

'Ben.'

'Ben,' she smiled with a nod. 'I'm Alice.'

We laughed as we took hold of each other's hand and gave a formal business-like handshake.

At that point the drinking-game group had come back into the room with new supplies. One of them, a short skinny guy with bushy hair that covered his eyes, had a row of drinks cradled in his arms, clearly stocking up for more than the one game. As he passed us he got pushed by one of his more robust mates, causing him to trip, knock into another mate and spill his drinks over everyone standing around him. I was fairly unscathed, but Alice received the majority of the beer-based tidal wave.

'Sorry,' the guy said evasively without looking at anyone in particular, picking up the now empty plastic cups from the floor before tottering off to the kitchen to refill them, the loss of alcohol causing him more concern than anyone's wet clothes.

'Oh crap,' Alice moaned, wiping some of the foamy beer off her orange dress with the back of her hand, flicking the drips onto the floor.

'Should I go get you a cloth or something?' I offered, gesturing towards the kitchen.

'No, don't worry. It's only beer – I'm sure it'll come out in the wash,' she sighed, looking down at the soggy material that had decided to cling to her toned body.

I couldn't help but notice her nipples which, thanks to the cold liquid, were standing to attention.

'Are you sure there's nothing I can do,' I flustered. 'You're soaking wet.'

'Easy tiger,' she giggled.

I joined in, shaking my head at my unintended sexual innuendo.

'I'll just get changed,' she shrugged, pulling the dress away from her body and giving it a little shake. 'It's getting late now anyway – I'm sure no one will notice if I slip away to my room for a bit. Maybe get changed into my PJs instead . . .'

'Sweet,' I nodded, looking around at the rest of the party, who seemed to be as drunk as I felt. The next round of drinking games had started, minus the bushy-haired guy who was still sourcing new drinks, Michael Jackson was blaring out of the stereo and a rowdy gaggle was attempting a comical dance-off, moonwalking around a few guys who'd passed out on the floor. Elsewhere in the room people were either in deep conversations or getting frisky with one another.

'Want to come up?' Alice leaned in and purred, tugging hold of my t-shirt in a playful manner that could only suggest one thing – she wasn't about to show me her PJ collection.

'Sure . . .'

We fought our way around the dance troopers, carefully avoided the gamers, passed the people still loitering on the stairs, and eventually made it to outside Alice's room. She removed one of her high-heeled shoes and fished out a key.

'The last thing you want at a house party is to go to bed and find it's already occupied,' she smirked, unlocking the door and leading us into the darkness.

As soon as she'd shut the door behind us, Alice, who I'd assumed to be fairly sweet and innocent, turned into a complete vixen – tearing at my shirt, ripping open the buttons and pulling at my jeans, pushing me onto her bed like a crazed sex beast. She was all over me – had me in her mouth within seconds.

The sex was angry and quick, full of grabbing, biting and slapping. It was a complete contrast to the loving nature of the night before, which was exactly what I needed. I couldn't stop Maddy from entering my thoughts, no matter how much I tried to push her away. I was so angry, so fucking angry. It was her that I thought about as I thrust deep inside Alice.

After I came, I cried, much to my embarrassment.

I was distraught that the only girl I'd ever loved didn't love me back, humiliated that I'd given such a huge part of my heart away to something that had only ever existed in my head and ashamed of myself for betraying my best friend.

Without asking any questions, Alice took my head to her chest and ran her fingers through my sweaty hair, running her hand over my forehead until I fell asleep.

I was grateful for the company.

Thankful I didn't have to spend the night in my bed, on my own.

The following Tuesday, once my lectures were finished for the day, I took myself off to the library to study. I wasn't able to get any work done in my room, the sight of it reminding me of the weekend's activities, so I thought sitting alongside other students hard at work might inspire me. It turned out to be fairly quiet in there – although that wasn't too surprising seeing as the sun had decided to grace us with its presence. I'm sure most students had opted to 'study' in the sunshine while they topped up their tans instead of sitting in the gloomy library, staring vacantly at a computer screen.

I was at a huge study desk on my own when Maddy came and sat down next to me. I didn't even have to look up to know it was her, the smell of her perfume, Ghost's Deep Night, gave her away, the sweet scent drifting in before she had. It was something that had always lifted my spirits, but on that occasion it made me squirm in my seat.

It was the first time we'd seen each other since she'd

stayed at mine. It was going to be an awkward encounter, after all – I assumed she was about to break my heart and let me down gently as she told me she was back with Robert, so I braced myself.

What took me by surprise was her mood – I could tell she was pissed off at something. Her breathing was heavy, as though she was trying to keep herself calm. Her face was flushed with what appeared to be anger. She swung the chair around so that she was facing me.

I struggled to look back at her.

'Did you sleep with Roger's housemate?' she asked in a quiet voice, her eyes darting around the room to make sure no one could hear us.

I was stumped.

I knew we were in dire need of a serious chat and that being with her again was going to be gut-wrenching, but I hadn't expected that curveball to be thrown into the mix. I was thinking it would be more of an explanation from her as to what had happened after she'd left mine and ran back into Robert's arms, forgetting that I even existed, along with some kind of apology – or possibly even making sure I wasn't about to tell Robert about that night now that they were staying together, just in case the guilt ever got hold of me and made me want to confess all. Those were the two scenarios that had run through my head as possible first conversations post 'that night'. Alice hadn't factored into it at all.

'Erm . . .'

'No point denying it. I've just bumped into him.'

'Who?'

'Roger.'

'Right.'

'Have you known her long?' she asked briskly, her tone thick with spite – I'd never heard her voice sound like that before, it was startling.

'No, I've just seen her around a few times. We've never actually spoken before,' I shrugged, suddenly feeling like a kid being reprimanded by their mother.

'Good to know she's someone you really care about,' she said sarcastically. 'Do you remember texting me?'

'No.'

'Well you did, telling me how much you loved me. Actually, I'm surprised you could bring yourself to tell me that while you were with her – I never knew you were such a multi-tasker,' she cackled.

I shifted uncomfortably. I did remember contacting her. I was still in the pub at that point. I'd been in the middle of sending my fifth and final message when Roger had called. I probably wouldn't have answered the call otherwise, but I'd picked it up by accident. I could also remember the drunken voicemail I'd left as I stumbled through town on my way to his house. They were all messages declaring my love, but I'd been unable to hide my sorrow in them, or my disappointment – luckily I couldn't remember exactly what I'd said. I was embarrassed enough at having contacted her so desperately.

'At least I know why you've been ignoring my calls since,' she added.

'Maddy, I'm sor –'

'And to think I actually believed you,' she interrupted, her eyes squinting at me in disbelief.

'Stop it,' I begged.

'That I told you I loved you, that we almost . . .' She hesitated as she once again glanced around the room. '. . . slept together. You told me you loved me.'

'I do.'

'So what happened?'

'What do you think happened?'

'Wow. I meant that much to you that within twenty-four hours you were sticking your cock into someone else.'

'Maddy!' I was shocked by the vulgarity of her tone, the explicitness of her language and the anger raging within her – wasn't I meant to be the angry one in that situation? Wasn't it me who had been royally screwed over by her?

'What happened? Once you got all those feelings out, you decided you didn't care as much as you thought you had? Or was I that much of a disappointment when you finally got me naked?' Her eyes bored into me, demanding a response. 'Well?'

I had nothing to give – no reason and no excuse.

'You've made a fool of me, Ben.'

'I haven't,' I protested, shaking my head at her words.

'You've made me feel like a complete mug. There I was thinking about you, about us, thinking about how we might be able to make this work, while all the time you were in bed with –'

'No, there you were, reconciling with Robert, Maddy. Don't try and play the martyr here, because you're really not,' I spat, taking the bait and allowing myself to be riled. 'So let's talk about that, shall we? Let's talk about how hours after you left me in my bed you were patching things up with Robert.'

She brought her hands up to her face in horror, her bullish façade slipping as tears sprang to her eyes. She shook her head profusely.

'I was trying to think things through,' she said helplessly.

'By getting back with Robert?' I scoffed.

'I didn't know what to do.'

'Seems like you made up your mind pretty quickly to me. It didn't take you long to forgive him.'

'I didn't . . .'

I sat silently as she tried to piece together her words. I couldn't look her in the eye. Instead, I focused on her hands in her lap, her fingers wriggling in discomfort, wringing the loose material on her skirt. She looked lost. All I wanted to do was embrace her and take that feeling away. In all our years of friendship I'd never been the cause of Maddy's tears, I'd always been the one to mop them up and make her feel better. It was agonizing to sit and watch her struggle.

'It's not that simple . . .' is all she managed before trailing off.

'From where I'm sat, it really is,' I said calmly.

'But I love you . . .' she mumbled as a tear escaped and fell onto her lap.

Her words gave me little pleasure.

'Did you tell him?'

'Of course not. I wouldn't . . .' she said, shaking her head, a sob rising from her mouth.

I took hold of her hand then, I couldn't resist it, my thumb rubbed the back of it.

In return she squeezed my hand.

Three times.

The gesture shocked me. Rebuked me into pulling my hands away.

'Maddy,' I sighed, my patience wavering slightly. 'I don't know what you want from me. You know how I feel. I opened up to you, finally told you everything I've ever wanted to say, but you're back with Robert. You clearly don't feel that love back.'

'But I do!'

'You have a boyfriend.'

'And?'

'That's a pretty big "and" right there.'

'Are you going to see her again?'

'Who? Alice? I dunno, I hadn't thought about it. I might. Why not?' I shrugged, confused as to why she was bringing up Alice – it seemed insignificant in the circumstances.

Defiantly, I wondered why there should even be a problem if I were to see Alice again. Maddy was back with Robert, leaving me on my own, once again. It seemed unfair that I'd be doomed to watching the two of them all loved up as though nothing had happened. Surely, I told myself, it was time for me to have someone of my own – someone to stop me from focusing on what I couldn't have.

'Right . . .'

'It makes no sense to just hang around, you know?'

'Yeah . . .'

'Now I know where I stand with you, that is,' I said. I loitered on that sentence for a while, offering a spot for her to interject and protest, but she didn't. I ploughed on.

'To be honest, Maddy, for the sake of our friendship and for Robert, I kind of think we should just forget it ever happened. It was only one night after all. We can put it all down to the drink and heightened emotions.'

The expression on her face as she looked up at me was one I'd never forget – one of shock, sorrow and disbelief. As though my words had literally slapped her across the face and simultaneously ripped out her heart.

'If that's what you want . . .' she muttered, looking back down at her hands.

I shrugged in reply, hating myself as I did it, not fully understanding why I was pushing her away so viciously. It wasn't what I wanted at all.

'Oh . . .' she looked as though she was going to say more, but decided against it.

My heart ached as she got up and walked away from me.

If only falling out of love was as easy as falling in it.

If only being with the girl I loved was as easy as all the songs on the radio insisted.

A day later the emails began. All the things that weren't said, that maybe we couldn't say face to face, written in safety from behind a computer screen. Saving us from having to speak the words out loud that we wouldn't have had the courage to utter in person, although perhaps leading us to boldly say things that we otherwise wouldn't have – the keyboard allowing us too much honesty, giving us too much bravado, making us forget ourselves.

Maddy sent the first one:

Look, I know you probably don't want to talk, you made your feelings quite clear yesterday when you told me to just forget the whole thing, but I have to get some things off my chest. I want to talk about this, even if you apparently don't. You might feel like acting as though it never happened, but I can't just do that. Not straight away. I feel like I need to explain a few things first. I need you to understand me.

I want you to know how much the other night meant to me. Never in a millions years did I think you'd tell me you loved me, that I'd hear I'd been so blind to what was going on in your head for so long. I thought I knew everything there was to know about you, but that was a pretty big secret you'd been keeping. One second you were my trusted friend and then the next – BAM – something more. You were offering me possibilities I never knew existed, a love that was more wholesome and honest than I'd ever thought possible – it felt enchanting. It felt right.

Because of the feelings you stirred in me, I was shocked when I found out about you and Alice. I felt like it lessened the importance of our night together and it made me feel a bit cheap and just another 'almost' notch on your bedpost. Am I? I hope not. I just can't get my head around how you can say you feel one way but then sleep with someone else straight away after. As they say, actions speak louder than words. Perhaps it's a guy thing, but it's not like you to do something so shitty.

I know you said about me jumping back into bed with Robert, but deep down you must have realized that wasn't the case. I couldn't have done that. We didn't. We haven't. And the reason for that was because I've not been able to get you and me out of my head.

Ben, you know I love Robert. I've been with him for five years, and have known him for as long as I've known you. He completely fell apart in front of me, something I wasn't expecting (you know he's usually so strong) and that threw me. I was prepared to hate him for what he'd done but when he was stood in front of me like that I faltered. I couldn't hurt him further when I could see how much agony he was in. Even when he left I wasn't sure what I was going to do. It wasn't as simple as I forgave him, forgot about you and we moved on to a happy-ever-after existence. I was coming to find you the other day to talk it all through with you, to try and make things clearer in my head. For me, there was still a big chance of you and me being together, or at least of talking and seeing what the possibilities were. I'd thought about it, a lot. But then I bumped into Roger. I felt crushed.

After seeing you yesterday, and hearing what you had to say, I called Robert and told him I was ready to put what he'd done behind us and move on. I was surprised that I'd done it when I put the phone down, but, if I'm honest, I only did it because I was angry with you. I still don't know what I want. It's all so raw still.

You're saying you want to move forward as though nothing has happened between us. After years of hiding your feelings you're certainly being very quick to brush them aside, as though they weren't as important to you as you proclaimed. Why are you giving up so easily, Ben?

I really don't know what to say to make all this better. You're my best friend and a huge part of my life. Can we meet up and talk? Go for a drink, or a walk, or something? Anything?

Deflated. That would be my one word right now.

I love you, Ben. Always have, always will.

Maddy xoxo

I was in my bedroom working when the email pinged through. Reading it caused me to drop everything I was doing, to get up, walk outside and go for a mammoth bike ride. I was out for hours, trying to process my different thoughts and emotions – each of them conflicting with the next.

I waited a few days before I replied. Not because I was trying to hurt her or punish her in any way, I simply didn't know what to respond with. Parts of her email angered me, while others made me sad.

None of it made me happy.

I sat in bed with my laptop on my knees trying to piece together some sort of response. All I wanted to tell her was that I loved her unconditionally, and that I would always be there waiting for her, but there was no point. She'd made her decision. Me harping on wasn't going to help matters. In the end I typed out a response in seconds and sent it before my heart had time to process its true feelings.

There's nothing to sort out, Maddy. I love you, but you're with Robert. It's that simple. I'll always be your friend, you know that.

Even I was disappointed with myself and my seeming lack of effort.

She replied within minutes.

It's not that simple and you know it! I love you too! I know some people don't believe that you can love two people at the same time – but I'm starting to think you can! You can and it's an awful feeling, because no matter what you decide to do about it you're always going to hurt someone.

And thanks for the short email. What about everything else I said?

My fingers hastily ran away from me as I typed a response straight away, against my better judgement.

Maddy, what do you want from me? You and Robert have shared five years together as a couple – we've had one night. Therefore you chose him. There's nothing I can do to change those facts, all I can say is I get it. I understand. What more do you want? My blessing? If so, you have it. Being in love with two people? Perhaps you're just saying it to flatter me. As it's only been five days I hope you'll be able to fall out of love as quickly as you fell in it. That should clear you of your woes.

As for you being another notch on my bedpost – how many girls do you seriously think I've slept with? Do you honestly think I treat girls in that way? You know me better than anyone so I'll try my best not to be offended.

I got with Alice that night because I felt like it and because you didn't give me any other option. Actions speak louder than words – yes, you're right. They do. Which is why Robert and you being together on Saturday spoke volumes. Instead of kicking him out, he stayed there and you talked things through – leading to him calling me! You could've given me some warning. In many ways it was the catalyst for the rest of the night. If it appears that I've brushed away any feelings then it's because someone handed me the broom. Not that I'm trying to lay blame on anyone else.

My feelings for you haven't altered, but my outlook on the situation has. We're best friends. You and Robert are my rocks. I know everything will be fine. At some point everything will go back to the way it was and we'll move past this. I don't think meeting up to talk about any of it is going to help either of us. I'm a bit busy at the moment, so not really free to meet up anyway, but we'll definitely do something soon.

Ben x

As soon as I'd sent that one I wished I hadn't. I wanted to disconnect and make things easier for both of us, but instead I'd added coal to the fire and prodded it aggressively with a giant rod. I only ever had love for Maddy, but the situation made me hide that, made me show her an ugly side instead, one that I hated. I suppose the same must have been true for her. We became vicious and snappy – something we'd never been with each other before, even when we were young and thoughtless.

Handed you the broom? Are you kidding me? You say there's no one to blame, but that's blatantly pointing the finger at me. How dare you. You're the one who started all this. You felt a certain way and bottled it up inside for years. Why not keep it locked up? You were obviously good at keeping it a secret. Why put it out there so that I have to deal with it too? Why wait until I'm heartbroken and drunk? Or was that your plan all along? Have you been waiting all this time for Robert to slip up so that you could jump in and make yourself look like the hero?

After looking at the screen for an hour, not knowing how to respond, I decided, instead of emailing back with further malice that I didn't mean, to put my laptop away, pick up my phone, and call Alice. I'd been putting off doing so because my head and heart were still feeling fragile and bruised, but I came to the conclusion that what they actually needed was a bit of TLC.

'Hello, you . . . Long time no speak,' she giggled, as she answered.

'Hey! Yes, I know. Appalling behaviour on my part.'

'Don't you know it's rude to leave a girl hanging like that?'

I couldn't help but laugh. 'I'm sorry, it's been a manic week.'

'I see . . . remind me, how long does it take to send a quick text these days?'

I could tell she was still smiling, even if there was honesty in her disappointment.

'I wanted to wait until I had time to call.'

'Hmmm . . . I see.'

'I was wondering if you fancied going out tonight? For dinner or something?' I said as I got up from my bed and paced around the room.

'Tonight? Are you really expecting me to drop all my important plans for you after you had sex with me and didn't call for a week?'

'Oh . . .' I suddenly felt stupid for having asked.

'Only joking,' she cackled. 'You'll only be saving me from a night in my PJs eating chocolate. Pick me up at seven.'

'Deal.'

I knew I needed to get Maddy out of my head and, as Alice came with no complications, she was a welcome distraction. That's what was appealing about her. That and the fact that she was ridiculously pretty and had a wicked personality to boot. If anyone was going to help me get over Maddy, I thought she would. Plus, let's not forget, I cried after having sex with the girl. I felt she deserved a little more respect than me never calling her again. A nice chilled-out dinner – I owed her that much.

When she answered the door at seven o'clock, we both stood there nervously, hesitant over how to greet one another. When I left her on the Sunday morning I'd kissed her goodbye – well, I had just slept with her, it would have been rude not to – but it would have seemed too forward to repeat the gesture then, when we were both totally sober and back to feeling like strangers again. So, instead, I stood there grinning at her.

She looked ridiculously cute with her hair bundled up in a high bun on the top of her head, her petite frame wearing a pale blue denim dress and with cream Converse on her feet, patterned with a design of dainty pink flowers. I towered above her, a fact I liked.

We didn't hold hands as we walked the short distance to the restaurant. In fact, we hardly spoke. Alice wasn't acting like the giggling girl I remembered her to be – instead she was suddenly demure and shy, with a preoccupied expression plastered on her face, making her seem wary. It troubled me.

For our date I'd picked a nice little Italian restaurant on the river – I'm ashamed to say it was a place I'd taken other girls previously. Antonio's had a great view, felt like an authentic Italian (the owner had the thickest accent to accompany his rather thick and dark moustache), and the food was delicious – much better than anything I could have knocked together. But best of all, it was relatively cheap – I was, after all, paying for it out of my student loan, or what I had left of it. Needless to say, I was on a tight budget.

As soon as we had sat down to dinner and ordered some wine, I decided to get to the root of what was going on with Alice.

'Are you okay?' I asked, taking the red cotton napkin from its fan-like position on the table and placing it over my lap.

Her eyes widened in embarrassment as she looked up at me.

'Yes!' she said slowly, picking up her own napkin and unfolding it. 'It's just I'm aware that we've done all of this the wrong way round.'

'Done what?'

'This,' she said, waving her hand manically between us both, the napkin flapping around in the air. 'You've seen me naked before even finding out my second name.'

'Oh, right,' I smiled, heartened by the sweetness of it all. 'So what is it, your second name?'

'Turner,' she said calmly, neatly placing the cloth over her thighs.

'Alice Turner.'

'And yours is Gilbert,' she stated with a coy smile.

'Yes!'

'See, I knew that. Oh, I don't know,' she sighed, as she put her head in her hands, seemingly embarrassed. 'I made it so easy for you. I don't usually do that. You know, what happened the other night. I'm surprised you even called. I wouldn't have if I was you. What a tart.'

I laughed, unsure how to respond. Alice was cute. Her girlie nerves made me feel protective – they made me want to reassure her. 'Well, I did. Plus, and I really don't want to point this out, but, if you're a tart, that makes me a tart . . . so at least we're in good company with our tarty ways.'

She let out one of her sweet giggles as she visibly started to relax.

Once the waiter, Antonio with his signature moustache, had poured us some wine and taken our orders – we'd both gone for spaghetti and meatballs, with a side of cheesy garlic bread – I focused my attention on finding out more about Alice Turner.

'So, come on, then. Out with it. I'm ready to find out everything about you.'

'Everything?' she asked, raising her eyebrows as she sipped on her wine.

'Yes.'

'That could take a while . . .'

'True. Good job we have time, then,' I shrugged.

'And I'm not that interesting,' she smiled.

'Maybe just some highlights into the world of Alice Turner, then. Give me five fun facts.'

'Ooh, the pressure is on!'

'Make them good,' I teased.

'How to make myself sound fun and desirable . . .' she pondered with a smile, as she rested her chin on the palms of her hands and tapped her fingers against her cheeks. 'Okay, fact one, I study English Language and am in my third year, which, yes, means that we've been in the same city for three years and never actually spoken.'

'How weird!'

'Not really. I've seen you around but you've usually been with a girl, a redhead, so I assumed you two were an item until Roger told me otherwise. Plus, I was dating this guy for most of that time – a loser. Unimportant,' she said, waving her hand to dismiss him further with a grimace on her face.

'Ha! Carry on,' I beckoned, wanting to swiftly move past the fact that Maddy had been brought up; something I didn't want us to dwell on for too long.

'Fact two, I grew up in Brentwood, Essex, with my mum, dad, and little brother, George.'

'An Essex girl?'

'Why does everyone say it like that?' she said with a bemused frown.

'Like what?'

'You know.'

'No . . .'

I did.

'Wipe that grin off your face, mister. Contrary to popular belief, us Essex girls do actually have brains – we're not all handbags and white stilettos.'

'Clearly,' I smiled, enjoying the glimpse of her feisty side.

'Fact three, I thought I was going to be a time traveller

like Dr Who when I grew up, until I found out that he was fictional and that it wasn't an actual job. So, now I want to be a journalist.'

'You followed up your argument about having brains with admitting you wanted to be a time traveller?'

'Ha! Fair play, but I was young.'

'Oh, forgiven, then,' I nodded, enjoying teasing her. 'So, what sort of journalist?'

'A features writer for some big, fat, glossy magazine!'

'Sounds great.'

'Gosh, these were meant to be interesting facts!'

'They are!' I laughed.

We paused as the waiter came back over with a basket of bread and butter.

'Okay, fact four, I have a slight obsession with giraffes. Nothing major, but I do have a giraffe onesie that I like to chill out in . . .'

'Sounds delightful. You've talked a lot about your PJs.'

'Have I?' she giggled. 'I do love a good pair of pyjamas! And fact number . . . oh, I've forgotten what fact I'm on. Fact whatever-this-is, I own, and wear in private, a pair of slippers.'

'Is that it?'

'Oh no, these are not just any slippers. These are a pair of blue Little Miss Bossy slippers – they're like big cuddly toys that go on each foot. I can hardly walk around when I'm in them, they're so huge, but they keep my feet warm . . . I just can't get rid of them.'

'Do you wear the slippers and the onesie at the same time?'

'Don't be ridiculous . . . I'd look stupid. Besides, they

clash. Believe me, I've tried it,' she laughed. 'Now, that's enough about me, I want to know all about you!'

'Well, I'm really not interesting. I don't have an animal onesie for a start.'

'But if you could pick an animal outfit to chill out in, what would it be?' she pushed.

'Ooh, that's a tough one.'

'You have to think carefully.'

'Maybe something like a koala? I imagine they'd be good to snuggle in.'

'Mmm . . . good choice,' she giggled.

The rest of the night flew by with ease. The hesitant start a distant memory by the time I dropped Alice off at her door hours later.

'It's been a great night,' I said as we stopped outside.

'It has . . .' Alice smiled, rooting through her bag and pulling out her front door key.

Before she had a chance to put it in the lock, I put my arm around her waist and pulled her in for a kiss – our first that night.

She started giggling as soon as it was over.

'What?'

'I don't know,' she smiled, looking up at me. 'Are you coming in?'

'Not tonight.'

'You're not?' she asked, sounding surprised, playing with the sleeve of my top with her fingers, her lips forming a little pout of disappointment.

'No . . . I usually save that until at least the third date, and I don't want you to get the wrong impression of me – or worry that I have the wrong impression of you.'

'I see . . .' she pondered, nodding her head.

'Hmmm . . .' I playfully sighed as I fiddled with the strap of her dress on her shoulder, tempted to go against my own valiant words.

'So you think there's going to be a next time?' she asked, raising her eyebrows.

'I'd like to think so,' I said, leaning in for another kiss. 'And a time after that.'

'If you're lucky,' she giggled.

I got back to five emails from Maddy. The first continued with the same angry tone as before, the middle three were wondering where I was and the last was more like the Maddy I knew . . . calm and reasonable.

> I'm sorry. I'm just going to put it out there right now. I'm being a complete twat. Getting angry with you isn't going to help things. My head's a bit messed up. Well, I say a bit . . . really I mean a lot. Of course I don't wish you'd never said anything. That was a stupid and pathetic thing to say. I'd never want to take away what happened the other night. I'll never wish it didn't happen. It was beautiful.
>
> I'm getting irate because I'm scared of losing you and I don't want that to happen. You know how much you mean to me. I know we'll be able to get through this – it'll just take time.
>
> Sorry for being a loser . . . and a crazy nutcase. Hope you don't think less of me. In fact, please ignore all previous emails. Off to seek professional help immediately. I believe they'll have a straitjacket waiting for me upon arrival. Ha!
>
> Let me know you're all right. x

I sighed as I closed my laptop and put it away, realizing that Maddy was always going to have the ability to draw me in. It was the way I'd conditioned myself to be over the years – my heart would always belong to her. Knowing that irritated me after spending such a great night with Alice, and, instead of it making me want to cool off things with her – after all, I doubted anyone could level up to the unrealistic pedestal I'd put Maddy on – it made me want to make more of an effort with her. I thought she deserved a chance.

Maddy and Robert were staying together, so I knew it would have been painful for me to remain single and watch the two of them together, acting as though nothing bad had ever happened between them. I didn't want to be sat on the sidelines pining after Maddy, yet again. No, I told myself, it was time to make some changes, and pursuing things with Alice was how to start. Plus, I imagined being with her would ensure that I'd definitely keep my distance from Maddy, stopping me from crossing boundaries once again. Not that I thought I would, but having obtained something I'd desired for so long, well, it increased my thirst rather than quenched it. The thought of being with Maddy was more real than ever before, I knew what I was missing, knew how we could be together, knew her body's secrets, the way it curved, the way it responded to my touch – they were no longer just little thoughts I'd imagined in my head, instead they were very real.

I knew I needed to push those thoughts from my mind, and divert that energy onto something else, before I ruined things beyond repair.

Alice was my only hope, so I decided to give her my all.

Maddy

Twenty-one years old . . .

I'd known and seen Ben almost every day for the past twelve years, but, following our passionate love affair, when I thought of him I was bombarded with visions of his face that night. The way he'd nervously smiled as he confessed his feelings at the pub, the way he longingly looked at my lips before kissing me, or the way his mouth grazed my body. Just thinking of the latter would cause a tug on my insides and a wave of excitement in my knickers – something I'd instantly feel ashamed of.

I was angry with him for sleeping with Alice, but what did I expect? Of course I could see everything from his point of view. The situation was so messy. In a way he'd given me a get-out clause, given me reason to turn my back on him and his words, but I had an internal need to know that he loved me and cared. I didn't want to feel that what we'd shared wasn't real. I needed to know it was more than a lusty night. I wasn't the sort of girl to drop my knickers for anyone who came knocking, after all. For the first time in my life I'd done something completely reckless and I hated the fact that it made me a bad person.

I bumped into Ben down the street from his house. Which, yes, sounds suspiciously like I was stalking him and trying my best to run into him . . . that would be a correct assumption to make. I wasn't sure what else to do. He'd stopped answering my emails, calls and texts when I'd turned a bit psycho in an email to him. Okay, it was several emails in the space of a few hours, but I hadn't meant to, I was just so frustrated by the whole thing and emotionally drained. Seeing as Ben was the only person who knew the full extent of my life's current affairs (bad choice of words, but you know what I mean) it seemed like he was the only one I could vent to. I was taking every ounce of anger I'd been feeling out on Ben thanks to the guilt that had decided to rear its ugly head, making me unable to vent such frustrations at Robert – even though he'd started the whole thing. How pathetic does that sound?!

The way I'd acted towards Ben was unfair and I regretted the emails straight away. He eventually sent a lovely reply back – he didn't just leave me in silence to hate myself (although he didn't relieve me of my torment for a whole twenty-seven hours and nineteen minutes), saying he completely understood and that all he wanted was for us both to be happy. It was the few days of silence that he followed that up with that led me to engineer seeing him that morning! I knew he was avoiding me and it's fair to say it was starting to make me go a little mad. So, one Thursday morning, when I knew he'd be heading for a lecture, I accidentally-on-purpose made sure I was walking in the opposite direction and that we would inevitably collide into each other at some point. I spotted his bouncing walk from quite a distance; it created a wave of affection and brought a smile to my lips, something I wasn't prepared for. He noticed me a few hundred yards away and continued to walk towards me. I took that for a good sign. As he got nearer I saw he was smiling, and the butterflies inside me went berserk.

'Hey, you,' he said casually as he got closer.

'Hey . . .'

Stopping when he was yards away from me, Ben rocked backwards and forwards on his feet in uncertainty, no doubt wondering what I was doing springing the surprise visit on him. Stupidly I hadn't planned what to do after bumping into him, which led to me looking like a complete idiot as I became tongue-tied. I knew he'd been ignoring me; I had just wanted to see him and check everything was okay. Force him into making some sort of interaction with me, but instead, I knew he felt cornered. Ben hated any kind of confrontation, always had.

The silence between us spoke volumes. It was one of those moments where subtext and body language said everything where words failed. I felt aware of every part of my body and ridiculously aware of his. The way he licked his upper lip with the tip of his tongue, ran his fingers through his thick hair and gave it a tousle, the way his eyes focused on mine briefly before looking down at the ground. The connection sent a bolt of unexpected pleasure through me as it instantly transported me back to his bedroom, back to his bed, back to the way he'd looked at me with fresh eyes – back to his secret smile.

Being so close to Ben was far more charged and awkward than I had expected, creating an astounding amount of conflict within me. I immediately wished I wasn't there and reprimanded myself for manipulating the ambush . . . but then, a large part of me wished I could just go up and kiss him. That it was my tongue licking his lips, my fingers running through his hair – and that we were back in his bed, picking up where we'd left off. I winced at those thoughts and wondered why my brain was so quick to betray Robert, the guy I was supposed to love with all my heart. The one I was trying to forgive.

'How have you been?' he asked, looking up at me properly for the first time, allowing his gaze to rest on mine for more than a split second.

'Fine,' I answered, unable to resist smiling at him. 'You?'

'Good. Really good.'

'Great.'

'Yeah . . .'

'You're looking good,' I blurted.

'Really?' he laughed, looking down at himself. He was wearing his normal ripped baggy jeans, with a slim-fit stripy blue and white t-shirt. He looked the same as normal, but there was something different about him, and I don't think it was solely down to my raging hormones. 'Must be the sunshine,' he offered as he gestured upwards.

'Yeah . . .'

An awkward silence fell upon us as we looked up at the blue sky above, as though we were inspecting the weather. We were far from relaxed together.

'Ben, is everything okay? With us?' I asked quickly, embarrassed to be even asking the question. It felt like such a silly and adolescent thing to ask. I wasn't used to speaking in that way to him. I'd never had the need to before.

His eyes rested on mine as he exhaled. 'Of course.'

'You've been avoiding me.'

'I haven't,' he shrugged.

'Are you really going to try and deny it?' I asked, raising my eyebrows at him.

'Okay, you're right,' he sighed, tugging on the strap of his backpack as he jiggled uncomfortably on the spot. 'I thought that it was for the best. Just for a little bit, mind. But I'm feeling better about everything now. You know?'

'I guess, but you could've given me some warning before you went MIA. I've been going mad with worry.'

'Ha! Sorry about that. I feel like I've got my head screwed back on again now. All I needed was some time.'

'But you're back now?'

'Yes! Definitely,' he beamed as he gave me a squeeze on the arm.

The arm.

Not the hand.

Just one.

Not three.

I couldn't help but feel sad as I noticed the absence of the two extra pulses.

'Robert's worried about you,' I said in a strained manner, aware that I was bringing up he-who-shall-not-be-named. 'I said you've been busy with work and stuff, but he wants to see you when he's down at the weekend. He's even mentioned storming into your bedroom and dragging you away from your desk.'

Ben laughed loudly.

'He thinks you're angry at him.'

'Oh. I see. I'll give him a call later.'

'Thanks.'

'Actually, talking about work, I'd better be going,' he

said, pointing his thumb in the direction he was meant to be walking in.

'Yes, of course . . .'

'Where are you off to?'

'Oh, I was just . . . wandering around,' I couldn't help but smile. I knew he knew I was there just to see him.

'Sounds great,' he grinned, slapping his hands against the sides of his thighs. 'Right, I'll speak to you later, Mad.'

He grabbed hold of me and pulled me in for a hug then. I'm not sure if it was just a habit that he'd forgotten to break or whether it was an urge like the ones I'd been fighting that had led him into the embrace. He lifted me up slightly and ever so gently brushed my naked neck with his lips. The sudden intimacy led me to inhale deeply as his being took over my body, eradicating all rational thought. The bubble that we'd previously found ourselves in had come back to cocoon us once more, making everything around us disappear within seconds.

The way he released me abruptly, jumping back in shock and putting distance between us once more, suggested the action had caught him off guard too. But, whereas I'd welcomed it, he hadn't. It alarmed him and caused him to flee.

'Must dash!' he said nervously, his cheeks flaming red as he launched himself into a fast-paced power walk away from me.

As I watched him get further away, one word sprang to mind – FUCK! It dawned on me that the next few months were going to be incredibly hard if my mind so easily disintegrated in his company, if his touch could generate such a colossal reaction within me. I wasn't sure how I'd cope.

'I've finally spoken to Ben!' Robert said with relief on the phone that night.

His call had woken me up. I hadn't been sleeping well for obvious reasons, but had somehow crashed out on my bed early evening without meaning to when I was trying to get some work done. The sound of my phone ringing roused me with a shock, making me disorientated.

'What?' I croaked, unable to hide my irritation.

'Ben! I've just spoken to him.'

'Oh really?' I asked, as I reached for the glass of water from my bedside table, trying to stop my head feeling so groggy.

'You okay?'

'Yeah, I was asleep.'

'It's only nine o'clock!'

'Really? Blimey.'

'So, like I was saying – I found Ben,' Robert continued. 'Turns out he wasn't busy with work like we thought, or joined a religious cult like I feared.'

'Thank God for that,' I laughed dryly.

'He's started seeing someone!'

'What?'

'Yeah, I know! What a dark horse. He goes missing for a couple of weeks and then comes back with a girlfriend. I'm surprised he didn't tell you about it.'

I thought back to that morning, he had seemed happier and lighter – I'd commented on it, he'd said it was the sunshine, but it was actually because he had a girlfriend.

Surely, I thought, after everything we'd been through, he'd have told me about something like that. Especially before mentioning it to Robert! I knew there was no way Ben wouldn't have known the impact it would have on me. I wondered, momentarily, whether it was Ben's way of getting back at me – showing me that he was fine, or highlighting the fact that he had options, lots more than I did. Even as I thought it, I doubted Ben would be so manipulative or calculating. It wasn't in his nature.

'We haven't really seen each other,' I lied. 'We've been busy.'

'Oh, right. I said to him about us going out when I'm next over at yours.'

'Yeah . . .' My mind was elsewhere, not paying much attention to what Robert was harping on about.

'I'll feel better once I see him,' he said meaningfully, alluding to how concerned he'd been about not being able to get hold of him. I hadn't spoken to Rob a lot in those two weeks, not wanting to rush into too much too soon, but every time we spoke he'd mentioned how worried he was about Ben. I knew he felt it wasn't just me he'd let down – that he had to clear things up with him too. 'Besides,' he said with a gentle laugh, 'I want to meet this girl he's left us for!'

'Already? He's only just started seeing her. Plus, I've got so much stuff on . . .' I said, trying to keep the panic from my voice. I did not want to go out with Ben and some girl he had just started dating. It was the worst idea I'd ever heard. I frantically tried to think of how to get out of it in a way that wouldn't make Robert suspicious, but nothing sprang to mind.

'Come on, we can double date like old times.'

'Do you really think he likes her that much? Knowing Ben he'll have changed his mind within a week.' I added a rather feeble laugh to try and make light of the subject and to dismiss the idea entirely. It didn't work.

'I don't think so. He seems really keen on Alice.'

'Alice?' I questioned, remembering her name from an email Ben had sent. Alice was Roger's housemate, the girl he'd slept with the night after being with me.

I couldn't quite get my head around that. From what Ben had said, he'd slept with her because he thought I was back with Robert, or because he was stupidly drunk. Whatever the reason, if Robert was right, the girl he'd vented those frustrations with had somehow become his girlfriend. I wondered how that had come about, what had urged Ben to turn a one-night stand into more.

It saddened me that he hadn't had the guts to tell me himself, that he felt it was okay for me to hear the information second-hand from Robert instead – that he had such disregard for me and my feelings.

It took every ounce of self-control to stop myself from calling Ben as soon as I got off the phone to Robert – which I did so in a grumpy and flippant manner, in the fastest way possible. A part of me wanted Ben to know how much his indifference was hurting me, but then, what right did I have to be to hurt or angry at him? As far as he was concerned I'd made my choice, he was free to do as he wished. It dawned on me that all I really wanted was to know that he cared about me still, and that I wasn't so easily replaced. I couldn't help but feel I'd been pushed aside. I needed to know that I hadn't acted so appallingly and been unfaithful for something meaningless. I didn't want it to be a drunken fumble to be ashamed of. My needs were selfish, but it irritated me that he wasn't willing to fulfil them.

I was also, for the first time in my life, experiencing jealousy. I was jealous of Alice even though I'd never met her. I was envious of whatever qualities she had that had led to Ben moving on so swiftly after declaring his love to me. I also resented the fact that she would be able to have Ben adore her in such a carefree manner, when I knew I couldn't.

By that point I hadn't spoken to Pearl like I'd planned, I'd let it all fester inside me instead, and avoided the girls as much as I could. On hearing that Ben was seeing Alice, that he was developing actual feelings for her, I decided I needed to talk to someone. I tiptoed across the landing to her room and knocked on her bedroom door.

'Pearl?' I whispered.

'All right, darling,' she growled. 'Come in.'

She was at her desk in her pyjamas, with books and loose pieces of crumpled paper covered in handwritten notes surrounding her. Her hair was gathered in a crazy pineapple at the top of her head – her favourite way of keeping it out of her face while she worked.

'Revising?'

'Doing what I can, but I fear it's a case of too little too late,' she said, swivelling in her chair and turning to face me.

I must have looked as troubled as I felt – as soon as she saw my face her own curled downwards in a frown.

'Dude! What's up?' she asked, as she stood up, took me by the arm, and led me to her bed to sit down.

'I don't even know where to start, Pearl,' I said, crossing my legs and picking up one of her pillows to hug, burying my face in it.

'Tell me. Is it all this stuff with Robert?'

'Yes and no,' I said, looking up at her.

'Go on . . .'

'I kissed Ben.'

Unshockable Pearl's jaw dropped. 'What? When?'

It's one thing admitting to yourself that you've done something wrong, it's another when you've got to tell someone else how much of a plonker you've been. Pearl stayed uncharacteristically quiet as I told her everything. From Ben and me getting drunk, kissing, having a fumble, him sleeping with someone else, him saying to forget it ever happened, to having to go on a double date with him, Alice and Robert.

'Hold on a minute. Rewind. You didn't sleep with him?' she said, holding her hand out and stopping me.

'No.'

'You just cuddled?' she asked, raising her eyebrows.

'Not quite, but in the end, yes.'

'Jeez, what are you even worrying for?' she sighed.

'It was more than that, Pearl. Cheating is cheating, whether it's a kiss or mind-blowing sex.'

'It's really not. It's totally different,' she argued, shaking her head dismissively.

'Is it, though?'

'Yes! Do you want me to go into detail to prove it? Remind you exactly what you could've done had you not stopped?'

'No, thanks,' I squirmed, knowing Pearl would go into a graphic description that would make even porn stars blush.

'Shame,' she sighed comically.

'It's not only that, though, I feel like I've fallen for him. That's got to be way worse than sleeping with someone.'

Pearl looked at me with confusion as her face crinkled up in bewilderment.

'Mad, your boyfriend did a really shitty thing. In response, you got rat-faced and kissed someone. That's all it needs to be. Don't go turning it into something else, especially if that person's now gone off and started screwing this other bird.'

'He said he loved me.'

It was almost the same thing I'd said to Ben, the same argument that stopped me from being able to get past the whole thing and accept that being together wasn't even a possibility.

Pearl looked at me and sighed. 'And then he did something even shittier than your boyfriend did in the first place.'

I'd never thought of it like that. It seemed ridiculous to me that, even after he'd slept with Alice, I was the one running around after him, emailing him with heartfelt words (and crazy ones), placing myself somewhere that I knew he'd turn up. I couldn't explain what had led me to do those things, or say what I was hoping to gain.

'I think you've freaked yourself out,' Pearl continued, standing up and pacing around the room, nodding her head as though she was agreeing with her own words. 'You've acted in a way that's completely out of character – Maddy, you're the most loyal person I know. You've shocked yourself and now you're trying to give it a greater meaning to justify your behaviour. Babe, you did wrong, but that one action doesn't define who you are.' She grabbed my hand in hers and patted it sympathetically.

'I just don't know what to do,' I said feebly.

'What to do about what exactly? It looks to me as though Ben is no longer an option,' she said matter-of-factly, perching herself back on the bed. 'You need to get him out of your mind, pronto.'

'How?'

'Do you still love Robert?'

'Yes.'

'Do you think you'll be able to forgive him?'

'I don't know. I think I might,' I shrugged.

Robert's cheating was something I'd found difficult to think about. It wasn't that Ben filled my head and pushed aside all thoughts of Robert's wrongdoings, more that it upset me too much to think about what he'd done. He'd hurt me far more because he'd risked the years we'd been together and made me question our whole relationship. Yet, I still loved him – and that's what left me irritated, annoyed and confused.

'Are you willing to try and work things out?'

Without much gusto, I nodded in reply.

'Maddy, a couple of weeks ago you two had your whole lives planned out together – take a leaf out of Ben's book. Pretend nothing has changed.'

'I don't know if I can do that.'

Pearl raised her eyebrows at me.

'Seriously? This is all over one night. Get a grip.'

I knew Pearl was going to offer blunt advice, she was always to the point in every situation with the inability to filter what she thought – and that was why I went to her over Flo or Jennifer. The whole situation had already become over-romanticized in my head, I needed someone to knock a bit of sense into me. She was right, I had to stop thinking of Ben in that way; if he was moving forward, I had to too.

I couldn't explain what had made me focus so much on Ben at that point and not on saving my relationship with Robert. It was like my brain had been taken over by some alien being. I knew, like Pearl said, I needed to get my head out of the clouds and focus on what I did have. I needed to work on things with Robert and see if what we had was salvageable.

I had to forget about Ben . . . but if only doing were as easy as saying when it came to matters of the heart.

The double date had been arranged for the following weekend. Needless to say I had no part in the planning – I left Robert and Ben to do that, it was enough for me to just turn up on the night. It was happening, it was inevitable, I just had to get on with it.

Me being there was a classic case of 'curiosity killed the cat'. After all, I could have made a last-minute excuse, but the truth was I needed to meet Alice. I wanted to know everything about her, what she looked like, what her voice sounded like, how she laughed, where she'd grown up, what her likes and dislikes were, what her taste in music was like . . . morbid curiosity meant I needed to know what Ben saw in her. Perhaps to understand, or perhaps just to see how I measured up in comparison.

The boys had decided to go bowling. Robert and I were the first to arrive, which meant we were there when Ben and Alice came through the door hand in hand and giggling their heads off. To say I felt nauseous would be an understatement.

I'd built up images of Alice in my head – I expected her to be tall, dark and model-like, but it was worse than that. She was extremely petite, around five foot two with a beautifully dainty frame. Her long blonde hair fell in waves around her shoulders and her hazel eyes had the most dazzling flecks of green in them. She was naturally beautiful. The kind of girl you knew would roll out of bed in the mornings and look amazing. She wore a floaty yellow dress which came down past her knees, its thin straps exposing her delicate shoulders and collarbone. Even in those first few seconds I knew there was something endearing about her, she radiated warmth.

'Here he is!' shouted Robert as he grabbed hold of Ben and gave him a manly hug and a bit of a wrestle, leaving me to smile in Alice's direction awkwardly, dubious as to how to greet her.

'Hi! I'm Alice!' she giggled coming towards me for a hug. 'You must be Maddy?'

'Yep. Don't worry, I won't be doing that to you,' I smiled.

'Gosh, thank goodness,' she laughed. 'I've heard a lot about you.'

I wondered what Ben had been telling her, causing my mind to falter momentarily.

'Sorry, got a bit carried away. I'm Robert,' said Robert breathlessly, breaking away from Ben and giving Alice a kiss on the cheek.

Ben didn't really look at me before walking in my direction and giving me a klutzy hug. It was brief and as soon as it was done he turned to the others with a smile.

'Let's do this!' he laughed as he grabbed hold of Robert and they galloped over to the counter like overexcited kids.

'Here goes,' I said, following them, feeling deflated that things were still on edge with Ben and me. But what had I expected? It wasn't as if we were seriously going to bounce back into being normal with each other after what we'd done, especially not with Robert around.

'Are we allowed to use the bumpers?' asked Alice next to me, pulling me from my thoughts.

'Oh . . . the boys don't usually let me, they tell me it's cheating.'

When we were younger the three of us had gone bowling and they'd allowed me to have the bumpers up, as it was my first time. Miraculously I'd won even though my ball had rebounded off the side each time I bowled, occasionally even a few times in one throw, creating a pretty zigzag pattern as they made their way down to the pins. The boys were understandably livid and told me I'd won unfairly. I might have been their best friend, but they were still competitive, especially Robert who sulked the whole way home. From that point onwards I was never allowed to use the bumpers again.

'Really? But I'm rubbish!' moaned Alice.

'Same here.'

Even though I'd been forced to play without the aid of bumpers over the years I was still terrible at the game. My problem was that I didn't have the patience for it. I was a just-throw-it-and-see-how-it-goes girl. I couldn't be bothered with the whole lining it up and getting your elbow in the right position malarkey.

'We're having the bumpers up, right?' said Alice sweetly as we joined the boys in the line for our shoes. It was more of a leading question than anything else.

Both boys looked at her with their mouths open, unsure of how to say no nicely – they were both aware that they were meant to be making a good impression on her.

'Erm . . .' started Ben. 'Oh, we didn't book a lane with them, I'm afraid.'

'Yeah, and usually you have to ask,' Robert answered, with an apologetic shrug.

'No, it's okay! They have those electric ones now . . . we just press the button on our control thingy and they pop out,' she smiled. 'I know how to do it too, so you don't need to worry about a thing. I'll do it.'

Ben and Robert just stared at her. I couldn't help but laugh. She knew the boys were trying to fob her off, and that they'd be too polite to argue with her. She turned to me and raised her eyebrows, trying not to laugh as she changed the subject. 'Are you going for laced or buckled shoes, Maddy?'

The boys needn't have worried, as even with the bumpers up, Alice and I were as crap as each other. We were lucky to get a couple of pins down each time. Clearly my win all those years ago had been more to do with beginner's luck than actual talent, and Alice couldn't help but laugh every time she took her turn, clearly feeling embarrassed by the whole thing. She'd go up full of gusto, line up her shot, and then keel over in a fit of giggles before she'd had the chance to throw it. Her giggle was infectious, though, and we couldn't help but laugh along with her.

Alice and Ben weren't as touchy-feely with each other as I'd feared they were going to be. They may have sat next to each other on the sofas throughout the game and looked deeply smitten, but they weren't there snogging each other's faces off, which was a big relief. In contrast, Robert and I were still distant from each other, or rather, I was avoiding having any sort of PDA with him with the aid of the whopping big barrier that I'd erected and had been unable, so far, to knock down. So, despite how hard he was trying to make things seem normal, they weren't.

At the end of the first game, which our sporting hero Robert obviously won, we stopped for some food. Burgers, fries and milkshakes were brought over to us at the lane, which we greedily devoured while sat on the comfy red leather sofas.

'I've seen you around campus before, actually,' said Alice to me as she popped a chip into her mouth.

'Oh, really?'

'Didn't Ben tell you? I thought you were his girlfriend,' she giggled.

'Something you two want to tell me?' Robert jokingly accused, nudging me with his elbow and raising his eyebrows at Ben.

I felt like a rabbit caught in headlights, completely

unsure what to say. So I just gormlessly looked from Alice to Robert.

'Oh don't worry,' Alice laughed at Robert. 'It's only because they were together that I thought that . . . there was clearly no chemistry whatsoever.'

My eyes flicked up at Ben, who was looking at me for the first time that night. For a split second the guard he'd put up slipped away and I could see the real Ben exposed, full of love and honesty. It was as though a magnetic force had been switched on, drawing me to him, making it near impossible to look away. It was a dangerous look to share in public. I felt ashamed as my insides tingled at the connection. I had thought being in the company of others would stop that feeling arising, that we'd be able to lock it away. But it seemed the inappropriateness of it made it more intense, and left it to linger and grow like an unattended fire.

'At least he's keeping other prowling guys away for you, Robert,' giggled Alice.

My eyes darted down to my food and stayed there, unable to look up. I felt Robert shamefully stiffen next to me and Ben shifted in his seat uncomfortably opposite.

Not noticing the sudden change in mood, or the fact that we'd all ventured into silence, Alice continued to place her petite foot even further into her mouth, 'That's what friends are for, though. Shame they haven't had someone returning the favour in Nottingham.'

A weak 'Ha' was all Robert could muster in reply. I almost felt sorry for him.

'Must be tough being away from these two, though,' she smiled, turning to Ben and me. 'From what I've heard you're quite the terrible threesome.'

It was clear that Ben hadn't told Alice anything about recent events in our group. I suspect it was a case of where to start and at what point to stop. She'd meant nothing scathing by her comments, she was just trying to make friendly conversation.

'Life's been very different, that's for sure,' I nodded.

'I bet Robert can't wait to get the crew back together.'

'Yeah, you're right,' he agreed, seeming to relax.

'So what are your plans? For after?'

'We haven't really talked about it yet,' I said, purposely being vague to end the conversation there.

'What would you like?' Alice asked Robert.

'I'd love us all to move to London. Maybe get a little flat or something.'

'Really?' I asked, in as bright a tone as I could muster, giving him a little warning look.

'Well, it's something we always talked about when we were younger, you know, moving in together as a trio . . .' he shrugged, trailing off, unable to hold eye contact with me.

'We haven't talked about that for years,' laughed Ben nervously, clearly as thrown as I was. 'I've no idea what I'll be doing . . .'

It was something that we had talked about a lot, but only when we were incredibly young – mostly before me and Robert had even started dating. It was a topic that, especially once we knew we were going to different universities, had been dropped. None of us knew realistically what the future was going to bring, we hadn't even talked about what came after our scrolls of paper were handed out at graduation.

Alice continued to push the idea, much to my discomfort.

'Are you telling me that if Rob found you all an awesome pad somewhere amazing you'd give up the opportunity to live with your two bestest buds? As if!' she laughed, looking at us as though we'd gone mad.

'I guess it depends on a few things, and besides, things change,' I smiled, hoping that the conversation would be dropped. In the end I decided to turn the topic of our futures back onto her – it seemed the safest way to stop me losing my rag. 'What about you, Alice? What are you going to do?'

'Well, I'm from Essex so I'll probably be heading back over that way. I've always fancied getting a place somewhere more central, though. Plus, most magazines and stuff are based in London, so it makes sense for me to be there.'

I glanced over at Ben to see him nervously looking around the bowling alley.

'We should probably play the next game,' he said, looking at his watch. 'We've not got long left!'

'I'm gonna kick arse this time,' giggled Alice. 'I can tell!'

'Good luck with that,' laughed Robert politely, clearly relieved to be getting back on his feet and away from the conversation.

As soon as we'd said goodbye to Ben and Alice and got into his car, Robert turned to me with his eyebrows raised.

'So, what do you think?' he asked, popping on his seat-belt.

'She's adorable.'

I really meant it too, even if it was painful for me to admit. Alice was bubbly and sparkly – a pleasure to spend time with. I understood what Ben saw in her, although I'd been shocked to see how different she was to me. We weren't alike in any way – appearance or personality. It bothered me and I couldn't put my finger on why – I hadn't expected a carbon copy, but I had thought she'd have a least a few qualities in common with me. In reality, I felt decidedly average around her, which irked me after Ben had made me feel so special.

'Ben seems really happy,' Robert added, starting the engine and pulling out of the parking space.

'Yeah.'

'I was really nervous about seeing him.'

'Really?'

'You know how protective he is over you – I half expected him to lamp me one.'

'He wouldn't do that,' I half laughed, half squeaked, in shock.

'You never know . . .'

'Things were fine, though, right?'

'I don't know. He seemed a little distant at first.'

'What, when you guys were jumping all over each other like apes?' I tried to joke.

'No, after that. When we were stood at the counter, it was like he had something on his mind. Maybe that's just me reading too much into it, looking for signs that something was wrong,' he frowned, nibbling on his lower lip.

'Must be,' I muttered.

It was possible that, like me, Ben had struggled with us all being together and acting as though everything was normal. It was also likely that being stood next to Robert once again had reminded him of our betrayal.

'He didn't say much about us all moving in together, did he?'

'None of us did really . . .'

'Do you reckon he wants to?'

'We haven't even decided what we're doing yet.'

'I know, but I assumed –'

'We've been through a lot lately, Rob,' I snapped.

I hated myself for saying that, especially as I'd not said it purely because I was still angry at him, more because I wanted him to drop the subject, at least until I could figure out a good reason for us not to live together. There was, after all, no way I was going to be able to live with both Robert and Ben. Just the thought of us all under the same roof was enough to make me feel queasy. The idea was completely inconceivable.

'But we're fine now, aren't we?' Robert asked with sadness. We hadn't even made our way out of the car park yet, he was still trying to work his way around its one-way system.

I looked ahead as I thought about his question. 'I hope we will be, but things take time. You can't just magic us back to normal. Too much has happened,' I exhaled.

'Yeah,' he nodded sadly, my words deflating him.

'Anyway, I'm sure Ben won't want to live with us when we're in the midst of coming through all of that,' I reasoned.

'I guess so . . .'

He pulled over and turned to me, gently taking my hand in his.

'You know how sorry I am about the whole thing, Maddy,' he said softly. His face was a picture of regret and sorrow, as his eyes searched mine. 'I love you with my whole heart. It'll never ever happen again. No one else could hate me more than I do for it. I was an absolute jerk.'

'It doesn't matter,' I said dismissively, annoyed that we were talking about his mistake once more.

'It does because I hurt you. I was wrong,' he persevered, lifting my hand to his lips and kissing it. 'I want you and me to live together, Mad. It's that simple.'

He pulled my hands into his chest and cradled my arms, causing my body to lean towards his. He kissed my lips softly.

It was the first time he'd kissed me since his confession, and the simple gesture made me feel overwhelmingly sad, reminding me of the love we'd shared and were close to throwing away. I knew there was something special, comfortable and loving between us – I just had to allow him to work his way through that barrier I'd built so that I could start seeing it again.

Ben

Twenty-one years old . . .

After our interesting double date, I walked Alice the short distance back to hers. Her front door was already in view when she turned to me and asked me in.

'Is it wise?' I asked, not wanting to take advantage. Up until that point we'd still been trying to keep things respectable by going on dates and getting to know each other properly. Not only was Alice a welcome distraction from other things that were going on, she was also great to be around. She lightened my mood and made the world seem like a less complicated, happier place. I wouldn't say she made me forget, but she certainly made me think about the Maddy situation a lot less.

'I think, now that we're several dates in, we can resume where we started,' she said with a cheeky grin.

'Oh, really?'

'Or, if you don't fancy that, we could chill on the sofa, watch a movie . . .' she teased.

'Your first offer was a bit more tempting, but I'll take either.'

I excitedly followed her inside.

She'd been wonderful that afternoon, full of all the charm and warmth that had attracted me to her in the first place. I needed to see her like that around Robert and Maddy, I needed to see that I had someone of my own who was special at last.

'So, do you think they like me?' she asked, once we were in her room and lying on her bed, facing each other – one of her housemates that I didn't know was watching TV in the lounge, so we'd decided to go up to her room instead – well, that was our excuse, anyway, but we both knew that was where we preferred to be.

'They loved you.'

That was definitely true of Robert, who wasted no time in leaning in and telling me how fit he thought she was, although later on he'd also winked at me whenever Alice did something funny or cute – she'd effortlessly won him over. As for Maddy, well, I'd watched her around Alice, I wanted to gauge her reaction for some reason – see how she responded to me being there with someone else. She seemed fascinated by her and watched her keenly for most of the afternoon with intrigue. I was surprised Alice had failed to notice.

'You sure?'

'What's not to love?'

'Whoa there, tiger, with the love talk!' she giggled.

Putting my hands on her hips, I pulled her on top of me and gave her a kiss.

'Before we get carried away . . . I have something for you,' she said, untangling herself from me as she pulled a large present from the side of her bed, offering it to me with a smirk.

'What's this?' I asked her, looking at the neatly wrapped gift and juggling it around, trying to work out what it was – it was soft and made no sound when I shook it; I had no idea what she was giving me.

'It's only something small,' she shrugged. 'I just thought it would make you smile.'

I tore apart the blue wrapping paper to find a koala onesie and couldn't stop myself from grinning as I kissed her once more to say thank you. It was the most thoughtful gift I'd ever received, I couldn't help but be blown away by the gesture.

'You really are the cutest little thing,' I said, cupping her face with my hands.

'Why, thank you! Once you experience the joy of this onesie, I swear it'll be hard to get you out of it.'

'Oh, but I hope you'll try.'

'Ben!' she squealed with laughter, giving me a playful slap on the arm.

'I'm joking . . . sort of. Seriously, though, thank you. It's so sweet of you.'

'Not really, it just gives me an excuse to wear my onesie around you and not feel stupid.'

'Ooh, ulterior motives, Miss Turner?'

'Made sense for when you finally managed to make your way back into my bedroom.'

'Crafty.'

As we sat there grinning at each other a thought popped into my head. 'Actually, Alice, I have to go home next weekend, for Maddy's dad's fiftieth. Fancy coming?'

If I'd spent a little more time thinking about it I'd probably have concluded it was a bad idea, but I hadn't. Sitting in front of her, basking in her sunshine, it seemed like a perfect idea.

'I can't just turn up uninvited.'

'I'm inviting you.'

'You can't do that.'

'I can, I was given a plus one on the invite.'

'But I don't know anyone.'

'Alice, I'm trying to ask you to come home with me and meet my mum, would you not make it so difficult?'

'Oh! I forgot she'd be there,' she giggled. 'I'd love to.'

Every social event, ever since Maddy and Robert had become an item, had turned into me being asked a million questions about my love life, which ultimately would turn into me being given sympathetic looks and told not to worry because 'it'll happen' if I just 'hang in there'. That's a whole five years of being made to feel like I was on the reject pile when it came to love.

I wasn't prepared to receive the same treatment yet again, as I watched Maddy and Robert act all loved up, as though the past few weeks had never happened. I'd decided I was going to have someone wonderful on my arm to avoid the glum chat. To make me feel like an equal and, hopefully, to help me enjoy what would otherwise be a very dreary night.

I knew Maddy wouldn't be overjoyed, but hoped she'd be able to understand that I couldn't just watch her walk away from me. I had to occupy myself – keep my heart busy.

Maddy

Twenty-one years old . . .

The weekend after our double date, we all went back to Peaswood. It was my dad's fiftieth birthday and a big party had been planned to celebrate. The hall in our local community club had been booked, a mullet-coiffed DJ hired and a few dozen blue and silver helium balloons had been puffed up for decoration.

After all the drama of the previous weeks I had been thrilled to be going home, back to familiar surroundings where everything was once so simple. However, our calm little house had been taken over for the weekend and turned into chaotic madness. With distant relatives invading us to share in the celebrations, there was a battle over the bathrooms, hairdryers and any tiny little space as we all fought to get ourselves ready for the party.

At seven twenty-five on the dot, once my hair was in a high bun and I'd managed to squeeze myself into my floor-length emerald dress, the taxis arrived. As the rest of the family cascaded into the waiting cars, Mum turned to me with her hand on her forehead.

'I completely miscalculated how many of us there were.'

'Huh?' I frowned, slipping my feet into my heels. 'I'll just squeeze in the back.'

'No, the driver won't allow that. You wait here and I'll send someone back for you.'

'But, Mum . . .' I whined, hating the idea of being left behind and having to turn up on my own.

'That way I can check everything's okay with the hall before everyone else arrives. Thanks, love,' she flustered, before giving me a kiss on the cheek and running out the door.

Rather bemused, I sat on the stairs and waited.

After about five minutes, the doorbell rang. I opened it to find Robert, looking dashing in a grey suit, his blond hair slicked back into a stylish quiff. Somehow, despite all the recent events and how much he'd hurt me, he still managed to take my breath away.

'Did Mum send you?' I asked, reaching for my clutch bag.

'Not quite.'

'What do you mean . . . did you ask her to leave me behind?'

'Maybe,' he smiled, looking nervous, still wary of how I might act around him. 'I just thought it would be nice to go together. We've not had a night out like this since, well, I think it was our sixth-form ball.'

'I guess not.'

'This is for you,' he offered, pulling a corsage from behind his back. A thick row of gorgeous pearled beads made up the band, on to which was attached a deep red rose. 'May I?' he asked, gesturing for my wrist.

I couldn't help but smile then. It was exactly the same as the corsage he'd given me on the night of our ball three years before, when he had, again, picked me up from my doorstep and escorted me.

'This is very nice,' I smiled, appreciating the effort.

'Thank you,' he said softly, looking bashful.

Once the house was locked up, I took hold of his arm and let him lead me to the taxi, where he opened and closed the door for me like a gentleman.

As the car started moving and we sat in silence with our hands entwined, I felt closer to Robert than I had in weeks. I shut my eyes and rested my head on his shoulder, allowing myself to enjoy the warmth I'll admit I'd begun to miss.

The car stopped sooner than I expected. To my dismay I opened my eyes to find we were outside Ben's house. Not only was he walking towards the car, but so was Alice – something I was completely unprepared for.

The joy I'd been experiencing suddenly vanished, I was back to the same unsettled feeling I'd had before I'd come home. Despite the effort he was making, I instantly became angry at Robert for not realizing he should have just kept it as the two of us.

After a courteous hello to Ben and Alice, I stayed quiet for the rest of the ten-minute journey, I sulked in the corner, allowing my frustrations to rise dramatically.

Needless to say, Ben's arrival at the party with Alice managed to get dozens of tongues wagging as our families speculated over the significance of it. They cooed over whether she could she be 'the one', like Ben's love life was some sort of prophecy to be fulfilled. It was all anyone wanted to talk about.

And they played quite the perfect couple. Ben had stuck by her side all night, taking care that she always had a drink in her hand, was introduced to everyone, and that they had fun on the dance floor – watching them slow dance together was excruciating. It felt as though Ben was flaunting his new relationship, letting me know that he was fine. He'd found someone else. Someone better. It hurt to be so easily and quickly replaced. And yes, I liked Alice. I thought she was a lovely girl, but I didn't want her perfectness to be rammed down my throat and to have all our parents talk about how great she was and how happy Ben looked.

Robert tried to continue being the gentleman he'd shown me at the start of the night, and was, to his credit, just as attentive as Ben was with Alice, but I rebuked and rebuffed every advance as I found fault with his every move. I became a grump for the rest of the night. I snapped at Robert more than was necessary, and generally walked around like I had a huge thunderous cloud above my head, threatening to strike him with a bolt of lightning whenever he irritated me. I'm surprised he remained by my side and didn't run for the door.

Unfortunately for me, when I snapped at him because he hadn't noticed his shoelace was undone (it seemed like a massive deal at the time), my mum overheard. She leaned over to me as though she was giving me a motherly embrace, but her hand clamped on my arm with a little too much pressure to be comforting.

'I don't know what's got into you, young lady, but snap out of it,' she hissed through her teeth, continuing to smile at the other guests who were looking in our direction. They were unaware that Mum was telling off her twenty-one-year-old daughter who was, I'll confess, acting like a five-year-old . . . and a spoilt brat.

The rest of the night wasn't much of an improvement – my mood stayed dark and stroppy, something that wasn't helped by me watching Ben and Alice like a crazy, unhinged stalker. I tried my best to avoid any conversations with our family friends and relatives, preferring to sit in the dark festering in my self-pity.

I hated Robert for shagging some slutty stranger whilst blowing apart our version of perfect and for thinking so little of me as he did so.

I hated Ben for ripping open my heart and then leaving it to bleed while he gaily sauntered around with his new girlfriend.

But mostly, I hated myself for not having the answers to make everything better.

Needless to say, I wasn't in the jovial mood required for parties.

Unfortunately for me and my new friend, the-big-black-cloud-of-doom, my room had been given away to family for the night, with Mum and Carol planning for me to stay with Robert. For once I wished our mums were stricter about us sharing a bed at home.

As soon as we got back to his box room I got into my nightie, curled up under the sheets and pretended to be fast sleep.

I'm not sure whether he knew I was faking or not, but after he'd got into bed and turned out the light, he faced me and let out a desperate sigh.

'I love you so much, Maddy,' he whispered.

I said nothing, but kept my eyes clamped shut.

'All I wanted to do tonight was remind you of a happier time, before I screwed everything up . . . I guess I failed.'

His breathing became erratic then. I'm not sure whether he had a lump in his throat or whether he was actually crying, but I wished he'd stop. It wasn't just him who'd failed us. I had too.

'I made a mistake. A stupid, horrible, mistake that I will regret for the rest of my life. I don't want to lose you. I couldn't bear that. You know, I'd do anything for you to forgive me, Mad. Just tell me how I can make that happen . . .'

It took a whole lot of stubbornness for me not to blub at his words. I was aware of how I was treating him and was annoyed at myself for being a complete cow as I tried to push him away – perhaps as a means to find atonement for my own mistakes. I still don't understand why Robert allowed me to treat him in the way I did, or why he didn't pull me up on my behaviour and tell me I was being unfair. He was probably scared of what might have happened if he did. I can't blame him for that.

The morning after the party I made my way downstairs while Robert was still asleep, hoping to make a quick escape back to mine. Instead, I was stopped by Carol. She appeared from the kitchen as though she'd been waiting for me, looking like she'd been up for hours with her short blonde hair perfectly set and her make-up reapplied.

'Want to come have a cuppa before you leave, Maddy?'

'Well, I really should be making a move, I've got to drive back today . . .'

'Come on, five minutes won't hurt. It would be good to sit and have a chat with you. I never get to see much of you any more.'

Guilt-tripped into it, I agreed.

'But I really can't stay long,' I warned.

Placed on the kitchen counter was a pot of tea, two mugs, a jug of milk and a bowl of sugar, and a basket of warm croissants and Danishes, confirming my earlier suspicion that she'd been waiting for me. Carol placed an apricot Danish (my favourite) on a plate and slid it in front of me before pouring us both some tea.

Feeling tentative, I pulled the pastry apart and nibbled on it slowly, anything to fill the silence that fell upon us. I could feel Carol looking at me, I knew she wanted to say something. I guessed she'd realized something was up with Robert and me and that she was trying to find out what. Carol was quite a nosy mum when she wanted to be – all our mums were. They always wanted to know exactly what was going on in our lives and to add their two pence worth to any situation, even if we hadn't asked for their advice. My plan was to act dumb, pretend she'd picked up on nothing and to dismiss the whole thing.

'Robert told me about what's been going on lately,' she sighed.

'Oh.'

Well, that completely threw me. Robert was always a high-achiever, a child for his parents to be proud of. I was surprised he'd risked denting that wonderful reputation by confessing to his mum, a woman who had often been very vocal with her thoughts on married men who strayed. You should have heard her talk about Ben's dad – he might as well have been the devil himself the way she went on.

'I can't say I wasn't disappointed, but I'm glad he told

me — that he's owning up to his mistake,' she said, shaking her head before hesitantly continuing. 'The thing is, Maddy, and I'm sorry to butt in like this . . .'

'What's wrong?'

'I saw the way you two were together last night. You and Robert.'

'I was just drunk,' I shrugged, with a lie. I hadn't touched a drop all night, it was the only way I could be sure I wouldn't say or do anything I'd end up regretting. It clearly hadn't worked, but I could only imagine the fallout if I'd had a drink or two to boot.

'Were you?' she asked, busying herself by pouring two sugars into her tea and giving it a good stir.

I stared into my mug and longed for the chat to be over. Getting pulled up for my bad behaviour by my own mum was bad enough, but having Robert's mum do it too was agony.

'I'm not saying you're wrong to punish him, not at all. What I'm thinking, Maddy, is that you have to either forgive him and move on, and try and make things work, or you don't.'

'It's not that simple,' I muttered.

Of course, Carol had told me off with the boys when we were younger for our general naughtiness, but that was always as a collective, I'd never been singled out. I knew she was talking to me in her kitchen because of the appalling way I'd been treating her son. I couldn't help but be sheepish. I didn't blame her for getting involved, though. After all, I'm sure any mum would be protective over their son. I knew she just wanted to help talk some sense into the situation.

'Oh, I know that. Believe me, every relationship goes through its testing times. It happens to the best of us.'

I looked up to see Carol raising her eyebrows at me, giving me a precarious smile.

It was a rather unsubtle hint that something scandalous had happened between her and Richard at some point in their marriage, although she failed to give any further information on when, which of them, or who with. She knew she'd made her point just by alluding to it – even couples who might appear to be perfectly close and happy go through their fair share of troubles. It also explained, if Richard were the guilty party, why she had such a strong reaction to others who'd done the same.

'It's how you pull through it all, darling, that lets you know whether what you have is worth saving or not. But you've got to be willing to try, otherwise there's no point in putting either of you through further heartache.'

'It's just difficult.'

'Relationships are hard work,' she nodded, agreeing with me. 'And, sadly, getting into trouble and jeopardizing what you have is far too easy in comparison. But I know my son, Maddy. He's made his mistake. He won't be making another one. You've got to learn to trust him again.'

'I just don't know how to begin to do that.'

'Patience, love and understanding will take you a long way.'

I cried then. Again! Years of growing up with boys had meant crying was hardly ever an option, but in those couple of months it seemed I'd lost all control of my tear ducts. They wept freely.

As Carol walked around the counter and put her arms

around me, I knew I had to release the anger that had been floating around inside of me. What was done was done. There was no going back and changing it. I had to move forward. Forgive Robert. Forgive myself.

The world had not decided to stop and grace me with some thinking time, it had, instead, pushed on and presented us with Alice. I knew that I had to move forward, I just needed to work out how. I needed to focus on what I did have, rather than what I didn't – just like I'd promised Pearl I would do the week before.

Robert wasn't Ben, but nor did I want him to be. He had a million of his own qualities that had made me happily fall in love with him all those years before. It became apparent in my mind that I needed to remind myself what they were, and be grateful for the amazing guy I had in my life.

Pearl was waiting for me on the sofa when I returned home that night, with a cup of tea and some much-needed chocolate Hobnobs. They made up a large part of her staple diet at university – I've no idea how she managed to maintain her size-ten figure with the number of packets she went through.

'How was it?' she asked, taking a biscuit out of the packet and dunking it in her tea. She pulled a grimace as she waited for my reply, rightly assuming that I wouldn't have had the best time of my life.

'Awful.'

'Crap.'

'I was a right bitch.'

'Oh dear. Still confused?'

'Actually, no,' I said with a smile, taking a gulp of my tea and reaching for the packet. 'I think I'm on the verge of having a mental clear-out. I should be fine soon . . .'

'Glad to hear it,' she smiled back. 'I've been thinking while you've been gone. I understand, honestly I do. You three have been inseparable for years and now this guy you've loved as a friend speaks up and turns it into something else. He gave you another option when things had gone a bit shit. But face it, he led you to a fucking big crossroads and then walked off with the map.'

'Ha! Great analogy.'

Pearl winked at me, but continued with her line of thought.

'What you need to realize is that you don't need that map. You just have to decide which road you want to take . . .'

'What's this? Is my cockney east-Londoner going all sentimental on me?' I joked, giving her a playful shove on the shoulder.

'No chance . . .' she laughed. 'All I'm saying is choose your love story and stick to it.'

Choose my love story and stick to it . . . I liked that. I liked that a lot.

I'd also like to thank all of our parents, not just mine and Maddy's, but June – you too, you've certainly been a mum to us both over the years. So thanks to you all for helping the three of us out and for being there with your endless support and pearls of wisdom. Whether we've asked for your input or wanted to hear it is a different matter but . . . only joking. You guys have always known best, so, thank you.

Ben

Twenty-four years old

By the time my twenty-fourth birthday arrived I was living in a flat share in Bethnal Green with Alice, and had been for over a year. We'd found the place on Gumtree – a room in a two-bed flat, on the fourth floor. It was tiny and meant we'd had to leave the majority of our belongings in my mum's garage, but it would do. It was cheap and central. We shared the place with an IT consultant called Kevin, who seemed to be out drinking most nights, so we usually had the whole flat to ourselves.

Before that, straight after university, I'd gone back to my mum's in Peaswood. Robert wanted us all to get a place together, but, for obvious reasons, I wasn't keen on the idea. I excused myself, explaining that I needed to find a job and save before I could even think about renting a place. He sulked for a bit but decided not to put any more pressure on me, thankfully.

It was strange being back in my old room, squeezed in with all my old toys and memories, and having my mum fussing over me again – but luckily Alice had moved in with her sister near Brick Lane, so I was there a lot, escaping the motherly furore – she was excited and it came from the right place, it was just overbearing after years of total freedom.

Being a newbie freelance Graphic Designer was tough. I had no contacts, no experience, just my portfolio filled with coursework. In fact, I guess the good thing about living at home with Mum was that I could get some internships and work for free, building up relationships as I went, hoping that it would build into something more. It did. I eventually fell in with a film production company, who employed me each time they were in production. Just that tiny chance opened up the doors to other great opportunities, and I was truly thankful. So, after a further two years at home, I was finally earning a regular-enough income to move out of home. I was thrilled – so was Alice when I asked her if she fancied living together. She was so unassuming and never tried to force me into thinking about the future and where we were headed – I liked that about her.

Robert and Maddy had moved home for the summer, as I had, but then quickly moved back out again. Robert had landed on his feet straight away and bagged himself a job as a PE teacher at a posh all-boys school in West London. As he was awarded a regular salary with twelve weeks *paid* holiday a year, they could afford to rent a pretty flat in Chiswick – a beautiful corner of the capital for yummy mummies and creative types. The picture-perfect couple fitted in nicely.

Maddy struggled to get paid work for her photography straight away, so, after years of studying decided to work in a local art shop instead – the plan was that she'd do that until something else popped up, but even after she started up her small, yet successful, business taking family portraits, she agreed to stay on there a few days a week. I think she liked the stability of knowing when she was going to have money coming in, plus they were lenient about her switching her days off if a shoot came up.

She still took her camera everywhere she went – eager to catch life at its best.

We all saw each other every Sunday, without fail, taking it in turns to travel across London to do so. They were still my bestest buds, although, by that point, Alice had been added to the mix, making us a neat little foursome.

Maddy had been right, things had got better over time. Not seeing her every day had certainly helped, although I'm gutted to admit that she never strayed far from my thoughts. The distance made me miss them both, but mostly her, and excited to see them each weekend as a result. The love I'd felt never faded, even though I was happy that a new love had blossomed with Alice – the sweetest girl I'd ever known.

I still visited my mum in Peaswood all the time. Yes, she did irritate me when I'd moved back home, but as soon as I moved out again I missed her terribly. My dad leaving when I was so young was an awful thing to deal with, but, by that point, I'd spent the majority of my life with it being just the two of us. I was used to it. I never forgot that, in many ways, I was her life. So despite me living elsewhere, I made sure I gave her as much time as I could so that she was never by herself for too long. Not that she minded being alone – she'd not had a man in her life since my dad left all those years ago, but I'd never heard her moan, making me wish I'd inherited some of her thick skin.

She spent most of her evenings either with, or on the phone to, Carol. Our mums were still as inseparable as they'd been all those years before when we were younger. It was great to know Mum had people around her when I wasn't there.

One Wednesday night, just after Christmas, I'd gone over to hers for dinner. Alice was covering an event for the magazine she worked for so I was on my own. I knew something was up as soon as I walked through the door. She couldn't stop smiling, as though she knew something but wasn't allowed to say. I said nothing, just waited, knowing she'd tell me whatever it was if she wanted to – thinking it was probably something village-gossip-related that I wouldn't be too interested in anyway.

We sat down to dinner (I was stuffing my face with her delicious homemade steak pie), when she finally cracked.

'Okay, okay, okay,' she said excitedly, waving her arms in the air, her grin getting bigger with each second that passed. 'I'm not meant to say anything, but then, you probably know already so there's no point us both pretending we don't know when we do.'

'What are you talking about?' I asked – I couldn't help but smile back, she was totally giddy over the news she'd been told, and I rarely saw her like that – like a naughty teenager, unable to keep a secret.

'Oh, give over,' she said, tapping my arm across the table, as though I was playing with her. 'You clearly know. I can see it on your face.'

'I don't, Mum. Honestly.'

'Why are you smiling like that, then?'

'Because I've never seen you act like this before, that's why.'

'Oh . . .' she said, suddenly unsure whether she should carry on or not. 'Well, perhaps I should keep it a secret, then. You don't want to hear it from me. Forget I said anything.'

'Mum! Go on, you can't leave it there.'

'Ah, it's just too exciting to keep from you, and there's no one else I can tell,' she practically screamed, bursting with happiness. 'Robert's gone and asked for permission.'

'What sort of permission?'

'Don't be daft. To ask Maddy to marry him. He went over to see Kathryn and Greg yesterday – Carol told me this morning. They're all so excited.'

I should have guessed it would happen one day. They'd been together since they were sixteen and had lived with each other for three years – it was the next step, we weren't kids any longer. The feelings it conjured shocked me – I was happy for them, but, mostly, I was sad. Sad that, if there was ever any doubt about the matter, Maddy and I would never have a chance of being together. It was a selfish thought, but it arose in me nonetheless, causing me to be annoyed at my heart for betraying me after all those years.

'Didn't he say anything to you?'

'No,' I said, managing to smile at my mother's beaming face.

'I expect he wanted it to be a surprise for you too. Oh, it'll be a lovely day for all of you really, not just them two.'

'Do you know when he's going to do it?'

'No idea, love. Next few weeks or months, though, I'd have thought. I don't think he has a ring yet.'

'Wow.'

'I know. Exciting, huh? Better get looking for a hat!' she beamed, unable to hide her excitement. 'Ooh, and, well, I know Rob's got two brothers, but I'm sure you'll be best man. You'll have to do a speech and everything. We can go through the loft and dig out some old photos. I think we've even got some from when I first met Carol. Yes, some great ones of you two eating ice cream in your prams, it's all over your faces.'

I played along with her joy, trying to ignore the panic stirring within me at the thought of losing Maddy, the girl I'd tried so hard not to love.

That Saturday night Alice and I were on our sofa watching *The Jonathan Ross Show*, tucking into an Indian takeaway – something we treated ourselves to more than we ought to. It was a bad habit that had lingered with us since our university days.

'Do you ever think about the future?' I asked, topping up our glasses of wine, of which we'd had quite a few – another bad habit that had carried over from student life.

'In what way?' she asked, mopping up some pilau rice that had escaped from her plate and fallen onto her lap.

'I dunno, what you think it'll be like?'

'Well, when I was six we were asked to draw a picture of what we thought the millennium would look like – I drew some elaborate flying car and a robotic dog. My teacher said I was unrealistic but imaginative . . . I guess I'm still waiting for my flying car to be invented,' she shrugged with a giggle.

'Not like that. I mean, where do you see yourself in five or ten years' time?'

'Oh,' she tutted, tapping her fork against the side of her plate as she thought of her answer. 'Editor of my own glossy magazine, with my own office overlooking the river – a vast upgrade from the shambolic mess I currently work in . . .'

'Nice,' I encouraged, watching her forehead crease as she contemplated her future.

'Living in a massive house with a swimming pool and a pink Ferrari on the swooping driveway.'

'Pink? Not red?'

'This is my vision, not yours. Am I being unrealistic again? Was my teacher right?'

'Not at all,' I laughed. 'You can have your pink Ferrari.'

'Good. I'll also be married to some charming man, whoever he may be,' she chuckled. 'And mum to a few delightful sprogs.'

'Sounds wonderful.'

'Doesn't it?' she laughed. 'You?'

'Same,' I nodded

'Editor of a magazine?'

'Obviously not, but the rest of it works.'

'Marriage and kids? Most guys our age would run a mile at the very thought of it,' she said, taken aback by the revelation as she raised her eyebrows.

'Not me.'

As we sat there smiling at each other, over our chicken tikka masalas, the next words spurted from my mouth before I'd even had a chance to think them through properly.

'Will you marry me?'

It wasn't just me they'd surprised – Alice's wide-eyed look told me that I'd completely caught her off guard too. Just like me, she hadn't been expecting it.

We sat in silence, looking at each other with our mouths open in shock.

'What did you say?' she asked, her voice wavering with emotion.

'I think I just asked you to marry me,' I laughed nervously.

'Did you mean it? There's still time to take it back, if not.'

'Do you want me to take it back?'

'Not at all . . .'

We laughed then, broke down in giggles over the grown-up thing we were committing to.

'So, will you? Will you be my wife?'

'Of course I will. Yes!' she beamed.

It was the most unromantic proposal in the world. Unplanned, unnecessary and done purely because I'd been scared of my own feelings. Petrified that I wasn't over Maddy and aware of just how much it was going to hurt watching her walk down the aisle towards someone else. I was in need of having my own future secured to give myself a little piece of armour, so that I'd be okay when that day finally came. It was the most selfish thing I'd ever done.

Maddy

Twenty-four years old

It was Ben and Alice's turn to head out our way that Sunday and, rather than stick to the High Road, we decided to go down to the Old Ship – a pub that sat on the river with great scenic views of the city. We'd found it the previous summer and loved spending our warm nights under the twinkling fairy lights which hung over their wooden benches. It was just as heaving in the winter months, but luckily we'd booked a table. The place was rammed with people who'd gone for walks along the river only to find themselves in need of warming up after being frozen by the bitterly cold December air – families fooled into not wearing enough layers of clothing by the bright blue skies.

Robert and I were sitting in our window seats, people-watching the walking ice-pops, when Ben and Alice arrived, both looking rather pleased with themselves as they fought their way through the other diners. Hugs, squeezes (not that sort) and kisses were shared before they whipped off their jackets and sat in their seats. The drinks hadn't even been ordered by the time Alice leaned across, unable to contain her excitement any longer, and shrieked out their news.

'We're getting married! Ben asked me last night. You're

the first people we're telling,' she giggled, before looking at Ben with admiration. 'We've not even told our parents yet.'

There was an indisputable momentary hiatus, which probably shouldn't have occurred, as Robert and I looked to Ben for confirmation. I knew the cause of my own surprise, but not Robert's.

'It's true,' Ben laughed, grabbing hold of her hand and beaming back at us.

They looked ridiculously happy and in love.

'Wow! Congratulations,' I smiled.

'Brilliant, just brilliant,' added Robert, with a slight edge to his voice.

It didn't take me long to notice the absence of a diamond ring, letting me assume the proposal had been a hasty decision on Ben's part. I wondered why. I'd thought Alice might have been pregnant, that Ben was keen to do the right thing by her and their unborn baby, but as Prosecco was ordered to toast their engagement and swiftly drunk by Alice, the idea was quickly erased. There was no baby. In fact, as the afternoon wore on, Ben revealed that he hadn't intended on asking the question, it popped out and surprised him just as much as it had Alice. Not that either of them seemed to mind its spontaneity; the fact that it was an off-the-cuff decision seemed, to them, to make the whole thing more romantic.

I liked Alice a lot. I even liked her and Ben together. Having her there, as a part of our group, had, in the end, made life easier for the pair of us. Everything was less awkward with her around. She made it easier to pretend certain feelings had never been an issue, that boundaries had never been crossed. I hadn't, however, expected Ben to ask her to marry him. Ever. The thought hadn't even crossed my mind.

I'd taken Pearl's advice all those years before, and reminded myself of her words regularly; that day was one of those times, as I realized I wasn't the only one who'd chosen their path and stuck to it. It occurred to me that, if Ben was willing to make such a grand gesture, prompted by the love he felt for Alice, I was far from his mind. I can't deny it, the truth stung probably more than it should have.

Alice radiated joy that afternoon, she had a real sparkle of happiness in her eyes – and talked non-stop. Clearly buzzing with elation as she reeled off endless possible ideas for their wedding, all the while smiling at Ben as though we weren't even there. The omission was probably a good thing, as neither of them seemed to notice the lull coming from our side of the table. Yes, I wasn't the only one dubious about the sudden announcement – Robert seemed off about it too. He acted strangely all afternoon, was quieter than usual and appeared agitated, not that he admitted to it.

'You okay?' I asked as we walked the short journey back to our house, holding hands through our matching black gloves. Even though we both had on our thick winter coats, mine mustard yellow, his black, the wind managed to work its way in and chill our bones wherever it could, causing my jaw to chatter uncomfortably as we talked.

'Yeah. Course,' he frowned.

'Weird to think that one of us will be getting married,' I laughed, trying to prompt him into a conversation.

'Yeah.'

'I never thought it would be Ben going first, though.'

'You're telling me,' he answered glumly.

'They both seem really happy about it.'

'Yeah.'

'Wondered if she was pregnant at first.'

'Me too.'

'She's not, though.'

'No.'

'You sure you're okay, Rob?' I asked, getting irritated with his monosyllabic responses.

'What? Yeah. Just got a lot on,' he sighed. 'School stuff.'

'Right.'

I knew he was lying, but didn't want to push any conversation involving Ben. My guess was that he was just disgruntled because Ben, his bestest buddy, hadn't shared the news with him first – or given any warning that it might have been a possibility.

It was also possible that he could have been a bit sad to realize that they were about to become even more divided than ever. Before I'd come along they'd been an indivisible duo, by each other's side night and day, but since we were eighteen they'd become more and more separated – first by university, then by living apart. I wondered whether he was worried marriage would separate them even further. Robert might put on a tough exterior, but his friendship with Ben was something he always treasured and valued highly.

Sometimes men were more complex than women gave them credit for. I left him to his own thoughts, knowing that, if he wanted to share them, he'd do so in his own time.

He never did.

Ben

Twenty-four years old . . .

Robert had decided to tell Carol about me suddenly popping *the* question. I knew this because on Monday morning I woke up to find six missed calls from my mum. The fact she'd tried to call so many times did not bode well. I could envisage the steam from her ears increasing each time she hit the redial button, only for her call to be left unanswered.

Deciding to bite the bullet and get the conversation over with, I called her back straight away from under my duvet, closing my eyes in preparation for the bollocking I was about to receive. Following our conversation the previous week I knew, once my mum found out, I'd have to own up to being a prize idiot, or plead ignorance . . . whatever I said, there was no way she was going to let me act as though I'd done nothing wrong, or let me get away with it.

'What on earth have you gone and done?' she shouted down the phone. I was glad Alice had already left for work, otherwise she'd have definitely heard her shrieking tone, and I've no idea how I'd have explained that one.

'I thought you'd be pleased,' I said. That was a lie. I knew Mum would be angry at me, I just hoped her anger would subside quick enough so that I could take Alice over to celebrate – the longer I left it the more suspicious she'd become; I didn't want her thinking my mum didn't like her. That was why I'd said we should wait before telling our parents – suggesting it would be nicer to do it once we had the ring and could tell them face to face. Alice, who, unsurprisingly, liked the idea of getting her finger blinged up first needed little convincing.

'You said you liked Alice,' I cheekily continued.

'Oh, I do, you know that,' she said, thankfully losing a bit of the honking volume in her voice. 'And, yes, I'm very pleased that Alice is going to be a Gilbert one day.'

'Well, then . . .'

'That's really not the point, though, is it?' she continued.

'Isn't it?'

'No, and you know it, Ben,' she said with exasperation. 'I told you what Robert had planned.'

'And?'

'And? And?!' she shouted. 'Less than a week later you've gone and ruined it.'

'How?'

'By getting in there first, that's how.'

'Mum, it's not like that.'

'Just tell me one thing, had the thought even crossed your mind before I told you about Robert asking Kathryn and Greg? Answer me honestly.'

I screwed up my face before giving her my answer.

'No.'

I couldn't lie about that, besides, it was more of a leading question than an actual inquiry – she knew what I was going to say before I said it.

'Oh, Ben,' she groaned.

'What?'

'What have you done?'

'Nothing, Mum . . . it's not going to affect him doing it.'

'Of course it is, he's not going to ask her now, is he? He'll have to wait – and not just weeks, months!'

I hadn't even thought of it like that, but Mum was obviously right. There was no way Robert would ask straight after I had – even if his own proposal was going to be properly thought through and planned. He wouldn't want his proposal to overshadow mine (he was gentlemanly like that) or, even worse, for it to look like he was only doing it because I had. Maddy would have hated the overlap of celebrations, and he knew it. I'd realized he was annoyed the day before – he'd been full of smiles when we first walked in but then hardly said a word after Alice told them, other than to mutter his congratulations. It occurred to me later that, having sought Maddy's parents' approval, I might have been next on his list of people to speak to about it – perhaps he'd have found a quiet moment at the pub to tell me – the idea made me feel crap. I'd been so apprehensive about Maddy's response that I hadn't even thought about what might have been going through Rob's mind.

Maddy didn't even flinch at the news. A smile broke out on her face within seconds as she showered us with congratulations, seemingly delighted for us. It put into perspective how little past events must have meant to her, forcing me into focusing on Alice, basking in her smile as I reminded myself of all the things I loved about her, why marrying her was a good idea and why I didn't need Maddy.

'Sorry, Mum,' I mumbled.

'A bit too late for that, isn't it?'

'I just didn't think.'

'You're telling me.'

'Okay, so I hadn't thought about asking before you mentioned it,' I rambled, hating the fact that Mum was clearly disappointed with me. 'But hearing that made me think about Alice and me, about our future and what I wanted. I admit, I stupidly got too excited about asking and it slipped out when I hadn't meant it to.'

I was greeted with silence from the other end of the line.

'Mum?'

'If I wasn't so annoyed with you I'd almost find that romantic, Benjamin Gilbert,' she laughed, as it became apparent she'd been holding back her tears.

I was grateful to have won her over.

'I rang Maddy earlier,' Alice told me that night, as she grabbed vegetables out of the fridge to go into the dinner. The chicken was already in the wok, so we were halfway towards sitting down with our stir-fry with sweet chilli sauce – I was ravenous, it already smelt amazing.

'Oh, really?'

Maddy and Alice talking on the phone wasn't something that happened all the time, but the two of them had managed to grow quite close over the years – hardly surprising seeing as we were all hanging out together every weekend. It would have been weird if they weren't friends.

'Yeah,' she continued, plonking a pepper, carrot and some baby sweetcorn on the kitchen side to be chopped and sliced. 'Well, I suddenly thought – remember that lovely shoot she did with that couple last year, when they got engaged?'

'Yeah . . .' I said slowly, concerned as to where the conversation was going.

I remembered the shoot – Maddy had taken the couple down to the river and snapped some great pictures of them together while they gazed lovingly into each other's eyes as though they hadn't a care in the world. I liked them. I thought Maddy had done a wonderful job. I mean, they were cheesy beyond belief, but I don't think it's possible to do such a shoot without a little bit of Cheddar being thrown in. All those lovey-dovey looks and smug faces as you congratulate each other on finding 'the one' – it's definitely not for the cynics out there. That's for sure.

'Well,' Alice grinned, looking pleased with herself. 'I thought we could do that.'

'Really?'

I was far too negative straight away, screwing my face up in horror. Alice was quite taken aback by the reaction, instantly becoming defensive.

'All right, not if you don't want to.'

'Huh?'

'If you think it's a stupid idea then we won't,' she huffed, picking up the pepper and aggressively chopping it into chunky rings before chucking them into the wok and stirring them in.

'I didn't say that.'

'You're being all hesitant and weird,' she said, brushing her fringe out of her eyes with the back of her hand.

'Am I?'

I was. I knew I was. I can't deny it.

'Yes. It doesn't matter if you don't want to do it,' she said dismissively, picking up the carrot. 'It was just a thought.'

'Isn't it a bit cheesy?'

'You didn't think so when she showed us them, in fact you really liked them.'

Like I said, I did. I couldn't argue with that.

'Won't it be weird having Maddy do it for us, though?' I suggested.

'She's your best friend, Ben. How many photos has she taken of us over the years?'

'True,' I mumbled.

'I just thought it would be a nice thing to do. Give our parents some lovely pictures of us,' she muttered, her face falling with disappointment. 'It's no big deal.'

'You're right,' I nodded enthusiastically. 'Let's do it.' There was no way I could possibly get out of it and I didn't want to upset Alice if it was something she really wanted to do – it was only taking pictures, after all.

'Really? You mean it?'

'Yeah. Why not.'

'Great,' she smiled, banging on the kitchen side with delight.

'So, what did Maddy say?'

'She said she'd love to – she was in the middle of something when I called, but she said she'd get back to me later on with some dates.'

'Marvellous.'

Maddy

Twenty-four years old . . .

I'd been sat on my backside in the rather dead art shop when Alice called. It wasn't manic and I wasn't busy. I just felt the sudden urge to get off the phone to her and call her back when I was mentally prepared.

Of course, I'd taken hundreds of photos of them before, they were all over my Facebook page, so it's not like I was averse to them being a couple or shied away from picturing them together. But taking photos of days out or when people are drunk and giddy is quite different to doing a shoot based on their love for each other. It's not that I felt I couldn't bear to see Ben and Alice together, or like I was worried feelings would start stirring in me again, more that I felt like I would be a big fat fraud taking the photos for them. *That* was my problem.

I sat in the shop for the rest of the afternoon and glumly thought about the best thing to do. In the end, after much deliberation, I came to the conclusion that I was worrying over nothing. If Alice had asked it meant that she must have spoken to Ben first, and if he hadn't been bothered about it then perhaps I'd been over-thinking it. Three years had passed since our one night together. I reasoned it was silly of me to keep thinking of it so highly and giving it such importance, especially as Ben was clearly so happy and in love . . . as was I.

I phoned Alice back later that night. Robert was watching the football in the other room and I'd just cleaned up after dinner. I sat at the kitchen counter, gulping on a large glass of rosé, while I waited for her to pick up.

'It's Maddy,' I heard her whisper, presumably to Ben, as she brought the phone to her ear. 'Hello, you.'

'Hey, Alice. So sorry about earlier, there was a sudden mad rush. All of Chiswick's loyal art collectors must have dashed out at once to find something new.'

'Not at all, don't worry,' she laughed. 'I should've called tonight when I knew you were at home. It just suddenly popped into my head and I got a bit excited about the idea.'

'Honestly, it's no problem at all,' I smiled, still finding her cheeriness as infectious as ever.

'So, what do you think? Are you up for doing something similar with us?'

'Yes, definitely. I think it'll be a lovely thing for you guys to do.'

'Nothing mad, we don't need to go crazy with it – just some of us wrapped up all cosy and walking along somewhere pretty would be lovely. Something nice and chilled so that Ben doesn't feel like an idiot.'

'That sounds doable,' I nodded to myself.

'Are you sure it's okay?'

'Definitely. Consider it an engagement present from us,' I offered.

'Oh, Maddy, thank you. That's so kind. We could even

do it when we come to you next, if you like? Save you lugging all your equipment across London.'

'Are you sure?'

'Yes! It makes sense.'

'Perfect. Robert can be my assistant and then we'll go have dinner afterwards.'

'Brilliant. Thanks again, Maddy.'

'It's a pleasure,' I insisted, bringing the glass to my mouth and sloshing more wine down my gullet.

Two Sundays later we took a leisurely stroll down by the river in the wintry sunshine. Ben and Alice hand in hand, me running ahead with my camera up at my face and Robert running alongside me holding my tripod, light reflector, spare lenses, memory cards and batteries, looking like a clueless (but enthusiastic) donkey. We snapped as we went, making most of the shots natural with Ben and Alice just talking and laughing with each other, looking all cosy beneath the mountains of layers they were wearing – Alice in a khaki fitted woollen coat, thick grey tights and flat leather boots, Ben in a sheepskin coat, faded jeans and chunky Timberlands. They did their best to ignore the fact that we were even there.

I was enjoying myself. I had my photographer's head on and had managed to detach myself completely from who I was photographing. My main focus was making sure the shots all looked good through the camera, that they were framed nicely by the sparse trees and river, and that I was positioning myself correctly so that I could capture them at their best. I was relieved to be finding it so easy.

Walking along we eventually came to a pretty bend in the river, offering a great view of London's skyline in the far distance. I instantly knew it would be a lovely spot to get a few more posed shots, if they were keen.

'Okay, shall we just stop here a second?' I called, getting out of the way of a nosy group of elderly people who had been trailing behind us, trying their best to see what we were up to.

'I was thinking you guys should rest against here,' I said, tapping the barrier by the river. 'It'll be great to get some close-up stills – I think we've nailed the whole romantic walking thing now. You're pros at that.'

'What should we do?' asked Alice as she jumped into position, holding her arm out for Ben to walk into, eager to get going straight away.

'Pose like you're in love,' joked Robert.

'Thank you,' I said, shooting him a warning look to shut up, knowing his input would deter us from what was going on. ' Just snuggle into each other a bit. We can do some of you looking at one another, away dreamily into the distance as you contemplate your lifetime of happiness together and then a few down the lens.'

I ignored Robert as he scoffed next to me. That jargon usually worked for others, but I'd forgotten I had Mr Romance-Is-For-Pansies stood by my side . . . although it probably was a bit much.

I raised my camera back to my face, ready to start shooting again. And that's where it all got a bit awkward. Whereas before Ben had looked comfortable, he'd suddenly become rigid and stiff, clumsily not knowing where to put his hands or where to look. He was far from relaxed.

Seeing as he kept stealing glances in Robert's direction and cracking jokes it looked like it was just because he was embarrassed posing in the romantic way I was after.

After they'd burst out laughing for the fifth time I lowered my camera and just raised my eyebrows at them both, willing them to stop.

'Guys!'

'What?' Robert asked innocently, trying his best to keep a straight face.

'Five more minutes then we're done. Can you save being idiots until then?'

'Just forget we're here,' smirked Robert.

'It's a bit hard with that clicking going off,' Ben moaned, pointing at the camera.

'Nothing I can do about that I'm afraid. It's the shutter,' I shrugged, becoming impatient with the pair of them.

'This is just weird . . .' he grumbled uncharacteristically.

'Hey,' Alice cooed, grabbing hold of Ben's coat and pulling him into her, dragging his attention away from what was bothering him. 'Close your eyes.'

Without saying a word he sighed and did as she said. I was sure he was going to burst out laughing again, but as Alice raised her head and rubbed her nose gently against his chin, his face started to soften.

'I love you,' she whispered after a moment or two, smiling contentedly at him.

Ben opened his eyes slowly and looked at his beautiful wife-to-be, his eyes full of doe-eyed love as his face expanded in a smile.

His secret smile.

But that time, it was for her.

Not me.

That was it. As the sun reflected off the water's peaks to make enchanting shapes of light dance majestically behind them, adding to the dazzling beauty of the moment, I took one single shot.

It was the perfect picture of the perfect couple, full of admiration, devotion and completeness. It was full of love – simple, pure and uncomplicated.

Ben

Twenty-four years old . . .

I'd never been very spontaneous when it came to love. I'd also never been able to show myself off as much of a romantic either. I'd always had too many feelings that I'd had to lock away, to hide, to avoid indulging in or risk exposing a one-sided love. What I loved about being with Alice was that I could feel something and declare it straight away. I didn't have to think it through carefully or hold anything back – I'd feel it and I could say it. It was that easy. Unfortunately, as I realized too late, it led me to make big gestures, like proposing, before I'd had a chance to think it through properly.

It took me a few weeks to realize I'd made a terrible mistake by asking Alice to marry me. The more I thought about it, the more certain I became of its error.

There was no doubting that Alice was a wonderful woman. She came along and unknowingly saved my heart from utter torment – she gave me hope and made my world a little brighter each day she was in it. But I couldn't marry her. The heart she'd helped to mend wouldn't let me, no matter how much I tried to convince it otherwise.

It might have taken days for me to regret, but sadly, it took me six months to rectify. We had by that point already booked the church for the following summer, a little place in Essex near where she grew up, and Alice was on the verge of going out with her mum and best friend to find her wedding dress. It was at that point I decided I couldn't have her trying on those gowns knowing that I was doubtful about the whole thing and that, irrevocably, we weren't going to be getting married. There was no way I could ruin that special moment for her – I wanted her to be able to enjoy it one day in the future, when she did eventually marry someone who deserved her. Not someone who'd used her as some diversion tactic to get over his own hankering existence.

She was sitting on the sofa, looking through the bridal magazines that had littered our flat for the last six months, when I broke the news to her. I hovered in front of her for a few moments before the words found their way, from the loop they'd been circling in my head, out of my mouth.

'I don't want to get married,' I said.

There was no way I could dress the issue up, or find an easier way to say it. I didn't want to be one of those guys who find faults in their relationships by blaming her for things she hadn't done as I pushed her away, or picking pointless fights in the hope that she would call the whole thing off. I knew Alice was perfect, and I'd meant it every time I told her I loved her, but that didn't change the fact that I didn't want to marry her. I couldn't marry her.

She froze.

She sat there, staring at the magazine as though she was trapped in its world of pretty dresses, blossoming flowers and a forever love, the world I'd promised her months before, but was snatching away from her so abruptly.

'Did you hear me?' It was a stupid question. I knew she'd heard. I just wanted to fill the silence, to get the agonizing moment over with, to stop it from lingering any longer than necessary. 'I don't want to get married.'

A wave of heat worked its way up my back and to my cheeks, burning them as I waited for her to react.

'What do you mean?' she asked quietly, her eyes still on the page in front of her.

'What I said,' I swallowed hard, forcing myself to stay strong. 'I don't want to get married.'

'Do you not like the church?' she asked feebly, her voice thin and panicked. 'Because we can change that. Or if it's the cost, we can invite fewer people. I don't mind doing that. It doesn't have to be anything big, as long as it's you and m —'

'It's nothing to do with any of that,' I said firmly and quickly, stopping her from coming up with more petty reasons for my sudden change of heart. Hating myself, I repeated the words — as though she hadn't heard it enough times already. 'I just don't want to get married.'

Slowly she closed the magazine, its pages fanning noisily in protest as their offerings were sent into darkness, banished from our lives and from the perished Gilbert/ Turner wedding. Her hands moved to cover the face of the glowing bride on its cover, as though her gloating happiness mocked Alice in her misery.

'Then why did you ask me?'

'Because I thought I did. Then.'

Her tiny frame seemed smaller and more fragile than ever as I watched my words smash away at her heart.

'What's changed?'

'I don't know.'

'Tell me,' she said, looking up, her glistening eyes boring into mine as tears made their escape, rolling down her cheeks. 'What have I done since then to make you think otherwise?'

'Nothing.'

'I must've done something.'

'You haven't.'

'Is it just marriage you're suddenly opposed to? Or is it a lifetime with me?'

'It's not like that.'

'But you don't want to be with me.'

It wasn't a question – it was a statement. I faltered at hearing her say it out loud. It sounded so cold, so final. For a moment I wanted to take it back, to retrieve what had been said, but I couldn't. I knew, whether I told her then or at the altar, I wouldn't be marrying Alice Turner. My heart wouldn't let me marry into a lie that I'd let fester for long enough already.

'Alice, I think the world of you. I love you.'

'Don't say that. Please, Ben, don't you dare say that.'

'But I do. It's true. There's nothing I wouldn't do for you.'

'Except marry me,' she jeered sadly, raising her eyebrows, defying me to contest her words. 'Or be with me.'

'Alice . . .'

'Is there someone else?' she asked curtly, cutting me off.

'Of course not.'

'You sure? There's not some girl who's caught your attention at work? Made you think twice about being stuck with me?'

'No.'

'Then why don't you want to marry me? If there's no one else and you love me, why don't you want to be with me any more?'

'Because it's not what I want.'

'And what do you want?'

'I don't know.'

'Why are you doing this to me?' she screamed, furious with my lack of substantial responses. She hurled the mocking magazine at me, the corner of its bind catching me on my forehead, cutting it and making it bleed.

'I'm so sorry, Alice,' I shouted back.

'Sorry you ever asked?'

'No.'

'Then what for?'

'For hurting you. I never wanted to do that.'

'You saying that doesn't make it any less cruel,' she spat. 'You're still breaking my heart and making me look like a complete fool.'

I hated that I'd turned the most happy, bubbly and loving girl I'd ever met into such a ball of anger – it was yet another failure to add to my ever-growing list of mistakes.

Robert was the only one who'd known that I was calling my wedding off and ending things with Alice. I'd phoned him the morning I planned to do it.

I'd been in our bedroom, surrounded by her things and pictures of us together with giddy faces on various holidays, funny trips and *that* picture, when I'd had an overwhelming urge to leave – to just walk out and avoid the confrontation as I broke her heart. The desire was so strong I knew I had no choice but to talk to her that night. Something had snapped inside me and I was worried that if I didn't act quickly my longing simply to flee would become a reality. I didn't want that.

Leaving our room, our home, I wandered into Victoria Park and walked round in circles for hours. Surprisingly, there weren't many thoughts spiralling around in my head, it seemed it had made its mind up. Instead it numbed my doubt and affirmed the end of our relationship.

At lunchtime, when I knew Robert would be at his desk and not in lessons, I sat on a bench by the vast lake at the bottom of the park, pulled out my phone and called him.

I needed to hear the words said out loud, before I said them to Alice, and the only person in my life who would not judge me for saying them or for making the decision was Robert.

'Are you sure?' was the first thing he'd asked.

'Yes.'

'Blimey,' he puffed. 'Have you been arguing?'

'No.'

'Cheated?'

'No.'

'Has she?'

'I hope not.'

'Why, then?' he asked, sounding confused.

'It's just not right.'

'Mate, it's not just pre-wedding jitters, is it? Because once you do this, there's no going back,' he warned.

'I'm aware of that.'

'I think you should give yourself some time before you do anything drastic. You might change your mind.'

'I won't.'

'How do you know? A few months ago you wanted to marry her. Maybe sit on it for a bit,' he suggested. It wasn't like Robert to hand out rational advice, but by then my mind had been set far too long to adjust my plan and reconfigure my emotions.

'I don't need to.'

'But you might wake up in the morning and regret it.'

'I might, but I doubt it.'

'I don't know what to say.'

'There's nothing to say. It's shit.'

'Yeah . . .'

Convinced that I couldn't be talked out of it, or persuaded to wait, Robert sighed.

'Stay at mine tonight.'

'No, you don't want me there, moping around.'

'Where else are you going to go?' he asked.

I hadn't thought of that. There was no way I could expect Alice to let me stay in the flat and sleep beside her, and I wasn't ready to go home and tell Mum. I didn't want to break two women's hearts in the one night.

'Please,' Robert pushed. 'Maddy's out with Pearl anyway – think of it as keeping me company.'

'Okay.'

Knowing it was just going to be us was all the convincing I needed.

He was ready and waiting for me when I turned up on his doorstep at eleven o'clock that night, armed with two suitcases of my belongings – the upshot to living in a tiny rented bedroom was that I didn't have much to take with me when I left. Robert took me inside, handed me a beer, and sat with his arm firmly around me while I looked straight ahead, wondering how I'd managed to make such a pig's ear of everything.

I couldn't help but be reminded of sitting next to him in my treehouse all those years before, when we were just nine years old. It struck me that, all these years later, he was still there to be my anchor. I didn't even need to ask for the voiceless comfort – he was just there to console me in the way he knew I needed.

That's when I decided he deserved better than a shitty friend like me, and it wasn't just Alice I needed to get away from.

Maddy

Twenty-four years old . . .

Ben stayed on our sofa for a week following his split from Alice. He left it a few days before heading back to Peaswood to tell June there wasn't going to be a wedding. Robert went along with him for moral support. Unsurprisingly she took it well, praised him for realizing something wasn't right and bravely acting on that rather than just going along with it because he was too scared to hurt Alice's feelings. He'd been anxious before seeing her, but once he had he seemed a little happier, as though he was ready to start moving forward.

Towards the end of his stay at ours, we were having dinner (I'd made us a Mexican feast) when Ben's future was brought up for discussion.

'So, any more thoughts, Ben? What's next?' asked Robert, before stuffing a taco into his mouth, taking care not to lose any of its filling. There was no tidy way of eating the dish – it was the only one he could eat like a slob and not have me moaning at him for it.

Ben sighed at the question, put down the taco he was eating and wiped his mouth with the side of his hand.

'Now there's a question,' he smiled.

'There's no rush for you to leave here!' I explained, not wanting him to think we were hinting that he'd overstayed his welcome. Robert and I had agreed that he was welcome to stay as long as he wanted, knowing he'd do the same for either of us if ever needed.

'That's lovely of you both, but, actually, I do have a plan.'

'Oh, really? Do share.'

'I've decided I'm going to go away for a bit.'

'Great idea, a holiday would do you the world of good,' Robert nodded, slapping him on the back in encouragement before turning his attention back to the food on his plate.

'Not quite a holiday, mate. I'm going to be away longer than that.'

'What do you mean?'

'I'm going to go travelling.'

'As in backpacking?' I squeaked in surprise.

'Ha, yes.'

'But why?' asked Robert, a frown forming as he looked back up at him.

'Why not? You said it yourself, some time away will do me good.'

'I meant a week in Tenerife, or somewhere slutty like Magaluf.'

'How long will you be gone for?'

'I don't know. A year, two years, maybe.'

'Two years? What? Why that long?' demanded Robert, unable to hide the disappointment of losing his friend for that long.

'Because there's a whole world to see.'

'And you want to go on your own?' I asked, trying to ask a few sensible questions seeing as Robert was working himself up into some sort of hysteria.

'It'll be good for me,' he shrugged. 'Do a bit of soul searching.'

'Soul searching? Ben, what's really going on? You suddenly got engaged, then broke it off and dumped the loveliest girl you've ever met for no apparent reason and now you're going off? Leaving us? Why?'

'Robert,' I warned, worried that he was being too hard on Ben after everything he'd been through.

'No, Maddy, I mean it,' he said gruffly. 'What's going on?'

'I need a change. Things weren't right with Alice, even though, yes – thank you for pointing it out – she was great,' he sighed, casually picking up another taco from the table and filling it with sauce, as though he hadn't just dropped a massive bombshell on his two best friends and told us he was about to move thousands of miles away.

Robert looked at him as though he'd gone mad. I must admit that even I found the whole thing to be a rather dramatic way of getting over whatever had happened between him and Alice, but it wasn't for us to dictate what he did or where he went. We were only meant to be there for him – something that Robert, in his shock, had forgotten.

'I'm going to say this, and I don't want you to freak out on me,' Robert said slowly, looking concerned. 'Is it because of your dad?'

'What?'

'Are you worried that you're like him? That you'd wake up one day and decide to leave?' he asked, his hands to the heavens as he looked at Ben imploringly. 'Because you're so far from ever being the coward he was. You're flipping amazing, Ben. You've got nothing to worry about.'

'Thanks for the text-book analogy. But that's really not it. I know I'm nothing like him,' he assured him, his spirits luckily not dampened by his words. 'This is something I've always thought about doing at some point, I just wasn't sure when.'

'You never told me,' Robert shrugged.

'Because I was in a relationship and I guess it seemed like an unrealistic thing to do. After finishing things, it dawned on me that if I don't do it now then I never will.'

'You can't just up and leave, you've got a good thing going here.'

'Have I?' he questioned, pulling Robert up on his words.

'Yes, with work. Think about all the contacts you've worked hard to make.'

'True, but I'm also twenty-four and still acting like a student.'

'You're an artist,' Robert declared passionately. 'Aren't you meant to be all floppy-haired, wearing baggy clothes and eating Pot Noodles?'

'Thanks. You're forgetting that, right now, I'm also homeless.'

'You can just stay here,' Robert pleaded, his arms waving in the air at the space around us.

'No, I can't do that.'

'Why not?'

'Because it wouldn't be fair. Besides, it's something I really want to do,' he insisted.

'When are you thinking of going?' I asked, interrupting them, having sat quietly listening to Ben continuously rebuke Robert's attempts at changing his mind for long enough. His rough approach wasn't working. Ben was set on his plan to travel; there was no way his decision was going to be swayed.

'Soon. In a few weeks. I've got to finish some bits on the film I'm working on and then I'll set off.'

'Can you even afford it?'

'Rob, I'm flattered that you want me to stay, but cool it. I'm going,' he said gently, leaning over and laying a hand on his arm. 'And don't worry – I plan on meeting up with a few friends for some of it, seeing what work they can throw my way to make ends meet.'

'You've really thought about it?' Robert asked sadly, sighing as he started to accept Ben's plans.

'I have.'

'I'm really going to miss you, mate,' he whispered glumly.

'You too.'

It was rare to see the boys get emotional with each other like that. I just sat there and let the moment happen, touched by its potency.

Robert went up to bed soon after dinner – the joy of having to get up at six o'clock each morning meant he was always left shattered by ten at night. Having Ben there meant he tried to fight it for as long as possible, but that night, in the end, when he could hardly keep his eyes open any longer, he'd been forced to cave in and retire off to our bedroom.

Ben and I were left to tidy up the dirty plates, saucepans and everything else I'd bashed around and used while making dinner that evening. Unfortunately, we didn't have the luxury of owning a dishwasher, which meant having to do the lot by hand.

'Are you honestly okay, Ben?' I asked, as we stood side by side at the kitchen sink, him washing, me drying.

'Yeah . . .' he sighed.

'Really?' I pushed, putting down the cream tea towel I'd been using and turning to look at him, scrutinizing his face for any flickers of betraying emotion. 'Because it's okay to say, if you're not.'

'Well, I'm not the best I've ever been. But I'll be fine,' he smiled sadly, bowing his head as he distracted himself with the washing up, tackling the big silver saucepan I'd cooked the chilli con carne in with a scouring pad, trying to remove all the black burnt bits from its edges.

'Your plans sound fun.'

'Thanks.'

'Not what I thought you'd be doing.'

'Me neither. Especially not at my age.'

'It's like a delayed gap year.'

'Yes,' he laughed. 'But I'm hoping my days will be filled with more enlightenment than parties and cheap shots.'

'Enlightenment?'

'Well,' he shrugged. 'I want to explore what's out there.'

'Where will you go?'

'South America first, for six months or so – tour around Ecuador, Brazil, Argentina, Peru, anywhere and everywhere. There are places you can go that do crash courses in Spanish. They'll probably be useful, seeing as I'll be on my own.'

'Let's hope you pick it up quicker than you did French.'

'Oi!'

'I'm joking,' I cackled.

'I'm pretty sure I was the only one of us three who could order a bottle of water over in Paris.'

'If that was the extent of your French after studying it for five years, I'll stick to my earlier statement,' I mocked.

'You cheeky monkey,' he simpered, holding up a wet hand and flicking me with the water dripping from his fingertips.

'Have you heard from Alice?' I asked when I eventually stopped laughing and started drying the silver saucepan Ben had finished washing.

'No. It's weird. I thought I would, you know?'

'Really?'

'Yeah, I expected to get something from her – an angry text or a teary drunken phone call, but no. Nothing. She's far too dignified for that,' he said sorrowfully, pulling the plug out of the sink and stepping backwards to rest against the counter as the water noisily drained away. He crossed his arms over his chest and let out a sigh. 'She must hate me.'

'I'm sure she doesn't.'

Even as I said it I knew I was lying. What girl wouldn't hate the guy who'd offered to make her his wife and then decided, without any apparent reason, that it wasn't what he wanted after all? But that wasn't what Ben needed to hear at that particular moment.

'Have you spoken to her?' he asked.

'Well, I've texted her a couple of times, but she's not really said much about anything.'

It was something I wasn't sure I should do, but I felt compelled to. I'd needed to contact her. I knew Ben was my best friend and that it was our job to help him through their break-up, but I'd grown to like Alice. I'd wanted her to know that I was thinking of her. The thought of what she must have been feeling and going through was horrendous. Understandably she was still fairly cut up, although she'd gone to stay with her sister, so at least she wasn't alone with her grief.

'It's hard knowing I've hurt her so much.'

'I bet it is.'

'I was such a jerk.'

'What really happened?' I asked. It was the one thing none of us had understood – even Robert.

He groaned gently and buried his head in his hands.

'It can't have been that bad,' I pushed.

'Okay,' he said slowly, fanning his fingers over his cheeks, stretching out the skin and pulling down on his jaw, as though to relieve some of the tension that had been building up. 'I realized I was marrying her for the wrong reasons. It wasn't fair on her.'

'Wrong reasons?'

'Yeah . . .' he murmured.

'What reasons were they?'

'I think it's best I don't go there.'

'Why?'

'Let's just say nothing good can come of it.'

I looked up to find him staring back at me, his cheeks bright red as a worried look fell on his face.

'Oh.'

'Yeah . . .' he sighed. 'That old chestnut.'

Silence fell upon us as the meaning of what wasn't said took shape. It hadn't been what I was expecting. I'd seen him and Alice together, the way he'd looked at her with complete admiration and wonderment – in my mind he'd clearly loved her far more than he had ever loved me. It had been blatantly obvious. Hadn't it?

'You know,' he said, abruptly standing up straight and making his way to the kitchen door, clapping as he did so to emphasize the end of the conversation. 'I'm shattered too, actually. I'd better go get some sleep. Got a busy day of planning ahead of me tomorrow.'

'Ben?'

He stopped, swivelled on the spot and faced me.

A sadness lingered between us as we took each other in.

There was so much I could have said, but in that moment none of those unsaid words leapt from my mouth. Instead, I stood there staring at him, my mind scrambled with confusion.

'Night, Maddy,' he whispered. There was no hope in his voice, no longing. Just defeat.

'Night, Ben.'

As I stood there, looking at the spot where Ben had been moments before, I was reminded of all the feelings I thought had long since disappeared. Rather than making me feel loved, they made me feel bereaved. I was standing in the kitchen of the home I shared with the man I loved, thinking of another man. I wasn't too keen on the type of woman that made me.

I felt for Ben and hurt because he hurt, but I couldn't allow what had passed to take hold of me. I loved Robert and the life we'd built together and I didn't want anything to come along and ruin it. I couldn't allow that to happen.

Ben

Twenty-four years old . . .

I sat on the sofa in the lounge with my head cradled in my hands, full of self-hatred. Unable to believe what I'd done, what I'd practically confessed. How stupid of me. How utterly vile of me to behave in that way when Robert had done so much for me. Even if that *was* the reason for my actions, there was absolutely no way I should have let it be known to Maddy. Ever. That hadn't been my intention when I'd agreed to stay round there. It hadn't even entered my head that it was a possibility. I was going away. I was purposefully freeing myself from the torment of the situation, so why on earth had I acted in that way?

The look she gave me, when she realized what I'd implied, I'll never forget. It was pitiful. She pitied me in that moment. There's no questioning that. Her jaw dropped and eyes widened at the crazy man standing in her kitchen who was clearly unable to move on from what had barely existed years before. She didn't need to say anything, the look said it all – she'd been mortified at my revelation. Bewildered.

The following day I moved to Mum's, telling Robert there was no point me sleeping on their sofa when I had a room of my own waiting for me back at Peaswood, along with a mum who I knew would be desperate to see as much as she could of me in the few weeks before I left.

I was gone before Maddy got home from work the next day, something I assumed she'd be pleased about.

Maddy

I hardly saw Ben again after that night. Not before he went off travelling, anyway. He went back to Peaswood and I faked a few social events when he and Robert met up. The only time I couldn't get out of it was the mini going-away party that June threw for him in their house. It would have been rather unfriendly for me not to go to that. But, seeing as all of our families were crammed into his mum's modest-sized lounge, there was no chance of us being alone together, which was a comforting thought.

It had been a lovely afternoon and wonderful to see how close our families still were after so many years of friendship. Our mums were continuously off gossiping with each other as they brought in more mountains of food (you'd have thought the whole village was coming – it was only us lot!), while the two dads lounged on the sofa and grunted about the football. Robert and Ben had everyone in stitches as they talked through stories of our childhood (tears, tantrums and laughter), reminding the parents how much of a nuisance we all were. I sat quietly, pigging out on the sausage rolls and chicken nuggets, and listened, feeling lucky to be part of such a close-knit group – although sorry that things had become so complex that Ben had decided to leave. It didn't seem fair.

As we left I hugged Ben goodbye on his mum's driveway. It was the truest hug we'd had in years. Our guards were dropped. I felt an overwhelming pang of sadness knowing I'd not be seeing him for a long time. I squeezed him tightly and breathed him in, holding back the tears at having his arms wrapped around me, holding me securely.

I'm ashamed to say that I walked away from him feeling relieved at knowing he wasn't going to be around confusing my heart once more with his almost-confession.

I waited until he'd left, and was firmly on South American soil studying Spanish in Ecuador, before I decided to tell Pearl of our encounter in the kitchen. We'd been in the Roebuck, one of Chiswick's great gastro pubs on the High Road, for about an hour and had already scoffed our way through steak and chips (her), and bangers and mash (me). We were about to dive into the sticky toffee pudding and salted caramel ice cream, which we'd decided to share because we were so full (but cheekily asked for an extra scoop of ice cream to be added), when I told her that Ben had, quite possibly, insinuated that he'd finished with Alice because he still loved me. It was enough to make her take her eyes off our dessert, for a split second.

'Let me get this right,' she said slowly as she pieced together the facts, waving her spoon in the air as she did so. 'The first time he told you he loved you he slept with someone else – the girl he got engaged to.'

'Yep.'

'And the second time he told you he packed his bags and went travelling? Seriously?' She shook her head at the madness of it, before taking another mouthful of dessert.

'Well, he didn't actually say it this time.'

'No chance you could've misread it?'

'None.'

'What is he playing at?' she asked, screwing up her eyes suspiciously.

'Nothing, he's gone.'

'Yes, and has left you behind, sat at home thinking of him. Crafty bugger.'

'I don't think that was his plan. I don't think he had a plan. You know Ben's not like that. I think he was just confused, he's been through such a tough time, it hasn't been easy.'

I stopped, knowing I was rambling in his defence.

'His plan certainly hasn't worked then,' she smiled, putting the last piece of pudding smugly into her mouth.

She was wrong, I told myself. I knew Ben, and I knew it wasn't some manipulative plan to stir up trouble. He'd innocently alluded to things. That was all. I'd brought up the conversation, I'd asked the questions, he had just answered them. As a result he'd momentarily opened the door to those old feelings and given us a glimpse of what was . . . but he'd left it there and slammed the door firmly shut again by going away. If he had wanted anything from me after that revelation, he would have made it clear then, rather than moving thousands of miles away from me. He'd closed the conversation before there was any real declaration of love, making it obvious he wanted nothing from me in return. There was no point in me running my mind ragged over what was clearly a slip following his break-up. There was no need for clarification.

Once again, I had to focus on my love story, the one I'd chosen, and ignore the feeling of elation Ben had caused to rise in my chest.

I'd be the first to admit that I'm not the most romantic guy in the world. I don't buy Maddy flowers for no reason – only her birthday or anniversaries – I hardly ever run her hot baths of an evening, I probably don't even tell her enough how gorgeous she looks – which she does, all the time. Especially today, Maddy. You look incredible!

So, because of my lack of effort in everyday life, I knew I had to do something seriously wonderful when popping the question . . .

Maddy

Twenty-five years old . . .

Robert had asked me to take the Friday before our nine-year anniversary off work, but wouldn't let me know what he'd arranged, insisting that he wanted to surprise me. We'd never done much for our anniversaries in the past. I think that was possibly the only downside to being friends before we became a couple – it made all that lovey stuff seem weird, making us both prefer to do something fairly chilled, like curl up on the sofa with a pizza or something. It's because of that and the fact that he wasn't normally one for big romantic gestures, or planning ahead, that made me so excited to see what he'd organized.

The night before I'd come home to find him waiting for me in the kitchen, wearing one of my aprons over the top of his trackie bottoms and t-shirt (it was what he'd worn for school that day). In his ruffled but delicious attire, he was stirring the contents of a pot on the stove. Just by the smell I could tell he was cooking a pasta sauce – one of the only meals he'd learned to make at university that was actually quite tasty. Not only was he cooking, but the table had been laid and decorated with a dozen red roses in a vase and some glittery heart-shaped sequins were sprinkled on the cream cloth. Two glasses of wine had been poured out in preparation for my arrival. I couldn't help but smile at the effort.

'This is all very lovely,' I grinned, putting down my coat and bag before walking over to him in the kitchen and inspecting the sauce he was concocting.

'You haven't seen anything yet,' he teased, leaning over and giving me a kiss.

'Really?'

'Yep,' he grinned. 'You're in for quite a treat.'

I let out a girlie giggle as I put my arms around his waist and gave him a kiss. 'I love you.'

'Good. Now, sit down, have some wine,' he ordered, ushering me out of the kitchen and into the dining area. 'Dinner won't be long.'

Once we'd finished the scrummy meal and our tummies were protruding from the carb-fest overload – there'd been a massive slice of triple chocolate cheesecake for dessert (shop bought) – I decided to fish for more information on the next day's activities.

'So, what are you planning for tomorrow, then?' I asked coyly, tilting my head and batting my eyelashes in an effort to win him over. Hoping he wasn't going to keep me in the dark any longer.

'Ah, I can't tell you that, but take this,' he said, handing me a red envelope.

'What is it?'

'Open it.'

I tore it open to find an anniversary card with a handwritten poem inside:

For nine years you've made me smile by being by my
    side,
I hope you know how much your love fills me with
    pride.
For three days we'll go away, it'll just be you and me,
So grab your coat and pack your bags, there's lots of
    things to see.

'We're going away?' I shrieked excitedly, jumping up from
my seat and standing in the middle of the room in surprise, unsure of what to do with all the giddiness twirling
around inside me.

'Yep,' he laughed.

'Where?'

'I'm not telling you that until tomorrow.'

'Rob, please!' I begged, with a desperate laugh. 'How
will I know what clothes to pack?'

'Oh, hadn't thought of that.' His face creased up as he
pondered over an answer. 'Just bring warm stuff that you
feel comfortable in. But also nice bits. Maybe a dress?'

'What?!'

'Trust me,' he said, standing up with a grin and kissing
me before piling up the dirty dishes and walking them to
the sink. 'You go get started, I'll wash these and then
come up.'

'You're washing up too?'

'Of course. Oh, and bring your camera,' he added over
his shoulder.

I couldn't help smiling as I made my way up the stairs
and pulled my empty suitcase from the airing cupboard.

As I opened it on the bed and started making piles of possible clothing to take, I thought of my own anniversary gift to Robert with horror. Even with just the home-cooked meal he'd made that night, he'd already outdone my stupid picture book. I grabbed a pile of sexy underwear that I kept at the back of my knicker drawer for special occasions and packed them inside the suitcase first, thinking they'd go a long way in balancing things up.

At five thirty the following morning Robert's phone played out its irritating alarm tune. For once I didn't mind it. I slid to his side of the bed and nestled into his warm body, my own body perfectly fitting into the nook of his armpit, as I rested my head on his shoulder.

'Morning,' I whispered, my hand sliding up his muscular chest.

'Morning,' he replied sleepily, lifting his head and giving me a kiss.

'Am I allowed to know now?' I smirked.

'Nope,' he teased, as he shook his head and pursed his lips together tightly, pretending to zip them up.

'But you said I'd find out today,' I moaned, shifting so that my chin was resting on his chest, half of my body splayed on top of his.

'Yes, but not right now.'

I pouted at him like a little child, hoping that would persuade him to tell me, but it didn't work – he was far too in-tune with my little feminine tricks and had clearly built up a protective shield against them over the years, rendering their power useless. I'd have to wait and find out whenever he was ready.

'It's so unfair,' I moaned – my last attempt in persuading him.

'You're such a monkey,' he smiled, craning his neck to give me another kiss.

'Please?'

'No!' he laughed, a smug smile forming at his mouth. 'Right, let's get showered – taxi's going to be here soon.'

'You mean, we're not driving?'

'No . . .' he teased.

My eyes widened with excitement. I'd no idea what Robert had planned, but the fact we weren't driving to wherever we were going was extremely intriguing. In fact, it blew any suspicions of what he had planned out of the water.

When, an hour and a half later, the cab dropped us off outside King's Cross Station, my head whipped round to Robert as a smile exploded onto my face.

'Are we . . .?' I asked with surprise, unable to finish the question.

His face creased up as he laughed in response. Ignoring the swell of early morning commuters who tutted as they made their way around us and into the station, he clasped at the lapels of my coat and pulled me into him.

'I thought it might be nice to go back and see where this little love of ours blossomed,' he winked, kissing me before pulling out two first-class Eurostar tickets from his pocket. 'But, this time, I thought we'd steer away from a smelly coach.'

'Paris!' I beamed in confirmation, throwing my arms around him and plastering his face with dozens of kisses.

'Although we'll probably still need these,' he laughed,

pulling away from me as he handed me two battered French phrase books. The same two we'd taken with us all those years before – they even had our names written in blue biro on the first page.

I couldn't believe my luck. It was the most thoughtfully romantic thing that Robert had ever done for me. I was astounded at the gesture.

I was still pinching myself as we pulled into Paris's grand Gare du Nord three hours later, *and* when we got in a taxi and took in the sights as we drove through the Parisian streets, *and* as we eventually pulled up outside our luxurious-looking accommodation, Hotel Vernet. A four-star boutique hotel, not far from the Arc de Triomphe, at the top of the Champs Elysées – the famous road lined with fabulous restaurants and expensive shops. Our hotel exterior was what you'd expect in Paris, its traditional stony cream surface patterned with horizontal lines, while at the bottom of its many windows sat intricately detailed black railings, woven with the green twigs of potted plants. Red canopies hung over each of them, giving the place an air of opulence, helped by its expansive glass entrance. It was a far cry from the shabby-looking place we'd stayed in before – it even had a lift, and a porter to take care of our bags as we checked in.

'This is amazing, Rob,' I said, looking around our suite – yes, a suite no less! Not only did the room have a stonkingly massive bed with an army-load of pillows laid on top of it, but it also had another room with a large cream sofa, a massive flat-screen TV and a desk – in case we felt the need to do any work while we were on our romantic trip. It was like nothing I'd ever stayed in before with its high ceilings and curtains that ran all the way up to them at the huge windows – there was even a box of Ladurée macaroons waiting for us on arrival. I took them to the bed and collapsed into the pillows while I popped a pink one into my mouth. Yum, strawberries and cream, I was in heaven.

'Glad you like it,' Robert smiled.

'Ah, I could stay here all day.'

'Oh really?' he said, climbing onto the bed and straddling me at my waist, taking a yellow macaroon and shoving it in his mouth whole, groaning at its deliciousness. 'That sounds like a very tempting idea.'

'Doesn't it . . .'

I pulled him down to me, hooking my arms around his neck as I licked his lips with the tip of my tongue.

'Maddy Hurst!'

'Yes?' I asked, widening my eyes innocently.

'You little minx,' he growled, nibbling at my lip.

I hadn't even had time to unpack the frilly knickers I'd packed before we started greedily tearing each other's clothes off.

Once we'd managed to untangle ourselves and leave our gorgeous hotel room, we wrapped up warm and wandered leisurely, hand in hand, down the Champs Elysées, taking in the vastness of it as we went, and stopping to eat crêpes (filled with Nutella and banana) in one of Jardin des Tuileries' restaurants for lunch.

We had decided to revisit some of our favourite spots from our teenage trip – starting with the Louvre, which had become increasingly well known since our previous visit thanks to the book (and film) *The Da Vinci Code,* making its glass pyramid even more famous than before. Dozens of people stood queuing, just to have their photo taken next to it, each adopting the same thumbs-up pose.

That night Robert had booked us into a restaurant for dinner, telling me to wear the smartest outfit I'd brought with me. We looked quite the dashing pair as we checked ourselves over in the hotel mirror before we left. Robert had put on a brown fitted tweed suit for the occasion and had even put a cream hankie in his breast pocket (extra posh), and polished his best black shoes so much that they gleamed. His short hair was waxed in a messy yet organized manner, finishing off the look nicely. Robert's slickly groomed appearance was hugely different from the sweaty state he would come home in every night after a day of sports with the kids. He looked scrummy. I'd decided (after lots of deliberation) on a tight black below-the-knee dress that hugged my curves and showed just the right amount of cleavage – enough to keep Robert entertained if I were to lean across the table at dinner, but not too much that other men would ogle inappropriately. With my hair curled and pinned to the side so that it hung over one shoulder, little silver hoops in my ears, and killer black stilettos with silver heels on my feet, my look was complete. Yes, we really did look dashing. I couldn't help but feel proud of how well we'd scrubbed up.

My jaw practically dropped as the maître d' guided us through the high-ceilinged restaurant. The chic room was covered in gold – from the sparkly chandelier that hung from the centre of the gold-encrusted ceiling, to the candelabras placed on each table which caused the glasswear to twinkle in the candlelight. The majestic feeling was taken further by classical background music being played softly by a pianist and harpist in the corner. It was like nothing we'd ever been to together before – it was so grand and sophisticated.

We were taken to a window seat, giving us a spectacular, uninterrupted view of the iconic Eiffel Tower.

Taking into account that we were in Paris, that it was our anniversary weekend, and that we'd just been given the best table in the restaurant, it's not surprising that I suddenly assumed Robert was going to be getting down on one knee that night. It had always been a topic I pondered over whenever we went away or celebrated a birthday or anniversary (or New Year's Eve, or Valentine's Day; anything that had a name attached to it, really). I was always speculating over when he might do it, but, sitting there amongst all that splendour, for the first time it seemed like it was likely to become a reality.

For that reason, the excited butterflies in my tummy went berserk, stopping me from eating or enjoying myself as I cheerfully watched Robert like a hawk for any further signs – checking to see whether he was quieter than normal, nervous in some way or acting shifty. I saw nothing. Robert looked calm and relaxed as he talked non-stop, ate off my plate (apparently making the most of my lack of appetite) and guzzled down the red wine. Each time our dirty plates were taken off to the kitchen, and we were left to gaze at the view, I'd stop breathing, thinking that it could be the moment Robert had planned to ask.

Nothing came after our starters.

Nothing came after our mains.

Nothing came after our desserts.

Nothing came after our coffees.

Nothing.

Once the bill was paid and Robert stood up to leave, I stayed sitting at the table in a state of shock.

'Let's stand outside and get another look at the Tower before we get a taxi back,' he winked.

My heart almost leapt into my throat at the wink, thinking it was him being suggestive – that the proposal was on its way. I gathered my bag and coat in haste, before grabbing his hand and following him outside.

Robert wrapped his arms around me from behind and gazed up at the Tower, its twinkling lights creating a magical atmosphere as they danced along the steel structure.

Stood there, in an embrace, I was again sure the moment would come.

I waited.

And waited.

And waited.

'It's nippier than I thought!' Robert eventually said in my ear. 'Want to head back?'

He wasn't proposing. The realization made me sad.

'You okay?' he asked, as we walked back towards the main road to find a taxi. 'Have you had a nice night?'

'It's been wonderful. Thank you,' I smiled, trying to ward off the tears that had been threatening to spill.

I'd never been so disappointed.

The following night, Robert suggested we take a walk and just see where we found that was nice for dinner. I was happy with that suggestion. Knowing how expensive the previous night had been, I expected Robert would be on the lookout for somewhere cheap and cheerful.

We wandered back down the Champs Elysées and through the Jardin des Tuileries (our feet seemed to automatically take us that way after having walked the route so often).

Robert stopped before the Louvre.

'I'm getting hungry now. Want to walk up there and see if there's anything good?' he asked, casually pointing up one of the roads.

'Yeah,' I shrugged, not too fussed.

I recognized La Ferme des Beauvais, the restaurant we'd visited with school, straight away. Perched on the corner with windows that covered the breadth of the external walls, displaying its name in silver-framed red lettering that curved like a rainbow on each pane of glass – although the lettering had started to peel at its corners.

'Are you sure that's it?' Robert asked with a frown, not looking too impressed with the place.

'Positive,' I squealed.

'If you say so,' he said dismissively.

'We have to eat in there.'

'Really? I don't remember their food being the most amazing thing I'd ever eaten,' he said, looking up the road and squinting at the other restaurants to find something better.

'I don't care. Come on,' I said, as I pulled him inside.

It was exactly as I'd remembered – the same red tablecloths covered the tables, upon which were tealights and single red roses. Even the pictures on the walls were still the same.

'Surely you recognize it now?'

'Yeah, I guess. A bit,' he shrugged.

I asked the waiter to seat us at the same table we were at before, causing Robert to laugh at me.

'What?'

'Nothing. You're cute,' he said with a wink. 'I like it when you're sentimental.'

'I want us to order the same too.'

'Really? You don't fancy trying snails?'

'Yuck, no,' I protested, screwing up my face.

'Okay. I'm up for that.'

'Although we are getting a dessert.'

'Of course. And wine.'

I gasped jokingly, 'What would Miss James say?'

Spaghetti Bolognese was ordered and eaten, washed down with French bread and copious amounts of red wine. Needless to say, it wasn't to the same standard of fine dining we'd experienced the night before, but we didn't care. We were relaxed, talking and laughing, making the most of each other's company.

Once our plates had been cleared away and dessert ordered (I'd gone for a chocolate and hazelnut pastry), Robert started to stare at me with a gooey expression, his face softening and a loving smile appearing.

'What?' I asked, a little perturbed – he rarely looked at me like that.

'Nothing. You're just so beautiful.'

It was at that point that the ever-familiar piano intro to 'All my Life' started playing through the restaurant speakers, prompting Robert to stand up and turn to me, as he gestured for my hand.

'What?' I giggled.

'Can I have this dance?'

'Here? We can't, people are watching,' I whispered, looking around at the handful of other couples who were enjoying their meals.

'I don't care,' he smiled, pulling me out of my seat and into his arms.

We slow danced on the spot, turning in little circles as Robert put his mouth to my ear and sang along to the words K-Ci and JoJo were singing. I closed my eyes and enjoyed the moment, thinking it was the perfect way to spend our anniversary.

Once the song had come to an end Robert stepped away from me and knelt down on one knee. Using two hands, he held up a sparkling diamond ring that he'd fished out of his jeans pocket.

'What the –' I started in shock.

'I'm not done yet,' Robert winked, stopping me from talking further. He blew out air from his cheeks, steeling himself before he continued. 'As you know, nine years ago we shared our first kiss on this very spot. It was the start of everything for me. You've always been such a huge part of my life, and I seriously don't know what I'd have done without you over the years. So, here's the question . . . Maddy Hurst, will you marry me? Will you be my wife?'

'Yes!' I practically screamed, dragging him up from his knelt position so that I could kiss him. 'Of course I will!'

A cheer rose from around us at my answer.

I was ecstatic.

I'm thrilled to say that in that moment no one else

entered my head. My biggest fear over the years about when that moment eventually came was that Ben would pop into my thoughts and ruin it. That somehow, my heart would hijack the occasion and use it to turn against me. But as Robert said the words, I was touched by nothing other than my utter love for him. He was offering me my forever and I couldn't have been happier.

'Did you ask them to play that song then?' I asked, when we were back at our table, unable to keep from gushing manically.

'Yeees,' he smiled.

'What? When I went to the loo?'

'Do you seriously still think we came here by accident?' He leaned his head backwards as laughter spilled from his opened mouth.

'What?' I asked. 'What is it?'

It suddenly dawned on me that the whole night had been planned – our feet hadn't just automatically walked up towards the Louvre, Robert had guided us.

'But you didn't even want to come in!'

'Yes, I did.'

'It didn't look like it.'

'I knew that if I'd told you I'd booked us in here you'd know I was going to propose.'

He was right, as the previous night had shown – any bit of effort on his part would have led me to that conclusion.

'It would've ruined it,' he added. 'But I also knew that as soon as you saw this place you wouldn't be able to resist coming in.'

'Very clever,' I laughed.

'I know,' he smiled, taking my newly ringed hand and admiring his handiwork.

The ring was absolutely stunning, but then, anything that sparkled would be. A single round diamond beautifully set in a dainty white-gold band. It was flawless.

'When are we going to tell everyone? Who already knows?'

'No one knows. I mean, I asked for permission last year and that was enough to get them all flapping around in a frenzy.'

'Last year?'

'Yes. Long story,' he grunted, rolling his eyes. 'But, anyway, I didn't even tell them we were coming to Paris.'

'No!'

I was shocked that he'd managed to keep the whole thing to himself – and plan it all on his own.

'One of them would've said something. Thought you'd enjoy going round and telling them ourselves.'

'That's a great idea! We'll have to do it straight away, though, there's no way I'll be able to keep this whole thing a secret. I want the whole frigging world to know,' I squealed.

'What about Ben?'

The question threw me.

'Huh?'

'When are we going to tell him?'

'Did he know you were asking?'

'No. I was going to tell him, but then all that shit with Alice happened. I didn't want to tell him before he left, thought it would be insensitive.'

'But that was ages ago.'

'Yeah, thought I'd let him settle. Figured we'd tell him together. Surprise him.'

'Let's wait until after we tell our parents, though.'

'Obviously.' He lifted my ringed hand and took it to his lips, kissing it softly. 'I love you so much.'

'I love you too,' I whispered.

I leaned forward and kissed him, forcing myself to focus on his lips, on the two of us together in Paris, and on the fact that Robert, who loved me so much, wanted me to be his wife. Our love was real. It had grown from the foundations laid in that very restaurant. It was offering me a future that I could depend on. I knew that I loved and trusted it.

Ben

Twenty-five years old . . .

I'd been in South America for five months, travelling from place to place. I started, as planned, in Ecuador at the Montanita Spanish School – it's surprising how quickly you can cut off from your previous existence when you're thousands of miles away, sat on a beach in the sunshine with new friends who know nothing about you. Needless to say, I told no one of the broken-hearted girl I'd left behind and, although I did talk about Maddy and Robert, I'd decided to not tell anyone about my other feelings. No change there, then.

I'd gone from Ecuador to Columbia, Brazil, Paraguay, Uruguay, Argentina, Chile and Bolivia, in that order. Catching buses and planes, or sometimes trekking if I was feeling super-adventurous. For the first time since university I felt liberated and carefree, ready to do anything or go anywhere that tickled my fancy – I fell in love with the sights again and again. Every day brought a new experience to treasure.

I listened to the thunder of the water at Iguazu Falls, Brazil, which was, quite awesomely, like something from *Jurassic Park*. Huge waterfalls splashed from every corner while I sat on a feeble-feeling viewing platform, unable to peel my eyes away – expecting a pterodactyl to fly overhead at any second. I was mildly disappointed when it didn't.

I soaked up the peaceful tranquillity of Lake Titicaca, watching the sunset as it caused a vivid array of colours to reflect on the expansive lake. Oranges, reds, pinks and purples swirled in the sky and in the water, making it appear otherworldly. Maddy would have loved it – the photographs I'd managed to take on just my bog-standard camera were insane.

Of everything I'd done on my trip by that point, sand-boarding down the dunes at Huacachina, taking in the obscene view as I went, was definitely one of my high-lights. Not only was I propelled off a sandy mountain at a ridiculously fast speed (it's a wonder I didn't scream like a girl all the way down), but the beauty of the world around me was breath-taking – massive sand dunes curved their way for miles around, eventually ending at the horizon where they were met by the deep-blue sky above. It was impossible not to feel in awe of it all.

The world was a big place with so much to offer, I was happy to greedily soak up as much as I could of it.

That day in November I'd arrived in Cusco, Peru. Getting off a long bus ride late-afternoon, I'd decided to chill in one of its town squares with a cold beer as I watched the locals around me going about their daily business. A group of old men, all wearing a mixture of grey and white trou-sers and shirts, had gathered on the adjacent bench to me, taking it in turns to talk passionately about something as the others keenly listened and nodded in agreement. I'd no idea what they were saying, but they were interesting to watch. Mothers wandered past, their babies barely visible beneath the multi-coloured blankets they were tied to their bodies with. All the while, at least a dozen stray dogs roamed around to different people, seeing if anyone would offer them scraps of whatever food they were eating.

It was while I sat there, in the Peruvian sun with my Peruvian beer, that I got a text from Robert asking if I was free for a Skype chat later that day. I hadn't spoken to him for a couple of weeks – it wasn't always easy to keep in touch, especially if I was off somewhere remote.

As a rarity, I'd treated myself to a private room in the hostel I was staying in for a few nights, knowing that I'd be camping a couple of days later when I joined the Inca Trail. I'd known I needed to get in as much decent sleep as I could before that. So rather than having a bunch of strangers around me as I tried to make the private call, it meant I was on my own, in my little single room, when the Skype call came through a couple of hours later.

When the image appeared onscreen I was surprised to see Maddy as well as Robert. Even though I'd spoken to her a few times since I'd been away, Maddy had usually found an excuse to flit in and out as Robert talked – busying herself with making the dinner or doing the washing. Sometimes she'd miss the Skype chat altogether – insisting she'd email me later on. Which she did, most of the time. I'd get the odd couple of vague lines about how everything over there was the same as ever, perhaps get updated on what the university lot or her parents were up to, but nothing really substantial or full of thought. I'd email her back my photos – not of me, obviously, but of the places

I'd been and seen. I liked to feel like there was still some communication running between us, that I hadn't managed to ruin everything.

I couldn't help but smile at the rare occurrence of having her join us.

'Mate!' boomed Robert, shifting the screen of his laptop, which he was resting on his knees, so that they were both nicely in view.

It may have been early evening for me, but it was late at night for them in England, and as a result the pair of them looked dishevelled and sleepy as they leaned into each other, dressed in their pyjamas ready for bed. I noticed they were on their brown leather sofa in the lounge, the one I'd been staying on before I'd left.

'Hey, guys,' I smiled back, waving with my free hand. It's a funny thing, I rarely waved hello at people when I greeted them in real life, but put a Skype call in front of me and it was the first thing I did. Always. Perhaps it was the novelty of being able to see people when they were miles across the other side of the world – I felt like I had to make the most of being seen, starting with that gesture.

They waved back, grinning manically at me as they did so.

I'd assumed they'd missed me.

'Nice to see you've still got your colour,' laughed Robert.

My olive skin had turned four shades darker on just my first day in Ecuador, something Robert was still shocked by every time we Skyped, continuously making it one of the first things he opted to talk about.

'Where are you?' asked Maddy.

344

'In Cusco, Peru.'

'That's where Paddington Bear's from,' she informed me with a knowing nod.

'Really?'

'Yep. What's it like?'

'Well, allow me to give you the guided tour of tonight's sleeping quarters,' I said, turning my iPad to show them the bare white walls surrounding me.

'Looks great,' laughed Robert. 'I like what they've done with the place.'

'Yeah, I know, very inspiring. I think they're worried that if they put anything up on the walls it'll get pinched.'

'They know what you travellers are like,' Rob winked. 'Where are you off to next?'

'Inca Trail – four days of hiking before arriving at Machu Picchu.'

'Sounds awesome.'

'I can't wait.'

I'd saved it until near the end of my stay in South America because it was one of the things I'd most wanted to see. I'd heard so many wonderful things about the ancient Inca city from other travellers who had been there – I knew I wasn't going to be disappointed.

'I've heard that's ultra spiritual,' smiled Maddy.

'Here comes your awakening. You'll be a monk before you know it,' laughed Robert.

I didn't bother correcting him that there weren't really monks in Machu Picchu. I didn't want to be an arse. Instead I just smiled and nodded.

'So, what's new with you two?'

At the question, something Maddy did caught my eye.

I saw her eyes widen as she glanced at Robert, a flicker of panic crossing her face as she opened her mouth to speak before closing it abruptly and pursing her lips together. Stopping herself.

Robert, however, was giddily smiling. He placed his arm around Maddy, pulling her into him as he planted a kiss on her forehead.

I knew what was coming before it was said.

'I've asked Maddy to marry me!'

Maddy sprang her left hand up and flashed the sparkling ring as clarification.

I clenched my jaw while my lips formed something resembling a smile.

'Wow. When? How?' I fired.

I had to ask the questions to give me time to steady myself, but I wasn't too keen on hearing the answers. I zoned out as Robert started telling me about Paris and how he'd tricked Maddy into thinking he hadn't remembered the location of the restaurant we'd all been to. I must admit, from what I heard, it sounded romantic.

My heartache wasn't like before when we were sixteen years old and I hadn't known their romance was about to kick off. This time I'd known exactly what was coming — my mum had, after all, told me he was going to ask at the start of the year. Part of me had expected the news every time his name appeared on my phone screen, causing a wave of anxiety as I picked up. I felt a little soothed that the moment I'd feared had finally arrived, that I wouldn't feel that same nausea when he called in the future.

This time I wasn't going to sulk, or cry to my mum, and I wasn't going to go off and sleep with another girl in a ridiculous bid to prove the impossible to myself, because for once I realized that the moment wasn't about me. It was about the two people I loved declaring their love for one another. I had nothing to do with it.

Being far away from home had given me the time I needed to reflect on the years I'd loved Maddy, and on everything that had happened over the previous decade and a half. Talking to other travellers, and hearing their tales of heartache, helped to put everything into perspective. Yes, it hurt, and yes, that pain was all relative to me and was real because I was living it, but I wasn't the only one in the world to feel that way. The difference was that other people were able to come out of such times and move forward, creating happier memories, new lives. Even though I thought I was moving forward with my life before – I'd had a good job, I was engaged – deep down I was waiting, although I hadn't told myself what for. For Robert to stray again? For Maddy to leave him? To realize she loved me? Whatever it was, it had stopped me, and that was something I'd realized while I was away. But I was the only one whose life was hindered by me pointlessly holding back. I was spoiling life for myself.

Maddy was happy. I could see that as I looked at her on my screen that day. She was visibly glowing as she gazed at Robert.

He made her happy.

She wasn't waiting for me.

I wasn't the guy for her.

That was when I realized that I'd never allow myself to stand between them ever again. It was yet another affirmation that I was wrong to ever have spoken up and act on my feelings. They were always going to end up together. I should have known that from the start.

'That all sounds magical,' I said as Robert came to the end of whatever he was saying.

'That's not all, actually,' he grinned. 'I was wondering if you'd be my best man.'

Mum had predicted it. I'd shunned the idea.

I was speechless.

I couldn't think of anywhere better to go and ponder over a broken heart than Machu Picchu – a deserted city built for the Inca kings on the peak of a mountain.

I was taking on that adventure with a mixture of people that the tour company had bundled together – a few travellers who'd been to almost all the same places as I had, an older couple from Canada who'd decided, after years of working hard, to stop and go see the world, and an English family with two sons who were a little younger than me. Our trek guide was a short tubby man called William, a local from Peru with limited English, meaning that, although he was eager to please, it wasn't always possible to get the information we craved. For instance, I'd heard many different theories about why Machu Picchu was built and who for and had loads of questions about it – but each time I queried him I ended up more confused. From what I understood, Machu Picchu had been built in the fifteenth century for the Incas to live in, a sacred place built by the people to show their devotion to their kings.

The walk getting there was mind-clearing enough. Even though our bags were carried by donkeys, it was still a struggle. The altitude made it difficult to walk more than five minutes before it swooped in and took your breath away, and when that wasn't an issue our legs occasionally went stiff from the number of stairs we had to scramble our way up. The plus side was that it forced us to stop and take a look at the surroundings.

I'd seen photos. I knew what Machu Picchu was going to look like, but as I climbed up the final uneven steps of the Inca trail and crossed through the Sun Gates to see it for the first time, I was overcome with emotion. Perhaps it was the exhaustion that made me feel that way, but I found myself having to walk away from the group to shed a few tears.

It was the first time in over five months that I felt part of a group and not a lone traveller. Yes, there were moments when I'd spend a few days with people here and there – but being on the Inca Trail gave the group a sense of unity. We were travelling towards something and did our best to help each other get there. It made me miss home. Miss Robert and Maddy and being a part of our team.

As I sat at the mountain's peak, overlooking the vast number of buildings that had been erected by worshippers who died to make their Inca kings happy, I thought of my two best friends. It hurt that Maddy had distanced herself so much from me and that I was becoming more of a stranger to her than someone she confided in. It was my own fault that things had become that way, but I missed her. I missed having her as a best friend to chat to every day. And as for Robert, I'd always felt like I owed him so much for always being there for me, but instead of repaying him I betrayed him. In many ways I'd started to wish that I could take the last few years back – transport us back to the days of innocence, when everything was far less complicated.

I was twenty-one when I drunkenly told Maddy I loved her. The way I acted following that showed my lack of maturity at the time. I should have talked to her and explained how I felt, not just acted out. I dread to think how I'd look back at the whole thing in my old age, with further years of worldly wisdom to draw upon. I wondered whether I'd cheer at myself for acting on impulse and seizing the moment, or reprimand myself for betraying a friend and acting so foolishly. I had a feeling it would be the latter.

I'd already known there was no way that I was ever going to get the girl, but hearing that she was getting married, that she'd be forever out of my reach, hurt. She'd agreed to marry Robert. No matter how she felt about me, the fact she'd said 'yes' to being his wife told me everything I needed to know.

I needed to forgive myself for the things I could not change, and move forward in the hope of salvaging the best friendship and love I'd ever known.

I wanted my friends back.

Paris served us well once and, as you are sitting here now you will know that it served us well a second time. I can't tell you how honoured I am to be married to the most wonderful woman in the world. Kathryn and Greg, I promise I'll take good care of her. And Maddy, I promise that from now on I *will* bring you home flowers for no reason at all, I *will* run you baths and I *will* tell you just how gorgeous you look.

So please, join me in raising a glass to my beautiful wife. The Bride.

Maddy

Twenty-six years old . . .

It's quite impossible to move forward and tell yourself that you're doing the right thing when everything seems to be making you question it. Weddings make you think for a start (and I'd been to two that year), as do love songs on the radio, romantic films or crazy dreams full of wacky scenarios and flashbacks – highly unhelpful. I thought of Ben a lot in the lead-up to my wedding. More than I should have.

It upset me that he kept springing into my thoughts. I couldn't understand why, when I was so happy, his face kept coming into focus to contest that.

And I *was* happy. I was completely happy with my life with Robert. That's something I can't stress enough. He was my best friend, he made me laugh every day, he challenged me physically and mentally, he was my ulti-mate pillar of support, always there, always loving, always giving. There was no reason for me to look else-where or consider the possibility that we weren't right together. We were, I knew we were, had done since day one.

But what did Ben taking over my thoughts mean? That's what I kept asking myself. Was it the Universe's way of telling me to think wisely before getting married? Was it suggesting I was meant to choose Ben? Or was he simply on my mind because I'd put him there.

A couple of months before my wedding, after driving myself slightly loopy, I decided to write an email to Ben, to get all my thoughts out in the hope that he'd be able to shed some light on the matter. I'm not entirely sure what I expected from him, but it helped to sit down and just blast out all my feelings. It helped me to organize them and see things more clearly.

That email sat unsent in my drafts folder for weeks. I thought about sending it time and time again. I'd look at it and reword bits, making sure it made sense, and that it truly reflected how I felt. It did, but something stopped me from typing his name in the address bar and pressing the send button. I let it sit there for as long as I could.

The night before my wedding I was in my old bedroom trying to sleep, but wasn't having much luck. I had too much nervous energy bubbling away inside me. It didn't help that my gorgeous wedding gown was hanging from the door of my wardrobe, demanding my attention — doing its best to tempt me out of bed and squeeze into it ahead of schedule.

Lying in the bed from my childhood, I thought about everything that could possibly go wrong the following day – the normal bride worries – but I also thought about me and Robert, about how far we'd come since our first smile at nine years old, to our wedding day. Thinking of our future, I knew we'd have a lifetime of happiness together. I knew, for absolute certain, that it was what I wanted.

Suddenly I decided I'd waited long enough.

I needed Ben to know how I felt.

I picked up my laptop from the floor and went into the draft folder of my emails.

I typed in his email address.

I clicked send.

Ben

Twenty-six years old . . .

Ben,

A few years ago I was told that, in order to stop my heart from being so torn, I had to choose my love story and stick to it. The thing is, I never really felt like I had a choice. You'd got with Alice and seemed perfectly happy, you never gave me cause to think otherwise. You also never fought for me or made me think that a future with you was a viable option. If I'm honest, it made me question if you'd ever really loved me at all. As a result I invested all my love and energy into Robert. I forgave him, and ended up loving him even more than I had before, because at that point I knew what it was like to be without him. I can't say I regret the decision or the years we've spent together. I'm incredibly happy and loved. As we both know, Robert is a wonderful man.

However, every now and then I think about you and what could have been. Not constantly, but it's been tugging away at me enough to keep you in my thoughts more than perhaps you ought to have been. For a while I thought I was having doubts – that it was my heart's way of saying it's you I love and should be with, but I've come to conclude that that is not the case. I DO love you, you can be certain of that, but I don't believe we're meant to be together, I don't think I'm meant to be with anyone. Instead that decision is one our hearts must make for themselves.

I know you didn't believe it when I told you I loved you all those years ago, but I honestly did, and still do. Completely and utterly. Just thinking of you makes me smile. I don't want to go through life without you there supporting me, and nor do I want you to be without my support and love.

Until now, I thought a part of me had been longing for you to come along and rescue me, but we both know I'm not in need of saving. Not in the slightest. There's nothing to save me from. I'm in love with someone we both think is amazing. I'll be full of happiness on the day of my wedding because I know that things are the way they should be.

So it's not because I don't love you that I'm marrying someone else, and it's not because you didn't love me that you stopped fighting for me or pursuing things. Instead, it's because we both have so much love for the one man who's been keeping us apart. He is OUR rock, OUR best friend, OUR Robert. It's not from a lack of love that we'll forever be apart, but too much.

You will always be in my heart and I know I'll love you forever.

Yours, Maddy

xoxox

Maddy

Twenty-six years old . . .

That was it.

There was no going back.

A surge of happiness bolted through me as I spotted him, staring back at me from the altar, looking simply divine. My wonderful man, Robert Miles – strong, reliable and loving. My best friend. I pursed my lips as my cheeks rose and tears sprang to my eyes at the very sight of him, looking more handsome than ever in his grey suit. His tall muscular frame visibly relaxed as his dazzling green eyes found mine, his luscious lips breaking into a smile that I couldn't help but respond to.

And then I stole a glance to the right of Robert, to see my other love, Ben Gilbert – kind, generous and able to make my heart melt with just one look. But he wasn't looking back at me. Instead, he had his head bowed and was concentrating on the floor in front of him; all I could see was the back of his waxed brown hair – the smooth olive skin of his face and his chocolate-dipped eyes were turned away.

His hesitance to look up struck a chord within me, momentarily making me wobble on my decision.

Suddenly, something within me urged him to look at me. Part of me wanted him to stop the wedding, to show me exactly how much he cared. Wanted him to stop me from making a terrible mistake ... but is that what I thought I was actually making? A terrible mistake?

I loved Robert, but I loved Ben too. Both men had known me for seventeen years – each of them had seen me at my worst, picked me up when I'd been caught in despair, been my shoulders to cry on when I'd needed to sob. They were my rocks. Plural. Not singular.

Yes, I'd made my decision. I'd accepted Robert's proposal, I'd worn the big white dress and walked up the aisle – however, if Ben had spoken up, if he'd even coughed suggestively, then there's a possibility I'd have stopped the wedding.

Even at that point.

But, as the service got underway, as the congregation was asked for any reasons why we should not have been joined in matrimony without a peep from Ben, it started to sink in that he was not about to start fighting.

He was letting me go ...

I did not stop the service.

I did not run off like the girls in films or books who decide at the last minute that their wavering hearts need to be with 'the other guy', who had been patiently waiting in the wings since forever. I did not have a moment of realization and 'put things right'.

There was nothing dramatic, no big outing of my scandal. Nothing. Just me, standing in front of Robert, telling him that he had my heart, that I would love, honour and obey him for the rest of my life. I declared my vows with love and determination, strength and clarity. Looking into Robert's eyes and remembering everything we'd been through, how he had been there for me, stood by me, fought for me. All the while telling myself that I was doing the right thing. I was making the right choice – because there was no other choice.

Never before has the term 'bitter sweet' been truer. I was marrying my best friend, the guy who made me laugh more than anything in the world, the one who I knew would do anything for me, but I was also saying goodbye to the possibility of the alternative love story – the one I had never and, from that point, would never, allow to have a proper chance.

My love story had been chosen. It might not have been the one others might have picked, but it was the one I was more than happy to live with.

Once the ceremony was complete and the register signed, we wandered hand in hand back through our gathered family and friends, smiling as they all cheered in delight, welcoming the newly formed Mr and Mrs Miles into the world.

That evening, during an unexpected break before dinner and the speeches, I stood outside, catching some fresh air in a trance-like daydream. I looked out at the candles that were beautifully placed on the vast green that was encased by towering trees, the sort the three of us had spent our carefree childhood climbing.

What a day it's been, I thought to myself with a sigh.

I'd been there for a few minutes when I heard footsteps coming towards me. My breath caught in my throat as I took a quick glance and realized who was walking in my direction.

Ben.

'You okay?' he asked, his voice low and quiet.

I nodded in reply and turned back to the view.

He stood next to me.

Side by side we watched the candles' flames dance and flicker, matching the twinkling of the starry sky above.

Without saying anything more, he took my hand in his and I instantly knew what was coming – those infamous three little squeezes, those longed-for three little unvoiced words, in the way he'd told me since he was just eleven years old.

One.

A bolt surged through me.

Two.

My lip wobbled.

Three.

My tears started to fall.

'I always will,' he leaned in and whispered, before slowly releasing my hand, turning around and walking away.

Ben

Twenty-seven years old . . .

I.
LOVE.
YOU.
That was what I'd wanted to say in those three little squeezes.

I knew I meant it.

I really did . . .

Being in that setting, with the emphasis of the occasion one of love and happiness, it was hard to escape the intense desire that took hold of me – making it impossible to ignore. I had an overwhelming urge to open my mouth and say the words out loud, but I couldn't. Instead I found another way to express what I was undoubtedly sure I felt. The words pulsed through my body and out of my hands into hers, the one I loved inexplicably.

Of course, it would be easy to brush the whole thing off and insist it was a crush, a silly little case of puppy love, but it wasn't. It was far more than that.

From the moment I saw Maddy she'd captured me. She had me completely gripped. I was fascinated with everything about her – the way she looked with her fire-like hair and flushed cheeks, the way her heart-shaped lips spoke with a softness and warmth, and the way she appeared so vulnerable as she exposed her caring heart. I adored her – it was that simple.

With Maddy in my life I felt whole. She added a magical sparkle that I'd never wanted to live without. And so I told her, with those three little squeezes. I had no agenda, no hidden plan or desire for anything to change between us – my only thought was to relieve myself of those feelings by communicating them in the only way I felt I could.

Three squeezes of love.

From me.

To her.

It was enough to know that she felt the same way back. I couldn't have asked for anything more from her. I wanted Maddy and my best friend to have a lifetime of happiness together, knowing that I would always be there by her side, loving her unconditionally in return.

As I let her go, into the arms of the best man I'd ever known, I felt a sadness knowing the best man had won – it just wasn't this best man.

I'm pretty sure everyone here knows who I am, but just in case there's anyone here these guys happened to meet when I wasn't glued to their sides, I'm Ben. I'm the best friend, well, best man for today.

When I look back at my childhood it strikes me that it was always sunny. Literally, if I were to recall a single tale from that time you can guarantee that the sun would be there, perched in the sky with her hat firmly on as she flamboyantly sucked on an orange Capri Sun and nibbled on some Party Rings. As I get older and I witness more cloudy and murky days than beautiful blue skies, I can't help but think there's something slightly off-balance with the way I've stored all those days in my memory bank. But, thinking about it, they all had one thing in common — nearly every story from my childhood, at least all of the ones with the sun shining, also contained two very special people. So, perhaps, what I actually remember is a feeling of warmth radiating from a special bond, rather than an accurate account of the weather in the nineties and noughties.

Robert and Maddy are my sunshine. Without either one of them I would be lost in a swarm of rainy days. So, thank you, guys, for pushing those dark clouds away and filling my days with light and laughter . . .

Epilogue

Ben

As I dropped my son off for his first day of school, I watched with a swell of pride as he gaily ran into the playground and played with anyone who showed the slightest bit of interest – he wasn't picky, yet. A friend was simply someone who flashed a smile in his direction and included him in whatever they were doing. He had no reason to be cautious or wary of their intentions. I hoped he had many more years of that delectable innocence ahead of him – before the school politics kicked in and taught him otherwise.

I wasn't the only one to become overwhelmed at that momentous milestone in my son's life. His mother, my wife, hastily fished around inside her brown leather handbag – searching for a tissue to mop up her falling tears.

'Hey – you okay?' I asked, as I put my arm around her and pulled her into my chest for a hug, kissing the top of her head and taking comfort from the familiar smell of her shampoo.

'I'm being silly. Sorry . . .' she mumbled, shaking her head slightly at the emotion continuing to mount inside of her. Unable to regain control of her breathing, she allowed soft sobs to escape as she continued to talk. 'He's just so grown up. Where did the time go?'

'He's still our little Scruff,' I assured her, using the nickname we'd given him on account of the fact that no matter what we dressed him in, and no matter how much we scrubbed him clean, our little tyke always looked like he'd been on some great grubby endeavour. His rosy cheeks and unruly dark curly hair didn't help to make him look any smarter.

She pursed together her lips and gave a little nod of agreement before exhaling and pulling her golden-brown hair away from her face. 'I just hope he likes it,' she shrugged.

'He'll love it.'

'But what if he misses us?' she frowned, turning to check on his whereabouts, her bottom lip pouting out in the same way our son's did – it was hard to decide which of them had picked up that little habit from the other. I wondered if she'd always pulled that expression, and whether it was just amplified now I had two gorgeous faces showing their scrummy bottom lips whenever they were worried and looking for comfort. Either way, they both had the ability to melt my heart within seconds. I wanted more than anything to resolve their woes, for them to know I was there, with them unconditionally – that they'd always have me for support. I was never going to be a dad who upped and left, or a husband who deserted his wife without a second thought. But then, why would I when I knew the two of them brought out the best in me and that I had everything I'd ever need within the four walls of my family home? Nothing would ever tempt me into tearing our happy existence apart. I knew that unquestionably.

'Kate,' I breathed, unable to stop a smile from spreading across my lips – she really was adorable. 'We've been stood where he left us for the last five minutes and he hasn't looked round once to check if we're still here. He's far too excited about getting up those monkey bars and having a swing.'

'True,' she sighed, as she brought her crumpled tissue up to her hazel eyes once more.

'He'll be home in a matter of hours, chewing our ears off with every little detail.'

With a nod, she smiled up at me, 'I know. You're right. We'll never be able to shut him up.'

'Exactly,' I laughed, leaning forward and planting a kiss on her forehead.

'Nice to see my wife's not the only one who's an emotional wreck,' Robert mockingly grunted before laughing, as he walked towards us with Maddy clinging on to his arm. Her face was as red and swollen as Kate's, leaving no doubt that she'd been finding the morning our little ones gained some independence just as tough.

'Shove off,' she choked, nudging him with her elbow, before covering her face and dissolving into laughter herself.

'And to think you used to laugh at your mum for doing the same thing,' I reminded her.

'God, I know. I'm an embarrassing mother already!' she sniffed, taking the tissue Kate was offering her and wiping her dewy face. 'I swear I saw her roll her eyes at me this morning too. Such attitude! She's five!'

'And it's only the beginning,' added Kate. 'It'll be worse in ten years' time when they've got all those teenage emotions flying around.'

'They probably won't even talk to us then,' Maddy muttered sadly.

'Yep. And everything will be our fault,' nodded Kate.

'Speak for yourself, I'm always going to be the cool dad,' answered Robert with a grin and a wink in their direction.

'Of that we've got no doubt,' Maddy replied with an eye roll. 'Shit – did she get that from me?'

We all laughed at the shock on her face.

'Seriously, though, I wonder what they are going to be like . . .' I marvelled aloud.

A silence fell upon the gathered group of adults, as we looked over at the children in the playground and started dreaming up different versions of the futures that lay ahead of us as we watched our babies grow and develop into fully functioning adults. What would become of us? But more importantly, what would become of them?

I was envious of my innocent little boy starting out on his first big adventure. Because school, no matter how insignificant and annoying it may seem as we get older and can't wait to get away, sets us on our life's path. It plants ideas for us to thrive upon, teaches us where we want to go and who we want to be – feeding us the notion that our dreams are limitless, that we can do anything if we believe in it enough and truly set our minds to it. But best of all, it encourages us to seek the friendships of others, to learn to lean on them for support and to console them in return. After all, it's the people you meet along the way who really make a lasting impression and who will, if you're lucky, stick with you for the rest of your life.

'We could spend a lifetime standing here thinking about

that,' mused Robert, breaking the moment. 'Want to come back to ours for some coffee instead?'

'We have biscuits!' grinned Maddy. 'Chocolate ones!'

'Sold!' laughed Kate, looping her arm through my red-headed best friend's and nuzzling her head onto her shoulder.

The two mothers had become exceptionally close – probably because our children had become as inseparable as Robert and I had been at that age. It was a comfort to see how much each of them valued the other's friendship – and how far we'd all come.

Before any of us had even nudged from our spot at the school gate, we all took a collective (and tentative) look into the playground, making one last check that all was calm and happy (and that our presence was still unrequired), before tearing ourselves away.

I left Isaac in the comfort of his new surroundings, but for the rest of that day, in fact, for many days, weeks, months and years to come, I wondered what stamp school would end up leaving on his heart. I hoped with every ounce of my being that he would have the pleasure of knowing love and heartache in the way that I did. It might sound strange me wanting my five-year-old son to experience heartache, but without it I wouldn't have met his mother – a wonderful woman who taught me just how uncomplicated falling in love can be when it is with the right person, as well as highlighting the notion that timing is everything. If I had met her earlier in life I've no doubt that I'd have made a complete mess of the whole thing. I wouldn't have been ready to receive her love or to give the love I'd spent years accumulating. I was unaware that it had been building up so intensely inside of me, longing to be given and bursting to cherish another being in all its entirety. When Kate came along I knew I was ready to open my heart again, but was as surprised as she was to discover its magnitude and strength – love oozed out of me like an uncontrollable tidal wave, happy to be freed as it quickly enveloped her in a tight embrace – promising never to let go.

Without it I wouldn't have him – my biggest challenge, yet my greatest achievement. Nothing on earth could make me happier than watching my son discover the world. He fills each of my days with happiness and pride, a feeling I know I'll savour and never let go. Ever.

Without that love and heartache I also wouldn't have the unconditional friendships I have with his godparents Maddy and Robert. I couldn't even begin to imagine what my life would have been like without the two of them by my side – if I'd become friends with other kids and hadn't even known them. Without them, I wouldn't be me. That's something I can be sure of.

Nor would my little boy have such a close relationship with Emily Miles – the beautiful little redhead who's every inch as wonderful, magical and spellbinding as her mum.

I tell myself that there's no significance in the way his eyes twinkle when he looks at her, that he talks about her nonstop, or the fact that he holds her hand whenever possible . . . but you never know.

Acknowledgements

Writing book one was easy – I didn't really have a deadline and was simply writing it for fun. Book two, however, was a whole other story thanks to the expectations I placed upon myself and the fact that life has gone a little bit crazy.

So, for keeping me sane I'd have to say a massive thank you to my agent Hannah Ferguson. Not only for continuing to believe in me, but also for getting me to believe in myself again once the self-doubt had started to seep through. Apparently it was all part of something I like to call 'Second Book Syndrome'. Phew. A special thanks to everyone at The Marsh Agency (who work alongside Hannah), for looking after me and making everything so simple.

As *Billy and Me*'s editor Claire Pelly took some well-deserved time away from her MJ desk to look after baby Tara (she's so cute – I've seen photos), I was left in the capable hands of Celine Kelly. Thank you for your ideas and inspiring pieces of cake.

Katie Sheldrake, Kim Atkins, Fiona Brown, Beatrix McIntyre and the wonderful PR, marketing, digital and sales teams at MJ – thanks for being so enthusiastic about my books and being lovely bubbly people.

To everyone who's messaged me on Facebook, Twitter and Tumblr demanding to know when they can get their hands on my next book — thank you for the support, I hope you enjoy it.

To all my wonderful friends — you rock my socks off!

Mum, Dad, Debbie B, Giorgina, Lee, Mario, Bob, Debbie F and Carrie — thanks for being the best family on the planet . . . my life is a lot easier and happier with you guys in it!

Tom, thank you for inspiring me with your many talents and encouraging me to nurture some of my own.

Crumb, you are our everything. I hope you grow to love with all your heart, to follow your dreams and to laugh daily. Thanks for all the kicks along the way — they weren't distracting at all.

Behind the scenes with
Giovanna Fletcher
and
You're The One That I Want

Are you #TeamBen or #TeamRob?

I loved Robert, but I loved Ben too . . .

In *You're The One That I Want*, Maddy finds herself romantically torn between her two best friends – Ben and Rob. Do you think she made the right choice? And, if you'd been in her situation, what would you have done?

If you're still undecided between Rob and Ben, find out who would be your best match with our simple quiz!

Do you believe in love at first sight?
A) Maybe. Though sometimes it can take a bit longer to see what's right in front of you . . .
B) Absolutely. When you find The One, you know

Physically, you're more likely to pick a guy who is:
A) Tall and athletic, with fair hair and piercing green eyes
B) Olive-skinned, with messy dark hair and soulful deep-brown eyes

The most important feature in a boyfriend is:
A) A good sense of humour – they have to be able to make you smile
B) Sensitivity – they need to be thoughtful and aware of your needs

Your biggest personality flaw is that:
A) You don't take anything too seriously
B) It's hard for you to open up and be yourself

Long-distance relationships:
A) Can be managed if you're both committed to each other. After all, absence makes the heart grow fonder
B) Put a lot of unnecessary pressure on the relationship and rarely survive. You want to spend every day with the one you love

What's your idea of the perfect date?
A) A trip to the local bowling alley, with nachos and milkshakes on the side. Retro, silly and lots of fun!
B) A quiet candlelit dinner at the local Italian restaurant. Intimate, peaceful and romantic

When it comes to showing how you feel:
A) Actions speak louder than words
B) It's better to put it in a letter – after all, words last forever

To demonstrate how much they like you, you'd prefer someone to:
A) Be spontaneous and sweep you off your feet in the heat of the moment – you can't plan these things!
B) Carefully create the 'perfect moment' incorporating all your favourite things – romantic gestures are the result of thoughtful hard work!

Now see how you did!

Mostly As

You'd be best matched with Rob. Gorgeous, sexy and outgoing he's the kind of boyfriend who'll protect you and cherish you – a great combination. Although he's suffered some lapses of judgement in the past, he won't make the same mistake twice and certainly knows how lucky he is to have you. Above all he's your best friend, and that means everything.

Mostly Bs

You'd be best matched with Ben. Sensitive, brooding and handsome, Ben would be a loyal and devoted boyfriend. Although he's occasionally led people on, with you he'd be committed forever, because he's loved you since the moment he first saw you. Above all he's your best friend, and that means everything.

Let us know if you're #TeamRob or #TeamBen on Twitter – we'd love to hear what you think.

Tweet **@PenguinUKBooks** and *@MrsGiFletcher* to let us know!

Giovanna's Top 10 Books

I think this list has the potential to change all the time (I'm always falling in love with new characters and storylines), but these ten books have certainly made a lingering impression and they're at the top of my lists when recommending to others.

1. *Jemima J* – Jane Green

This was the first chicklit book I ever read – I was still at school at the time. The character Jemima J was just so relatable and I don't think I'd experienced that feeling so strongly before reading this book. She was imperfect, and she let her imperfections rule her – define her even. Being a teenage girl, her insecurities rang true with my own body worries at the time.

2. *My Best Friend's Girl* – Dorothy Koomson

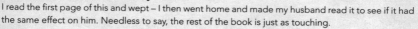

I read the first page of this and wept – I then went home and made my husband read it to see if it had the same effect on him. Needless to say, the rest of the book is just as touching.

3. *P.S. I Love You* – Cecelia Ahern

Dying husband writes letters to his wife from beyond the grave . . . seriously? Anyone who says they weren't moved by this is either fibbing or has a heart of horrible cold stone. Read the book before watching the film!

4. *Playing Away* – Adele Parks

I guess I'd class this as the first saucy book I ever read – although, on reflection, I'm not entirely sure how naughty it actually is. It's been years since I read this, but I just remember being gripped by it.

5. *Me Before You* – Jojo Moyes

Oh gosh . . . I honestly can't think about this book without getting emotional. I picked it up to pack in my suitcase the night before I went on holiday once and ended up reading half of it (sod the packing). It's thought-provoking and gut-wrenching.

6. *RSVP* – Helen Warner

I was asked to read this for my blog a few years ago. When I started reading it I had no idea what to expect, but I fell in love pretty quickly – not just with the storyline, but also with the writing style. Thoroughly enjoyable and engaging.

7. *Birdsong* – Sebastian Faulks

As you might be able to tell from my list so far, I'm quite a sucker for romance. So throw a war into the mix along with a love that has everything battling against its existence, and I'm a goner.

8. *The Age of Miracles* – Karen Thompson Walker

The days are getting longer, bringing with them severe consequences and danger as people try to deal with the changes they bring. Such a simple idea, courageously told through the eyes of a young teenage girl.

9. *The Secret* – Rhonda Bryne

Years ago I was introduced to this book by a great friend and it totally changed my outlook on life. Instead of focusing on the negatives I've learnt to look at the positives. Needless to say, I feel a whole heap happier for doing so!

10. *The Dinosaur That Pooped Christmas* – Tom Fletcher and Dougie Poynter

The inclusion of this book has nothing to do with one of its authors being my husband . . . Ha! Seriously, though – I've seen how much both guys have cracked up writing this set of books and, in turn, how much children have giggled their way through them. Books don't have to contain millions of long words to be great – they just have to capture the imagination.

Giovanna's Top 10 Movies

I know I'm going to kick myself for forgetting some classics, but these are the ones that came to the forefront of my mind. Do you promise not to judge me after you see my list of favourite films? Promise? Okay, here goes . . .

The Notebook
Need I say more? It's the ultimate love story that gets me every time I watch it. I never get bored of Noah and Ali's story. And that ending? Oh man . . .

I Am Sam
I don't think this is really well known, but it's been one of my favourites for over a decade. Sean Penn plays a father with a developmental disability that results in him battling for custody of his daughter (Dakota Fanning). Set to a Beatles soundtrack this film is touching, humorous and heartbreaking.

Fifty First Dates
I love this film! Mostly because I have a huge love of anything with Adam Sandler in it, but (along with the humour you'd expect) this one provides more innocence and romance.

Cinderella
This was a difficult choice as I could've easily put *Sleeping Beauty*, *Snow White* or *The Little Mermaid*. All four are about growing up and feeling the need to belong . . . and finding your Prince Charming, of course. Surely every girl has one of these princess stories in her top ten?

The Sound of Music
This reminds me so much of my nan. It was one of her favourites and she got us all hooked on its charms. I loved the idea of being part of an all-singing, all-dancing family who roamed the hills in their floral outfits. I'm pretty sure our love of this film was what resulted in me, Giorgina and Mario continuously putting on shows for my nan. I'm guessing we weren't as good as the Von Trapps, though – she was always asleep by the end of our performances.

The Wizard of Oz
Judy Garland is one of my all-time heroes and this has to be one of the best films ever made. Simple! I played Dorothy in my local drama group's production of this when I was nine years old . . . the majority of things that have happened in my life since have snowballed from doing that show. To me, it's a story about believing in yourself – not a bad lesson to learn.

Grease
Another film from my childhood – but obviously far cooler than The Sound of Music – Grease taught me everything I needed to know about attitude and being cool. I had no attitude and I was not cool in the slightest, but that didn't stop me thinking of myself as a Rizzo over a Sandy.

Breakfast at Tiffany's
I first watched this film a few years ago (yes, I was late to the party), and was instantly mesmerized by Audrey Hepburn with her effortless poise and beauty! The film is romantically bonkers. It's easy to see why this is such a classic and still highly thought of.

Forrest Gump
This film came out when I was nine years old. I can remember my parents going to see it at the cinema and them coming home and saying how much they enjoyed it. It was years before I was allowed to watch it myself, though. *Forrest Gump* contains so many beautiful morals and eye-opening thoughts, not least the comparison of life with a box of chocolates. The simplicity and innocence captures your heart from the first flight of that soft white feather to the last.

Titanic
I went to see this at the cinema when I was twelve years old with my best friend Sarah Tayler, our mums and siblings. It's a flipping long film and all that water made me need a pee half-way through – but aaaaaaaah! It's just so blooming romantic, heartbreaking and tragic.

Giovanna's Top 10 Songs

Ha! Each of these categories is showing how much of a loser I am . . . But I'd gladly belt out any of these tunes in the shower!

'Somewhere Over the Rainbow' – Judy Garland/Wizard of Oz
This is my favourite song in the entire world. Ever. I walked down the aisle to it on my wedding day and it's the song I've sung to my bump throughout my pregnancy. It holds so many happy memories for so many different reasons.

'Dream a Little Dream of Me' – Mama Cass
When I started drama school we performed a play called *Beautiful Thing*, in which one of the characters was obsessed with Mama Cass – and so my own little obsession started.

'Bubble Wrap' – McFly
I could actually add a whole heap of McFly songs here . . . in fact, this whole list could be comprised of songs that my talented husband has penned. *All About You, Love is Easy, Corrupted, Lies* . . . What geniuses those guys are! This song is just beautiful, though, and I love the idea of bubble-wrapping your fragile heart.

'My Way' – Frank Sinatra
This song reminds me of going over to my Aunty Ann's house and taking it in turns to go on the karaoke machine. When this song came on everyone would gather round and there'd be high-kicks galore.

'I Want You (She's so Heavy)' – The Beatles
I know, I know – with so much choice from the world's most iconic band, why on earth have I gone for this one? Well, I became a bit obsessed with it at one point and would happily listen to it over and over again. It's mean, moody and a tad sexy.

"Til There Was You' – The Beatles
Well, it's hardly surprising that I've got two songs from this band on the list – I couldn't resist. This is a flipping awesome song about the world coming alive when falling in love – so romantic and very catchy.

'Smile' – Charlie Chapman
If you read the lyrics to this song you'll see that it's fairly tragic and haunting with its 'grin and bear it' attitude – but, I love singing this one.

'Moonriver' – Audrey Hepburn
There's something terribly melancholic, yet hopeful about this song, and that's why I love it. Plus Audrey sings it so beautifully in *Breakfast at Tiffany's*.

'Feeling Good' – Nina Simone
There are so many versions of this song, but Nina's is simply the best with her soulful rendition.

'Easy' – The Commodores
This is the first song I ever slow danced to with my husband and it was subsequently the first song at our wedding. It's actually about giving up and leaving the one you love, but it took on a different meaning for us. Thankfully.

Giovanna's Top 10 Romantic Spots

For this I'm going to add a few spots that'll mean nothing to others, but a lot to me . . . but obviously there'll be the standard romance-inducing settings too!

Paris
There's a reason why Paris is known as the most romantic spot in the world – and that's because it unquestionably is! Everything is in walking distance and there's nothing better than walking hand-in-hand with the one you love down those Parisian streets – stopping for macaroons or putting your padlock on the 'Love Lock' bridge.

Sylvia Young Theatre School (the old building that's now owned by someone else)
This has to be on the list because I met my husband there fifteen years ago and it's also where he proposed. You just never know when you're going to meet the love of your life, or how things may pan out in your future . . .

One Marylebone, London
This is where I got married, so I think it's worthy of a place on this list as it holds a whole heap of magical, beautiful and romantic memories. If I could live one day over and over, it would have to be my wedding day!

Jade Mountain, St Lucia
This was one of our honeymoon destinations, and it certainly didn't disappoint. Full of wonder, luscious beauty and zen . . . I'd love to go back – maybe for our ten-year anniversary!

Walt Disney World, Florida
Yes, to some it might appear to be just a theme park, but really it's so much more. It's a place where magical dreams and imagination come alive. Plus, what's more romantic than running around with your partner without a care in the world as you giddily smile at anyone who glances in your direction? This was the second stop on our honeymoon, and that's basically what we did. ;-)

The Maldives
I've never been, but it's somewhere I REALLY want to go one day. Just the thought of being somewhere so quiet and tranquil in a little hut over the water . . . ahh! Delicious!

Byrant Park, New York City
I actually discovered this wonderful little park on my own when my husband was off having a meeting but I took him back there later on. It's simply gorgeous with its outdoor library and copious amounts of places to eat and drink. A glorious setting for lovers or happy people!

The cliffs next to Griffith Park, just north of Dee Why, Sydney, Australia
I don't know the actual name for this location – but short of giving you its co-ordinates, the above description is the best I can do. I spent five weeks in Australia at the start of 2008 and had a gorgeous picnic in the sunshine here (although we did get a puncture driving to it).

The Ivy, London
I just love this place so much… it's where we tend to go every anniversary. We're creatures of habit - once we know we like somewhere, we tend to stick to it!

Venice, Italy
I used to go to Venice all the time as a child. However, it's not somewhere I've ever been as a couple. It's quite similar to Paris in the sense that it's all about walking down little streets, eating great food and drinking lovely wine. It sure sounds romantic!

Giovanna's Top 10 Things That Make Me Happy

Aside from my husband, family and friends . . .

Smiles

Just like yawns spread, so do smiles. I can guarantee that if you smile at a stranger it's highly likely that they'll pass that smile on to someone else . . . how lovely.

Hugs

Not from strangers (that's just weird), but there's nothing better than a good old hug from a friend or family member. I could sit and hug for hours. It's just so loving, warm and makes me feel really secure. Hey, maybe I'll start up a hugging club . . . want to join?

Chocolate

Any type of chocolate makes me happy; that is a simple fact that I cannot shake. But if I had to say one type in particular, I'd have to go with Ferrero Rocher – I find them highly addictive and regularly need to hide them from myself if they're in the house. I'd actually go as far as to say that Ferrero Rocher is one of the best things about Christmas as we always have them in a big bowl in the centre of the coffee table . . . I'm pretty sure I'm the only one who munches through them!

Nutella

Ahhhhhh . . . Some might be dubious about the inclusion of hazelnut spread on this list – but it seriously makes me happy. I could eat it by the spoonful. That's actually how I reward myself after a good day of writing – around four or five o'clock I head into the kitchen, deliriously salivating as I pull out a spoon and reach for my little jar of heaven. Ha!

Elderly People

Okay, this might sound like an odd thing to include, but there's nothing lovelier than taking some time to talk to an elderly person. They're more experienced in this game called life than the lot of us – and such conversations (which always seem to be naughtier than I'm expecting) always leave me with a smile on my face.

Children

Yes, from one extreme to the other. I love children. They're so innocent, truthful and funny. If I'm at a wedding I'd much rather hang out with the children, pulling the craziest moves I can muster, than being all civilized with the adults.

Music

Music is so emotive and freeing – whether you're bashing (some sort of) rhythm out on the drums or screaming along to your favourite band as you do the hovering. It's fantastic. Obviously there are happy songs and sad songs, but bizarrely even the sad songs make me happy . . . funny how they do that. Sometimes wallowing in self-pity is actually quite nice. As long as it's not a regular thing, of course!

Cats

When people are sick and tired of you giving them hugs (it's happened) you can always count on a feline friend to sacrifice themselves for your pleasure. Judging by their purring they get a lot out of it too!

Pictures

Whilst I believe that people should make the most of every moment and not be looking at life through a camera lens, capturing special moments is so wonderful. I have loads of photos around my home of my loved ones laughing and being silly – or places that hold a specific meaning. Catching glimpses of them really helps to brighten my day.

Books

From a very young age I've been happiest when my nose is buried in a big book. I love reading about people's relationships, about their hopes and fears, their dreams and aspirations . . . books are wonderfully inspirational and I couldn't imagine my life without them!

I haven't included cake . . . but I love cake. Cake makes me VERY happy. If a cake happens to be reading this, don't you worry your fluffy little insides – I love you millions. My love for you knows no bounds. My love for you is limitless.

AND SEEING TWO MAGPIES! This is something that makes me SUPER happy . . . seeing one just turns me into a crazy nutter.

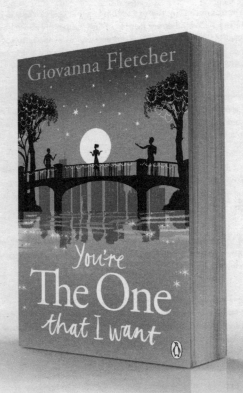

Discover *Billy and Me*, Giovanna Fletcher's
gorgeously romantic debut novel!

Read an extract now . . .

Me

When I was four years old, all I ever wanted was to have a weeing Tiny Tears doll. I'd never been into dolls really, but when my best friend was given one for her birthday I decided that a doll that cries actual tears and wets itself was exactly what my life lacked. After hassling my parents for a few weeks they eventually caved in – although, if I'm honest, it captured my attention for about a week and then the poor thing was left in a puddle of her own mess (oops!). I have no idea what became of her, but I'm guessing my mum sold her at a car boot sale or something similar.

When I was eight years old all I ever wanted was to appear on Live and Kicking and dance with Mr Blobby. There was something about that big dopey pink and yellow spotted blob that had me entranced for hours. Sadly, my desire never came true – but I still hold my Mr Blobby cuddly toy as one of my most treasured possessions and he happily accompanies me to bed every night (despite his missing eye).

When I was ten years old all I ever wanted was to be a Spice Girl. I used to drive my mum and dad crazy, running around the house, shouting out the lyrics to Wannabe whilst performing a little dance routine I'd made up. I was constantly putting my hand on my hip and swinging it out to the side, making a peace sign with my other hand and shouting 'Girl power!' as loud as I could. I loved them so much that I even named my goldfish Ginger after

Geri — my favourite Spice. I was devastated when she decided to leave. The Spice Girls with no Ginger just wasn't the same, and so my passion to become one of them simply ended (after crying my eyes out for hours, of course).

At some point that extrovert little girl who used to sing to anyone who would listen and dance without a care in the world, became painfully shy and bashful. I suddenly became less confident at school and around other people — preferring the company of a good book to an actual human. It's bizarre how everything changed; at primary school I was the girl everyone wanted to befriend, but by secondary school I had become awkward and tried my best to avoid everyone. I hated attention, people asking me questions or putting me in the spotlight; I preferred to blend into the background unnoticed. I felt safer that way. On the odd occasion that anyone would attempt to hold eye contact with me I'd usually end up shaking like a leaf or turning bright red, causing me to stare at the floor for the rest of the day. Actually, I did have one friend, Mary Lance, who was equally as socially inept as I was. I say we were friends — but in reality we hardly ever talked to each other, so I guess she was more like a silent partner. It was just nice to have someone by my side at lunchtimes or in class, someone who wouldn't pry into my life. I think we took comfort in the fact that we weren't alone.

At the end of my A levels, when the rest of my year had either secured a place at university (Mary went off to study dentistry at Sheffield) or planned to take a gap year so that they could travel the world, I was still unsure of what I wanted from life. I decided to join those taking a gap year, although not to travel. Wandering aimlessly around the globe and experiencing what the world had to offer did have its appeal, but I just wasn't quite ready to leave my home or my mum at that point. I was simply going to stay in my home village of Rosefont Hill, deep in the Kent countryside, and get a little job to tide me over until I decided what I wanted to do with my days.

I started my job hunt by dropping off my CV in the village shops — there weren't and aren't that many to target. We have a bank, a library, a post office, Budgens, a florist, a few clothes shops, a hardware store, a café and a teashop . . . hardly the most riveting high street ever! The last place I entered was Tea-on-the-Hill, perched on the hill's peak, with great views over the rest of the village.

As I entered the teashop, my eyes wandered over the seven tables covered in mismatched floral print tablecloths, each surrounded by two or three chairs — all different shapes and designs. The cups, saucers and teapots being used by the customers were also contrasting in their patterns. Absolutely nothing matched, but bizarrely it all fitted together perfectly. The smell of freshly baked scones filled my nostrils and 1950s jazz played softly in the background. I was staring at a secret little den for women — why had I never been in here before?

Flying around the room was a woman who I guessed was in her sixties. Her grey hair was set in a big rollered quiff at the front, with the rest of her curls held in underneath a net. I watched her dart between customers — taking orders, bringing out food and stopping briefly for a little natter here and there. She continued to keep a calm smile on her face, even though it was clear that she was running the shop alone.

I stood at the counter and waited for her to come over, which she eventually did whilst wiping her hands dry on her pink floral apron, which covered a glamorous light blue dress underneath.

'Hello there, dearie. Sorry about the wait. What can I get you?' she asked, with a broad smile and kind blue eyes.

In the previous shops I'd walked into I had just wanted to throw my CV into the manager's hands and then bolt for the door, instantly feeling uncomfortable as panic started to consume me, but there was something about this woman that had me rooted to the spot. I even held her eye contact for a few brief moments and almost felt comfortable doing so.

'Actually, I came to drop off my CV,' I said, as I fumbled through my bag and pulled out a freshly printed one. The lady took it from my hands and casually glanced over it.

'Have you ever worked in a shop before?' she asked, squinting at the paper.

'Yes, a florist's,' I said quietly.

'So you already know how to greet customers with a friendly smile?'

I nodded politely as I felt her scrutinize me from head to toe, the smile still plastered on her heavily wrinkled face.

Perhaps I should have told her at this point that I'd spent most of my time there washing dirty buckets in the back room out of sight and not with the customers at all; but before I could speak up she'd moved on.

'How many hours are you looking for?' she asked.

I hadn't thought this far ahead, but one glimpse around the room told me that I'd gladly spend a lot of time here. 'As many as you can give me.'

'And — one last thing — do you like cake?'

'I love it,' I said, giving her a nervous smile.

'Good to hear! You're hired. You've come in at a very good

*time actually, my last waitress unexpectedly quit yesterday — with
no explanation!'*

'Really?'

*'Sadly, yes . . . although she was a grumpy chops so I'm not too
bothered. I'm Molly, by the way.'*

*'I'm Sophie.' I offered my hand for her to shake but she
looked at the hand, grabbed it and pulled me in for a warm hug
instead. I can remember actually gasping at the intimacy, as it
wasn't something I was used to. At first I felt rigid and stiff but
once the shock had subsided it became strangely calming and
pleasant.*

*'Now, do you have any plans for the rest of the day?' she
asked softly, releasing me from her embrace.*

I shook my head and shrugged my shoulders.

*'Great, let's class this as your first day, then.' She slid a tray
with a pot of tea and a cup and saucer in my direction. 'Go take
that to Mrs Williams, the lady in the cream blouse with the purple rinse to the left — the one with her nose buried in* Bella. *I'll go
dig you out an apron.'*

*Picking up the tray I made my way over to Mrs Williams and
carefully placed the pot of boiling tea in front of her. She lowered
her magazine and peered up at me over the top of her glasses; I
instantly recognized her from out and about in the village.*

'You're new here,' she stated.

'Yes, I've just started. Literally.'

*'You live in Willows Mews, don't you? Your mum's that lovely
lady at the library.'*

'That's right,' I nodded, shyly.

'Aw, she's ever so kind — always helps me take my books

home. I've got greedy eyes when it comes to books, you see!' She let out a childlike chuckle and screwed her eyes shut. 'Send her my love then, won't you, darling,' she said, whilst pouring out a cup of tea and stirring in two sugars.

'Will do, Mrs Williams,' I said, as I walked back to Molly at the counter.

'You're Jane May's daughter?' Molly asked.

'That's right,' I said, with a slight nod.

'I thought so. Well if you're anything like her then I'm lucky to have you on board,' she said with a kind smile as she held out her hand and gave me an apron.

My first day working in the teashop whizzed by in a blur — there was one hairy moment when a plate managed to slip out of my hand, fly through the air and smash rather loudly into a billion pieces, causing me to blub dramatically — but other than that it went quite smoothly.

My gap year flew by before I'd even had a chance to think about what I wanted to do next, and so I extended it to two years . . . then three years . . . then four, until I suddenly realized that I had no desire to go to university at all; I was happy where I was, and am still just as happy eight years later.

Although I'd started as a waitress, Molly put a lot of faith in me and taught me all she knew about baking cakes and service with a smile. Every day we bake fresh scones, muffins and cakes, and experiment with new recipes, whilst putting the world to rights. At sixty-six years old Molly is continually being told by her doctor that she should be slowing down and starting to take things easy — but she's not one to listen.

I didn't just find a passion and career path when I stumbled

upon Tea-on-the-Hill that day; I also found a best friend. Look-
ing back now, I know Molly had an inkling of who I was as soon
as I walked into the shop. I also believe that, knowing who I was,
there was no way she would turn me away without helping me,
because it's in her nature to help those in need of healing; and I
certainly needed some of that.